Team Player

A Bobby McRae Novel

By Bill Farley

Team Player
By Bill Farley

Copyright © Bill Farley, 2018
Mount Pleasant, SC

All Rights Reserved. Except as permitted under the U.S. Copyright Act of 1976, no part of this publication may be reproduced, distributed, or transmitted by any form or by an means, or stored in a database or retrieval system, without prior written permission of the publisher.

This book is a work of fiction. While references may be made to actual places or events, the names, characters, incidents, and locations within are from the author's imagination and are not a resemblance to actual living or dead persons, businesses, or events. Any similarity is coincidental.

Cover Design by AM Design Studios
Distributed by Bublish, Inc.
www.bublish.com

ISBN-10: 1-948543-09-5
ISBN-13: 978-1-948543-09-5

Dedication

For my wife, Judy, always my first editor and support system, who doesn't really carry a 9mm in her Vuitton shoulder bag...at least not all of the time!

1

No one was more surprised than I was to find Jerry Kendall on the front porch of my cottage at the end of a rural road in South Carolina. Well, maybe Jerry Kendall was more surprised, but I couldn't ask him because he was dead.

Not being a psychic, I didn't know he was dead until I checked his pulse, which had ceased to exist. His body was still warm so that left two possibilities: he'd found his way here and collapsed and died or he'd been dumped here while he was still alive. Neither option would have made Jerry feel any better.

I'd been relaxing in front of the TV, zoning out on a TMC play of the movie "The Big Sleep," of all things, and sipping a bourbon/rocks when I thought I heard a noise outside. I'm not totally paranoid, but it was after 11:00 p.m. and I don't exactly have any nearby neighbors down at the edge of the marsh.

I slipped my little all-purpose weapon, a sweet Ruger .380 out of the drawer in the side table, padded to the door and flipped on the porch light. That's when I saw good ol' Jerry staring up at me. He was wearing hiking boots, a pair of jeans and a plaid Pendleton shirt even thought it was around 85 degrees out even at this time of night. My first thought after "What the hell is he doing here?" was "How the hell did he manage to die stretched out staring straight up?"

I'm not a forensic guy but a quick examination of the body yielded no obvious cause of death. No gun shot wound, stabbing, strangling that I could determine. And, I didn't want to get too intrusive and screw up a crime scene, assuming that this was a crime scene.

Rather than call 911, which was my first thought, I went to my little card file and fumbled around for a private number I'd gotten a few months before from the County Sheriff, a nice guy with a great cop name – Cal Major. I'd done an article on him for one of the local newspapers down here and he'd liked meeting me, shooting the breeze and seeing himself praised in print. He gave me the card and said that I should call him at any time if I wanted to get together or needed his help.

His phone rang four times before I heard his sleepy voice "Major here." I apologized for the hour, refreshed his memory as to who I was – he remembered clearly – and gave him the thumbnail of Jerry's demise.

"I'll have a car at your place within 30 minutes," he said. "I'll alert the Coroner's office. Once our boys get there, they'll give 'em the signal to roll." Cal paused for a moment. "You know you don't want to move the body or mess with the crime scene, right?" Then, "Bobby, is there anything else you want to tell me about this before I let the dogs loose?"

I knew what he meant. He had to ask. If I was somehow involved in Jerry's death, it would be smart for me to give him the heads-up before the deputies, the coroner, the CSI guys and the media showed up. I gave him the short form of the Jerry Kendall story and he hung up to start putting the wheels of justice on the move.

The long form of the Jerry Kendall story wasn't much more than what I had given the Sheriff. I had known Jerry when we both lived and worked in L.A. I had a pretty good job at Avante Entertainment, doing marketing, advertising and pr for the movies, videos and TV shows the company produced and distributed. Jerry worked for the company as well. He was about ten years older than me, and I never exactly understood his job except that it involved overseeing a lot of people in the financial arena.

By that I don't mean that he had anything to do with the tens of millions of dollars that the big stars and directors got for projects, but he had plenty to do with the other tens of millions of dollars that went to a host of production costs from craft services to props to locations, facilities, contractors and much more. And, he was pretty much the only guy who did.

When I met Jerry, he was a divorced man with no kids and no particular interest in re-marrying. I was single and having a pretty good time enjoying the attractions of Hollywood. So, we hung out from time to time. Kendall was a nice guy, a generous guy, and a decent story-teller and over a period of about five years we had dinner or double-dated or just hit a saloon to tell each other lies maybe two dozen times.

Still, it wasn't as if we were compadres. When my big break came – I won a pretty decent chunk of cash in the California State Lottery, believe it or not – I had to decide whether to keep my day job or not. I decided not. The company had a nice little farewell party for me, which Jerry attended, and we promised to keep in touch, which, of course, we didn't.

I made arrangements to sell my condo in Westwood and my Beemer, bought a used small RV and set off on a six month wandering pilgrimage through America that eventually took me to the Carolinas. The first time I saw Charleston, I fell in love with the city. In Los Angeles, a historic building was anything built before 1972. In Charleston, history stretched back hundreds of years and included the Revolution, the War of 1812, plantations and slavery, the Civil War and more.

With my windfall, I could have lived in the city but part of me has always been a little country. So, I bought a place 30 miles north of town, on the edge of the Francis Marion National Forest, and settled in to become a Southerner.

In the year that had passed between my departure from Avante and the Hollywood life and the late Mr. Kendall's final appearance on my stoop, I had had virtually no contact with anyone from L.A. I like clean breaks and, evidently, so did all the people who had previously been my "close friends and associates."

Truthfully, there was no reason for anyone from L.A. to have sought me out. I had burned those bridges and made it clear that I was moving on. So, how and why had Jerry Kendall found me? The how was pretty easy to answer. These days, it's almost impossible to hide unless you're in the Witness Protection Program, and I wasn't trying to hide.

Maybe Jerry just acted on a whim and Googled me. There's certainly plenty on the Internet if you enter my name: interviews, articles, professional references and, if you have a general idea of where I am and my age, how to contact me.

But, he didn't contact me. He just showed up down here unannounced, 2500 miles from his home and not an easy place to find under the best of circumstances. So, why? I looked out the front window and saw the blue lights of a Deputy Sheriff's car moving slowly down the dirt road. They weren't using sirens because there was no need when they already knew that one person was dead and the other had a connection to their boss and wasn't about to run. So,why?"

2

Manigault, South Carolina

Once the cops and the Coroner had left with Jerry Kendall's lifeless form in a black zippered bag, I had the local press to contend with. Not that this was a major imposition. I'd always been attracted to journalism and worked as a stringer for a few good-sized newspapers. Even when I was working full-time in the movie industry I still kept up my credentials with the US News International syndicate to maintain my status as a member of the Fourth Estate. I like the news media and I feel comfortable with them. And, down here, doing an interview is a piece of cake compared to standing in the spotlight in L.A. or New York.

The local TV and radio stations, notorious for their laid-back coverage of most stories, never sent a crew or a reporter, relying on a report filed by a rumpled, pleasant middle-aged woman from the local newspaper who showed up after a tip from the Sheriff and wrote a very accurate, very dry account of the incident. And, that was that.

I called Cal Major in the morning and thanked him for his kindness. I also asked him to update me on anything his people might have uncovered during the course of their investigation. He promised to do so, but I sensed in his voice that his department had no clue at all what had brought a Hollywood studio executive across the country to expire on a former friend's stoop. It seemed as if this would be a one day story that would just disappear from lack of connection to anything else.

To explain, if Jerry Kendall had been a member of a chorus line in a Broadway musical and had been born in Charleston or spent a year or so living here, his death would have been front page news for a week. This city has a chauvinism that is incredible. If a meteor smashed into Seattle killing 10,000 people and our local editors discovered that a Charleston couple had died in the tragedy, the headlines would read, "Comet Strikes Washington State: Two Charlestonians Dead." As a Californian, Jerry Kendall was nothing more than a footnote to the crime blotter.

Not to me, however. I couldn't begin to understand what had transpired. I leave my job in L.A. I settle in a quiet hamlet in South Carolina. Out of nowhere, a guy I knew pretty well in California shows up at my house, dead. And no one seems to know what he died of or why.

I'm not an investigator by nature, but I have a genuine curiosity about the world around me and why things happen. I kept turning this whole bizarre situation over in my mind and reaching no conclusions whatsoever.

One key question was: how had Jerry Kendall gotten to my front porch? Fortunately, the Sheriff's investigators were able to answer that pretty quickly, at least in part. A taxi cab receipt in his pocket – leave it to an accountant to save the receipt, probably hoping to expense it – led them to the dispatcher, who had sent a cab to a hotel near the Charleston airport to pick up one "Arthur Sweeney." Evidently, Jerry was a little paranoid just before he became a lot dead. The driver said he'd picked his fare up mid-afternoon and driven him East of the Cooper and past Mount Pleasant on Route 17. When he asked his passenger for his final destination, "Sweeney" just said, "Right here." The cabbie estimated that the drop-off point was at least three miles from where he was told by the investigator that my dirt road met the highway. Kendall must have not wanted anyone to know where he was headed and just walked the rest of the way. That would account for his shirt being sweat-stained and his shoes coated with dust. Why remained a mystery.

And mysteries seem to have followed me all my life. Long before I found Jerry Kendall flat as a flounder on my deck, I was a kid growing up in a tiny town in Western New York with a dream that my high school sports successes might win me a scholarship to some name brand college. A fluke gang tackle halfway through my senior year football season took out my left knee and it was a mystery why all of a sudden those big time schools didn't remember my name.

Two surgeries and three months on crutches later I enrolled in junior college instead. My major was criminal justice, but I discovered that I liked a lot of other subjects as well – history, literature, even art and journalism. The school newspaper gave me a chance to try my hand at news reporting.

I cruised through my major at the top of my class. Then another mystery: why there were no police jobs available anywhere nearby and why did the state troopers told me politely "thanks but no thanks."

My options were limited so I checked out the Army, figuring I could pick up some useful skills and take advantage of the G.I. Bill to get my BA degree one day. It was no mystery that the Army wasn't crazy about signing up a recruit with a bum knee. I tried to convince the induction doctors that it was just a flesh wound. They weren't buying but I must have sounded so committed to serving my country that they sent me to a military hospital for almost two weeks of intensive testing.

Here, the mystery was why a guy being checked out for his knee injury should have been given so many non-physical tests. I took intelligence tests, aptitude tests, attitude tests, vision tests, hearing tests, problem solving tests, psychological profile tests and some tests I didn't understand at all. Plus, I was interviewed by half a dozen officers I'm pretty sure were psychologists or psychiatrists.

At the end, I was told that the Army didn't think I'd ever make it through basic training, and that even if I did, I'd never be certified for combat. That was supposed to worry me, combat being the road to higher ranks. Actually, I was delighted. I had only planned on putting in my time and getting out in the first place. Doing it without being put in harm's way seemed like a terrific idea.

However, there was another option. The Army had quietly instituted some experimental new training procedures geared toward recruits they felt might have "special skills." If I signed up, I'd go through ten weeks of modified basic training. If I made it through, I'd get three months of more specialized training. If I survived that, I'd be sworn in as regular Army and given my MOS and my first assignment.

That sounded like a pretty good deal so I agreed. I was posted to a base in North Carolina where I started training with twenty other guys, all of whom had been through similar testing. When I heard what real basic training involved, I understood that we were getting very special treatment. In our "barracks" we slept two to a room. We had our own little mess hall with great food. And we had no pre-dawn runs or marches in full gear. Aside from an hour of physical training every day, all of our activities were in the classroom or on the firing range. We even had homework. It was like college with free meals and guns.

Around week eight, the major who was our mentor – he certainly wasn't a drill sergeant - gathered us all in a conference room. A sergeant wheeled in a cart with a stack of what looked like briefcases on it. These were really sturdy looking and secured with heavy-duty combination locks. We each were given a briefcase with a sticky note on it with the lock's combination. The major told us we would have five minutes to memorize the combinations for our cases. He went on to explain that inside each briefcase we'd find a complete life history of someone we'd never met, because that person didn't actually exist…yet. When we opened our cases we'd learn who we were to become. Over the next two weeks, we'd be expected to learn everything about our new identities: where we were born, who our parents were, whether we had any brothers or sisters, where we went to school, where we went to church, what kind of car we drove, what sports we played, what music we liked. Everything.

From that moment forward, we were to respond only to our new names, even if questioned by a senior officer. We would be tested regularly so it would be to our advantage to learn everything possible about our new identities. To become them. If at the end of our ten weeks we had not mastered this assignment, we would be dismissed. Oh, and also from that moment forward, all of our training would be classified.

The major gave us about ten seconds to absorb what he'd just said. Then, as the sergeant snapped up our sticky notes he barked abruptly, "Open your briefcases!" Three guys couldn't remember their combinations and were told to leave the room. I never saw them again. I nailed mine. It was like my Social Security number. Once I locked it into my memory, it was always there. I could tell you that combination today.

The same went for the contents of my briefcase. To me it was a game, like play acting. I even made up some "facts" about myself that that Army hadn't included. By the end of basic training, I <u>was</u> my new self. Two more guys washed out and were sent home. I was sent to a place in Virginia that looked like a former horse farm. There were only nine other guys in my unit, all of them operating under their new identities. We didn't have much downtime to chat about our lives. When we did, we did so as the new men we'd become.

For three months, we lived in nicer quarters with better meals and even a happy hour with wine and beer before evening chow. But, relaxing wasn't part of the curriculum. The specific details of our training were highly classified, so even now I can't go into the particulars. It was intense, though. We studied hand-to-hand combat, small arms and sniper fire, surveillance and counter-surveillance, coding and decoding, covert operations and more. Now, we actually did have a tough drill sergeant. As he put it, "Y'all gonna practice the 3-D method. Defend, disable and dispatch. You're gonna defend yourselves and disable your enemies. You may never have to dispatch 'em, but if you do, you'll have the tools."

How that fit with our getting a smattering of knowledge in subjects from international law to music appreciation, wine tasting and formal etiquette was another mystery to me. Later, it all made perfect sense.

All of us made it through the three month course and were split up again, each getting a new posting and a new MOS. I was designated as an intelligence liaison and, to my surprise, commissioned as a second lieutenant. I'd made it into an Army that I never knew existed.

3

New York, New York

I was posted to New York City and billeted in a tidy, wood frame house in a residential neighborhood in Queens. I shared the house with three other guys, all of whom I had to assume, were also operating under their new official identities. Instead of fatigues or dress uniforms, we were all issued small wardrobes of extremely nice, custom fitted clothes – suits, shirts, ties, shoes, the works. I guess the idea was that we all look like young businessmen, not special services soldiers who's been taught the "3-D' lessons

In fact, as I looked over my new housemates, I noticed that we all looked pretty much alike. We were all white, over six feet tall, athletic, shorthaired and what you might call "clean cut". Thinking back on training, it flashed on me that all of the recruits who made it through, even the three black guys and two Hispanics, had that same basic look. To this day, I have no idea what that was all about.

We never talked about each other's assignments. In fact, we never talked about much of anything. Unless we were commenting on the weather or some sports event, just about anything personal and interesting we could say about ourselves would have been a lie. One guy did break the weird code of silence. He said he had to ask himself what exactly we were being trained for in the long haul, and whether we were all being trained for the same things. He also said he wondered if we were somehow all interchangeable, and maybe even disposable. No one else wanted to pursue that conversation.

Despite those few misgivings, I was determined to get as much out of New York as I could. Just being there seemed really cool to me. Growing up in the western part of the state, I always thought of "the City" as the most exciting place in the U.S. which was basically true. Getting the opportunity to actually live there, even in a less than upscale neighborhood, was a real treat. From Little Italy and Chinatown to the bright lights of Broadway to Harlem, the Bronx and even Staten Island, I explored Gotham with every free moment I had. I'd never been much for art as such but even the museums fascinated me. I considered taking in an opera, but decided that I wasn't ready for that much culture.

For a single guy, even Army pay can stretch pretty far, particularly if your idea of a big night out is taking in a movie. In my hometown, we only had one movie theater and that showed only one film at a time, for two weeks at a time. It was forty minutes each way to the nearest big city with any sort of choice in what you'd see. It also helps the budget if your idea of a fancy dinner consists of two cheeseburgers or a few big slices of sausage pizza.

Of course, I wasn't living in New York City in order to have a good time. In less than three weeks the fun and games ended, except for those breaks we'd get later on between our assignments.

I got my first orders from a major in Manhattan. He told me to "dress for success" and be at his office in two hours. And, bring a toothbrush. I took the train into the city and went straight to the Major's office in a non-descript government building a few blocks from Grand Central.

Without much explanation, my "control" gave me two pages of information to read, memorize and destroy. It was my first run, so I studied the information sheets for maybe fifteen minutes. The Major finally interrupted me. "Time. Hand over the papers and take this."

He handed me a very handsome leather attaché case, with a sturdy lock that I'd be able to open because I'd just memorized the combination from the info two-sheeter. I was starting to sense a pattern here.

Before I could ponder much, the Major interjected again. "Please tell me you've got all your…" He paused. "… gear on your person." I told him "no worries." I had all my gear, and I now knew what my "gear" was from the check-list on those sheets I'd memorized: 9mm Glock, shoulder holster, one spare magazine; S&W .380, ankle holster, no spare magazine; arm knife (right arm carry); all necessary identification including Army, Department of State, driv-er's license, credit card(s) and my "new" passport, which already had entry and exit stamps from a dozen countries in place. I must have loved to travel.

There were a couple of other items to my "gear," items that I probably shouldn't even talk about now. I was never told what the attaché case – it was almost always an attaché case – held. It was easy enough to figure out through common sense and what little interaction I had with the other guys in my unit that we were couriers for a very secret array of documents, strategy reports, sensitive intel and other things that the sender or the recipient determined to be a danger to convey by any other means. They were probably right.

The Major handed me my commercial airline tickets. I think I flew military half a dozen times in all. He wished me good luck and God speed and I was on my way.

4

Eastern Europe

In its own way, the Army prepared me to be a corporate executive long before I had any inkling that I'd become one at Avante Entertainment. It taught me how to dress, how to act, and how to travel - a lot. In my first eighteen months on the job I logged more than a quarter million miles, mostly to Europe and Asia, with a few missions to South America and some in the U.S. and to Canada and Mexico. In all, I only had half a dozen or so incidents to deal with. They were mostly low level wise guys trying to snatch my case in the hope there'd be something valuable inside. With them I got to use two "D's" of my "3-D" training. Both worked.

Then I pulled a run to an Eastern European consulate in a city I knew nothing about. My flight was late and I arrived at the grey, gloomy air terminal around midnight. The place reminded me of a Greyhound station in West Texas. I never checked any luggage so I just hustled into the airport with my carry-on and my attaché case looking for my driver. Instead, I saw an attractive young woman holding up a cardboard sign with my name on it. I identified myself and she told me the airline had received a call that my car had been cancelled and that I should find alternate transportation.

That was unusual but not unprecedented. I headed for the taxi stand which was, predictably, empty. Less than a minute later a lone cab came around the corner and plowed through the pouring rain to stop right where I was standing. I jumped in and gave the driver a card with the consulate's address in English and the local language. We set off through a maze of narrow, winding city streets as the rain became even more torrential. Finally, the driver told me in his broken English that he couldn't see where we were going and had to pull over and wait for the storm to pass. I wasn't crazy about this idea but my options were limited. Plus, I couldn't see out of the windshield any better than he could. Then, he took a quick turn into a really tiny street that looked a whole lot like an alley.

Speaking slowly, as if that would make any difference, I asked "Why are you turning in here?" He didn't respond. But, an instant later, the door on my side was wrenched open and I was grabbed by the arm and half dragged, half-tossed onto the pavement. Luckily, my reflexes were good and I stayed on my feet. The big guy who had pulled me from the cab had lost his grip and was maybe five feet away. In his hand was a very large knife that actually gleamed in the dim light in the alley. I back-pedaled hoping I had some room behind me as he lurched forward with the knife in striking position for my abdomen.

I didn't have time to present my weapon but I had a hard shell attaché case in my right hand. I swung it fast and caught him under the chin. As he fell backward,

I kicked him in the groin as hard as I could. I couldn't savor the moment because the cab driver had appeared on the scene, groping at his waist to try to free a handgun of some sort. Training and practice kicked in for me and I retrieved my 9mm from its shoulder holster just as he started to raise his weapon. A quick shot to his head, a dark spot blossomed between his eyes, and the gun dropped from his hand.

All this happened in maybe five seconds, so I was pretty completely disoriented. But, not disoriented enough to miss the first bad guy making it to his hands and knees and groping for his knife. At that moment, everything became slow and clear. He grasped the knife and started to his feet. I remembered the old line "Never take a knife to a gunfight" and thought "Fuck it" as I coolly shot him in the head as well.

Damn! The third "D." Two shots and two kills. At least I assumed it was two kills because neither of the other guys seemed to be moving. Now what? An American in a hostile country guns down two locals. That's not going to look good in the morning newspapers.

The rain continued to pour down and I was getting soaked as I waited for the inevitable sirens and lights as the gendarmes responded to shots fired. Astonishingly, after several minutes, there was no such response.

Cell phones weren't common then, at least not in this backwater, so I had no way to communicate with any of our people and get some advice on what to do next. I jumped into the cab, grabbed a couple of Kleenex out of my pocket so I wouldn't leave prints, and backed out of the alley. Of course, I had no idea where I was or how to get to the consulate, but I caught a break a few blocks away when I saw what was obviously a tavern of some sort with the lights on. I dumped the cab down the block and hurried into the saloon to call the consulate and tell them to exfiltrate me, pronto.

After a solid night's sleep, I was awakened by a steward who brought me a fresh pair of fatigues and, of all things, paper slippers like you might get in a mental hospital. I guess my shoes were still in bad shape. He also told me I was expected for breakfast in the Green Room in thirty minutes.

I quickly showered and shaved and headed for breakfast as ordered. In addition to the ham, eggs, toast and coffee on the table were the vice consul, the protocol officer and another unnamed guy in a grey business suit. He had to be their CIA man. The vice consul asked me to relate all the events of the past twenty four hours and, in between bites of breakfast, I did.

When I finished my recitation, the CIA man piped up. "Your story seems to check out. Your weapon was discharged recently and two rounds are missing. Of course, you could have been firing into the air just for fun…or some other reason."

I was pretty sure "some other reason" meant he thought I might have faked the incident just to make myself look good. He went on. "The local authorities have no record of shots fired, much less two dead bodies in an alley. And, there was no taxicab found where you said you dumped it."

"Wait a second," I jumped in. "First, it's pretty obvious now that the woman in the airline uniform was a plant to get me into that cab. Second, how could my clothes have gotten that messed up unless I was rolling around in the rain in some alley? Third, how could I have gotten anywhere in this city, much less to that tavern, without being in a cab? You know, the one I stole that no one seems to be able to find."

The vice consul intervened. "Please don't think we disbelieve you. We simply have to check out everything like this very carefully. If you did shoot and kill two attackers, and we have no reason to think that you did not, we're just at a loss as to how to account for their being no bodies and no getaway cab."

Mr. CIA stuck his two cents in again. "Had you been drinking or taking any drugs, legal or illegal, at any time during the past forty eight hours?"

I ignored the three beers I had downed the night before last and answered, "No." Just then, a door opened and a young Marine lance corporal entered with a blood test kit. "Then you won't object to a blood test?" the CIA man said.

I rolled up my sleeve; the Marine stuck me and siphoned off three vials of my blood; he left. Abruptly, they all left, with the protocol officer suggesting I enjoy my stay at the consulate but not leave the grounds. For anything.

I found a little library well stocked with current American magazines. Reading them kept me going for a few hours. Then, it was time for lunch. I was served a roast beef sandwich and some odd looking potato salad and just as I began to dig in the whole gang reconvened, plus a full colonel with more fruit salad on his chest than an all-you-can-eat buffet.

The colonel took over. "Your tests came back negative. We believe your story. It's most likely that your attackers were anti-government terrorists. How they discovered your itinerary we're still working on. The probability is that after you dispatched those two men their back-up team a few blocks away saw the cab leave and assumed that their driver was aboard. On a dark, rainy night their vision would have been compromised. When they realized their mistake, they must have taken off after you but saw you enter a public place where taking you out would have been a problem. So, they retook the cab, carted off the bodies and lived to fight another day."

I was very relieved to see all the others, even the CIA guy, nodding in agreement. Then, the colonel said that I would be issued a complete set of fatigues, plus shoes, and put on the next military flight back to the U.S. at 6:00 a.m. the next day. My other clothes would be cleaned and forwarded to me in New York. Oh, and I had to leave all my weapons behind, too.

Without saying so directly, the colonel suggested that if the two dead men had, indeed, been radical fighters, their comrades would seek revenge. The consul, the Army and, I have to assume, the CIA guy wanted me out of the country disguised as an ordinary soldier ASAP. All I could think was that this kind of crap never happened to me in Paris or London or Rome. So much for Eastern Europe.

If that mission was a bust out, it was a day at the beach compared to what awaited me in New York. I'd barely gotten home when I was called into a different Army office downtown near Wall Street. There, I was confronted by a panel of a major, a colonel and a one star, all with folders in front of them which had to be my service records.

The general started things off. "Thanks for coming in, Lieutenant. You've had a rough mission and handled yourself admirably. You also have an exemplary service record. Much as the Army would like you to remain in service and move ahead with your career, it is in the national interest that you be officially separated, honorably, of course, effective immediately."

Before I could protest, the colonel chimed in, "According to reliable sources in the field, the attackers you dispatched were not radical insurgents. They were agents of the state's secret police. Nonetheless, their mission was the same, to steal the highly classified documents you were delivering no matter what the cost to you. The Army's only politically viable course of action is to wipe you off the official books."

Next, it was the major's turn. He explained that although I would technically be a civilian, I would still be required to honor the confidentiality of my classified service and missions. And, I could be recalled for additional training and even active service if I were needed. On a positive note, he explained that there would be a financial separation package to tide me over, I would keep my GI benefits, and, as they were all tailored for me, I could keep my wardrobe.

I felt as if I'd been beaten so badly that I was taking a standing eight count. Then, the major turned the proceedings back to the general and I expected the knockout blow. Instead, he reached into his uniform jacket pocket and produced a small box, which he opened slowly before showing me its contents. "That's why it is an honor to present you with the Bronze Star for valor. Congratulations, Lieutenant."

5

Los Angeles, California

As I'd expected, Jerry Kendall's demise was not a major story in the South Carolina media. Nor, a Google search revealed, had it made much of an impact even in Los Angeles. A brief article in the Times noted that "Jerome Kendall, 58, an executive at Avante Entertainment, had died, apparently of natural causes, in Manigault, South Carolina. Kendall was believed to have been on a vacation trip at the time. Kendall had been involved in the production of a number of Academy Award-nominated films and Emmy-nominated television series during his long tenure at Avante. He is survived by his ex-wife, Ann Marie, a non-pro." So much for a life and a career.

About three weeks after Kendall's unfortunate arrival at my residence, I called Cal Major. He generously took my call, although he had nothing new to report. Toxicology had not identified any deadly substances in Jerry's body, and forensics had found no obvious cause of death. As far as the Sheriff's department was concerned, this poor bastard had traveled all the way to my place just to suffer a heart attack and die. Somehow, that just didn't make sense.

Because I had the money to take off on a whim, I started planning a trip to L.A. I wasn't keen on revisiting the scene of my previous career, but I thought that checking in with some people who knew Jerry and worked with him, and touching base with my old contact Captain Terry Bates at the LAPD might give me a sense of what had happened, and why.

I fly first class these days, because I can. Even so, there are no direct flights to the Coast from Charleston and there's often a fairly lengthy layover in Charlotte or Dallas-Fort Worth. My outbound flight was listed as taking seven hours so I settled in to relax and enjoy the ride.

My thoughts wandered to my years at Avante Entertainment and how I wound up a pretty important player in an industry I basically knew nothing about. After I was summarily "drummed out" of the Army, I was pretty depressed. I had to leave my Army billet and find somewhere else to live in the city. I didn't want to go back to my home town in Western New York, but I didn't have enough money to survive for more than a month or two where I was.

One night, I was sitting at the bar in a crowded "meat market" saloon on First Avenue, hoping I might meet a really interesting woman. I'd met a few targets of opportunity before in this joint, but no one with "long term prospect" written all over her. About three drinks in, I thought I heard my name called out from somewhere in the crowd. At first, I didn't react. I'd been trained not to respond to my own name, and that training had stuck.

I heard my name being called out again and turned tentatively, prepared to deny who I was in case this was some sort of trap. It wasn't. Bulling his way through the crowd toward me was Frank DeAngelo, a tremendous quarterback for our biggest rival high school back in the day. I was only a sophomore when I ran for two touchdowns and caught for one, racking up the points that cost him the biggest game of his senior year.

I wondered whether he was still pissed and ready to start a fight. He wasn't. He was just glad to see a familiar face. We grabbed a semi-quiet table to catch up. I told him about JC, my problems getting a job, and my stint in the Army, about which I was purposely vague. Turns out that while I was improving my mind, then serving my country, he was one of the lucky ones who'd gotten a police gig. His uncle was a county politician.

Frank had put in a few years on the force before taking a chance on a security position with a growing entertainment company, Avante, in New York City. He thrived in his new environment and after a year was promoted to supervisor. Next, he'd made manager and was taking down good money and living nicely in Greenwich Village. When he found out I was out of the service and had no master plan for my future, he suggested I drop by his office and fill out an application for a security guard slot.

That sounded great and two weeks later I was hired. It was an entry level position. I was basically a night watchman, working 8:00 p.m. to 4:00 a.m. But, it was a start. Better, Frank offered me a place to stay if I'd help with the rent. And not wake him up when I came home from the job.

Working the night shift wasn't particularly exciting. On the other hand, it put me in contact with some very interesting creative people who did their best work after hours when the rank and file had gone home. Then, I got lucky again. One of the executives in marketing, Wes Burnside, always worked late. I'd stop by his office and chew the fat with him, mostly about sports. Somehow, the subject of my educational background came up and I told Wes that while I was first attracted to police work, I really liked writing and had done well in two advertising courses.

Wes took some advertising and marketing ideas he was working on and gave them to me to look over. They seemed really slick to me. Then, he gave me some more tentative campaigns and asked me to study them and see what I would do to make them better. I liked this a lot and always got back to him quickly with multiple new ideas.

About four months into my gig at Avante, Wes handed me an inter-office memo requesting recommendations for young, up-and-coming copywriters who could reach out to the youth market. He said I'd be a fool not to apply for one of those jobs, because I had talent and they had a future. I did, and to my amazement, I was accepted into the program. The rest, as they say, is history.

When I touched down at LAX, my first move was to rent a fire engine red convertible and drive it to one of my favorite hotels, the Beverly Colonnade on Wilshire Boulevard. I arrived in time for a great steak dinner in the hotel's four star dining room and began planning who I'd touch base with in my quest for the truth about Jerry Kendall's death

My first call was to Derrick Pettit. Derrick was Senior Vice President , Finance and Development for Avante and a guy who had no particular love for yours truly. That said, he seemed to be a decent guy and Jerry Kendall's pal. Pettit's assistant, a pert brunette named Alicia, remembered me and put me through. Derrick actually seemed pleased to hear from me and we made a lunch date at Le Chateau, an industry eatery on the Strip. I assumed that Pettit would pick up the tab, not because of any deep affection for me but because he had a virtually unlimited expense account and liked to use it.

I arrived a few minutes early and ordered an Absolut Gibson at the bar. I wish I could say that the maitre'd greeted me effusively and inquired about my absence and what projects had kept me from the restaurant's portals. But the truth is, I had rarely dined at Le Chateau, or The Laurel, or any of the other boites where entertainment executives and celebrities went to see and be seen. Most days at Avante, I ate lunch at my desk.

I'd had an expense account and plenty of invitations for lunches and dinner. But, I'd also had a bit of an inferiority complex, if that's the right term. Most of the people at my level were film school grads or MBAs from fancy colleges and had years of experience in the business and tons of great connections. I felt I had to work harder and longer to justify my increasingly important jobs.

Derrick hadn't changed a bit. He's the only black man I have ever know who could carry off grey slacks, Gucci loafers with no socks, a white-on-white shirt, blue blazer and an ascot. Today's ascot was, I think, puce. Only around 5'5", he always reminded me of Sherman

Helmsley, the actor who played George Jefferson in "The Jeffersons." Derrick was always "movin' on up" and he'd been very successful at doing so because he was smart, aggressive and very, very confident.

"Bobby, Bobby, Bobby" he effused, clasping my hand more firmly than necessary while cradling my elbow in his other hand. "You are the proverbial sight for sore eyes!" Derrick was always full of shit, which was part of his charm. He, of course, was, in fact greeted with considerable enthusiasm by the maitre'd, in part, no doubt because of the $20 he pressed into his palm each time he walked through the front door.

After Oysters Rockefeller, a traditional Le Chateau salad and a "mini steak au poivre," Derrick and I got down to business. I told him what I knew of Jerry's departure from this earth and Derrick nodded solemnly.

Wiping his mouth daintily with his napkin, Pettit offered, "Jerry was a fine man and a good friend. I feel cheated for not having had the opportunity to say a last good-bye. Over the past few years, he and I had grown even closer." Derrick's eyes seemed to mist over, but I'd seen that move before. He was as good an actor as he was an upwardly mobile executive.

"So, what was his life like, since I left the company?"

"It was good. He had gotten a nice bump in title and salary. He seemed happy. You know Jerry. He was always dating. Actresses, models, pretty girls or all sorts. Just before his death, he'd seemed to have connected with a new girlfriend that some of us thought could be the one. As usual, he was very reticent and evasive. Yet, he seemed smitten.

"I'm a Cancer, so I naturally tried to use my pincers to squeeze information out of him. To no avail. All I could ascertain was that they were getting serious and that she was 'exotic.' I was eager to meet this mystery woman and fully expected to do so at the premiere party for Micky Silas' latest film- his last release has grossed more than $150 million for us to date, by the way — but Jerry showed up alone.

"I was reluctant to press him too hard on why she was not with him, but I asked anyway. He was, shall we say, uncomfortable with my questioning and rapidly changed the subject. I noticed that he also seemed a bit more jittery than usual. I remember hoping that it was not coke. You do recall that he had fairly serious affection for cocaine back in the 80s."

I nodded thoughtfully, although I had had no idea that Jerry had been a coke head. Then again, in that time frame it would have been the rare individual indeed in the business who had not sampled the Bolivian Marching Powder.

"This girlfriend have a name, Derrick?"

"I'm sure she does," he quipped, sipping at his Kir. "But, I don't know it. Nor do I know where she might be today. Because Jerry had access to many sensitive files in the financial area of the company, we obtained a court order to search his home —which is still under lock and key, by the way. There was no girlfriend and no indication that there had ever been one.

"That's something I can't figure out. In his own odd way Jerry was popular with the ladies. I met many of his dates over the years. Finally, he hints that the 'right one' has come along. But, he never identifies her, never introduces her to anyone and when the poor bastard bites the dust, there's no trace of her. Ideas?"

I admitted that I had no clue and thanked him for lunch. We parted amicably with promises to stay in touch and get together soon, promises both of us knew we would never keep. I walked out into a gray Los Angeles afternoon no wiser but with even more questions about the last days of Kendall's stay on earth.

6

Los Angeles, California

My lunch with Derrick Pettit hadn't been very productive. All I'd gleaned was that Jerry had claimed a girlfriend that no one had ever met and now couldn't be found, and that Avante Entertainment had evidently been concerned enough about his access to money and financial info to search his home after his death. That seemed a little odd. If the company already had his computer and his files from his office, why would they think that he might have something at home that would be of value? Or, that might be somehow incriminating. And, if so, incriminating for whom?

Two p.m. on a sunny afternoon in L.A. is as good a time as any to relax and revisit old haunts, so I steered my rental down Santa Monica Boulevard toward the Pacific. At Ocean, I hung a left and continued along the coast to Venice. A right on Rose and I pulled into the parking lot at the north end of the beach.

Venice has always been one of those rare places that actually delivers on what non-Californians think of as the L.A. lifestyle. Everyone at the beach is an equal, and most everyone at the beach is a little bit nuts, or at least very eccentric. I strolled past the 3 for $10 T-shirts joints and the vendors offering hundreds of pairs of sunglasses at $5apiece. I stopped for a few minutes to listen to one of the omnipresent groups of Peruvian musicians —at least I think they were Peruvian; they might have been Bolivian – playing their haunting tunes on primitive flutes. I gave a wave to the East Indian guy in the turban on roller blades who plays the electric guitar through a portable amplifier. And I watched a group of around fifteen Hispanic guys performing some pretty amazing gymnastics.

Lunch had filled me up, but I always have room for a beer or two so I slipped into one of the bars along the concrete "boardwalk" and enjoyed a cold Dos Equis while watching the beautiful people go by on skates and bikes and the just plain ugly people strolling by in Speedos and two-pieces that did nothing to conceal often enormous rolls of belly fat. Yes sir, there's something for everyone at Venice Beach.

I couldn't leave without hitting that peculiar stretch called Muscle Beach. Behind chain link fencing, dozens of enormous – some might say grotesque – males postured between bouts of hoisting ridiculously loaded barbells, executing hundreds of shoulder dips and engaging in even more arcane forms of bodily punishment. Everyone, of course, was deeply tanned and oiled to a brilliant sheen. Even the black guys.

In an odd way, I felt a simpatico with the Muscle Beach denizens. When I'd first moved to L.A. and had more time on my hands, I'd fancied myself a potential bodybuilder. I joined the I.F.B.B. – the International

Federation of Bodybuilders - which entitled me to not much except a ton of flyers and newsletters encouraging me to attend or participate in competitions, all of which offered the prospect of winning a title, such as Mr. San Luis Obispo.

I also joined the famous Gold's Gym, which had gotten its start in a little storefront in Santa Monica and was rapidly morphing into a major "health club" chain nationwide. Southern California was the mother ship for entrepreneur Joe Gold's enterprise and his gyms there attracted some of the biggest names in the game. Among its alumni were Arnold Schwarzenegger, Franco Columbo and Lou Ferrigno.

Naturally, all of the other guys were lifting Herculean amounts of iron, while I was doing my best just to keep one step ahead of some of the female body builders. One day, I was working very hard at the bench press, which was one of my best and favorite stations. A guy I'd never seen there before had offered to spot me, and he looked as if he knew what he was doing. So, I took a deep breath, added 20 pounds to my personal best and hoisted 330 pounds – twice. He tried to urge me on to a third rep, but I was finished.

When I sat up and cleared the bench, he slapped me on the back and slammed two more 45 pound plates onto the bar before pumping out eight good reps without breaking a sweat. At that moment, it became clear to me that I was way out of my league. I joined the "Y" where I could exorcise my adrenaline on simple machines like the Nautilus and still maintain a passable physique.

My Muscle Beach reverie was interrupted by a soft voice that inquired, "Do you mind if I take that seat?" I was on a bench just outside the fencing and had plunked my little carry-all bag next to me, taking up a space. I looked up to see a gorgeous woman who looked to be in her late 20s or early 30s. Blonde – natch – wearing short shorts, flip flops and a tube top that looked as if it had been sprayed on.

"Be my guest," I offered gallantly, moving my bag to the ground.

She lifted her dark, wrap-around sunglasses to expose a pair of green eyes that would have put emeralds to shame. "Sorry to impose. I don't get down to the beach as much as I'd like these days, and I always enjoy spending a little time watching the 'show' at Muscle Beach."

I considered regaling this other-worldly creature with my own career as a body-builder, but quickly decided that there were many other ways in which I could go right ahead and make a complete fool of myself.

"I used to live and work in L.A. Now I live back East – in the South. I took a little trip out, part business, part pleasure, and thought it would be fun to revisit some of the attractions that always made L.A. unique. This is clearly one of them."

"I agree," she said, her voice as pleasant as her smile.

A few moments of silence passed, then she asked, "Why did you leave Southern California, and where do you live in the South?"

I'm naturally a bit of a suspicious person, and a gorgeous babe going out of her way first to sit next to me on a park bench and then to engage me in small talk got my antennae up and working. Immediately, I wondered if she were a hooker on the prowl. But, prostitutes didn't generally hang out at Venice Beach. The competition from amateurs would be too great. Plus, this woman exuded a healthy glow that wasn't consistent with a life on the street, plenty of drugs and the occasional beating by a pimp. I couldn't figure her.

"I worked in the entertainment industry for a few years. I enjoyed it a lot. But, I felt as if I'd reached my limit in terms of advancement. Then, lighting struck. I came into a bit of money I hadn't anticipated. Not Bill Gates money, but enough to keep me in beer and cigars for a while. So, I quit my job, picked up stakes and headed across country. When I got to South Carolina, I looked around, liked what I saw, and decided to stay. And, I've never looked back. So, what's your story?"

She gave me another big smile. "Not as exciting as yours, I don't think. I grew up in Indiana, basically in farm country. I went to community college for two years..."

"Ah, so did I," I interrupted.

"So, you weren't a Rhodes Scholar either," she countered with the hint of a chuckle.

"Hardly."

"Like so many young girls who people always told they were pretty and fun and bright, I thought that if

I could just get to Los Angeles, I might make it in the movies, or on TV or as a model. I was able to survive as a waitress for a few years until I realized that for every pretty girl who wanted to become a star there were a dozen more just as pretty and a lot more talented. So, I adjusted my expectations. But, I love it here and don't ever want to leave."

I really liked this girl. She was a knock-out with a warm personality and a realistic assessment of what life was like on the Hollywood scene. Yet, I couldn't get a handle on why she had singled me out to tell her story, particularly as she hadn't spent ten seconds watching the "show" at Muscle Beach that she had claimed to be the reason she wanted a seat.

That notwithstanding, I was about to ask her if she'd like to join me for a margarita when she glanced at her wristwatch, flipped down her shades, took my hand and whispered, "Well, it's time for me to get back to work. Do enjoy your trip down memory lane here in L.A." Then she was gone, swallowed up in the throngs of locals and tourists surging by munching hot dogs and cotton candy and soft ice cream cones.

I sat there for a few more minutes pondering our surreal encounter. The angle of the sun was lowering and the glare was starting to irritate my eyes. I usually don't wear sunglasses unless I really need them, but now seemed like one of those times. I couldn't recall if I'd packed a pair in my carry-all, so I reached down to look. It has a zipper closure, which I think is always a good idea even if you're not carrying serious valuables around. Or sensitive government documents. But, it was partially open. I reached in to rummage for the specs, but before I located them I ran across what looked like a business card. On the back was written, in violet ink and with a distinctly feminine hand, "Call me" and a 213 telephone number.

The plot had surely thickened. As I contemplated the depth and breadth of my hugely masculine appeal, I turned the card over in my hand. The other side read, "Detective Allison Simmons, Homicide Division, Los Angeles Police Department."

7

Los Angeles, California

My trip to L.A. was becoming little more than a stroll down memory lane. Frankly, I was starting to believe that that's why I came back in the first place. Jerry never meant that much to me. We were friends but not life-long buddies. I was sorry that he was dead, and sorry that he chose to travel cross country to make my front porch his final resting place. The Sheriff and the County Coroner agreed that there was no indication of foul play, although I sensed that they were both giving me a funny look, as if I knew some secret reason why he was in South Carolina in the first place and just wasn't saying. When all's said and done, I'm not only a newcomer "from off," meaning not born and raised in the Lowcountry. I'm a Yankee to boot and immediately somewhat suspect.

I just had the feeling that the circumstances of his showing up – dead or alive – so soon after I'd left the company and told virtually no one where I was headed was more than a bit odd. If Derrick Pettit had known anything, it wasn't evident. Still he wasn't very forthcoming and he was one of the few people I could link to Jerry both professionally and personally. I know they both liked to gamble a bit and would take long weekend junkets to Vegas a few times a year, so they had to be somewhat close.

I'm hardly a professional investigator, although I've conducted and been the subject of enough interviews to have a pretty good sense of when the other party is being aggressive, defensive or deceitful. Derrick just seemed neutral – unhappy that Jerry was dead, but not particularly concerned about the circumstances. Of course, if Kendall had had an enlarged heart or an aneurysm he could easily have just have keeled over and croaked. His location would have been sort of irrelevant. Nonetheless, he wound up on my doorstep.

I drove into West Hollywood and made a pit stop for a beer at a saloon on Melrose not far from the Pacific Design Center. It was one of the first joints I hung out in when I arrived in L.A. A funky place with cheap drinks, decent bar food and good music, it drew a young, attractive crowd, especially on Friday and Saturday nights. I made it a point to drop by every few weeks for more than a few years until one night when I hit the men's room and, after washing my hands, took a fast glance in the mirror to see if I had to slick back my hair. It may have been the beer or the hit of a joint I'd taken out back, but the guy looking back at me wasn't all that attractive and certainly couldn't pass any longer for young.

I left the john and as I eased my way through the crowd the sensation that I was the goofy uncle at a party for his teen age niece swept over me. I couldn't wait to get outside into the cool night air, hop in my car and get away. From that moment, I never went back after 6:00

p.m. although I would pop in for a burger from time to time. So, I indulged in another few moments of nostalgia before I decided what move to make next.

By the time I started my second beer I'd nailed down two for-sures. The first I was reasonably certain I could arrange, a dinner and some catch-up with the one and only Tara Fukimoto. Her very Japanese mother loved "Gone with the Wind." The second, not so certain, was Captain Terry Bates of the LAPD.

I always called Tara "the one and only" because she got a kick out of hearing it. It was really an in joke because the only one who knew that it meant "the one and only person who believes that Tara has a career in show business" was me.

That sounds mean, but it's really not. Tara Fukimoto is one of the most upbeat, optimistic and resilient people I've known. At, at five feet nothing and 95 pounds with silky black hair down to her waist, she could also be one of the toughest. The Fukimoto family had fled the Coast for Minnesota after WWII. Quite a few family members had been interned by the federal government after Pearl Harbor and they had no particularly pleasant associations with California.

Tara was born in a place called Bemidji, which I believe translates from the Native American as "colder than a son-of-a-bitch." I looked it up on a map and it was about as far north as you can get before you have to learn the words to "God Save the Queen." Aside from its huge statues of Paul Bunyan and Babe the Blue Ox, Bemidji couldn't have had much magnetism for an ambitious young Japanese girl who envisioned herself wowing the world in the bright lights of Hollywood.

As a dutiful daughter, Tara finished high school with high honors, earned her B.A. from the University of Minnesota with an eclectic course of study that included drama, theatrical production, filmmaking, chemistry and two semesters of "The History and Practice of Shamanism." Immediately after graduation and a big party her parents gave for her, she left them a very nice note and hopped a Greyhound for Los Angeles, five hundred bucks in her pocket, no contacts and little idea what she would do when she got there.

But, get there she did and in short order had an apartment with two roommates, a Mo-Ped to get around town, and a brutal schedule of acting workshops, singing lessons, dance classes, improv and stand-up showcases, evenings at Equity waiver plays, open mic nights and even poetry readings.

How Tara managed to keep herself afloat was always a mystery. Evidently her folks had forgiven her and were sending her a few dollars and care packages now and then. To her credit, she always seemed to have some sort of job. One week she was bagging groceries at Ralph's. Another, she was waitressing at a diner on Olympic. For quite a while she actually called on her ethnic roots to be a part-time hostess at an upscale sushi bar in Beverly Hills. Long story short, she was a survivor.

Unfortunately, she apparently wasn't much of an actor, singer, dancer, comedian, poet or any other sort of performer who would achieve stardom in front of the footlights. I can attest to at least part of that statement because I first met her at one of those open mic nights at a fairly popular second tier comedy club. Her jokes fell flat; she tried a quick song-and–dance and boos were heard; time was running out when she began desperately shouting an original poem as she was hustled off stage.

Now, I'm not a predator like the wolf. I don't circle the herd and look for the lame to go after. At least, not all the time. In this instance, I actually felt sorry for the kid. I worked my way backstage with a small greasing of the security guy and asked her to join me for a drink. That's when I began to get to know her.

End result, we went out a few times, neither of us thinking anything serious was developing and both of us correct. But, a friendship developed that lasted over many years. I think what cemented it all was when after hearing for the tenth time how disappointed she was that her show business career wasn't working out I suggested the obvious: production. Her eyes lit up. "Production! That's it!!! I'll learn how to write and produce and direct and make my contribution to the industry behind the scenes. How do I start???"

I didn't have the heart to tell her that production wasn't all that easy, but I did have some juice with a few of our own producers and directors and I got her her first production assistant job on a sitcom pilot. She never looked back. Turns out, Tara was a great schmoozer and networker although, once again, not a great talent. Still, over the next fifteen years or so she was never out of work for long, picking up an associate producer gig on an indie film, an AD credit on a documentar and whatever else she could hustle up on a dazzling array of failed network series.

Unlike so many of us, Tara Fukimoto had never fallen prey to the Peter Principle and reached her level of incompetence. She would never be a star or even a big-name mover and shaker out of the spotlight. Nonetheless, she was definitely in show business, albeit in a sort of minor league way. She was perfectly capable of handling any number of low to medium level jobs on a set. People liked her, so when the larder became thin and the rent was due something would always come along to keep her above the waterline for a few more months. Plus, by her own admission, she had met and charmed – at least for a night or two – quite a few hot young stars. All good for her book of memories.

I hadn't seen Tara since one night around five years ago when we got together for some Thai food up on Hollywood Boulevard and wound up back at her place doing some 'shrooms she'd gotten from "the Best Boy on the 'Mark Salem Show'." Everything in her life – even drugs – was better if it were connected to "the industry." And, I'd only talked with her once after that, just before I left L.A

I went back to my hotel, got a number for her. Once I heard it I remembered it as the same one she'd always had. I'd give her a call in the morning. Then, I called Det. Allison Simmons at her Parker Center number. I left a message.

8

Los Angeles, California

Tara Fukimoto was ecstatic to hear from me. Of course, Tara Fukimoto is ecstatic about a lot of things, most of them dramatically unrealistic. However, I had a real offer for her that I knew would be hard to refuse – dinner at Leaves, an expensive and celebrity-filled bistro on Robertson not far from the Beverly Center. Tara loved expensive meals and she loved rubbing shoulders with celebrities even more. We agreed to meet there at 8:00 p.m.

Surprisingly, my call to Terry Bates went almost as well. The Captain took my call after a brief ten minute hold and said he'd make time to see me the next day. I didn't know what our meeting would yield, so I called the hotel desk and extended my stay by two days. After all, I had no pressing engagements back in South Carolina. I didn't mention my strange contact with Detective Allison Simmons. Neither did he.

It's easy to kill a day in L.A. Between a little window shopping on Rodeo Drive, a run up the Coast Highway to Malibu, a brisk workout at the hotel's health club and a refreshing nap, it was soon time to connect with Tara.

I arrived ten minutes early, even though I knew from experience that dining at Leaves usually meant you'd be seated thirty or forty minutes after the time of your reservation. I knew that Tara would be there on the dot. Naturally, our table wasn't ready so I grabbed a seat at the bar and ordered a Jack Daniels, rocks.

A few minutes later, Tara breezed in wearing a blue silk long dress embroidered with gold dragons. She was proud of her ethnic heritage and knew how to use it. The dress clung to her body which was both good and bad. Good, because it fit her very well. Bad because Tara, frankly, didn't have much of a body. I yielded my bar stool to her and she ordered a "ladies" drink.

The noise level was high at that hour, but I wasn't paying attention and Tara didn't care. After a perfunctory air kiss she turned her attention to eyeballing the room. Big names were few that night but I spotted Jim Lampley of HBO and NBC across the room and he gave me a thumbs up. Tara waved vigorously at Jim, probably thinking he was interested in her which, knowing Lamps, wasn't entirely out of the question.

A nice surprise was Jimmy Kimmel coming in with several of his writers from the show. I'd known Jimmy since his "Man Show" days and we still kept in touch. He came by to catch up but I didn't have time to tell him much other than that I was only in town briefly on some personal business. He said that if I were staying for a few days I should call his assistant and come by the show; he had some great guests lined up and we could grab a pizza afterward. I thanked him and seriously considered his offer. Jimmy has a terrific Green Room.

Tara spotted Neil Patrick Harris, Angelina Jolie and Leo DiCaprio but since neither of us knew any of them personally it was just a spotting. Nonetheless, Tara jumped up three or four times to kiss-kiss guys who meant nothing to me but who were evidently industry types she had worked with and wanted to impress. They all seemed happy to see her. Tara's that way, extremely likeable but, unfortunately for her, extremely forgettable.

Then, sauntering in from the patio came my old colleague Derrick Pettit, accompanied by a guy in an expensive suit with dark, wavy hair. Around 5'10 and beefy, he exuded substance and success. Derrick had to pass right by me to get to his table – evidently he had either more juice than I did or an earlier reservation. We greeted each other heartily and I introduced him to Tara. Derrick introduced his companion as Carl Wolf, a producer he was working with on some potential projects.

Carl was very personable with a dazzlingly white smile that had to be all caps. Interestingly, he seemed to have a slight lisp, almost an affectation. His diction was otherwise perfect but perhaps the lisp was explained when he mentioned that he had begun his career with Televisa in Mexico before moving into independent production in the U.S. He did look just a trace Hispanic, but not at all Mexican, at least not in the sense that most of us who had lived in L.A. would consider Mexican.

Derrick explained that we had worked together for many years and that I had retired to a "life of leisure" in the South. Carl inquired what had brought me back to Los Angeles and I told him that I was looking for some information on a personal matter. He nodded thoughtfully, as if he really cared.

Then, out of nowhere, I found myself asking Carl if in his dealings with the studios he had ever run across my old friend Jerry Kendall. I saw his eyes narrow ever so slightly and I think I detected him glancing quickly toward Derrick. "No," he said, "that name means nothing to me. Of course, in this town you can't know everybody."

Derrick and Carl moved on and shortly Tara and I were seated. Tara being Tara she ordered the most expensive items on the menu, from the lobster salad entrée to the filet mignon wrapped in bacon and the crème brulee. I didn't care. It was only money.

I was more interested in what Tara knew. I should explain. Ms. Fukimoto is not only a star-fucker, she's an industry hound. She subscribes to all of the trades and logs on to all of the blogs and talks to anyone and everyone in the business about who is doing what to whom and why. And, because she is basically ingenuous and charming, people tend to open up and tell her things as well. In short, she's a one-woman gossip factory. If she had channeled her interest and energy into a web site of her own she might have made a fortune on the Internet or as a syndicated columnist. But, she couldn't give up her dream of being a mogul.

After some preliminary chit-chat, I went for the jugular. Had she heard about the unfortunate demise of Jerry Kendall and if so were there any rumors floating around that might be helpful to me. Tara sipped on her

Cosmo, a libation she'd taken up as a result of her addiction to watching "Sex and the City."

"I remember Jerry Kendall because I met him with you at a premiere. It was either 'As Good As It Gets' or 'Good Will Hunting.' I remember it had 'good' in the title. He seemed like a very nice guy. A bit bland, but nice. There was a little item in Variety about his dying unexpectedly somewhere out of town and leaving no family. He was a studio accountant of some sort, right?"

I explained that he was a little more than an accountant and that the "out of town" where Jerry had gone to meet his maker was on my front porch in South Carolina, which explained my sudden return to the Southland.

"I'm sorry," she said, her eyes downcast. "I didn't mean to be so casual. I didn't know."

"Tara," I said, "I didn't expect you to know anything about Jerry's death or to be affected by it. You scarcely knew him. What I'm wondering is whether you picked up any vibes about oddities at Avante or any other industry scuttlebutt that might have any relevance to why he came to me out of the blue and why he wound up dead."

She shook her head. She couldn't remember his name ever coming up except for his brief death notice. Then her eyes brightened. "This may mean nothing, but a few months back there were several blind items in the columns about financial improprieties at one or more studios involving international businesses with shady connections. Avante wasn't mentioned, but neither was any other studio, at least not specifically. I think the source was Andy Albert's column. That's all I remember. Do you think that means anything?"

I had no idea. Blind items were a dime a dozen and these didn't seem to hint any anything tangible, at least if Tara's memory were accurate. I thanked her for her help and suggested she keep her eyes and ears open and give me a call if she thought of anything. I slipped her my card with my new information, paid the bill and walked her out into the cool night air.

As the valet brought her car up she kissed me on the cheek, more personally than her initial air kiss. "I'd like to invite you back to my place but I have an early call tomorrow. I'm associate producer on a commercial for a new combination cola/coconut drink and it could be a springboard to lots more work."

I smiled. "That's OK, Tara. I have a big day tomorrow myself. Call me if you think of anything and I'll give you a ring in a few weeks to catch up."

Her eyes momentarily seemed misted over with passion. Then, she whispered breathlessly in my ear "Look. Behind that umbrella on the patio. It's George Clooney!!!"

9

I'd only been to Parker Center a few times in my life, once to get my press credentials and once or twice more to get together with Moise Gandell, one of the strangest men I have ever known but a terrific crime reporter and occasionally a very helpful adjunct to my studio business, usually advising me on how to keep certain celebrity indiscretions somewhere between low profile and disappeared. I never knew much about his background, but he was established enough to have a crappy little office right in the LAPD's headquarters building.

Moise weighed at least 350 pounds, which at around 5'6" was one hell of a lot of weight to carry And, his office consisted of a four foot wide metal desk, a phone and an old Royal typewriter, all of which were surrounded by decades of randomly piled copies of the Los Angeles Times, the old Herald Examiner and plenty of other obscure publications I'd never heard of.

I don't know if he had a home, because he always seemed to be at Parker Center, day and night. Once, I walked him to his car. He was actually leaving the building to check on a source. Except for the driver's seat his entire car was filled with old newspapers, too. I would have loved to drop in on him but the poor bastard had died a few years back. Evidently he expired on a Friday night and no one found him until Monday. Turned out he wasn't just hugely overweight, he was 89 years old. Go figure.

Terry Bates' office and lifestyle were 180 degrees from Gandell's. Terry had a plush office with a reception area staffed by not one but two gorgeous assistants. His desk was like the deck of an aircraft carrier, and his computer gear was state-of-the-art. The flooring was parquet with several rich, Oriental rugs. The walls were festooned with certificates and citations and newspaper and magazine articles, all extolling the virtues and accomplishments of Terry Bates.

Despite his obviously healthy ego, he was a charmer, and anyone admitted into his inner sanctum was treated like a dignitary, even me. After offering coffee, a soft drink or –wink, wink – something a little more adult, Mark ushered me over to a cozy nook off the main office and we sat in twin leather chairs chatting like old pals having cocktails at the country club.

Terry already knew that the purpose of our get-together wasn't to relive the old days, but he couldn't resist schmoozing me a bit before getting down to business. Unfortunately, business wasn't much.

The Lieutenant expressed his sympathy over Jerry Kendall's untimely passing, while admitting that he'd never known the man. And, he told me how unfortunate it was that Kendall had arrived on my doorstep not only unannounced but deceased. He shook his head thoughtfully and compassionately. "It must have been a great shock."

That said, Bates had little more to offer. Obviously, the case was not in the LAPD's jurisdiction and they had received a report from the South Carolina authorities indicating no signs of foul play. Despite the fact that Kendall's residence was in L.A. there was just no connection and no reason to investigate.

"Come on, Terry, "I tried. "The guy was a long-time executive with a major studio. One day he just picks up and leaves everything behind to track down a colleague who wasn't even a close friend, then dies en route. You can't tell me that doesn't tickle the Spider-sense in that cop brain of yours."

Bates chuckled. "Yeah, yeah, yeah. It looked weird to me. But if the locals didn't see any reason to investigate and since no one else was kicking up a fuss, LAPD couldn't and wouldn't have any horse in that race. But…"

Terry paused as if pondering whether to give me some morsel of information he had "just thought of." I knew he was full of shit. Nothing he did was uncalculated. He kneaded the bridge of his nose before proceeding.

He seemed almost in pain as he asked, "Do you know Robert Raskin?"

"I'm not on his Christmas card list." I answered, "but of course I know who Robert Raskin is. He's the most prominent trial lawyer in Southern California and one of the legal top guns in the nation. How does he fit into this picture?"

"Well," Bates sighed, "he was Jerry Kendall's attorney and is the executor of his estate."

I couldn't imagine how a financial management guy at a studio, even one fairly high up in the food chain, would even know a legal superstar like Raskin, much less have the wherewithal to be able to retain him. Plus, why would Kendall need a top shelf defense attorney as his lawyer?

Sensing my puzzlement, Bates said, "We all asked the same questions that are going through your mind when Raskin – rather, one of his flunkies – called the Chief and asked for a meeting. You don't turn Raskin down so I was tasked with setting things up. The Chief and I and Raskin met for steaks and drinks and the counselor asked for a favor."

Now, my interest was piqued. No, it was whetted. No, I wanted more. "And, so...???"

"This doesn't leave this room, OK?"

I nodded assent.

"Raskin wanted us, very discreetly, of course, to do a CSI type screen of Kendall's condo. He said he didn't anticipate we would find anything out of the ordinary, but he was disturbed by his client's actions in recent months and a closer look by professionals would put his mind at ease. We wouldn't need a warrant because as executor he would give us complete access to the premises, which was not a crime scene, of course.

"All he asked was that we conduct our search in complete confidentiality, report any and all results solely to him, and make certain that no record of the investigation would appear on any official documents. If the LAPD could assist him with this, there would be a more than generous contribution to the Widow's and Orphans Fund through a foundation that could not be traced back to him."

"So???"

"So,what??? What would you have done??? This guy could be a huge pain in the ass to the department or, in certain instances, a real asset. We assigned some of our best and most discreet guys to go over the place top to bottom and gave him his report."

"What did he think you were going to find?"

"Who knows? Bugs. Wire taps. Drugs. Kiddie porn. We had no idea."

"What did you find?"

"Not a damn thing. Jerry Kendall's must have lived like a Franciscan monk. There was nothing that would implicate him in anything. Nothing at all."

I hadn't really expected any revelations. But, I was surprised about the Raskin connection, the Raskin intervention, the LAPD acquiescence and the finding of nothing of interest at the Kendall condo.

"So...???"

"Ball's in your court, good buddy. If I were you, I'd place a call to Robert Raskin and see if he'll meet with you. There might just be something he'd rather discuss with a friend of the deceased than with a police officer."

Captain Bates stood briskly, extending his hand to indicate our meeting was over. "Great to see you again, Bobby. Good luck and give me a call any time."

I asked one more question before I left him. "What ever happened to Moise Gandell's old office here at Parker?"

Bates smiled. "I think we turned it into a broom closet. That's about all it was good for. But good old Moise, now there was a genuine character!"

I held back on asking another question. "How did Det. Allison Simmons fit into this picture and why had Terry Bates not mentioned her or she mentioned him?"

10

I left Terry Bates' office feeling as if he had given me a tidbit of information but not a full meal. That wasn't a complete surprise. It had always been something of his MO to tease with a fact or two but hold back on the really important info until it was to his advantage to say more.

When I hit the street, I dialed Det. Simmons' number. No luck. Her voicemail picked up. I thought to myself that this woman was going to be a hard one to figure. Then, before I even reached my car my cell rang.

"McRae here."

"Hi, Bobby, It's Allison Simmons. How'd go with Terry Bates?"

"I just called you and your voicemail picked up. I thought you were out of the office."

"C'mon. Don't tell me you never screen your calls. It's the only way I can avoid the real crazies."

"And, I'm not included in that category?"

"Not at present."

"So, when do we meet?"

"I'll be free for dinner around 7:00 tonight if that works for you. How about Ernesto's in the Valley."

I had to think about that one for a moment. "You mean the Mexican joint in North Hollywood?"

"Yeah. It's right there on Lankershim between Moorpark and the freeway."

"All due respect," I said, "I can afford a fancy BH place, and I'd like to treat you right. Why Ernesto's?"

She paused momentarily. "Thanks for the offer. It might surprise you but I get my fair share of opportunities to rub shoulders with the glitterati. Ernesto's is good for three reasons. One, it's dark and it's not likely there'll be any LAPD brass among the customers. Two, it has really good down-and-dirty Mexican food. Three, it's around the corner from where I live. Good enough?"

"Good enough."

I took the afternoon off for a workout at the hotel gym followed by a refreshing nap. The older I get the more I agree with Ronnie Reagan, may be rest in peace. There's nothing like a little daytime snooze to bring you back up to speed.

I drove out of the garage a little before six, remembering that during rush hour there was really no easy way to get over the hill. Coldwater Canyon seemed the best bet so I gave it a shot. Predictably, traffic was stop and go all the way to Mulholland before lightening up a bit on the way down into the Valley. Also predictably, a sickly brown haze lay over Sherman Oaks.

I took the Ventura east, got off at Lankershim and pulled into Ernesto's parking lot just before 7:00. Simmons was right. The place was plenty dark. I didn't see her inside so I grabbed a seat at the bar and ordered a Dos Equis. It was almost ten after when I felt a tap on my shoulder.

"Hi, sailor. Where ya been.?"

I said, "Right here, waiting for you. And it was soldier, not sailor, if that makes a difference."

"It might," she said, squeezing my arm. "I'm in back. I thought you'd find me. When you didn't show up I came looking for you. Let's go."

Allison led me to a back table where she was already set up with a basket of chips, a bowl of salsa and one of those huge margaritas that look as if you could launch a canoe across them.

"Let's order, then we can chat."

I ordered the biggest, most humongous carnitas burrito on the menu and Simmons wasn't far behind, choosing a combo platter that might just have choked a Clydesdale. It looked as if an interesting evening were beginning.

I tossed out the opening gambit. "So, aside from my natural charm, what attracted you to me?"

"Bates," she replied. "You probably know as well as I do that he's more of a politician then a cop. He worked

himself off the street and out of the bag faster than anyone I'd ever heard off. After a few years in high profile
assignments with Vice and Narcotics he worked a little
Fraud then nailed down the PI gig. In a year or two if the
Chief doesn't resign or get fired and Terry doesn't get the
job, expect him to run for office, probably Mayor.

"He'd do well in a run for Mayor because he'd be
an attractive, articulate candidate for a city-wide office.
If he had to make a run at Council or County Super-
visors he'd be handicapped because those guys all have
their constituencies pretty buttoned up. Plus, the Mayor
doesn't really have to do much in L.A. except look good
and not step on his dick."

I have to admit that it was a little disconcerting to
look at a woman who could have been the poster girls for
some Midwestern county fair and hear her talking like a
tough, inner city pol. It made her even more interesting.

"I take it you don't care for Terry Bates…"

"Au contraire. He's been good to me. And, I've been
good to him. Which is why when Jerry Kendall went
belly up and his hot-shot lawyer asked for a low profile
look into his home and personal effects, I was picked to
head the team. That's what led me to you."

"Really."

"Yup. I'm not lying when I tell you that there was
nothing remotely suspicious about Jerry Kendall's place.
I don't know if he was gay or not, but he sure could have
been. Everything was perfectly in place, not even a couch
cushion askew. Maybe be was just a fussy bachelor.

"However…there were a couple of odd finds. One, his rent was paid in full for the next twelve months. He'd cut the check just three days before he left town. Second, his leased Mustang, the one we found at LAX, also had more than a year to run. Third, he had what looked to be an expensive leather monogrammed notebook on his desk with all kinds of weird notations, none of which made much sense. And, among those notations two names appeared multiple times, often marked with a red circle. One was yours."

That struck me as both interesting and odd. "So, you decided to contact me as a person of interest?"

"More or less. Because Kendall's demise wasn't considered a homicide, there was no reason to consider you a suspect. But, let me back up a bit. What Terry Bates probably didn't tell you was that a week before Jerry bailed we had a Jane Doe homicide in Holmby Hills, of all places. Mid-thirties Hispanic woman, well-dressed, and clean as a whistle. No ID of any sort. Labels cut out of her clothes. No signs of violence. Just dead in the bushes by the side of the road."

Simmons took a long swig of her enormous margarita. "Her prints weren't in the system so she was just another stiff, except for two things. She was carrying a Berendi purse,very expensive, and it had an itsy-bitsy serial number under the flap of the change pocket. It didn't take much effort to find out from the Beverly Hills Berendi retailer that this particular purse was never sold in the U.S. In fact, it had only been on the market for about 18 months in South and Central America before it was dropped."

I asked about the second thing.

"The Coroner called her as a respiratory failure, no known precipitating factors. That would have been that except for a tech in the Coroner's office who owed me a favor. She let on that she'd seen a few similar deaths before back home in Nicaragua. They were curare poisonings."

I'd heard of curare but always associated it with old-timey murder mysteries like the Sherlock Holmes stories.

"What led her to that supposition?"

"Respiratory failure with no proximal cause. A tiny, and I mean tiny, puncture wound at the nape of her neck that could have been caused by a needle-like projectile fired from a blowgun, which is the customary method of killing with curare. The killer could have nailed her silently. She might not even have known she was hit. A wound like that wouldn't have felt like much more than a mosquito bite. Once she toppled over, the killer could have pulled out the dart and split."

I asked, "Did the post-mortem show any signs of curare?"

"Unfortunately, no. Curare apparently dissipates pretty rapidly and after a few days leaves no traces. Because Jane Doe wasn't officially a homicide, there was no detailed look at her for about a week. So, end of story."

"So, how does this connect to Jerry Kendall?"

"She had his business card in her bag. Was it planted? Who knows? He was called in for an interview and shown her photos but he claimed he'd never met her, or at least couldn't remember meeting her. He stated that in his business he hands out a lot of business cards and sometimes people he gives them to pass them along to others, thinking that he could be a good contact for an aspiring actor, or director or whatever. So, end of story. Then, of course, he disappeared until he turned up at your casa."

I was stumped and admitted it. I'd known Kendall to be a pleasant guy, someone you could have a cocktail with now and again, but not a serious player. After his divorce he dated a lot, but mostly women his own age or close. Widows, divorcees, "industry singles." To place him with a hot, much younger Hispanic woman was a real stretch.

Out of curiosity, I said, "Let's go back to those crazy notes you found at his place, the ones you couldn't figure out. You said two names were written down several times, often circled in red. One was my name. What was the other?"

"No one we could get a handle on," she said, sucking down the last of her margarita and waving her glass at the waiter for another. "Just some guy we couldn't place at all. A non-person. Some guy named…"

The hairs on the back of my neck stood up and I tried not to show any expression. The other name in Jerry's notebook was my identity in the Army's special services program.

11

I think I managed to deep six any reaction when Detective Simmons told me the "other name" that had appeared circled in red in Jerry Kendall's notes. At least, she gave no indication that she had made any sort of connection.

Instead, she suggested that we cap off our dinner with some tequila shooters, water back. I had no objection to that although I knew I had to be cautious. She lived nearby. I had to make it back over the hill without getting snagged by the LAPD. Unless, of course, she was setting me up for an invitation to stay the night.

I have to admit that that would not have been an offer I would have refused. Allison Simmons was really something. In heels, which I noticed she had changed to before our "date" she stood about 5'7". Her shoulder length blonde hair looked to be natural and her body was sensuous and lithe. I guessed her to be around a 36C with a 22" waist and maybe 34" hips. Maybe I read too many men's magazines.

Facially, the best analogy I can come up with would be Morgan Fairchild. Absolutely perfect skin. Pale blue eyes. And just the hint of the bitch that made her even more interesting. On the other hand, I had noticed that her fingernails were not quite as long as mine. They looked as if they'd been bitten down and then filed to make them look even. Maybe she wasn't as secure in her self as she seemed.

"So," I began, "Once you saw my name in Jerry Kendall's notebook, what led you to contact me?"

"Captain Bates. He knew right away who you were and where you had worked. He agreed that you probably had nothing to do with our Jane Doe or with Kendall's death but might be able to shed some light on one or the other."

"So...?"

"Well, you weren't exactly covering your tracks very well, which is a good sign that you didn't have anything to hide. I went over to Avante – phone calls can tend to be overlooked or just not returned – and badged my way into HR. They were more than willing to provide me with plenty of information on you. Senior executive. Worked his way up through the ranks. Relocated from New York City to LA early in his career. No harassment charges. No financial improprieties. Nothing out of the ordinary. Then, one day, you just resigned and left."

I've been told that as I matured I had started to look like NFL Hall of Famer Howie Long. I could kind of see that. Unfortunately, despite his fearsome reputation as a defensive lineman for the Oakland Raiders, Long looked like a pretty genial guy. So, it was hard for me to put on a scowl and try to intimidate Detective Simmons. Nonetheless, I did my best.

"O.K. Because Jerry Kendall's business card turned up on your DOA and my name turned up in some scribblings in his fancy notebook, you came after me, right?"

Allison reached across the table and patted my hand. It wasn't an affectionate gesture. It was more like, "now, now, calm down you moron."

"I was only following up on leads. You were never a suspect."

"So, why the clandestine meeting at Muscle Beach?"

"I just like to have a sense of who I'm dealing with. It's like the old saying that a good trial lawyer never asks a question he doesn't already now the answer to. Once Bates told me who you were, I called my contacts at the credit card companies and hit pay-dirt on the first one. Because of the LAPD's good relationship with the credit folks, and a hint that you might be implicated in an investigation, they were only too pleased to cough up your recent transactions.

"Bingo! You bought a ticket – first class, if you please – to LAX and were leaving in two days! You used your card to reserve a car   and to book a room for four days at the Beverly Colonnade. The rental company had no problem giving me the make, model and tag on your car, and the Beverly Colonnade handed over your room number. I just tailed you a little until you went to Venice Beach, then made contact."

I thought to myself, "Crap. She's not only good, she's not embarrassed to admit that she shadowed me, and that I was too dumb to notice."

"O.K.," I tried. "If I wasn't a suspect why didn't you just introduce yourself and we could have had a nice chat. I mean, why all the cloak-and-dagger stuff"

"Bobby, first of all that's my style. Secondly, you have at least some experience with police procedures. You must know how dull my job gets sometimes. It ain't all 'Law & Order' and 'CSI' and 'NCIS'. My job can be pretty boring. So, it's fun to use the tools we have at our disposal. Helps keep our technique sharp. Plus, from what I could find out about you, you weren't one of those assholes who'd get all bent out of shape and start yelling about police harassment and lawsuits."

"And, you also figured that I'd be really less likely to object to being contacted by a hot babe." Allison Simmons almost seemed to blush just a bit.

"Yeah, well, I deduced that you weren't gay, so, sure, I thought you'd be flattered, or at least interested."

As long as we were putting our cards on the table, I tried another angle. "So you gave me an opening to get in touch with you, presumably still on official not personal business. That raises the question of where do we go from here, and why do you seem to want to keep our contact off Terry Bates' radar."

"I could handle another round of drinks if you could," she said. I sensed she was buying time.

Trying to lighten the mood, I said, "Sure. But if I get pulled over on the way home, I'm going to expect you to bail me out and provide me with a reasonable alibi."

"Happy to do it," she whispered conspiratorially. "Just make sure you get nabbed in LA and not in the county. Those sheriffs can be real dick-heads."

The drinks arrived and we hammered them back. Actually, I wasn't feeling them at all but I didn't want Simmons to know that. Maybe she'd open up a bit if she were getting a little tipsy and thought I was, too. No such luck.

"As we were saying…?"

Allison looked at her watch. Never a good sign.

"O.K. I'll level with you. I don't have a partner right now. He's on administrative leave and chances are he's not coming back on the job. He stepped on a few brass toes. Since he got pulled, I've been kind of floating – filling in. I need a few good cases under my belt to get back on the 'A team' and it looked like the Jane Doe homicide and the Kendall connection might have been a big help. Now, I'm not so sure. But, with not much else on my plate, it seemed like a situation I should pursue.

"And Bates?"

"All due respect, Captain Bates was never much for doing legwork. If a case was complicated or difficult, he'll figure out some way to sidestep it and pass the buck. He was always more interested in moving up the ladder than in solving crimes. Like I told you, we get along fine. That doesn't mean I tell him everything I'm doing or everything I know. He has a way of mentally logging that kind of information in case he can use it to his advantage somewhere down the road.

"He gave you up pretty quickly, which is a little bit unlike him. Usually he wants a quid pro quo. He gives you; you give him. So, I was a little suspicious. Maybe he was just trying to be helpful. I mean, he knows my situation. Maybe he had some ulterior motive. I haven't been able to get a handle on it either way. So, in my view it's best that we keep our contacts between us. Sound conspiratorial enough for you?"

Right about that time I started to feel a glow that signaled me that maybe the drinks were starting to kick in. I could feel a little flush on my face and I could sense a tingling as I gave Allison Simmons another quick once-over. Yeah, she was a cop, but she was also a hottie. Maybe this could lead to something.

"So, is our case closed, now that you've had a chance to follow me, trick me and interview me?"

She reached into her purse, pulled out a little compact, and slowly and deliberately checked her make-up. Saying nothing, she took out a pale, pink lipstick and very carefully applied it to her bowed lips. I was ready to leap over the table and jump her bones right in front of the meandering mariachis.

Once she had completed her touch-up, she said demurely, "I don't believe so. There may be more to all of this than either you or I know. I'm going to pursue any leads I can find. I think you'd do me, the justice system and yourself a big favor if you'd do the same."

That wasn't exactly the response I had been anticipating

"Well, guess I'll hit the road back to Beverly Hills. I should probably catch a flight back to South Carolina tomorrow or the next day. It's cold enough that the sea trout should be running, and they always give you a good fight."

"Yes," Allison said, "you probably should head back over the hill. I have a full day tomorrow so I'll just thank you for a lovely evening and wish you well with your fishing, and with any other good fight you get involved with. Let's stay in touch."

Before I could even make a counter offer, she was up and out the door and into the night. The drive back over Coldwater was frustrating, perplexing and very, very much alone.

12

Los Angeles, California

Despite my pretty transparent and ineffective ploy to convince Allison Simmons that our dinner at Ernesto's was her last chance to hurl herself at me, I hadn't really planned on leaving Los Angeles before I satisfied my curiosity about a few things.

How did Jerry Kendall's business card wind up in the Jane Doe's bag? How did my alias wind up in Jerry Kendall's fancy notebook? Why had Terry Bates given up the Robert Raskin connection so quickly? Why hadn't he mentioned Detective Simmons? Why had Detective Simmons given me so much information about her sweep of Jerry Kendall's home? Why had Detective Simmons stressed her good relationship with Captain Bates but clearly conducted her investigation of me without his knowledge?

Not knowing the dynamics of all these players, I just concluded that the LAPD was a strange organization. The other questions would have to remain unanswered at least for now.

I knew that I needed to get a face-to-face with attorney Raskin, but figured that he'd be unlikely to take a call from some stranger from South Carolina, even if one of his clients had decided to check out on that guy's door step. So, I took a page from Allison Simmons' playbook and "badged myself in" so to speak.

At 10:00 a.m. I parked my rental in the garage under the building where Raskin had his office, took the elevator to his floor and announced my self to his receptionist, a pruny-looking woman in her mid-50s who looked as if she had last smiled when George Washington made it across the Delaware. The name plate on her desk read, "Rose Hatchet." Maybe there is a God.

"Bobby McRae. I'm a journalist and I'm here to see Mr. Raskin."

She gave me a look as if I had said, "I am a cockroach."

"You do not have an appointment."

It wasn't a question.

"I do not. But Mr. Raskin's client Jerry Kendall died at my front door and I may have information that he would find of value."

"I see. You'll excuse me for a moment."

Although she had a telephone and an intercom and a computer on her prim desk, she left the room and disappeared into Raskin's warren of offices. Ten minutes passed before she returned.

"Mr. Raskin has a very busy schedule today. However, he has authorized me to inform you that if you return at 1:30 p.m. he can make a small amount of his time available to you."

I thanked her and left, wondering what her personal life could possible be like. Maybe she spent her idle hours watching documentaries about prison guards or reading biographies of Eva Braun.

At 1:30 p.m., precisely, I was back in the reception office. Ms. Congeniality informed me that Mr. Raskin was ready to meet with me and buzzed me into the inner sanctum. I was both impressed and pleasantly surprised. The famous attorney had a very nice office. Parquet floor. Massive mahogany desk. Oriental rug. Numerous degrees and professional honors on the walls. But, it was not huge and not festooned with images of the lawyer and his many celebrity clients. The only photos in evidence were of him with his family. Overall, it was not much larger or richer than the office where I'd eventually ended my own career.

Raskin himself, however, was as I might have expected. Not a big man. Maybe 5'9" and 170 pounds. He had a rich head of silver hair and a face that could have been carved onto Mt. Rushmore. Clothes? Nothing but the best. Saville Row, most likely. Only two rings on his fingers but one about three carats of diamond and the other a thick, gold wedding band. Even his necktie was a vintage Countess Mara. Robert Raskin clearly put a lot of stock in first impressions, but was equally aware that he didn't want to overplay his hand.

"Mr. McRae," he greeted me. "I know that you were a friend and colleague of my late client Mr. Kendall. I'm pleased to meet you and I hope that I might be able to be of assistance in providing some closure to this unfortunate incident."

The guy was slick. No big surprise.

"I wasn't aware that you were a journalist."

I answered honestly. I told him that I had worked on and of as a stringer for the wire services, had established LAPD press credentials, and was affiliated with a Southeastern U.S. regional news organization. I had mentioned my journalism to give his receptionist a reason to bring me to his attention, but my real mission was, as stated, just to find out what I could about why, and how, Jerry Kendall died at my home.

Robert Raskin rubbed his nose. "I'm as much at a loss as you are. I have no tremendous insights. All I know is what the Charleston County Sheriff's office recorded, that Jerome Anthony Kendall expired of natural causes, most likely proximal cause, respiratory distress."

"Mr. Raskin," I asked, hesitatingly, "Why did you request a discreet LAPD crime scene investigation sweep of Jerry Kendall's home?"

Raskin paused momentarily. "I assume that you have spoken with Captain Terry Bates."

"Affirmative."

Raskin responded, "I have the luxury of being able to request certain favors from the LAPD. As I'm sure you are aware, we are on opposite sides of many issues. That doesn't make us enemies. Just parties to the same conundrums.

"When a client acts irrationally, disappears from his home and job without notice, and turns up dead in, you should pardon the expression, Nowhere, South Carolina, a conscientious attorney has a responsibility to follow up and try to find out what happened."

I gave him my best dead-pan stare. "So, what did you find out?"

A good poker player, Raskin said not much. "Not much."

"Not anything, or not much?"

Raskin ostentatiously looked at his Omega watch. "Not anything."

"Well, "I said, I wouldn't mind the opportunity to take a look around Jerry's place. It's not a crime scene, so the LAPD probably wouldn't object How do you feel about giving me access to the premises?

Raskin steepled his hands and looked into the nether distance. "I hadn't considered that, but I believe it could be arranged. I'd have to have one of my associates accompany you, of course. I'm the executor of Jerry's estate, so I have to protect its assets. If that were acceptable to you, I believe it could be arranged."

"Make it happen, "I said. "I can stay around as long as it takes. Naturally, I'd prefer to do it sooner rather than later because I have a life a whole continent away. But, I appreciate your assistance."

Raskin countered, "I can do this. But, I trust in your discretion. On the very unlikely chance that you should identify anything that might piqué your journalistic radar, I would demand that you report it to me and allow me to review it and respond to it before you went public in any other way."

"Absolutely."

We had apparently reached an agreement, which seemed solidified when Raskin reached across his desk and shook my hand, But, I wasn't finished. "That's a deal," I said, "but it leaves out one very important piece of information."

"Which would be???"

"Jerry Kendall, at least the Jerry Kendall I knew and worked with, was a man of modest means. He was by no estimate a pauper, but by no other estimate a mogul. Why did he need one of the nation's most famous defense attorneys in his corner, and how did he afford you???"

Robert Raskin was anything but a fool. He had to know that unless I was a blithering idiot, I would have to ask this or a similar question sooner or later.

The attorney spoke slowly and deliberately. "Jerry Kendall and I grew up together in a small town outside Cleveland. We were pals from kindergarten all the way through high school. I was a football player – not a star, but a player. Jerry was first trumpet in the marching band.

"After high school, we both went on to prestigious colleges. I was enrolled in Harvard. Jerry made it to Yale. I went on to a law degree. Jerry took a Master's in Accounting. Neither of us ever expected to wind up in the glitz and glitter of Hollywood, but both of us did. No question —I was more successful than Jerry, although he was more successful than most. It's all a matter of perspective. But, he was my buddy, one of my oldest friends. He didn't ask for much or require much, so how could I refuse him?"

Raskin seemed worn out by his recital of the Kendall connection.

"You know I'm the executor of Jerry Kendall's estate. For whatever personal reasons, he didn't have a will. He asked me to draw up a living trust. Then, he specified that the trust not be made public until one year after his death Naturally, I can't tell you the specifics, but you are mentioned in his trust."

"Well, if he left me even a pair of cufflinks, I'd be happy, "I replied. Raskin checked his calendar and told me I could take a look at Jerry's place the next day.

13

Los Angeles, California

The following morning I drove to the mid-Wilshire district and was lucky enough to find street parking only a few blocks from the older building where Jerry Kendall had lived. It was an attractive masonry building with no particular outstanding characteristics not far from the famous if redundantly-named La Brea Tar Pits.

My appointment was for 11:00 a.m. and as I'd overestimated the difficulty of finding a parking space, I was more than 30 minutes early. I like my coffee so I went into a convenience store just down the street, thinking that I would pick up a brew and maybe a croissant to enjoy on a park bench in the sun before meeting up with the lawyer's assistant.

As I stepped into the Quik Stop, I recognized the man behind the counter. Unless I was mistaken, and I didn't think I was, he had been a clerk at another store I used to patronize in Brentwood. What made me feel certain was the large, dark mole on his right cheek.

If I were correct, his name was Hassan, and he was an Arab. He was looking down at a newspaper of some sort and not paying much attention as I walked to the counter. I cleared my throat and tried a phrase I remembered from my special services training, "*mien beykalemni?*" which, I think means roughly "What is your name?"

He looked up, startled to hear that question from a tall, pale Caucasian with a brush cut. He looked me up and down before answering, queroulously, "Hassan." Having apparently succeeded with my first foray, I tried, "*momken akhod* – can I have" before running out of gas and just saying in English, "a black coffee and one of your nice rolls."

He looked so perplexed that I broke down and said, "Hassan, it's Bobby McRae. I used to come into the store where you worked in Brentwood. I'm back in town for a few days and I was surprised and pleased to run into you!"

"Oh, now I recognize you," be exclaimed. "When you spoke to me in Arabic, I didn't know what to think. You used to like the raspberry cakes we had on Thursdays and Fridays."

"That's me," I admitted. "I picked up a few phrases in your language and thought it would be fun to surprise you. I'm just in town for a few days. So, why did you leave the old store?"

He told me that he'd quietly put away a few dollars every pay day and when the opportunity came, he and his brother bought their own store on Wilshire Boulevard. "Life is good, now," he said with a big smile.

We chatted a bit, and I finished our conversation with, "*ashoufak baAdein,*" "I look forward to seeing you again."

He replied, grasping my hand in friendship, *"rab-bena yebarkak"* - "God bless you!"

I enjoyed my coffee and roll in the morning sun before moving on to the lobby of Jerry Kendall's apartment building a few doors away. Like so many older apartment building lobbies in Los Angeles, this one had been designed to be staffed by a doorman. But, those days were long gone. Instead, it was a sparsely furnished space with two upholstered chairs, one nondescript couch and a scattering of wall mirrors and antiquey wood side tables, several of which held magazines that were undoubtedly months if not years out of date.

In one of the chairs sat a young man who appeared gaunt to the point of being cadaverous. He had wispy brown hair, large ears, and a nose that seemed a bit too large for his face. As I crossed the lobby, he looked up. "Mr. McRae?"

I allowed as that was who I was and he stood up, or rather, unfolded. He was tall, a shade taller than I am, and very, very thin.

"Linus Parkin," he introduced himself. "Mr. Raskin asked me to accompany you to Mr. Kendall's apartment. He requested that we spend no more than one hour examining the premises, that nothing be removed, and that you give him a call after your inspection."

Linus looked like a guy who probably didn't spend much of his time in comedy clubs. Attempting to warm up to him, I tried, "So, you're an intern at the prestigious Raskin law firm. Pretty plum deal, eh!"

"Actually, I am a paralegal," Parkin responded, in funereal tone. "I have completed all but a few courses toward my law degree and anticipate becoming one of Mr. Raskin' associates by next year."

I hoped that Linus would be researching or writing briefs, not litigating or representing the firm in public. By the same token, dry as he was, he seemed to be a nice person, so I made a note to myself not to judge lest I be judged.

Kendall's apartment was on the tenth floor, ten floors constituting a "skyscraper" in most of L.A. We entered and I have to admit, I was surprised at what I saw. The apartment was not gigantic, but it was certainly roomy. I counted two good-sized bedrooms and what appeared to be a combination office/media room. There were two full-size bathrooms, a large, well-equipped kitchen, a very large living room and a substantial balcony with a nice view toward Century City and, on a clear day, possibly the ocean. It occurred to me that even though I had known Jerry for many years and we'd shared drinks and meals numerous times, I had never been to his home. I couldn't recall if he'd ever been to mine.

What surprised and impressed me more than the generous size of the place, particularly for one person, were the furnishings. The living room gave the impression that it was never actually used. I'm not much on interior design terms, but the expressions "rococo" and "baroque" both sprang to mind. The room was filed with what appeared to be period antiques, ranging from overstuffed armchairs to heavy sofas, a dark wood sideboard, gilded lamps with elaborate fabric and beaded shades and what I recognized from some magazine article as a "fainting couch." On the walls were numerous high-quality prints. At least, I think they were prints because I'm reasonably sure Jerry couldn't have afforded originals. Their styles ranged from the Impressionists to the Romantics to the Old Masters. To my eye, it amounted to a mess. But, I guess art, like beauty, really is in the eye of the beholder. Even the telephone looked like something from a French film from the '20s.

By contrast, one of the bedrooms was what I would call Colonial, the other Rustic Cabin, and the office/media room was Danish Modern. The kitchen was elaborately French all in blue-and-white with butcher block counters, one of those hanging racks with copper pots, a commercial six-burner stove and all manner of kitchen gadgets and knick-knacks that would have done Julia Child proud. As for the bathrooms, they were simple, unadorned contemporary and bland. It was as if the apartment had been designed and furnished by half a dozen different people.

Just out of curiosity, I tool a look in the huge, stainless steel refrigerator. It held a bottle of Absolut vodka, opened but barely touched, one and one half lemons looking worse for wear and one large onion that clearly needed to be tossed. Despite his high-tech kitchen, it didn't seem as if Jerry cooked very often. Or, he might have planned on not cooking much in the future. The freezer yielded even less information. Three Weight Watchers dinners, a half pint of raspberry sherbet and an unopened box of White Castle cheeseburgers.

As I wandered through Kendall's apartment, Linus shadowed me, silently. Finally, I turned to him and asked "What do you think?"

He answered, "Eclectic, to be generous." Obviously, Linus was a man of few words.

Alert to the fact that my time was limited in the late Jerry Kendall's domicile, I moved along quickly. My perfunctory search of his bedroom produced little at first. What could a single guy have other than a few suits and dress shirts, some khakis, a pair of jeans? I had the same set of threads in my own closet. Then, two things happened that definitely attracted my interest.

The first was when I looked into Jerry's sock drawer. It was a sock drawer like any other sock drawer. White socks. Brown socks. A few black dress socks. But, when I squeezed a bit, one pair of socks yielded something lumpy, and interesting. I kept my discovery to myself because Linus was right at my shoulder.

"Linus," I said. "Could you possibly get me a glass of water?"

He left the room and I retrieved an odd-looking .38 caliber round and a key from his sock plus several thousand dollars in hundred dollar bills. Etched into the key were the numbers 1328-17. Instead of the bullet being solid lead or jacketed, it looked like solid lead but it felt light, almost soft, and it was nearly black in color. I picked up the shell and key in a Kleenex and left the cash in place.

Linus quickly returned with my glass of water and I thanked him for his kindness. We had twenty minutes or so before our visit was supposed to be over so I poked around as best I could, mentally cataloging whatever I could.

Nothing jumped out at me. Jerry Kendall's apartment was a bit weird, but it didn't yield any significant clues about his departure, his death or anything else. I guess I'd hoped to find a blowgun or a treatise on South American poisons or something that might link him to the death of the Jane Doe. But, no dice. Of course, since the police had already combed through the place and found nothing it would have been unlikely that a civilian from South Carolina would have had any luck.

The one thing I didn't find that gave me pause was a monogrammed leather notebook, the one with my name and my Army alias. Allison had been very specific about it. Had she taken it as evidence, and if so, evidence of what? Had she turned it over to Terry Bates, or Robert Raskin? Who would have wanted it, and why? I had no idea.

As I pondered these questions, Linus Parkin intoned, "I believe our hour is up, Mr. McRae. Is there anything else you would like to inspect before we leave?"

"No, thanks" I said. "This has been very helpful." But, hopefully, not nearly as helpful as the strange cartridge and key in my pocket might prove.

14

Manigault, South Carolina

Traveling to or from Charleston International Airport is always a pleasure. The compact facility is always clean. The employees are cheerful and courteous. On arrival, your luggage slides down the conveyor belt almost before you've arrived at baggage claim. There's plenty of safe and relatively inexpensive parking only about 50 yards away. And it's never crowded or chaotic.

Because my flight from L.A. arrived late at night, just before the sleepy airport closed down – imagine LAX, Kennedy or O'Hare shutting down for the night - I was in my car about ten minutes after we touched down. I felt pretty refreshed after a healthy nap during the flight. The plane had been half empty so I had stretched out across a three seater.

The somewhat grungy Dodge pick-up I drive most of the time cranked over on the first try and I was on my way home, through North Charleston, across the Cooper and the Wando Rivers, and through the Town of Mount Pleasant on Highway 17. Natives have told me that the "real" Mount Pleasant ends at Bowman

Road, just before where the 526 crosses 17. They really don't recognize the stretch north of Bowman as legitimate. I can kind of see their point. The Old Village area of the town is seriously older homes, streets canopied with giant trees, quaint shops, the fishing boats at Shem Creek and a lot of history.

To the north are the bright lights of a major shopping center, the Isle of Palms Connector, the gas station and shops at Highway 41 and a number of developments with hundreds of homes that were built as recently as this decade. There's even a Wal-Mart surrounded by a cluster of shops and a Kohl's department store. We're not talking about a mini-Los Angeles, here, but to the locals, all this building and lighting and such is tomfoolery pandering to Yankees who have moved to the area in the tens of thousands to enjoy the weather, the beaches and the golf. Of course, they're right.

That's why when I decided to settle here I headed further north. I'm not one of those hermits who shuns human contact and lives in a shack with no electricity or running water. I'm also no good at growing my own vegetables or killing my own meat. I can fish, but I don't always catch. So, I'm grateful to have supermarkets and restaurants and hardware stores within striking distance. But, I'm delighted I found a cottage on a dirt road with a little dock on the Intracoastal Waterway. Makes me feel a little more a part of the land.

As I passed the traffic signal at the brightly lighted entrance to Park West, then the discreet signage for the roads into Charleston National Country Club, my eyes were getting heavy despite my onboard nap. It was a relief about ten minutes later to turn onto the narrow paved road that lead to the even narrower dirt road that services the half dozen residences on the water in my little nameless community.

My cottage, and that's basically what it is although I've invested in some upgrades that meet my needs, is about 50 yards off the main dirt road on its own dirt road. As I made the turn past the signs stating "PRIVATE PROPERTY – NO TRESPASSING" I could see its lights glowing. I always set timers when I've going anywhere for a few days. I'd say it's just force of habit. Compared to most of the places I've lived, this area is like the Peaceful Kingdom. Except for North Charleston, which has its share of bad guys, an area crime wave generally consists of a rash of bicycle thefts or more than the usual number of over-enthusiastic drinkers taking to the roadways.

As I pulled into my parking area, the motion sensor floodlights kicked in illuminating a large sign I'm particularly fond of. Its image is a silhouette of a large man pointing a huge handgun directly at the hapless visitor. The legend is "Forget the Dog. Beware of the Owner." I can be a little simple-minded at times, but I amuse myself.

As I shut the truck off and sat listening to the ticking of the engine as it cooled in the night air, I thought. "Maybe that sign is an omen. Maybe I should get a dog." I resolved to address the issue at some future date, but not right now.

I'd picked up my telephone messages remotely when I was in California, not that they'd amounted to much of anything. A pretty attractive divorcee I'd met at the gym had suggested we get together for dinner and a movie; my old buddy James, who now lives in Boca Raton, was just checking in and wondering when I might be coming to Florida; my bank had called with a free checking offer; one of the local small newspapers inquired when I might be available to handle a few personality profile assignments; all nice stuff but nothing that required immediate attention.

Mail was another matter. I decided to leave unpacking for the morning and dive into the large box of correspondence that had accumulated. I was fortunate in that one of my neighbors in "the holler" as I jokingly called it, had agreed to take in my mail. He's the only person I trust with a key to my place. His name was Jerome Ravenel and he's a retired, much-honored Captain in the Charleston Fire Department. His surname was one of a handful of renowned names in the area that included both white and black families, a legacy of the slave-holding days.

I saw that Jerome had left me a note: "I noticed that you had an overstock of beer in the refrigerator in the garage. I didn't want to have you at risk for this surplus of suds putting such a strain on your ancient Kelvinator that it might simply yield its spirit and expire. So, I helped myself to a few bottles. Well, maybe more than a few bottles. Let me know when you are receiving company."

Jerome had a wry sense of humor. He also turned a nice phrase. More to the point, he had a very interesting history. His great grandfather had fought for the Confederacy in the Civil War, or, as it's more commonly know in these parts, "The War of Northern Aggression." Jerome was known and loved by just about everyone in the area, not only for his service as a firefighter but for his leadership in a number of community organizations and charities. All in all, he was quite a guy.

What made his story all the more interesting, at least to me, was that he is a black man. Six feet tall. Ramrod erect. Grey close-cropped hair. He reminds me a lot of Morgan Freeman. He's smart and intellectually curious, and he has a silly side as well. He loves practical jokes and considers me his current prime target. More than once I'd gone down to the dock to fish and found a water snake in my tackle box or panicked to see my john boat drifting twenty or thirty feet off shore before I realized he'd cut it loose but secured it with a sheet he'd attached below the waterline.

His mother, Miss Lucille, is still alive and very active. She plies the art of sweetgrass basket making, part of the Gullah tradition that stretches back at least two hundred years in South Carolina, and whenever the weather is good she can be found sitting by her ramshackle wooden shed selling her beautiful, intricate craftworks and charming tourists with tales of the Old South. It's hard to resist Miss Lucille, and I'm a good example of her appeal. I really have little use for beautiful baskets, but I've already bought at least a half dozen from her and will probably buy more.

Jerome and his family represent a long tradition of being connected to this area, and Jerome himself has a distinction that impressed me from the start. He was the first person to mention to me the existence of an organization called The Southern Gentlemen's Society. He did so in passing as a part of my cultural acclimatization.

The SGS is comprised of about fifty men, mostly in their sixties and seventies, who have distinguished themselves in their respective fields. They meet regularly, not to show off their resumes, but to let their hair down and act like real people. They have a strong affection for Southern values and traditions and the tidy "clubhouse" they maintain not far from where I live is festooned with the Stars and Bars and dozens of framed photos of Civil War heroes and historic documents. Yet, they are by no means nostalgia buffs yearning for a return of the pre-war society.

The SGS isn't strictly speaking a secret society, but it keeps a low profile Not long after I arrived in the area, I was asked to interview Dr. Aloysius Pinckney, the esteemed jurist and scholar, for a local magazine. It was my impression that the Judge had founded the SGA. When I researched him, I was intimidated. He was a direct descendant of Charles Pinckney, one of the signers of the Constitutionnd a hero of the first rank. The Judge himself had served as a state legislator, as a two-term Governor, as the presiding judge of the State Supreme Court, and as Professor Emeritus of the School of Law.

Long story short, he agreed to the interview, our one hour commitment stretched to three, concluding with cocktails in the tiny garden outside his office on the Peninsula, and a lasting friendship. He liked the fact that despite my Northern roots I was something of a student of the war and shared his views that slavery had been on its way out in any event and that economics and tariffs were the major issues behind the conflict. When my article came out he sent me a hand-written note of thanks and promised that "Much as you may wish to, you will not be able to shed me or my friendship."

I took that to be only Southern hospitality and hyperbole. But I was wrong.

15

Manigault, South Carolina

After tossing dozens of pieces of obvious junk mail, separating my magazines and coupon flyers and envelopes and opening important correspondence from my banks and credit card companies, I turned to the meager stack of actual personal correspondence. I was not surprised at how few letters I received from real people, the trend toward e-mail letters having already escalated to the point at which I always opened my computer account with trepidation, reluctant to face the scores, even hundred, of messages that had to be waded through. True, I could quickly delete most. I had no interest in increasing my penis size – well, only a modest interest and that tainted by my belief that mail order nostrums would likely not make me the next John Holmes. And, I neither wanted to earn big bucks working at home, buy land in Patagonia or assist a deposed Nigerian prince in retrieving his rightful billions of dollars by sending him my personal financial information.

On the actual correspondence side I found a dinner invitation from a very lovely divorcee living in Wild Dunes, but the date for the dinner had passed while I was in Los Angeles. I promised myself I would call her and beg forgiveness. Ace Hardware sent me a nice $5 off card for my next purchase. That would come in handy the next time I needed a torque wrench, which would probably be never. St. Andrew's Presbyterian Church extended its arms to me if I wished to visit for services and perhaps become a member. I did not. The rest I decided could wait until later. Then, I noticed a square, off-white envelope that was thicker than the rest and looked like another invitation.

Indeed, it was an invitation, and the return address was the home on the Battery of my interview subject, Dr. Aloysius Pinckney. Hand-written in an elegant cursive, Dr. Pinckney it requested my presence for "cocktails and casual dinner" and the opportunity to spend some pleasant time with a few of his close friends.

This seemed like a big deal to me. As a newcomer and single guy, I hadn't yet been invited many places, particularly East of the Cooper, where young families and retired couples dominated the social scene. And, I was always eager to meet new, interesting people. I had to believe that as such a Charleston icon, Dr. Pinckney would have plenty of those. The date for the gathering was ten days away, so I had time to hustle to the local Belk department store, purchase some decent note paper, and hand-write my letter of acceptance.

When the appointed date arrived, I reviewed Dr. Pinckney's invitation. He had somewhat cryptically suggested that the evening would be "relaxed and informal" so I compromised between a business suit and jeans and a Hawaiian shirt by donning pressed chinos and a traditional blue blazer with a dress shirt but no necktie I also picked up a nice bottle of Shiraz, hoping that he liked red wine.

Parking on the Peninsula is never very easy, but I was able to secure a spot on the street only two blocks from the Dr.'s home, not surprisingly among the finest residences in Charleston, on the aptly-named Rainbow Row. One of the most famous images of Charleston, this very old section of the city boasts numerous traditional Charleston homes with their facades painted a riot of pastels.

A brief walk over the rough cobblestone sidewalk that I had been told dated to the late 1600s and I was at the front door of a pale turquoise three story wood frame house built in the classic Charleston style, with a gate to the street leading into a landscaped courtyard. Up a short flight of stairs was the piazza, essentially a long, narrow morning porch with hanging plants, a brace of wooden rockers and a wood-framed swinging glider. Several doors, including the true front door, lead off the piazza. All of the homes at the Battery were designed with the same configuration to capture the on-shore breezes in an era before the advent of air conditioning.

I turned the handle on the iron gate and found it locked. There was no "door bell" apparent. However, a short, knotted rope protruded from an iron grommet set into the stone just above the brass address plate on the stone wall. I pulled it and a distant bell sounded, its tone reminding me of a marine bell buoy. I have no idea how the mechanism worked or where the bell actually sounded. But, within thirty seconds a dapper, grey-haired black man in butler's livery appeared to open the gate.

"You must be Mr. McRae," he said with a big and evidently sincere smile. "Dr. Pinckney is expecting you."I was still new to the protocols of the South, yet it seemed appropriate to offer him my hand, which he took readily. "And your name?"

"I am Isaac Porcher." He pronounced "Porcher" in the uniquely South Carolinian manner, as "Po-SHAY."

"My family has been in service to the Pinckneys in one manner or other since before The War."

I had no difficulty determining which "war" he was referring to.

Isaac led me into the house and to a parlor where Judge Pinckney and several other men were enjoying cocktails and nibbling hors d'oeuvres. To my amazement, I already knew all but one of them. I had interviewed and written about Charleston Police Chief Irving Fein; similarly, Eustace Delacroix, the renowned painter whose depictions of landscapes and ante-bellum plantation life were expensive and much-coveted art objects, Meklin Smythe, whose ramshackle farm and butcher shop off the beaten path in Meggett drew customers from throughout the state and who catered virtually every major barbecue event from Columbia to Beaufort, and Dr. Edmund Perry, chief cardiologist at the Medical University of South Carolina.

The lone guest I had not previously encountered was not a stranger to me either, as I had read and enjoyed his fascinating articles about the life and times of the Lowcountry. He was a teacher by trade but a historian by inclination and the photo that accompanied his weekly columns in one of the local newspapers showed him wearing a bushy brush mustache and a distinctive slouch hat. Samuel P. Archibald.

I shook hands and acknowledged the men I already knew and introduced myself to Mr. Archibald with sincere plaudits for the education he had already given me about my new home through his entertaining and enlightening writings. He seemed genuinely pleased that I was a fan.

My next surprise was how Spartan were the snacks. Three kinds of cheese – a Brie, a very sharp Cheddar, and a semi-soft with green veins, a plate of apple slices and a pile of Ritz crackers. Dr. Pinckney was pleased to receive my bottle of wine and offered me a drink from his ample sideboard bar. I chose three fingers of Gentleman Jack, rocks, and Isaac gave me an generous pour.

After perhaps 30 minutes of small talk ranging from local and national politics to the next Spoleto Festival to the difficulties in raising hardy bougainvillea in the South we were ushered into an elegant dining room. The long, dark wood table with damask place settings and heavy silverware was lighted by a chandelier with so many facets I estimated it would take two weeks just to clean.

We took our places, the Judge offered a brief grace, and a smiling black woman – Isaac's wife, as it turned out – entered the room pushing a rolling cart topped with several silver covered serving dishes. She placed them on the table flanking Dr. Pinckney and retreated to the kitchen.

"Now, gentlemen," the Judge intoned ceremoniously. "Our guest, Mr. McRae, is a newcomer to our hallowed turf. He is not aware of some of our more arcane traditions. Presumably, he is anticipating a sumptuous repast, perhaps Beef Wellington or Squab under Glass. I hope and trust that he will not be disappointed with the more pedestrian fare upon which we dine when we gather. It is our way of escaping the seemingly endless rubber chicken dinners, 17 course extravaganzas and heavy-duty 'Southrun' barbecues, oyster roasts and tradi-tional meals we endure because of our positions in soci-ety and the need of our peers to reinforce their South Carolina identity.

"All of us are men of substance in our respective fields of endeavor. Yet, when all is said and done, we are just men, met in camaraderie and simple in our wishes and our tastes. So, let us all enjoy!"

Aloysius removed the ornate lids from the serv-ing salvers to reveal a huge, steaming meatloaf, a giant mound of mashed potatoes, a brimful gravy boat and a platter of what appeared to be succotash. In a separate glass bowl was a heaping service of applesauce.

"Let's dig in!" shouted Chief Fein, and dig in we did. I was both amused and astonished that this group of local luminaries would forsake French cuisine and even such regional favorites as she-crab soup and shrimp and grits for such a common meal. It was delicious and I gained a new respect for these guys who could undoubt-edly dine on larks' tongues and veal seven days a week but enjoyed just being guys.

After dinner, the Judge suggested "At the risk of being labeled politically incorrect, I'd like to suggest we repair to the verandah for some small but very tasty Cubans I have secured through means which will not be revealed. Isaac will pour us all a nice cognac and we can continue our conversations. Perhaps our new friend Bobby McRae will regale us with some tales from his many glamorous years in Hollywood."

We moved to the verandah, where a cool and pleasant breeze was, indeed, blowing in from the harbor. The cognac was mellow and the cigars were superb, at least to my untutored palate. We all shared in the conversation but it quickly became apparent that Dr. Pinckney had structured this gathering to put me in the spot light as the outsider whose life and career was entirely different from anything these men had experienced. They were hardly star-struck, but all evidenced a serious interest in what my life and my work were like in the exotic world of the entertainment industry on the Left Coast.

To be honest, I was not unhappy being the center of attention. I had been blessed with some extraordinary experiences over the years, and my colleagues were eager to hear my stories and to pick my brain with pointed and intelligent questions. Also, I had plenty of experience being interviewed on camera, for newspapers and magazines and on nationally syndicated radio shows. I'd hesitate to label myself a ham, but others might not be so kind.

Isaac returned to refill our snifters and also to whisper in the Judge's ear.

Aloysius Pinckney tapped an empty water glass to get our attention. "One of our invited guests this evening had a previous commitment, but promised to join us for a drink après. He is on his way upstairs now."

Thirty seconds later, the door to the verandah opened. "I believe you two gentlemen are already acquainted," the Judge said. Jerome Ravenel stood in the doorway, wearing a blue striped seersucker suit and carrying a slim leather binder which he placed on the table.

"Mr. McRae, you and Mr. Ravenel have established a bond since your arrival in our beloved Charleston. He is not only your friend, but he is also your sponsor. Mr. Ravenel is a member of the Southern Gentlemen's Society, as are we all, and as are many more good men.

"With Jerome's strong recommendation and based on the pleasure these members of the steering committee have had in spending time with you both as a reporter and as a friend, we would be honored if you would accept membership in our band of brothers."

I was stunned. I had anticipated only a "thank you" dinner from the Judge after his article was published. That Jerome was a member of this group astonished me. This was no longer the Old South. That they would also extend such a hand of brotherhood to a Yankee such as me was amazing.

I raised my glass and with a lump in my throat said, "I can think of no higher honor. Of course, I accept."

16

Manigault, South Carolina

Despite my totally unexpected acceptance into the Southern Gentlemen's Association, and much as I tried to get in the habit of being a modest country squire with no responsibilities, my thoughts kept turning back to the Jerry Kendall situation. For the first time, I considered reaching out to my control at the Army and looking for some help. I mean, what good was it to have a top security clearance in an organization with tendrils into the whole country's intelligence apparat and not be able to use it?

I had my control's code name and direct phone line memorized, as well as my own crypto calling card. It had been made clear to me when I was officially mustered out that I would still be kept on the books by the Army for special training and possible assignments. The Army hadn't been hesitant to call in that chip, either. I'd been called to fourteen day sessions at various bases half a dozen times and mobilized for actual service once, during 9/11.

It was no trick for me to get some time off when the service needed me. I was always even or ahead in my work and my bosses just assumed that I was an active reservist. In a way, I actually looked forward to the advanced training. It was mental as well as physical. In addition to hands-on experience with new weapons and weapons systems, I learned a lot about strategy, tactics and the world of geopolitics. I'd never been much of a linguist, but I had to pick up additional phrases in languages including Farsi, Pashtun and Arabic. During one session, I spent a great if grueling three days under the command of an Iraqi-born British SAS officer, a true special forces tough guy.

When America suffered the tremendous blow of September 11, 2001, I was one of I assume a great many specialized soldiers immediately mobilized and issued BDU's and sidearms. Unfortunately, once I'd been mobilized, the Army didn't seem to know quite what to do with me. It was probably the same for all the other guys in my situation who were called up.

Like most veterans, even veterans of unconventional services such as my own, everyone wanted a piece of the action. Unfortunately there were few opportunities for those of us who weren't combat qualified.. The sum total of my 9/11 service was four weeks on duty leading a squad of reservists posted to the Palm Springs Airport. It was truly crappy duty. We weren't even issued ammunition for our weapons. I guess if we identified any Middle Eastern terrorists, we were supposed to bludgeon them into submission with our rifle butts. The only good thing about the assignment was its proximity to two Indian casinos. When I was finally pulled off, I left feeling as if I hadn't contributed much to protecting the nation.

My last call-up before I left Avante and Los Angeles was a different story. My colleagues and I weren't exactly heroes, but we handled ourselves well enough that we all got commendations. Which, of course, were classified so we couldn't share them with anyone.

This training session began with a bus ride from L.A. to Edwards Air Force Base, a sprawling place about an hour and a half northeast of the city. In all, there were thirty-six of us assembled, and, for the first time, we didn't get comfortable accommodations. We were housed in a spartan barracks at a remote corner of the base and fed MREs, not hearty, fresh cooked meals.

At 0500 the next morning, we were rousted out and stuffed into two Huey helicopters in full battle gear, including SAWs, light machine guns, grenades and mortars. During the flight our commander, a colonel, briefed us through the radios imbedded in our helmets.

In brief, we were to be dropped off in the desert with no GPS or other navigational gear and minimal supplies. We would have two Bradleys and an APC at our disposal. Our mission was to locate a distant settlement, reconnoiter it, enter it and neutralize any enemy combatants. This would be a live fire action, the twist being that our weapons, and any weapons employed by the other side, would shoot nothing more lethal than marking projectiles.

As the rugged master sergeant shepherding us put it, "You'll be part of the biggest, best paintball combat ever." He urged us to take our mission very seriously and never to aim for the face, because the projectiles could cause considerable harm. We'd have standard body armor and so would the enemy. Then, the choppers left, not to return until we radioed base that we had completed the mission.

It took us nearly two days to locate our target, a compound of adobe-style structures, some two stories tall, in the middle of nowhere. At least from a distance, shielded by the dunes, it seemed to be a peaceful scene. Women drew water from a well and tended to a small vegetable garden. A few men went behind the building to what turned out to be a pen with several goats and a cow. The rest of the men squatted in the sun smoking and talking.

We saw no weapons at all and no evidence that this might be a haven for enemy combatants. After observing virtually all day, we pulled back to our temporary HQ and put our heads together to plan for the next day. A guy named Mullens, the only Lt. Colonel among us, took the lead.

Col. Mullens broke us up into fire teams and sniper teams with himself with three other special services guys hanging back to handle radio communications, logistics and the firepower of our vehicles if needed. I was on Fire Team #1, charged with breaching the main door and securing whatever lay behind it. The other teams were to move to the remaining three sides of the structure along with their sniper back-ups and enter the facility through side doors and windows. By 0530 we were all in place and primed for the assault. Just as the sun rose over the barren dunes to the East, we moved in.

As our team reached the main entrance, we saw no signs of resistance, or even any awareness that we were there. On the signal from HQ, I tried the door, and it swung open. In the dim light, I could see a number of people sleeping on mattresses strewn about the floor of a large mostly empty room. Having expected hostile fire and explosions, our entry was pretty anticlimactic. Lacking any better idea, I shouted as loudly as I could, "U.S. Army! Everyone on their feet!!!"

That's when it hit the fan. One woman opened her eyes and shrieked. Then another, and another. The men bolted to their feet, shouting and waving their fists as they cursed us, presumably in Arabic. The handful of small children in the room ran to their mothers sobbing. It was just chaos. Evidently, the other fire teams encountered much the same scenario – no shooters, but plenty of folks who were both terrified and angry that their home had been invaded by a bunch of Army yahoos brandishing weapons.

It took about an hour before we were able to corral all the civilians, patting down the men but steering clear of the women, hoping they weren't carrying guns under their burkas but not wanting to breach protocol in dealing with Middle Eastern females. When we had them all in one place, our guy with the best Arabic explained that we would be moving them out of the structure to temporary quarters which would be provided by the U.S. Army until it was safe for them to return. Of course, we knew they were only actors, as we were, too, but the point was to make this exercise as realistic as possible. One member of each fire team was dispatched to assist in herding the civilians toward the area we had staked out with our vehicles.

Long story short, we took control of the facility with no losses on either side. At first. Once we'd cleared the building of its occupants, we sat around wondering what we were supposed to do next. There was no manual with instructions of "what you do after you have successfully won the engagement." So, we had a meal. And, we played some poker. And we had another meal. And, we set up our watches and went to sleep. But, not for long.

Around midnight, we were attacked. Aerial bombs lit up the night sky. Smoke and tear gas canisters were lobbed into the building. Enemy snipers opened fire with their paint-ball weapons from all four quadrants. Worst of all, enemy combatants began appearing seemingly out of nowhere in our midst. I "took out" one guy with a gut shot from my M-4, then two of my comrades "bit the dust" from enemy small arms fire.

The whole facility was dark as pitch and we scrambled around trying to avoid exposing ourselves to incoming fire through the glassless "windows" while also maintaining some cover within the building itself. We had no idea how the enemy had infiltrated us or how the snipers had encircled our position.

One of those answers became clear when we radioed our base camp. We were informed that the armored logistical support had been withdrawn because of another pressing threat, so we were on our own. That was clearly in the plan all along. The proper response to this situation was to get some of our best shooters onto the roof with night vision glasses and let them try to clear out the bad guys. Just off the main room was a ladder and we sent four guys up to assess the situation.

The other problem was figuring out how many enemy had already entered the building, where they were located, and how they had managed to get past our security. Room by room, we worked in teams of two to clear each area. All of a sudden, a simple structure we had perceived simply as a group residence had become a honeycomb of narrow passageways, blind corridors and hiding places for bad guys with weapons.

My partner and I entered what looked to be a cooking area and before he could raise his weapon an enemy popped up from behind a counter and dropped him with a head shot. I was so pissed that he'd shot at the head that I gave him a three round blast that sent him reeling. "Dead man!" I shouted, just so he'd know that he was out of the fight.

I should have saved my breath because no sooner had he dropped to the floor another enemy popped out of what looked like a closet and blasted at me with an AK. Luckily, he was a lousy shot, and didn't hit me at all. It may sound ridiculous, but I calculated that he was just too close. Had he been ten feet or so further away, he would have been able to sweep his muzzle over me and, theoretically, cut me in half. But, close as he was, he couldn't get a decent angle on me.

On the other hand, I was able to get a great angle on him, although not with my weapon. I grabbed a broom that was leaning against a counter directly in front of me and swatted him across the turban. He put up his hands to protect his head, dropping his weapon in the process, and I chased him across the room whacking him with the broom and thundering "Surrender!"

The poor guy undoubtedly thought that instead of the well-disciplined "soldiers" he's been attacking in previous maneuvers, a complete lunatic had slipped into the U.S. Army's ranks.

"Awright awready" he yelled, dropping any pretense at being a Middle Eastern fighter. "Leave me go, ya nut." I thought he sounded just like some of the guys I'd known in New York, particularly the ones from Brooklyn.

I poked him in the ribs with the handle of the broom a few times for good measure as I backed him up against the wall.

"O.K. Muhammad," I barked. "Give it up. How did you and your buddies breach our security and get inside???"

"The name's Al," he said, "and I can't give you that info."

I was feeling pretty tough at this point, so I waved my broom at him threatening, "Oh yeah? Oh yeah?? You want some more of this?

"No, man! Cut it out!!! There's a tunnel from the storage building out back that leads under the main building. It's got three trap doors with ladders covered by 'prayer rugs'so we can sneak in at night and catch you guys off guard. Usually it works pretty well. Tonight, maybe not so much. I'll show you where they are."

Well, Al was willing to dress like a camel jockey, hide out in the desert for war games, be shot at and subjected to potential injuries by bomb, gas etc. but he was unwilling to get whacked in the chops by a bunch of straw attached to a stick. Score one for the US of A!

Frankly, in those few moments, I had begun to like Al. But, that's not always an asset in combat. So, as soon as he'd shown me where the trap doors were, I shot him dead anyway.

17

The phone call I received from Derrick Pettit was more than a surprise. Not only had I not anticipated hearing from him again on the Jerry Kendall situation, but what he had to tell me was actually a shock. Pettit apologized for calling me so late in the evening, it was nearly midnight, explaining that he did not want to call from his office "for reasons that would soon become clear."

"As you know," he began, "I had a warm and cordial relationship with Jerry Kendall. We socialized, and occasionally took a quick trip to Las Vegas to exorcize our respective gambling demons. Jerry was not a person one could get tremendously close to, however. He kept his emotions and his aspirations close to the vest. That being said, I felt I knew him as well as anyone could."

Pettit paused, as if catching his breath before revealing what was to come. After Jerry disappeared and then turned up deceased at your residence, it was my responsibility to pick up the pieces, put his accounts in order and help in the selection process for his replacement. What I found was not a positive picture of a dedicated financial executive. Although on the surface his books appeared to be impeccably maintained certain occasional irregularities began appearing as I delved further into accounts payable.

"First, I discovered several vendors I was unfamiliar with and which were not listed in Avante Entertainment's approved contractor file. Then, I spotted absolutely legitimate vendors who were being disbursed amounts that seemed to me to far exceed the value of their services.

"Not to belabor the point, but my thorough examination of Jerry Kendall's actions over a period of more than ten years led me to the conclusion that he was embezzling from the company. He was cautious at first, misappropriating a few thousand dollars here, a few thousand dollars there. Over time, he became more confident in his ability to conceal his thefts and occasionally remitted tens of thousands of dollars to bogus recipients. Over the course of his embezzlement, I estimate that Jerry Kendall was responsible for losses that may amount to one million dollars or more."

I was stunned. Meek, mild-mannered Jerry Kendall had been skimming Avante to the tune of more than a million bucks??? How could that be? And, what the hell had he done with the money. I'd seen his home in L.A. and it was consistent with what a studio executive at his level would have been able to afford. Maybe even a little less than he could have afforded. If he were really a crook, why did he become one and where did the cash go?

"Derrick," I said," I'm dumbfounded. The last thing I would have pegged Jerry as would have been an embezzler. Three questions spring to mind. One, what did he do with the money? Two, where does Avante go from here? Three, and this is one that I imagine neither of us can answer, what does this have to do with Jerry turning up dead on my doorstep?"

I took a deep breath while waiting for Derrick Pettit's answers. A dark thought had crossed my mind that I didn't want to share with him unless he had already considered it and left me no choice than to address it. Did Pettit or anyone else at Avante Entertainment believe that I was an accomplice to Jerry's alleged crime, perhaps as a recipient of or a conduit for the purloined funds???

Derrick sighed. "Let's begin in reverse order. First, no one connects you to Jerry's criminal activity. There's simply no reason to do so. I was much closer to him that you ever were. He reported to me. If guilt by association were the issue, I'd be at the front of the line, not you. Second, this situation has been reviewed at the highest levels within the company. The decision, endorsed by the Board of Directors, is to let it go. The alleged embezzler is dead. It is unlikely that he has left an estate that can be tapped into to make Avante Entertainment whole. At least, that's the sense I get from his attorney and executor, Mr. Raskin. The fact that a highly-regarded financial executive was able to skim so much money from Avante is an embarrassment but, in itself, not significant enough to affect the company's bottom line

"So, rather than drag Kendall's name through the mud posthumously, Avante is willing to write off the losses and move on. There will be no public acknowledgement of the embezzlement and no involvement of the legal system Case closed."

Pettit paused before addressing my first question. "As to where the money went. The company hired a well-regarded private investigation firm to find answers. On the whole, they came up empty. The faux vendors and contractors were generally postal drops that were discontinued or moved regularly. The legitimate recipients could explain the excess payments to our satisfaction. Jerry had no known bank accounts where he could have stashed large amounts of cash. And, as you observed, he lived modestly.

"Three possibilities exist for the disposal of the funds. One, Jerry liked to gamble. However, I've been with him on junkets and while he liked to think of himself as a player, he rarely dropped more than two or three thousand over a long weekend. And he went to Las Vegas no more than two or three times a year. Two, drugs. As I told you, Jerry once had a cocaine problem. But, in recent years, he seemed to have it under control. I knew that he did a few lines from time to time, but I never saw him truly wasted. Three, women. Jerry was not very slick socially. As I understand it, his wife divorced him because he was just plain boring, in bed and out. Nonetheless, he had a taste for beautiful, exotic women. Perhaps paying for them was a major consideration."

"I follow your drift," I interjected. "A million dollars is a significant amount of money. He already earned a good salary and didn't live extravagantly. If you're right about his only occasional drug use and his more or less modest gambling, women might be at least part of the answer.

"But, I've been to his home and given it a pretty clean sweep. There was no evidence that a woman or women had even been in the place. I mean, it was almost Spartan. The furnishings were pretty strange, but he had virtually no food or liquor in the place. How could he have a wild social life without leaving any traces?"

Derrick paused again. "Bobby, I'm a pretty serious-minded guy with no real secrets. Can I trust you to keep this next piece of information between us?"

"Well, sure. I have no reason to want to compromise you or your position"

"Around the time of the first financial improprieties – which I was completely unaware of, bear in mind – Jerry asked me if I wanted a share in what he called 'The Champagne Castle'. The idea was to have three or four guys kick in to rent a little pied a terre not far from the office which we could take turns using for whatever purposes we chose. I wasn't in a serious relationship at the time so I told him to count me in.

"What Jerry came up with was not much more than a small apartment, but it was located on the 'penthouse floor,' actually the roof, of a '30s apartment building in the flats of Beverly Hills. One big living room/ dining room area with a large screen TV; a small functional kitchenette; two decent sized bedrooms and baths. The best part was a tiny private elevator that ran from the lobby directly to the apartment. Apparently some wealthy eccentric had it installed decades ago for the same reasons that we would be using it in 2011.

"Jerry called it the 'Champagne Castle' because it sounded cool to women and also because the only refreshments generally available there would be fine wines and champagnes.”

“So, you became a charter member of the 'Castle',” I asked.

“I did. But I soon regretted my decision. When all was said and done, I was not cut out to swing. I didn't feel comfortable with professionals, and when I tried to make something work with a woman from the 'real world' three things tended to happen, all bad. First, I would feel as if I were falling in love, which, intellectually, I knew I was not. Second, I would think of my job and worry about what would happen if this came out. Third, despite what you may have heard about African-American sexual prowess, I would sometimes pull a limp noodle. So, after about a year, I bowed out.”

“But the other guys, including Jerry, kept the 'Castle' going?”

“As far as I know. Jerry and I never really discussed it after I left. He seemed to enjoy the concept a lot, so I have to assume that he remained the principal if not the only other member.”

“Well, Derrick,” I said, “I truly appreciate your sharing this information with me. I know it couldn't have been easy for you, and for Avante. We'll probably never know why Jerry did what he did or how it led to his death, but perhaps he's better off now than living a lie.”

“Yes, Derrick Pettit replied, “perhaps so.”

18

Derrick Pettit's confidential revelation about Jerry Kendall caught me completely off guard. Of all the scenarios I could have come up with to explain why Jerry was dead and why he died on my doorstep, major league embezzlement was not among them.

I poured myself a stiff Gentleman Jack, Jack Daniel's premium brand, and plunked myself down in one of the rockers on the front porch. A full moon was just rising over the ocean and it seemed to welcome rumination. Sad to say, my attempt at sorting through the situation crashed and burned in less than fifteen minutes. So, I decided to make a few probing telephone calls.

First up was my old friend Tara Fukimoto. Her number rang four times before going to voicemail. "This is Tara. I can't come to the phone right now. If this is about work, try my cell phone or call my agent right away." She gave both numbers.

At the beep, I said, "Tara, it's Bobby. Hope you are doing great. I wanted to talk with you about a few things. If you get a chance, call me…"

"Bobby! Just screening my calls. So many crazy people out there. You back in town???"

"No ma'am. Still in South Carolina. How've you been?"

"Great, great, great! AP on a national beer commercial and AD on an indie film starting up next month. Life is good."

The amenities having been established, I filled her in on why I was calling. Without getting into specifics, I asked her to keep her ear to the ground particularly in regard to any rumors of fraud involving Avante. I explained that I had come into some information that had been provided to me confidentially and that I had no way of corroborating without implicating my source. I didn't want her to stick her neck out, but if she heard anything, to let me know. She agreed immediately and said she'd put her feelers out discreetly. Then she added, "I'm thinking you will be back in L.A. soon. We can pick up where we left off. Call me…or else!"

I assumed she was hinting that we'd have a nice dinner and go back to her place or mine and do hideously enjoyable things to one another until dawn. Of course, I also knew Tara's track record of having an "early call" each time we'd gotten close to sex recently. I wasn't counting my chickens.

By the time we rang off, the moon was high in the sky. It was one of those warm, breezeless nights that make you think of magnolias, pralines, shrimp and grits and all the things that are sweet about the South. But, I couldn't appreciate the Dixie mood. Derrick's call kept bouncing around in my mind.

Another Gentleman Jack and I checked my old, battered Rolex. It was almost 1:00 a.m. in the Carolinas, but only 10:00 p.m. on the Coast. I pulled her business card out of my phone book and dialed Det. Allison Simmons. Once again, voicemail intervened. "This is Allison Simmons. If your call is personal, please leave me a message. If it pertains to police business, please call my office. In either case, I will do my best to get back to you as soon as possible."

Again at the beep, I left my message. "Hi, Allison. Bobby McRae here. I'm back home in South Carolina. I just had a conversation with a former colleague who shocked me with some revelations about Jerry Kendall. Of course, he swore me to confidentiality, so I have to tread lightly in terms of what I can and can't say. Be that as it may, I felt that even in general terms this information might be of value to you and your Jane Doe investigation. Call me whenever it's convenient and I'll fill you in." I left my home number and that was that.

Against my better judgment, I was about to pour yet another bourbon/rocks when the phone rang. At first, I couldn't find it. Then, I remembered that I'd left it out on the porch. I caught it before my own voicemail kicked in. "McRae here."

Allison Simmons breathy voice returned the salutation. "This is Allison. I just got your call. What are you up to?"

Somehow, she made that innocuous greeting sound like "What are you wearing…and can I tear it off with my teeth?" Or, that could have just been my overactive libido and my whiskey imagination.

"Well, sweetheart," I tried, "I'm just settin' here in my rockin' chair watchin' the moon rise and listenin' to the hounds bayin' in the distance. Just a typical night here in the land of the Spanish moss and grand ol' plantation homes."

Allison laughed, briefly. "Cut the corn pone, Bobby. You may like where you live these days, but you're about as much of a native Southerner as Calvin Coolidge. So, what have you got for me?"

I trusted Det. Simmons, but I also felt an obligation to Derrick not to involve him in anything over and above our conversation. Without mentioning him specifically, I summarized our talk. A ranking executive at Jerry's and my former employer had conducted an audit that appeared to show that Kendall had been embezzling for at least a decade. He'd started small, but upped the ante when he realized how easy it was for him to get away with his con.

In total, the audit showed that he may have swindled Avante Entertainment out of more than $1 million before he disappeared and turned up dead. Nothing about his lifestyle pointed to where the money might have gone. However, he had had a cocaine problem at one time; he like gambling; and, he had a weakness for beautiful, exotic women. Allison already knew as well as I did that his apartment showed no signs of women being present. I held back on telling her about the "Champagne Castle" and I made no mention of the odd .38 caliber bullet and the key I'd pocketed at his place or the five thousand dollars in cash in his sock drawer.

Allison took her time digesting this new information. When she did respond, she said, "Jerry Kendall wouldn't have been the first financial guy to wake up one morning and realize that he was handing out a lot more money than he would personally ever see. You need a pretty strong rabbit to put in charge of guarding the lettuce patch.

"If he were doing blow, that could account for some of the money. If he were a serious player, that could account for another chunk. If he liked expensive ladies, it could have been a trifecta. Maybe my Jane Doe was one of those five grand a night hookers. I wish I knew, but we still don't have a positive ID on her and probably never will. One thing's for sure, based on prints at least, she was never in the system."

"So, what's your gut feeling?" I asked.

"It's too soon to say. I just picked up another case, a homicide in Bel Air. Nasty one, too. A "seventy two going on forty" ex-ingénue raped and beaten to death in the home she inherited from her fifth husband. Whoever did it really didn't like her because he, or she, chopped of her head. I've got two good leads, but this one has put Jane Doe on the back burner for a while."

"Damn! That's like something out of a TV show. How do you deal with violence like that?"

"I deal. We all deal. And where do you think those television shows get their plot lines from, their fertile imaginations???"

I told her I understood that my little information wasn't a priority. She thanked me and said softly, "I'm glad we met, Bobby. The last time we were together, our evening ended too soon. Do you have any plans to come back to L.A.?"

Her tone had softened. A lot. To my semi-addled brain, she sounded as if she regretted our not sleeping together and was tossing out an offer that we might give it a second try if I came into town.

"I truly can't say. But, if I make it west, I'd love to take you to a terrific dinner and spend as much time with you as you can spare. Is that a deal?"

I thought that was pretty Sinatra-walking-off into-the rain-under-a-streetlight of me.

"You know it would work for me, don't you?"

"I never know anything, but sometimes, I can hope…"

I could hear jazz saxophones moaning in the background of my mind.

Then, Allison said, "Have you discussed this telephone conversation with your source with anyone other than me?"

I felt I could be honest with her. "As a matter of fact, I have a good friend in Hollywood – a woman who's a free lance producer/director and a great source of industry gossip. I asked her to get back to me if she heard any rumblings about financial shenanigans at Avante. But, I didn't give her any specifics."

"Do I detect some pillow talk, here?"

I think I actually blushed. "Not so's you'd notice. She's just one of those characters you cultivate over time and who you've helped out and want to return the favor."

"Good. Well, I'd suggest you keep this between us and your 'gossip maven.' No reason to involve anyone else."

Maybe it was the onshore breeze cooling me down a bit, but Allison's voice seemed to take on a bit of a chill.

"Between us chickens. I'd not let Terry Bates in on this new information. That O.K. with you?" That struck me as an odd request.

"It's probably nothing. It's just that Terry can be a pit bull at times. Give him a little intel and he'll go to any lengths to find out where it came from, who passed it along, whether it's reliable and, most important, whether he can use it to squeeze someone to his advantage. It's just his style."

"I understand, "I said. "I'll keep Captain Bates out of the loop. And if – no, when – I get back to Los Angeles, I expect you to honor your commitment to a terrific evening."

She promised to clear her calendar. I hung up and sipped the dregs of my drink thinking about Terry Bates. "It's probably nothing," she'd said. And she was probably right.

19

Manigault, South Carolina

Morning in the Carolinas didn't seem all that cheery as I awoke from too many bourbons and all the, new information my brain had been working on while I slept.

As I soaked up my coffee and contemplated what to do with the rest of my day, I remembered that I had planned to make a trip to one of the big box stores to stock up on huge quantities of non-perishables plus plenty of other stuff I'd never use.

A quick dip in the chilly Intracoastal followed by a hot shower helped, and by one o'clock I was able to get behind the wheel and headed down Route 17. I returned a few hours later and about $300 dollars poorer with a truck full of items that took me almost an hour to unload and store in my two refrigerators and what space remained in my cluttered garage. I probably didn't need those four pounds of peanut butter stuffed pretzels or the two gallons of olive oil, but, hey, you never really know what will come in handy. And, I didn't plan on making another big stocking up trip again anytime soon.

Just as I stuffed the last package of meat into the freezer, I noticed that my message light was on. I had two calls. The first was from Jerome Ravenel, wondering if he might come by and ask me for a favor. The second was from Carrie Ann, the good-looking divorcee from the gym. She said she hadn't seen me working out for a while and wondered if I was out of town and, if not, if I was OK. She'd been planning to take in a play by a group of local actors with her best friend, but the friend had "gotten a better offer" from a guy she had her eye on. So, Carrie Ann wondered if I might be available to go with her.

I called them both back, leaving a message for Jerome to drop by as soon as he could because I might be going out for the evening. Then, I rang up Carrie Ann and told her I'd be delighted to enjoy a play with her but, tonight at least, I wouldn't have time to finish up what I was working on, get dressed, and take her out for a nice dinner. She was cool with that and suggested we might have a drink and a light snack afterward. Fine with me! What had started out as kind of a crappy day was beginning to look up by the hour!

I decided that another shower and a shave would be in order, and after I'd completed my "ablutions" – a word, oddly enough, that Jerry Kendall had liked to use to sound intelligent and "upper crust" – I rewarded myself with a modest "libation" – yet another Kendallism – on the porch. I didn't have to pick Carrie Ann up until 7:15 and it felt good to just relax.

Then, the bushes to my right parted and Jerome Ravenel appeared. "Yo, Jerome!" I called out. "Get your butt up here and I'll pour you a premium Jack Daniels!"

Jerome smiled – he had one of the warmest smiles I'd known in a long while - and allowed as he might indulge himself in just a tiny taste. I poured him about three fingers and didn't notice him objecting.

Even though I was cleaned up and dressed for the evening, I knew I couldn't just sit and chat forever, so I asked him what was on his mind. Turned out it was nothing major at all. He was doing some repair work at his house and needed to go to the Home Depot and get a little lumber, some dry wall and a bunch of other construction stuff. Only, his brother, who had a nice Ford 250 diesel pickup, had to be in Georgetown. So, Jerome needed a way to carry his materials from the store to his home. In short, he wanted to know if he could borrow my truck for a few hours.

To me, that was a non-question. Of course he could use the Dodge. The only quick calculation I had to make was whether I might be staying at Carrie Ann's place overnight. We'd never done it, but this could be the night.

"Tell ya what, Jerome. If you can come by around 10 a.m. you're on." I knew that whatever happened I could be sure to be home by then. If he needed the truck all day after that, it'd be just fine with me. I had my little 850 Harley in the shed if I needed to go someplace. And, of course, if I needed a car for any reason, I had quietly bought an almost-new Caddy, a 280Z and a cherry '57 Chevy and stashed them in a barn I rented just up the road. I enjoyed owning them but I didn't drive around town showing them off.

Jerome appreciated my help and promised that the next time he bagged a buck, I'd be getting some venison steaks and sausages. I told him that wasn't at all necessary, but, if he forced the meat on me I'd feel obliged to accept.

We had a good laugh and I yielded to the temptation to add just a pinch more Jack to my tumbler before he departed. "If I'm not up," I called out to him, "just look under the left front tire. I'll leave the keys there. If you need any help with some carpentering, give me a shout. I'm no good at that stuff, but I make a great cheering section." Giving me one of those great smiles while flashing me the bird, Jerome disappeared back into the brush.

My evening out with Carrie Ann went well. I knew I liked her looks, and her personality was a perfect match. She was an Alabama native who'd moved to Charleston when her husband was transferred here in his bank job. Then, she found out he had at least one girlfriend on the side. After a few more strained years of marriage, they decided to call it a day.

I gather that he was pretty successful and that she got a decent settlement, because although she worked only part-time at a boutique down in Belle Hall, she dressed well, lived in a nice condo in the Old Village and drove a Lexus that was only a couple of years old. I'm not one to pry, and she didn't volunteer any information, so I don't know if she was a college graduate or not. Of course, neither was I, unless you count my AA in criminal justice. But, she seemed pretty smart and she had just a hint of that Southern Belle accent that I admit I'm a sucker for.

Long story short, the play – locally written, produced and acted in – was a lot better than I had anticipated. We both agreed that there was a lot of talent in the area.

When we got back to her condo, our night together ended pleasantly with a discreet kiss. I sensed that while she was interested in me, she wasn't ready to take things to the next level. I respected that. She wasn't one of those needy women who had to have a man at all times. As for me, I could wait. Maybe we'd get together; maybe we wouldn't. So be it. We'd had a nice time, and I looked forward to doing it again.

I stopped for a night cap at Charley's, a great roadside saloon where a lot of locals and transient bikers hang out, and shot some pool with a couple of local types I recognized from previous visits. Not wanting to take a chance on an accident or a ticket, I cut myself off after two beers, arriving home just around 1:30 a.m. To be on the safe side, I stuck my car's remote under the front left tire, as I'd told Jerome I would.

Then, I went to sleep, thinking "life is good."

20

I slept well. I even had a little dream about Carrie Ann. Just a pleasant meander through a country meadow. I guess I'm a bit of a romantic, after all.

That idyllic moment was shattered when my eyes snapped open and I sat bolt upright in bed. I can't say whether it was some weird sixth sense or a throwback to my military training. I knew something was wrong.

For an instant, I saw thin streams of sunlight coming through my wood-shuttered front windows. Then, there was a blinding flash and a powerful explosion rocked my house. Instinctively, I rolled out of bed and hit the deck, protecting the back of my head. The explosion was quickly followed by the crackling sound and the acrid smell of fire, not a good wood fire, but something ugly and evil.

The possibilities raced through my mind before it became clear. Something had happened to my truck – and Jerome had been coming by to take it to Home Depot! I jumped up, yanked on a pair of shorts and sandals and raced through the house, stopping in the kitchen to grab the little fire extinguisher I kept next to the stove.

I didn't know how much good it would be, but it was better than nothing.

I threw open the front door and was came face to face with my Dodge parked 20 feet away engulfed in towering flames. I ran to it shouting, "Jerome! Jerome!!!" and spraying the driver's side door with foam. The heat forced me to back off. I wanted to get into the cab to save Jerome, but I couldn't get closer. I could feel my hair starting to singe. Behind a curtain of CO2 I made one frantic lunge, smashing the window with the butt end of the extinguisher.

Out of nowhere, a pair of vise-like pincers grabbed both my shoulders and hurled me backward. They were hands, Jerome Ravenel's strong, bony hands. I stumbled sideways trying to retrieve my balance. "Jerome! You O.K.???" He was slapping dirt and embers off his clothing and looked as pale as a man of color could.

"I'm OK, Bobby. Now get back!"

"What the hell happened???"

"Tell you later. Now, grab your hose and do what you can. But stay back as far as you can. I'll make the calls."

Jerome ran into the house and I raced to unspool my garden hose. A pillar of fire a dozen feet high licked at the overhanging tree limbs. I took a position behind the big oak to the left of the porch and gave the torched truck the best dousing I could. It wasn't enough.

Minutes later, Jerome was by my side. "No way you can save the vehicle," he said. "Fire and sheriff are on their way. Just keep the flames down."

Because I live out in the sticks and nowhere near a fire hydrant, it took nearly fifteen minutes for the fire department to arrive, bringing both a tanker and a pumper. While they got to work swiftly and efficiently, Jerome took me aside.

"I called the Sheriff direct and also my old buddy, the chief arson investigator. They'll all be confidential about this."

"About what? I don't even know what happened. I'm just glad you're OK."

Jerome wanted to talk fast before the investigators arrived. He told me that, as we'd planned, he came by at 10:00 a.m. He glanced around the house and saw no signs that I was up and about, so he retrieved the keys I'd left under the front tire.

He said he'd gone back and climbed up onto the porch, figuring he'd knock softly so if I were awake, he could tell me he was leaving. At the last minute, he changed his mind and turned toward my truck. "Then I stopped," he sighed. "I'd like to think my next move was based on my years of fire-fighting. It may have been. I picked up a little scent of gas. That seemed odd because it was as if you'd overfilled your tank, but you'd told me you were low and I'd have to throw a few gallons in on the way to the lumber yard. But, it was more likely dumb luck or my weakness for novelty. I saw that you had one of those remote start gizmos on your key ring. So, I walked back about twenty feet to see what kind of range it had, and pressed the button. That's when the truck blew. Knocked me to the ground, but at least I wasn't in the driver's seat."

"What do you think went wrong???"

"I don't think anything went wrong. I think everything went right, except you weren't sitting behind the wheel when the engine cranked over."

"What are you saying?"

"Bobby, your truck was rigged to explode. I don't know how just yet and I certainly don't know by whom. But, this was no accident. You were supposed to join the choir celestial this morning. When Captain Carmichael gets here, we'll be able to put some pieces together and figure out what the detonator and accelerant were. But there's no doubt in my mind that someone wanted you dead."

I was absolutely stunned. If Jerome were right, someone tried to kill me, and it was only by chance that neither of us had been blown to pieces and incinerated. This was almost beyond belief.

The firefighters had the blaze under control quickly and were just mopping up when the Sheriff and his driver arrived, followed by Captain Carmichael and two assistants in a county fire department van. The assistants went to work on what was left of the truck while the rest of us went back onto the porch. I offered coffee to everyone and went inside to put a pot on the stove.

When I came back with the coffee, we sat watching the investigators probing through the remains of the vehicle. Jerome deferred to the Sheriff.

"Bobby, what light can you shed on this unfortunate incident."

"Not much, Sheriff. I drove the truck last night without any problems. I parked it right where it is now around 1:30 a.m. I went to sleep and woke up just before the explosion and fire."

"I'm not so much concerned with that timeline," the Sheriff said, "as I am with whether you can identify anyone who might have had reason to want to cause you harm. Has anything happened recently that might have caused any individual or individuals to contemplate killing you? Could this have anything to do with a former associate of yours turning up dead on the very porch where we are now sitting?"

I couldn't imagine any connection between the two events, but at the Sheriff's prompting I gave him the Cliff Notes on my recent journey to Los Angeles, my meetings with the LAPD and Jerry's famous lawyer, and also my strange call from Derrick Pettit informing me that Jerry Kendall had been a coke user, a gambler, a horn dog and an embezzler.

Jerome shook his head. The Sheriff whistled as if stunned. Capt. Carmichael stood up and left to supervise his team.

"Bobby," the Sheriff said softly, "there's plenty of reasons why your sticking your nose into Mr. Kendall's death may have resulted in the trashing of your vehicle with the intent to trash you as well. I'm not in a position to make any wild guesses on this one, but I'd surely advise that you consider this a little more than a warning shot across your bow. If Carmichael's boys conclude that your truck was rigged to blow – and I have little doubt that they will – my department will do everything possible to find out who did it.

"That said, I'm pretty sure that it wasn't anyone local. You haven't been around here very long and, even though you're a Yankee, you don't seem to have pissed anyone off enough for them to want to whack you. My guess is that this could well have been a contract hit, possibly out of California."

Jerome jumped in. "Bobby, while you were inside we came up with a little battle plan. If someone wanted you out of the way, they'll be eager to find out if their little plan worked. So, the arson report will remain sealed. My years in the department give me a little juice to make sure than these things can be kept under wraps unless and until the details are needed.

"The Sheriff has agreed to have the official report on this incident suggest that a faulty electrical connection caused an automotive fire that resulted in the destruction of a vehicle. No more, no less. If this makes the newspaper, and I doubt that it will, it will be two or three sentences on page eight, and probably won't even mention your name."

Jerome paused, "Sheriff?"

"The upside to keeping this quiet is that it will frustrate whoever was behind this probable murder attempt. The downside is the same. When there's no news about one Bobby McRae being toasted in his truck, your assailant will have to assume that you are alive, and still a danger. So, you'll have to take some additional measures to protect yourself. And, you'll have to spend some time analyzing recent events to see if you can come to any conclusions about who might have it in for you."

"Meanwhile," Jerome chimed in, "you might consider investing in an alarm system for the house and even some remote-activated floodlights at key spots on the dirt road. And, you might want to take that silly sign down and actually get yourself a dog."

21

I decided against a dog, at least for now. I decided against photo-electric cell activated floodlights, because it was pretty obvious that whoever rigged my truck hadn't driven down the dirt road. Perimeter security was out of the question. Every time a squirrel brushed up against one of the wires I'd be diving under my bed. I compromised by having a few extra locks installed in the house as well as a simple alarm system that would just make a lot of noise if anyone tried to break in. Living where I did, putting in one of those systems that "alerts" a home office and then they call the cops would be ridiculous. Any bad guy with half a brain could be in North Carolina before law enforcement could possibly respond. And, I invested in a few more weapons, most notably a Remington 870 shotgun with a custom pistol grip, a folding stock and a laser sight. If the sound of a pump shotgun being racked doesn't scare off a bad guy, a load of buckshot will.

Otherwise, life returned more or less to normal. I took my john boat out a few times, catching mostly trout, and rarely ones big enough to be keepers. I went to the gym. I read and watched some TV. Of course, I had some interesting conversations with my insurance agent, who eventually agreed to compensate me just about as much as I had wanted for the truck. Damn. I missed that Dodge already. It had been good to me.

Once I had the logistics of my personal protection more or less under control, I decided to try something I'd never tried before. I gave in and called the emergency number in Washington, identified myself as Raoul and said I had a message for The Doctor.

A bland female voice said, "One moment, Raoul."

Seconds later, a male voice barked, "What's your situation?"

I replied, "My situation is that I've recently been the target of a car bombing, and I'm looking for some help in figuring out who did it, why they did it and how I can avoid becoming a human marshmallow if they try it again."

The Doctor took what seemed like a long while to respond. "So, you're not in an emergency at the moment?"

"Not that I'm aware of, but a hit team could be lurking in the woods as we speak. So, can you guys help me or not?"

"Raoul, this line is supposed to be used only if you are in imminent danger on a mission. Is that the case?"

"I just told you. My vehicle was blown up in front of my house. Isn't that enough???"

I could swear I heard him sigh. "Every case is different. In general, I'd say that yours isn't an emergency. But, talk to me."

I ran through a brief history of Jerry's death, my visit to L.A. and my attempted murder by a person or persons unknown. He seemed unmoved. Then, I asked him for his help. I told him that I needed some information on several people connected with my recent activities.

"Whoa, whoa, whoa," he snapped. "I'm on a secure line, but you're not. I'm not sure this office can help, but I do know that discussing these matters on an open circuit just won't fly. Stay home tomorrow until you hear from us, understood?"

I agreed and without any further explanation, he rang off.

Feeling a lot frustrated and a little pissed off, I hopped on my bike and cruised up to Pawley's Island, where I had a nice meal, wandered through the little stores and came home to watch some HBO.

The next morning, I was having a cup of coffee along with some bacon and eggs when I heard a truck that seemed to be wheezing and squealing down my dirt road. I slipped the .380 in my pocket and propped the shotgun next to the front door. Moments later, a FedEx van turned into my drive.

The delivery man stepped out and looked legit. He knocked on the door so I opened it. "Mind signing for this package, sir?" I signed, and he sighed, "Do you get many deliveries down this, uh, road, sir?"

I was a little bit nervous about opening the box, but I did when I spotted the return address in suburban Virginia. It was a simple telephone with one or two extra buttons. I tried the hot line number and got the same neutral female voice.

When The Doctor came on the line, he said, "I see you received our package. Go to the lower right, find the button marked with a star and hit it."

I did as I was told and the line seemed to go dead for several seconds. Then, The Doctor's voice came back, sounding a little bit as if he'd stepped into a cave. "I can hear you," I said, my own voice taking on a bit of a reverb.

"Of course you can hear me. We're on the telephone. But, now we're scrambled. Use this instrument to contact me. And don't lose it! Now, what can I do for you?"

I told him that I needed information on several people, among them Captain Bates, Det. Allison Simmons, attorney Robert Raskin, Derrick Pettit, Jerry Kendall and a Jane Doe found dead in Los Angeles approximately three months previously.

He sounded irritated. "Raoul, we're not the FBI. We're not the CIA. We're not the NSA. Not that that would matter anyway, because none of those guys share information with each other anyway, much less with us. We're just a small part of the U.S. Army associated with the Department of State. You're asking a lot."

"I know I am," I replied, "but you have to have resources that I don't. Can't you just make a few inquiries and see what turns up?"

The Doctor let my question hang.

"No promises. I'll see what we can do. Give me what you've got."

I ran through the story once again, this time in detail.

There was silence on the other end of the line as he presumably considered all my information.

"Today's Thursday. Give me a few days, maybe until next Tuesday or Wednesday, and I'll get back to you. I'll call on this phone, so keep it nearby."

"Next Tuesday or Wednesday," I snapped. "Can't you guys work faster than that?"

"You know, for someone whose major claim to fame is wasting a couple of Balkan thugs, you've got a bit of an attitude."

"Hey, man. I thought our operation was 24/7!"

"You may be 24/7 but that's above my pay grade. I go home on the weekend, paint the picket fence and play ball with my kids. I'm not a cloak-and-dagger type. So, keep your shorts on. I understand that you're upset about being the target of a potential car bombing, but if you want my help you'll just have to go along with the program. Like I told you, were not an investigate agency. We have some contacts, and we'll do what we can to get you some helpful information. But, you gotta cool your jets."

I had to admit that he had a point. I'd been a target, but there was no reason to believe that I would be one again. And, he didn't have the resources to give me any solid answers, particularly about the Jane Doe. I apologized and thanked him for trying to help.

I hung up both frustrated and disappointed. I guess I'd expected something more James Bondish, maybe "M" leaping to assist me or "Q" promising some exciting new gadgets to help me unravel this mystery and smash the bad guys. Instead, I'd gotten a bored bureaucrat reluctantly agreeing to look into my case.

I took a tumbler of Gentleman Jack onto the front porch and surveyed the scorched area where my truck once sat. Through the trees, I could see a pretty substantial cabin cruiser making its way down the Intracoastal. I did a few mental calculations and decided that while I might be able to afford a nice boat like that I probably wouldn't use it enough to justify the cost. Still, it would be kind of cool.

Another bourbon and I started to feel a little better, well enough to consider the prospect of some female company. I dialed Carrie Ann. After the fourth ring, her voicemail picked up. "Hi, this is Carrie Anne. I'm in Atlanta visiting my sister and I'll be back in a week. If you need to reach me…" and she gave her cell phone number.

I thought to myself, "You should never leave a message saying you're out of town. That's an open invitation to having your home broken into." Next, I thought, "Bobby McRae ain't getting' no lovin' tonight." So, I whipped up a mess of shrimp and grits and decided to settle in with a good book.

22

My social calendar wasn't exactly going gang-busters, but my appointments seemed to be picking up speed. First, Jerome called to let me know he'd spoken with Captain Carmichael of the arson squad.

The Captain's men had concluded that my ride had been incinerated by a pretty simple yet sophisticated explosive device, a few ounces of plastic explosive detonated by the vehicle itself. The bomb was wired to the alternator so when the engine turned over, it blew. And, as it was situated directly under the driver's seat, it was clearly intended to give me a big lift I hadn't counted on. The fuel line from the oversized tank I'd had installed passing through the same general area guaranteed a quick, fierce burn.

According to Jerome, the Fire Chief and the Sheriff were willing to sit on this one, at least for a while. They'd quietly do some investigation, but there wasn't much to go on other than to see if there were any local sources for the explosive. They surely wouldn't be finding any fingerprints or DNA on what was left of the vehicle, and their guess was that whoever had planted the bomb had arrived by water and carefully covered their tracks on land when they left.

For now, the incident would remain a fire due to mechanical failure, and, in the absence of any new information to the contrary, that's what my insurance company and any news media that cared enough to look into it would be told.

I was grateful to everyone involved for sweeping this under the rug, however temporarily. They knew and I knew that this would buy me some time to sort out why it had happened and who might have been responsible.

Unfortunately, my next call was of almost no help at all. The scrambled phone burred and The Doctor was on the line.

"I checked out as much as I could," he drawled. "Nothing out of the ordinary came to light."

"That's your report?" I snapped.

"No, that's my summary and conclusion. If it makes you feel any better, I ran the names you gave me and didn't find either any skeletons or any closets. The guy who dropped dead on your stoop was an accounting/finance type who evidently never even got a jaywalking ticket. The two cops, Bates and Simmons, are exactly who they say they are. He's an upwardly mobile type with a solid record as a street cop, a detective, and now the Chief's right hand man for policy and public information.

"Detective Simmons is also clean, although her former partner is currently under suspension while IAB looks into some shady dealings he's said to have had with gangs, specifically narco-gangs.

"Who else? Raskin. Top defense lawyer. Attorney to the stars. Makes a ton of money and lives in Beverly Hills with his wife of 30 years and two of their three daughters. The third daughter is working for Paramount as a director trainee and living with two other girls in the Hollywood Hills. Mr. Pettit was Kendall's boss. But you knew that already."

"So, that's it???"

"Pretty much. Reviewing your jacket in the service, there's no indication that anyone foreign or domestic was after you. At least that should be reassuring."

"Listen," I interrupted, "since I last spoke to you I've learned from the county sheriff and the fire department's arson investigator that my truck was blown up by a plastic charge. It's been logged as a mechanical malfunction while I try to sort this out. Now, you're telling me that nobody's after me and this was just some sort of mad bomber fluke???"

"I'm not telling you anything because I'm not assuming anything. You asked for information on some specific individuals and I got it for you. It seems to be that absent some military or national security connection our business is completed.

"Oh, one more thing. Your stiff, Kendall, must have been a big fan of Hispanic culture. He's taken four trips to Mexico, Mexico City to be precise, in the past five years. You'd think that living in L.A. he'd get enough tacos and burritos by just driving down any block. And, your Jane Doe is just that, a Jane Doe."

"Thanks for nothing," I said, as politely as I could manage. "Now, go fuck yourself."

It realized that it probably wasn't a great idea to piss off The Doctor, but I was steamed. This anonymous guy was supposed to be my lifeline, and he couldn't even come up with any decent information on a handful of civilians, who might have been involved in my questioning how Jerry Kendall got killed. And that questioning was looking as if it were behind nearly surprising me with the same fate.

I mulled this over for a bit and concluded that I might have been reacting to his attitude alone. Maybe there just wasn't anything important to find out about any of the people I'd asked him about.

All I could think of to try was an end run. It might not work and it might backfire on me. But, I had to give it a try. I got Information and dialed the Pentagon.

Actually, calling the Pentagon isn't that hard in and of itself. It's getting through to anyone important that's the trick. I asked the operator to put me through to Lt. Col. Thomas Matthews, who'd been promoted from Major. The male voice answering his phone identified himself as Sgt. Edward Slattery and asked my name and the nature of my call. I gave him my special services name and said I was under the Colonel's command on an interagency mission.

Slattery put me on hold for about a minute and then came back on the line. "Colonel Matthews is just finishing a briefing. If you can hold a few minutes longer he'll be with you." Bingo! Of course I could wait a few minutes. I would wait all day to get his ear.

I took the phone out on the deck and plopped down in a rocker to wait. About five minutes went by before I heard the Colonel's brusque salutation, "Matthews here, Lieutenant. What's your situation?"

As succinctly as I could, I summarized the events from Jerry Kendall's death to my own truck bombing."

"So, you are not in imminent danger?"

"No, sir. Not so far as I know."

The Colonel cleared his throat. "First, as you should understand, the hotline you called is intended only, and I stress only, to seek assistance when you are, one, on a mission and two, in clear and present danger. That office is not the information desk at the public library."

He paused, then proceeded. "Your contact may have been unduly abrupt. He was following protocol. If you had had any other non-urgent business to discuss, you should have brought it to the attention of my office. Is that clear?"

This conversation was going from bad to worse. "Yes, sir, sir!"

"One sir will suffice, Lieutenant. Now, I'd like to be of some help to you but we're not face-to-face and I'm not in a position to discuss this any further without being on a secure line, which is…"

"…right here on my coffee table," I interrupted.

"What's right here on your coffee table?"

"An Army issue scrambler phone. My contact over-nighted it to me after we talked."

"Jee-sus," the Colonel snorted. "Maybe that office does need some looking into. To be candid, most of those staffers are special services prospects who never qualified for field work. Maybe some of them are still ticked off and taking it out on decorated operators like yourself. Call me back right away on your scrambler."

"I can make outgoing calls on it?"

"Of course. It's a damn telephone, isn't it?"

"Yes, sir." And, I called him right back.

The Colonel himself picked up and began talking right away. He told me that everything we said would be recorded and that I should be succinct and to the point. I went through my story as simply as possible, sticking to the facts and not adding in any of my own speculations.

"To your knowledge, no indication of any foreign involvement or any direct connection to your Army duties?"

"None that I can think of, sir, but, aside from training with the service I've been a corporate desk jockey for a lot of years so maybe my instincts are a little rusty."

"OK" the Colonel sighed. "In my estimation the fact that some person or persons attempted to take you out with ordnance typically associated with a clandestine operation is enough for me to make some inquiries and call in a few chips if needed. I'll need about forty-eight hours. Does that work for you?"

"Roger that, sir. Shall I stand by to hear from you?"

"Affirmative. I'm going to shoot for 1600 hours, day after tomorrow."

"I'll be standing by…with one eye on the wire!"

"Right. Keep a lookout and don't take any unnecessary chances while I try to help sort this out. Oh, and one more thing…"

"Yes, sir?"

"One of the main reasons I'm willing to go out on a limb like this is your record. I trust your skills and your judgment, and I don't think you're one of those guys who takes himself too seriously."

The Colonel paused, as if pondering whether he should go ahead and say what was on his mind and on the tip of his tongue. He decided he would.

"You know, all of our field exercises are thoroughly videotaped, don't you?

"I didn't actually know that, sir. But, common sense would hint that the Army wouldn't put operators through full-out drills without expecting to get some assessment of their capabilities."

"Exactly. During your most recent field exercise, you handled yourself commendably."He paused again.

"And, you also gave me and a select few of my fellow officers a little break from the life-and-death nature of the drill. It's not often we get to smile, much less laugh out loud, when reviewing the tapes."

He was losing me until he chuckled, "If I had the power and the decoration existed, I'd put you in for a medal for conspicuous innovation in employing an unconventional weapon. I've never before seen an enemy combatant disarmed and dispatched with a broom. Frankly, more than one senior officer up here nearly wet his pants when you nailed that guy. I even had to burn a few copies for their private archvies!"

I wasn't sure how to react so I just offered,"Well, I used what was right there at hand. I guess I was looking for a …clean sweep."

"OK," the Colonel said, "Don't go stand-up on me. Using that broom was smart, effective and funny – under the circumstances. Just don't think you can get away with a stunt like that in real combat. Oh,and when you have an enemy subdued, don't go ahead and shoot him dead, at least if there are any video cameras around.'

23

Manigault, South Carolina

With not much to do until I heard back from the colonel, I found myself at loose ends. Nothing I wanted to see was playing at the movies. I didn't have the concentration to pick up a good book. The only woman I was remotely interested in these days was out of town. So, I called Jerome.

"Have your nerves recovered after the big blast" I asked him.

"Pretty much back to normal. All in all it wasn't much worse than the time those propane tanks blew at the old railroad yard fire. Just more of a surprise. Anything new on your end?"

I couldn't tell him exactly what channels I had opened up so I just alluded to some contacts I'd worked with over the years. I told him my first attempt hadn't yielded much information but that I was expecting more info in a day or two.

He told me to be careful and let him know if he could be of any help.

"There's one thing," I said. "I haven't had a chance to spend any time at the camp the Gentlemen's Association keeps up in the woods. "Anything going on up there in the near future."

"Nothing planned," Jerome answered. "But, tell you what. Why don't I call a few of the fellas. Suggest we just meet up for an hour or two, say tomorrow evening. Play some cards. Have a drink. Maybe brainstorm a little on your recent situation."

I allowed as I was a little bored and more than a little apprehensive and wouldn't mind a quiet evening with the excellent company of some of the Association members. Jerome said he'd pass the word and see who might be available. At the very least, he and I could go to the camp. With the prospect of free drinks and maybe some sandwiches undoubtedly a few more members would be on hand.

We set the date for a five o'clock happy hour the next day and I promised to deliver some foodstuffs to go along with the camp's always copious supply of bar essentials.

After filling up my rented truck with three bags of snacks, breads and cold cuts at the market, I picked up Jerome and we headed up route 17 to the camp. Even though we were half an hour early, we weren't the first to arrive. Jerome told me that the lime green Jaguar convertible belonged to Artie Farmer.

That name seemed familiar and Jerome explained that Artie had played for nearly ten years on the PGA tour. He was one of those golfers who always finished somewhere in the money, even winning a few times in some of the lesser tournaments. But, he was destined never to get rich. That's when a very wealthy golfer with a yen for his own home course built what's now known as Carolina Coast Country Club and hired Artie to be its first, as so far only, resident professional.

While still competing a few times each year, now on the Senior Circuit, Farmer carved out a nice life for himself at the Club, not only as the golf pro but as a canny investor who traded golf tips for stock tips with many of the highly successful members. As a result, the kid who learned the game by caddying for duffers at podunk courses throughout the South became an esteemed member of Charleston society and a frequent board member of some of the most influential civic and charitable organizations in the Lowcountry.

We dragged in my contributions to the evening and found Artie already enjoying a tall Scotch out on the verandah overlooking the marsh. In lime green trousers that matched his car and a blindingly white polo shirt, Farmer looked like exactly who he was – a prosperous golfer who had no quarrels with the fate life had laid out for him.

Next to arrive were Judge Pinckney, Police Chief Fein, Sheriff Major, Fire Chief Huger and artist Eustace Delacroix. Last to arrive were two more members I had not yet met, E. Jasper "Jazz" Thomas, managing editor of The Daily Chronicle newspaper and Sumter Karl, anchorman of the Channel Three television news at 6:00 and 11:00 p.m.

After a round of drinks and the obligatory catching up and jibing at one another, Judge Pinckney suggested we convene around the big green felt covered card table and see what the pasteboards had in store for us.

Before the first shuffle and deal, the Judge reminded us that under South Carolina law, playing any game involving cards or dice was a criminal offense. "And, playing any of those games for money raises the ante from a venial to a mortal sin."

His admonition fell on deaf ears as the obscure 1802 law is almost universally honored in the breach not in the observance. "Nonetheless," he continued, "to stay within the spirit if not the letter of the law, we'll continue our practice of playing for colored toothpicks. Then, at the conclusion of the games, if any of us wants to square their accounts, they can do so privately.

"Sheriff Major, could you please distribute 100 toothpicks in three denominations -let's call them 10, 25 and 50 - to tonight's players?"

With the deal rotating and each new game being dealer's choice, we ran through Texas Hold 'em, Seven Card Stud, Five Card Draw and the aptly named No Peek for around ninety minutes and were about to count our toothpicks when two quick chirps from a police siren broke through the wooded silence, accompanied by a rapid blue light strobe.

Judge Pinckney raised his eyebrows. "I would hazard a guess that our two friends from the Fourth Estate are about to become a part of a major story on an illicit gaming raid. Or, this new arrival might be an invited guest from the Midlands, Special Agent Mike Kelly of the Federal Bureau of Investigation.

"I'm hoping for the latter because the FBI has no authority over strictly state concerns such as gambling laws, so he'd have neither motivation nor authority to run us all in!"

The Judge knew all along that Agent Kelly would be dropping by. He'd called ahead to let Pinckney know that he had to be in town from the Columbia head office and the Judge insisted he join us.

Kelly bore little resemblance to the stereotypical motion picture and TV FBI agent. No taller than 5'6 and weighing in at about 130 pounds, the sandy haired agent looked more like a fast food cashier than a federal lawman. It wasn't until considerably later that I learned about the much-honored exploits in his nearly 25 years with the Bureau, personally taking down big-time drug dealers, mob kingpins white collar criminals, kidnappers and more.

Agent Kelly worked the room, introducing himself to those of us he didn't know and amiably sparring with old friends.

Then, between puffs on what he described as "a mellow Dominican, from Cuban seed," Judge Pinckney casually turned the conversation from general banter to me.

"As you all know, Mr. McRae here is both a rather recent transplant from the Sodom and Gomorrah of Hollywood to our sylvan shores and, in point of fact, the newest member of our modest organization.

"Despite Bobby McRae's brief tenure as a Charlestonian, he has managed to woo a few fair damsels, make something of a name for himself as a writer and interviewer and become the focal point of two extraordinary occurrences, the untimely death of a former colleague on his front porch and the destruction of his vehicle, evidently by a bomb, not more than a few meters from that very aforementioned front porch."

"Tonight's gathering was cobbled together just for our usual fun. But, with so many representatives of both law enforcement and the news media present, I'd like to suggest that Mr. McRae fill everyone in on his involvement in these two incidents. If he'd be so kind as to do so, perhaps among us we might be able to assist him in his quest to determine just exactly what the FUCK is going on here!"

With that, the Judge took another puff on his cigar and leaned back in his wicker armchair, beaming. And, all eyes turned to me.

I'm not unaccustomed to talking to the media, or to law enforcement for that matter, Nonetheless, I felt pretty much put on the spot, or perhaps under the microscope.

Sumter Karl, the patrician, silver-haired anchorman broke the silence. "Bobby, I believe you know that in the South, or at least here in the Charleston market, our news gathering is a bit different from what you've likely been accustomed to in Los Angeles and New York.

"Down here, we're more cooperative than competitive. That's not to say that we don't relish the occasional scoop, but that's not our sole goal. The print media have more staff than TV does, and often break news items first. Then, while they have the ability to deliver lengthy, analytical reports, it's up to television to reach all those folks who don't read the paper as well as all of those who do but can also benefit from the immediacy and visual impact only TV news can deliver. Jazz, would you agree?"

Thomas was in mid-gesture, rolling up the sleeves of his tailored blue-and-white striped Oxford cloth shirt as if he were about to grab a soft pencil and dive into marking up some feckless reporter's copy.

"I believe you've summed the situation up nicely, Sumter. Of course, that's what you folks in TV do – sum things up nicely. We who labor as ink-stained wretches are burdened with informing the populace in exquisite detail about, and with implication of, what snippets of news they have witnessed on TV sandwiched between commercial messages and network entertainment promotions.

"More to the point insofar as this evening is concerned, I believe we are united in making any statements, comments or observations completely off the record. The axiom is that nothing is <u>ever</u> off the record, so if anyone present has a long-lost sexual dalliance or axe murder preying on his conscience, I'd suggest holding your tongue. But, as for Mr. McRae and his life and times, I'm confident that all of us – and I include our brothers in blue, so to speak – can assure confidentiality."

Nodding heads and murmurs all around. Then, Agent Kelly said smiling, "As best I can determine, the only one with primary jurisdiction here is you, Sheriff. So, if you're on board, I think we're OK to let Mr. McRae spill whatever beans he may have."

Truthfully, I would have felt a lot more comfortable just regaling the guys with some stories about wild Hollywood parties or some of the dumb things I'd seen celebrities do. I'm sure they would have enjoyed a little peek behind the Hollywood tinsel façade. Unfortunately, that didn't seem to be an option.

So, without further delay I began the story of my recent years. I held back only a few details, such as the keys, cash and strange bullet I found in Jerry Kendall's apartment and my personal opinion on Detective Allison Simmons as my own target of opportunity.

Of course, I completely skipped over my years with the Army and the Department of State, as well as my Bronze Star and my deep cover second identity. I wasn't concerned about my fellow club members, but I believed that if I brought up the subject the FBI would soon have a dossier on me, if they hadn't already.

A drink and a half later, I'd disgorged all the information I felt comfortable sharing and wrapped up quipping, "So, that's my story and I'm stickin' to it!" I hadn't been expecting a bravo! or even a smattering of applause. I also hadn't been expecting the somewhat awkward silence that followed.

I was about to try to lighten the mood by suggesting, tongue in cheek, we open the floor to a little Q & A when Judge Pinckney cleared his throat. His gesture had the same impact as a speaker tapping on an empty water glass to get everyone's attention.

"Bobby, "the judge began, "you've done an exemplary job in summarizing the unusual experiences you've had since moving here to our community. Now, it's our responsibility to review the facts you have presented to us and utilize our respective expertise and experience to suggest why these incidents took place and what they might mean to you in the days ahead."

I nodded, noticing that several of the men in our group had inched forward on their chairs, apparently concentrating on what would come next.

"Before I served on the bench," Judge Pinckney continued, "I put in a few years as a state prosecutor. With that background in mind, I'd like to begin."

"The demise of Mr. Kendall was ruled as due to natural causes. There were no indications of foul play. However, his body was cremated before further tests could be effected that might have raised questions about the initial verdict. Bobby, you then traveled to Los Angeles to try to determine why a former colleague who you say not a close friend would have arrived unannounced on your doorstep, only to die before seeing you.

"You returned to South Carolina without any answers. Then you heard from Mr. Kendall's former boss who revealed to you that Kendall had been involved in embezzling a rather considerable sum of money, and that the studio had been unwilling to prosecute.

'Next, your neighbor Jerome Ravenel was nearly killed when an explosion ostensibly meant for you destroyed your truck in your own driveway. The county fire chief's office and the sheriff's office agreed to report this occurrence as a mechanical malfunction rather than the planned detonation they believe it to have been. This was to confuse the perpetrators who could only guess at the efficacy of their explosive and whether it had even been determined to be an anti-personnel device."

"The idea being," Artie Farmer interjected, "not to let the bombers know that their plan had bombed!"

That got a good laugh and I thought we were going to move on to some more idle banter and then head home. I hadn't counted on the judge. "If no one has any immediate questions or observations, I'd be honored to leap into the breach," Pinckney suggested.

"Separating the facts into those a prosecutor would consider truly relevant we find ourselves with an embezzler who made off with millions of dollars from the company he worked for, which was strangely disinclined to prosecute him alive and is apparently not seeking to recover any of those losses after his death.

"We find that same embezzler traveling cross country for no apparent reason only to die – or, possibly, to be killed – on the doorstep of a former colleague at the same company, Bobby McRae.

"Interestingly, less than one year ago, Bobby, you abruptly quit your executive job stating that, despite the daunting odds against it, you had won a significant amount of money in the California State Lottery and no longer needed to work. You left the glitz and glitter and the throngs of starlets in Tinseltown to move to Charleston, a city you had never before visited, to live in a rustic cabin in the woods in an unincorporated area remote enough that is not yet a part of any municipality."

The judge paused, seemingly for emphasis. "A stickler for detail might raise a few minor questions, such as, 'How did Mr. McRae rise so swiftly through the ranks of his company? What was his true relationship with the deceased? Even in the face of having pocketed a substantial sum in lottery winnings, why did he leave Los Angeles, rather than simply buy a mansion in Beverly Hills, put a brace of Rolls Royce in the garage and continue living the Hollywood good life.? And, of course, why did his vehicle explode on the one morning when it was to be driven not by him but by his friend and neighbor, Jerome Ravenel?"

Suddenly, I started feeling a lot more than uncomfortable and all eyes in the room seemed to be riveted on me.

"This is hardly a court of law,' Judge Pinckney said somberly. "I am simply raising some questions that would likely be posed if it were."

"What springs to mind, gentlemen, is the core question from which radiate all manner of issues in respect to criminal activity. That is, 'cui bono' roughly translated from the Latin as 'who benefits?' Absent any heretofore undiscovered candidates, Bobby, one could speculate that the one most likely to benefit would be, you."

24

The unpleasant silence that followed seemed to be a signal to call it a night. Jazz Thomas was the first to speak. "Well, gents, I'd better be heading downtown. Have to check the bulldog before it hits the street."

Thomas must have just re-watched "The Front Page. These days, and especially in smaller markets, there was no "bulldog," the first edition that major metropolitan newspapers print just after midnight. In fact, in Charleston there was only one edition of any newspaper, the one that arrived on doorsteps around 6:00 a.m.

Sumter Kraft followed suit. "Got a busy day tomorrow myself. Have to be in Walterboro by noon for a remote broadcast in our 'Your Lowcountry' series."

Artie Farmer tipped his empty highball glass to his lips, looking as if he really wanted another Scotch but with so many lawmen present was thinking twice about taking his chances with a DUI.

The other members started to head for the door. Jerome and I had already volunteered to stick around and clean the camp before heading home.

Agent Kelly stood and walked over to shake my hand. "Nice meeting you, Bobby. Say, would you mind walking me out to my car? I want to pick your brain for some scuttlebutt on a few of those celebrities I'm sure you know. My kids would kill me if they found out I'd spent an evening with a movie studio guy and didn't come home with some juicy stories."

We headed up the long dirt road to where Kelly had parked. One the way, he said softly, "You know, the Judge has both an extremely probing mind and a very fertile imagination. It's a combination that's interesting."

"Roger that."

"Military?

"Once upon a time."

Agent Kelly nodded thoughtfully at my non-answer. "Any skeletons in your closet?"

"Nothing incriminating, Agent Kelly. The only skeletons I can think of might be related to my teenage dating. But, they're buried so well even the Bureau couldn't dig them up. Not that the FBI would want to."

We reached the front fender of his unmarked official Bureau sedan and paused. "You know, the state of California has an anonymity policy on its lottery winners. Names aren't disclosed unless the winners waive their right to privacy."

"Agent Kelly, I'm clean. I don't know why I was a big winner. I didn't even play very often and I just did the Quick Pick. In a perfect world, my winnings would have gone to some poor soul with eleven kids, no job and terminal something. But, they didn't. And the main reason why I retired when I did was because I was feeling burned out at the studio.

"Don't get me wrong. Avante was terrific to me. I started off as a nobody rattling doorknobs on the security graveyard shift in the New York office and through no fault of my own worked my way up to an executive job with more responsibilities and better pay than I'd ever imagined.

"It was just that after fifteen years or so I'd done pretty much all I could do, and I was getting antsy. I wasn't sure what to expect back out in the real world, but I thought I should take the opportunity I'd lucked into a chance to give it a shot."

A hint of a smile flickered across Kelly's face. "You know, despite that anonymity rule, a properly executed subpoena would open the Lottery's records files quicker than a can of Spam.

"Of course, if you're legit, no worries. Your winnings would eliminate motive. At least <u>one</u> motive. As for means, right now there isn't any. If Kendall just up and died, which is how it's been ruled, means isn't a factor. Naturally, opportunity is a different story. You'd have had to lure him to your cabin. But, located where you are, there'd have been no witnesses other than the occasional owl."

His smile broadened and I sensed he was just needling me, at least in part. Fishing out his wallet, he handed me a business card. "You know the Bureau has no horse in this race, for now. If you ever want to get in touch with me, even if it's just to grab a cup of coffee and talk, give me a buzz up in Columbia. Are you planning on going back to L.A. any time soon?"

"I just might be. There are way too many loose ends floating around. I'm thinking I might sleep a lot better if I could put some answers to my questions."

Kelly took a fancy pen with a built-in flashlight out of his shirt pocket and wrote on the back of his card. "Bud Bianco's the SAC in the L.A. office. He's a terrific guy and knows just about everybody who counts. If you run into any snags, he can at least give you a heads up on what to go after and what to steer clear of. Use my name."

I thanked him and headed back to the cabin where Jerome had already put most everything in order. "I'm about ready to head out, Bobby." He hesitated, then asked, "You aren't planning on bumping me off on the way home and leaving my body for the turkey buzzards, are you?"

He broke out in a big grin and all I could think of to say was, "You shithead!"

The next morning I was the one with the head. It was buzzing from too many bourbons and a pretty fitful night's sleep. I'd learned enough in my criminal justice courses and watched enough cop shows on TV to know that the most innocent guy can look guilty as hell through circumstantial evidence. But, me???

A pot of coffee, a grapefruit juice and some rye toast brought me up to a decent consciousness level, so I wasn't surprised when the scrambler phone rang. As good as his word, it was Colonel Matthews.

"Lieutenant McRae here," I answered in what I thought sounded like a crisp, military salutation. Because I wasn't on official business, I wasn't really sure which of my names to use.

"We're not on official time here, Bobby. Just call me Jack. I've got some info for you. I'll run through whatever I was able to find. Stop me if you want to ask questions or get me to slow down. It's not all that much."

He was right. There was nothing much on Kendall except that he had no outstanding debts and liked to take vacation trips south of the border.

Captain Terry Bates' bio was a little juicier. In his day, he'd climbed the ladder faster than most, probably in part because his wife was the only daughter of a very prominent businessman who owned several dozen fast food franchises and a local magazine. The old man was also a significant financial backer of city and state office-holders, among them the current Chief of Police.

Add in his own self-generated high profile and it was no surprise when Bates became the Chief's protégé. He was even spoken of as a top candidate to be the next Chief, maybe even the Mayor of LA.

Robert Raskin was nationally known for his successful defense work in some very spectacular high-profile murder cases, including one where he and his team got an acquittal for a pair of twin college basketball stars who everyone with an intelligence level higher than a clam was convinced had brutally murdered their gorgeous twin girlfriends. In short, he was really good and had never personally been accused of filching as much as a candy bar.

The colonel even checked out Jerome Ravenel, coming up with a tidbit I hadn't been aware of but that didn't surprise me. As a young man coming up in rural upstate South Carolina, he'd been something of a civil rights firebrand and been both beaten and arrested numerous times. Once the national tumult died down a bit he moved to Charleston where he became one of the first black men to become a firefighter and, eventually, the city's first black chief.

Derrick Pettit also turned out to be pretty much what he seemed to be. Jack confirmed that he'd grown up in the Bay Area, did his undergraduate work at San Francisco City College, earned an MBA from Stanford and became a CPA.

"We focused on criminal databases. The only reason he popped up is that he's an accountant. The FBI loves keeping track of accountants and attorneys. Half the Bureau is bean counters and lawyers So, nothing much on Mr. Pettitt. Too bad he wasn't a Small."

That seemed like an odd thing to say. I replied, "Well, he is small. Maybe 5'6" on a good day."

"I didn't mean little small. I mean it's too bad he isn't <u>named</u> Small. There are files thick as a phone book on that family."

The Smalls must have captured the colonel's attention. He said that they were also a Bay Area family whose children grew up in the 60's and 70's.

"There were seven boys, and all of them had names that began with the letter 'J'," he said. "Jeremiah, Jonah, Joshua, that sort of thing. All Bible names. The oldest was Josiah Small and that's who most of the records are on.

"This was all before your time," he noted. "Josiah became a radical around the time of Malcolm X and the Panthers. His specialty was explosions. The government has him linked to at least a dozen bombings – university research labs, right wing publications, public buildings like a police station in Wisconsin.

"All in all, he was responsible for as many as 18 deaths and millions in property damage. But the law couldn't lay a glove on him. He was that slick.

"Your bombing is why I mention this, not that Josiah Small, or Shabazz Ali as he liked to call himself, could have been responsible. He's been on the lam since 1974."

Jack paused. "Ali's big mistake was hooking up with a group of rich, anti-war white kids who called themselves The Subterraneans.

"They'd taken credit for two or three mass demonstrations, riots more like it, in New York when Ali arrived to show 'em how it's really done

"Unfortunately for him, their enthusiasm for explosions wasn't backed by much practical experience. One of the home-made bombs they were working on in their fancy brownstone blew prematurely. Killed four of them and took out a good chunk of Ali's left hand. That's how the FBI ID'ed him. From the fingerprints on the two fingers he left behind."

According to Colonel Matthews, Shabazz Ali went deep underground, got his wound treated, and made it across the border to Canada. That's when his trail went cold. The assumption was that's he'd wound up seeking asylum in some country with a beef with America, probably in North Africa.

For all of his short career, Small/Ali had been a bullhorn for anti-war, anti-government, anti-U.S. rants. Suddenly, he was silent and despite years of effort the United States couldn't find him, much less bring him to justice. Finally, the government just threw up its hands and decided Ali was either dead or no longer a threat to America.

"That's about all I could come up with, Bobby" Colonel Matthews said. "I don't know how much help all this will be to you.

"Frankly, I don't know why you're pursuing this. If the alleged bombing of your truck is any indication, it's pretty obvious that some person or persons doesn't want you poking around anymore. Since you're not a cop and you have no official standing in any investigation, you might do yourself a favor by just backing off."

I thanked Matthews and told him how much I appreciated his standing up for me in my dust-up with The Doctor and all his help in checking out the people I saw as somehow connected with Jerry Kendall's death.

It was pretty clear that from here on in, I'd be on my own.

25

Manigault, South Carolina

Despite what I'd implied to FBI agent Kelly, I had no immediate plan to return to the West Coast. All of the information I'd been able to gather on everyone I considered to be associated with Jerry Kendall's death amounted to nothing special. The facts shed no light on who might have been responsible for blowing up my truck, or why. I had to assume that the blast had been meant to kill me. But, in the wake of its failure, there'd been no follow-up attempt.

I'd pretty much put the whole situation on the back burner, in part because my post-holiday dance card had filled up fast. Among the observations I'd been able to make once I settled in to my new life in South Carolina was that the residents of The Holy City and its environs are extremely charitable, and that they also believe that there's no time like the present for a good party. As a result, the Christmas season never ends with New Year's Eve. It continues on into January, February and beyond with a staggering array of fetes, galas, balls and just plain blowouts to benefit good causes from curing breast cancer, heart disease, kidney disorders and much more to women's rights, gay rights and historic preservation. You name it.

There's a substantial corps of Charlestonians who'll open their homes, their hearts and their wallets for just about any noble mission, and there are others who won't support every cause that comes along the pike but will move heaven and earth to give to and work for their own pet charities.

On top of all this partying and giving, which also includes the growing and increasingly affluent suburbs such as Mount Pleasant, Isle of Palms and Sullivan's and Daniel Islands, every other person you meet seems to be a volunteer for something. And, not just donating an hour or two once in a while to giving visitors directions at the local hospitals. These people work hard, all year round, and many of the most prominent local professionals will take weeks off from their lucrative practices to provide medical, dental and legal assistance pro bono to other South Carolinians as well as to strangers in far-flung places from South America to Africa and Asia.

I was pretty amazed when I learned all of this. About the only solid advice my father, rest his soul, ever gave me was "never volunteer," a sentiment echoed by my first mentor in the Army. On the other hand, I've never been a cheapskate when it came to tossing some money in the basket for organizations I believe in such as The Salvation Army, the SPCA, and a mixed bag of civil rights, human rights and libertarian groups, including the anti-marijuana laws lobby. I mean, our jails are packed with people who didn't do anything worse than smoke a weed, for Pete's sake!

Once I really had some serious cash at my disposal, I expended my charitable horizons to include a few of those charities that seemed to mean so much to the movers and shakers in my new hometown. I was no Rockefeller Foundation, but I had little problem giving away a few thousand dollars here and there to help with all the good work.

Much to my surprise, my modest largess paid off in ways I hadn't anticipated. I got on lists. Of course, this meant that everyone and his cousin with an axe to grind - Saving the Salamanders, Equality for the Clumsy, A Cure for Bad Hair - began bombarding me with solicitations. That was the downside, but it wasn't much of one as the wackier groups were easy to ignore.

The upside was that I began getting invited to a lot of those big bashes and blowouts at which long money was raised for the high profile charities. There were plenty of them. Charlestonians will find a reason to celebrate just about anything, from Mardi Gras to Groundhog Day to the opening day of the Riverdogs' minor league baseball season.

I would have liked to believe that it was my great native charm that brought me into at least the fringe of local society, but I'm pretty sure it was the contributions. Of course, my last name being the same as that of a family that owns one of the major restored plantations in the Lowcountry might not have hurt.

Once I decided to come out of my cave and take a look at the social whirl, I was surprised once again. Turns out that there is a significant population in the area of fairly well-to-do, quite attractive, youngish women who find themselves at loose ends either as a result of divorce or widowhood. By contrast, there are far fewer reasonably attractive - and charming! - middle-aged men with interesting, even exotic backgrounds and no need to work for a living. Let's just say that I became something of a hot commodity.

While I danced and drank myself through the party circuit, meeting and, hopefully, impressing a procession of female doctors, lawyers, interior designers, entrepreneurs, college professors and the ubiquitous real estate agents, I didn't have much time to dwell on the other issues that had entered my life with the death of Jerry Kendall.

Still, many a quiet night by myself in the still darkness of my woodsy hide-away, I turned everything over again and again in my mind, wondering if I'd missed some important fact, and if anyone would ever solve the mystery of how all those elements fit together.

It was in the midst of one of those musings that Jerome Ravenel stomped up onto my front porch and called out, "Former second-class citizen in need of an adult beverage. Chop, chop!"

Despite any and all adversity, Jerome always had a way to make me smile. I invited him in, poured us both healthy drinks and, despite an uncharacteristic February chill we repaired to the front porch and broke out two decent cigars.

With relatives and friends all over South Carolina and throughout the South, Ravenel was often out of town, visiting his far-flung network of family and acquaintances. Although he never presented himself as a role model of any sort, it was evident that a great many black people, the term "African- American" never having really caught on in Dixie, looked up to him, respected him and sought his counsel. From humble beginnings at a time when Negroes with roots in slavery were often considered no more valuable than barnyard animals, he had educated himself and built himself a tremendous career as one of the first black men to make his mark in big city government.

It was clear to me that he spent much of his retirement time, and perhaps his retirement money, traveling around from big cities to tiny hamlets offering advice, encouragement and a helping hand to young blacks who hoped to be as successful one day as he'd become. In his quiet, unassuming way, Jerome had likely done more for a generation of young black men and women than a dozen flamboyant politician/preachers.

Tonight, he was in a relaxed, reflective mood, so the time seemed right to ask him a personal question about the past. "Jerome," I said, "Back in the day, did you ever know a guy named Shabazz Ali?"

Jerome puffed on his cigar before answering. "Shabazz Ali. I can't say I <u>knew</u> him, but I knew <u>of</u> him. Fact, I first heard about him back when he was called Josiah X. He was really just a kid then, but he was already locked in with both the Black Panthers and the Nation of Islam."

"When you say you knew <u>of</u> him," I tried, "do you mean you'd only read about him in, like, TIME magazine or something? Or, did you know him better than that?"

Jerome swung his rocking chair around so that he was looking me straight in the eye. "I never met the man. I was never involved in the Panthers or the Muslims, either. I knew Ali by reputation only."

"Here's the thing, Bobby," he went on, "When I was coming up, the black folks in this part of the country were just trying to nail down a few very simple things. The right to vote. The right to a decent education. The right to sit where they wanted to on a bus or at a lunch counter. Nobody I knew was trying to overthrow the government, or kill all the white folks or change the world."

He paused. "Some of these other guys had very different ideas. They believed that black people in America had been trampled on for centuries and that now was the time to turn the tables. Every one of them was shouting 'Burn, baby, burn!'

"Aside from a few hotheads here and there, I never knew anyone who really agreed with them, much less supported them. But, they couldn't be ignored. In their own twisted way, they were our icons, our champions, the niggers who wouldn't take no shit from Mr. Charlie. They wore uniforms and black berets. They carried guns and weren't afraid to use them. They talked a great ballgame and then blew up a few things just to show they weren't kidding around.

"Were they heroes? Not to my way of thinking. Nonetheless, they were smart, serious black men who weren't afraid to take a stand for freedom and put themselves and their lives on the line to get it. So, yeah, I knew all about them. I'm not saying I agreed with them, but they couldn't be ignored."

My mild-mannered buddy had become more passionate as he talked. His voice rose. His fists clenched. Even the cadence of his speaking voice seemed to change.

"So, what was your position on everything that was going on?" I already knew at least part of the answer to that question.

"I knew Dr. King and Ralph Abernathy really well. I worked with them. They were just trying to keep bread on people's tables, to keep their kids in good schools, to keep redneck, bigoted muthafuckas from beatin' and killin' men and women just for the *crime* of being born black. I did my share of sit-ins and went on the Freedom Rides. I did jail time and I got beaten up by mobs. But, I never, ever said that all white people were no good. It's the Martin Luther King Jr. legacy that we're seeing today, not the Panthers' or the Muslims'. Some of the richest, best known and respected, most powerful people in America today are black. We've even had a black man in the White House. But, we didn't get where we are by hatred and killing."

Jerome stopped talking abruptly and took a healthy pull on his drink.

A waited a long beat before asking, "So, in your view, where did Shabazz Ali fit into all of this?"

Ravenel sighed. "He was right up there with Eldridge and Huey and Bobby and their kind. The difference was that while they were tough and mean-spirited and smart, he was all those things plus ruthless. Word on the street was that if Ali had his way there'd be mass rapes and murders of every white man and woman in the country, except for a handful of rich radicals who could kiss his black ass and give him the money he needed to plan bombings that would kill innocent people."

I asked, "Do you know what happened to Ali?"

"All I know is what I read in the papers. He was in with some crazies in New York who accidentally blew themselves up. The way I heard it, he was at the front door of their fancy brownstone paying a Chinese take-out delivery guy when the bomb went off. The story is that he was hurt but not killed and he managed to escape to somewhere. Good thing he wasn't killed. Can you imagine how embarrassing it would have been for a dangerous militant to be taken to the morgue covered with egg foo yung and fortune cookies?

"As far as I know he's never been heard from again. If I had to guess, I'd say he had himself some phony papers, made it up to Canada and then pitched his tent in some other country that also hated America, maybe Algeria."

Jerome leaned back in his chair. He looked spent from retelling his part in the history of black America's struggle for civil rights. "So, what's your interest in Shabazz Ali?"

"Nothing special, "I vamped. "I just ran across his name somewhere. Knowing you, I figured you must have been a part of the civil rights movement. I thought maybe you might have known him."

Our conversation turned to college basketball and the upcoming March Madness. Jerome had another drink, finished his cigar and said good night before ten.

I went inside and turned on the news, more to get the weather forecast than anything else. By the time I flipped the TV off and headed to bed to read a new mystery novel, my mind was made up. I was going to go back to L.A. and snoop around some more, preferably unnoticed, to look for some way to tie everything together.

26

Before I could leave for Los Angeles, I had to take care of a few details close to home. Jerome had convinced me that if I wouldn't get a security system or a big dog I should at least sink some posts at the head of the dirt road and stretch a good strong chain and between them. Plus, a bogus sign he had made up stating "No Trespassing – Hazardous Material Site." I wanted to make it "Nuclear Waste Site" but Jerome felt that was going too far.

As usual, he agreed to pick up my mail and keep an eye on the cabin for me. And, I installed a half dozen pretty decent variable timers so that some lights and the TV would go on randomly after sundown.

My next stop was Second Carolina Bank, an institution I'd picked because I felt that any bank that could take pride in being #2 probably was a pretty down-home, friendly place. Most of my serious money was elsewhere, in a handful of major banks and with brokers up North and out West. But, I kept a good chunk of liquid assets nearby and handy. I also had a big safe deposit box with some of my most important papers and documents.

I brought a leather attaché case to the bank and made my first stop the safe deposit vault. I had the key and the assistant manager had no problem letting me access the box without showing my more ID than that. I wondered whether big city banks would be so easy. It took me only a few minutes to pick through the contents of the box and remove all of the documents for my other, Army/State Department identity.

I had a valid passport, Army and State Department laminated ID cards, an official silver shield with "Special Agent" emblazoned on it in gold. It didn't state "Special Agent" of what. I'd applied for and received a driver's license, a library card, even a gymnasium membership card in my other name. And there were the two legitimate bank cards, one credit, one debit, both in the same name.

I put the safe deposit box back, went to a teller's window and withdrew $9000 in cash, mostly 50s and 100s. No reason to draw attention to myself by taking more so the bank would have to file paperwork with the government.

After I tied up a few more loose ends, I booked myself first to New York City and then on to LA. I could have flown West through Charlotte, but I had some business to take care of in the city. I didn't bother with a return ticket from California because I had no idea how long I might be out there.

After I arrived in New York and settled in with my modest luggage at The Graham, an unassuming but comfortable and reasonably priced hotel close to Chelsea, I set off to find the two most important items in

Manhattan. A slice of the best, thin crust sausage pizza in the world and an unmatchable vendor cart watersoak, a Sabrett hot dog that had been simmering all day in truly grungy water served on a plain hot dog roll with brown mustard and sauerkraut. L.A. had lots of fancy ethnic restaurants and Charleston was turning into a gourmet's paradise, but nothing could beat NYC street eats.

Before I left home, I'd bought a "throw-away" cell phone and loaded it with 1500 minutes, more than I thought I'd ever need. In New York, at least, it's not as if I had a lot of friends to call and get together with. I hadn't lived in the city all that long and most of the time I'd worked nights. So, the people I met weren't exactly the cream of society.

But, then there was Lane Lander. I'd called her from Charleston to tell her I'd be passing through New York and she seemed genuinely excited to see me. I suggested we take in a Broadway show but she'd seen all the ones that interested her. We settled on drinks and dinner and plenty of catching up.

When I first met Lane, her name was Lainie Moskowitz and she was a kid just out of school, a junior publicist in Avante Entertainment's home video division. The only reason I'd met here was because she was such a hard worker that she rarely left the office before 8:00 or 9:00 p.m. She was a mousy little thing, maybe 5'2", skinny, with sort of stringy brown hair and black Buddy Holly style eyeglasses. Glamor was not part of her vocabulary.

On the other hand, Lane was obviously really smart and determined to get ahead in the world. She planned on making a mark for herself in the entertainment industry. It didn't hurt that she had enough upbeat, positive personality for three girls. When it came to enthusiasm for life, she was a cheerleader without pom-poms. Everybody liked her.

After I moved to the West Coast offices, we stayed in touch. Once or twice a year, when she was in L.A. or I was back for meetings in New York, we'd grab a bite. In between, we'd call or e-mail pretty regularly, sometimes actually on business but more often to share jokes or the latest gossip about our co-workers.

Lane's work ethic clearly paid off for her. In no time, she was promoted to publicist, then to manager of publicity, then to director of publicity, and. finally to Vice President, Publicity for the division. Most recently, she'd taken a step back in title but a big step forward in salary and responsibility as National Director, Corporate Communications. In this company-wide position, she handled media relations, investor relations and even some governmental relations for all of Avante's businesses.

Along the way, Lane had made only one misstep, and that she could now at least laugh about. She'd fallen in love with and after a brief courtship married a guy named Jack Lander. I never met Lander, but I knew about him from reading and seeing his picture in the trades. He was a big, handsome, charismatic bullshit artist who worked in A&R for one of the big music companies. It used to be said that the way you could tell that Jack Lander was lying was that his lips were moving.

Lander had been married before, which Laura knew going in. Actually, he'd been married twice before, which she didn't know, at least for a while. Evidently the two former Mrs. Jack Landers had caught on pretty fast that their hubby was way too fond of blow and that his frequent "scouting" trips to locations such as Vegas revolved more around hookers and craps tables than "finding the label's next breakthrough stars."

Eventually, Lane, too, had had enough and made Jack a three-time loser. However, she kept his name and shortened hers from "Lainie" to "Lane." "It's a better show biz name," she'd explained. "It has class, and alliteration and marquee value!" I felt bad about her brief bad marriage, but I admit I kind of liked her new name.

I rang her up at her office and we decided to meet right after work the next night. We'd rendezvous at the bar in the Oxbridge Hotel, a slightly decaying but still classy old school hotel a few blocks from the Avante Entertainment building. As for dinner, Lane suggested a famous steak house on 52nd St. That seemed an odd choice. This place was a New York landmark, an expense account joint with huge steaks and even huger prices. Its ambiance was overwhelmingly masculine, sort of a cross between Madison Square Garden and an old-time Irish saloon. Then, I remembered that lots of little girls really liked to eat. I made the reservation for 7:00.

Just thinking about food made me hungry again so I went for a Gotham trifecta. I caught a cab down to Canal Street and walked around for a while, checking out the hundreds of knock-off vendors, all of whom swore their merchandise was real. Unfortunately, I didn't need an Omega watch for twenty-five dollars. However, I could use a Louis Vuitton wallet for eight bucks. When you're carrying fake ID, it never hurts to present it in a good-looking package.

After a hearty and satisfying dinner of egg roll, chicken lo mein and pork fried rice, I headed back to The Graham to eat a few candy bars and read a paperback thriller I'd picked up at the airport. I was fast asleep before Jimmy Fallon could get through his monologue.

27

Next morning, I slept in. After bacon, eggs, potatoes, toast and java at a Greek coffee shop down the block I headed out to go shopping. I didn't need new clothes. I already had all the wardrobe I'd need down in South Carolina and as much as I wanted for L.A. in my suitcase and carry-on at the hotel. I was looking for a few special items I knew would be easier to come by in New York than in Charleston, at least without raising a few eyebrows.

First stop was lower Broadway and Macchio Brothers, a full-service print shop Avante had used for years for its corporate brochures, earnings reports and other high volume printing needs. Macchio's was one of the best, most reliable printers in town. If you got to know Angie Macchio, grandson of the founder, you might learn about some of the other services they could provide.

What I was after today was somewhere between legitimate and not. But, without asking any questions, Macchio Brothers would most likely be able to help me out. Working off my actual Army and State Department credentials, I simply wanted to have them run me up a few hundred business cards. They had to look like the real deal, and they have to list me as "Special Agent," same as my silver badge. This was the kind of job Macchio could handle without breathing hard. Thirty minutes and fifty dollars later I had 250 great looking business cards in their own black leather case.

The case even had what looked like it had some sort of official seal stamped into it. Angie told me that if I could wait a few hours, he could run me up a T-shirt and a windbreaker with the same "Special Agent" info front and back. Tempting as it would have been to wear to the beach, I said thanks but no thanks.

Next, it was back to Times Square, a much cleaned up Times Square but one that still catered to some exotic tastes, if you knew where to look. Close to Eighth Avenue was a store with the catchy, kitchy name, "Veronica Electronica." There really was a Veronica, the wife of the owner, Manny Kopnik. They named the place for her because they specialized in all manner of electronic gizmos, and because Kopnik doesn't rhyme with anything, at least not with anything good. Veronica is around 5'10" and resembles a cross between Cher and Morticia from "The Addams Family." Manny is maybe 5'4", mostly bald and looks as if he could be someone's Uncle Bernie. They're a great couple.

The front of their very chic high-tech boutique offers everything for the upwardly mobile New York family: computers, HDTVs, security systems, remote cameras, baby monitors, "Nanny Cams," the works. The storeroom, one level below ground and not open to the retail public, is their private stock. That's where Manny and I headed while Veronica smooth-talked the yuppie customers up front.

Without revealing much of what I planned to do, mainly because I didn't have any idea what I planned to do, I got some good suggestions from Manny. When all was said and done, I walked out with a briefcase filled with "spy gear" including some very expensive GPS homing devices with a tracking station, a miniature voice activated recorder, a tiny digital camera with "fantastic resolution, and a snap-on long lens with more magnification than a telescope." I added a pepper gas pen with extra cartridges, a fake cell phone that was actually a 100,000 watt stun gun and a foldable remote listening device. I turned down a pair of night vision goggles even though Manny said they were the best around and "on sale this week only."

Some $1500 later, all in cash, I was about to leave when I asked Manny's advice on a few more things. "I'll need a knife I can carry concealed, but a really nasty knife. Also, I may be dropping in on some people who haven't prepared for my visit by unlatching their doors."

Manny thought a moment. "Jose's Souvenirs down the block. Jose has some front-opening switchblades that'll penetrate an inch of plywood, or whatever else you have to penetrate. And A-Plus Locksmith around the corner on Ninth. Ask for Larry. His brother's a stiff, but Larry will know how to help you out."

Two more stops and my briefcase now contained a truly vicious auto knife with a tempered steel stiletto tip and razor sharp blade edges. Also, a cute little plastic packet filled with picks and shims and a few other items one might use to open a door without resorting to explosives. I'd had enough training in the service to understand how most normal locks work. I'd never be a safecracker, but these tools would get me through your everyday house or apartment door. I'd also found a great pair of horn-rim plain glass specs at Jose's and took them to give myself a new look.

When, how, where and why I was going to use all of these great gadgets remained a mystery. I just felt better having them on hand because, you just never know.

Back at the hotel I stashed my acquisitions, showered, shaved and headed out to meet Lane. I arrived at the Oxbridge a little early and was glad I did. From my seat at the bar I could keep an eye on everyone coming into the room. I'd be able to duck anyone I might not want to see.

Better yet, as things turned out, I was able to spot a lone young woman when she entered the bar and swept the place with her eyes as if looking for someone. It took me a beat to realize she must be Lane. I hadn't seen her in maybe five years, at least since her divorce. I wasn't prepared for the changes.

Her plain brown hair was much darker, almost black, and styled in a short shag. The eyeglasses were gone, undoubtedly in favor of contacts, which made her big brown eyes luminous. Under a form-fitting expensive fur jacket she wore a deep red mini-dress that matched her deep red lipstick. Her tall high heels were a burgundy patent leather. She even seemed to be noticeably bustier than I remembered. In short, she was a sophisticated, New York career woman. And, a babe. Glamor was no longer not in her vocabulary. It was her vocabulary.

We exchanged the obligatory Hollywood air kiss so as not to muss her make-up and she ordered a Sweet Rob Roy to my Tanqueray martini. Her choice of cocktail seemed odd and old-fashioned but, then again, the Oxbridge had the aura of a different era and perhaps Lane just liked very sweet drinks.

Trying not to trip over my own feet – or tongue – I raised my glass as in a toast and said, "Lane, you look fantastic!"

Raising her glass in response, she said, "I know."

When she saw that I didn't know how to react, she broke out in the same old cackly laugh she'd had as Lainie so many years ago.

"Don't be such a putz, Bobby. Of course I know I look great. It's taken me a lot of work – and cash - to look this way. First, I had to remove every external evidence of Lainie Moskowitz. Then, little by little, I had to create a new image. I think I did a pretty good job of it. Underneath it all, I'm the same knucklehead you knew and loved when we were still young and foolish. Well, I was young. You were just foolish."

She paused, took my hand in hers, and whispered, "Yes. I got new tits, too."

I almost choked on my drink I laughed so hard. Lainie or Lane, she hadn't changed a bit. Only, now, she was gorgeous as well as funny and smart.

I was right about her appetite not having changed, though. At dinner, she knocked back a jumbo shrimp cocktail, an 18 oz. sirloin, sides of mashed potato, onion rings and spinach along with another Rob Roy and the better part of a nice bottle of Valpolicella. And bread.

In between mouthfuls we laughed until tears came to our eyes as we reminisced about some of the crazy people we'd worked with and the completely insane problems we'd had to solve along the way. She told the story about how one of her bosses had gotten so mad about the constant breakdowns of his office photocopier that he'd unplugged it, rolled it into the men's room and held it hostage until the company promised to get him a new one. I told her about how we tortured this one summer help kid, some exec's nephew who'd been foisted on us and nobody liked. One of the nicest things we'd done to him was take transparent tape and tape down the button on his telephone receiver. When anyone would dial his extension – and we did it plenty – his phone would ring but when he picked up there'd be nothing there but a dial tone.

Lane was about halfway through an Irish Coffee served in a glass the size of a flagon when she turned serious. Reaching out, she took both of my hands in hers and stared into my eyes.

"We had some great times, Bobby. But through it all, you never once tried to hit on me. Why?"

I was speechless, and she could probably hear the gears in my mind meshing, trying to come up with an acceptable answer.

"Well, I guess…"

Before I could finish what I hoped would be a cogent thought, she pulled her hands away, chugged the remainder of her Irish Coffee, then stuck her tongue out and gave me a raspberry loud enough to be heard three tables away.

"I'm just pulling your chain, Bobby. No one's been a better friend to me than you, even if you are a homo."

"Hey, now wait!"

"You are just too easy to fluster, man. Stop taking me seriously. I'm loving life and seeing you here in my city is making me love it just a little bit more. Come on. Let's blow this peanut stand and go back to my place. You've seen Lainie Moskowitz 2.0 and I'm betting that you approve.

"Now, let me show you how Lane Lander lives. It's comfortable and quiet and I have a well-stocked bar. Plus, I'm pretty sure that your showing up in Manhattan is connected with some scheme more nefarious than simply catching up with a kid who used to look up to you because without a lot of fancy degrees you made your way up the ladder in a big entertainment company and never lost your humanity."

What could I say, but "Sounds good to me."

28

New York, New York

As soon as Lane gave the cabbie her address, I knew that life was treating her well. I picked up the fare and gave the driver a healthy tip when he dropped us off at a canopied, doorman building on East 75th St. just off Central Park. The doorman, a fairly typical overweight Irishman in a hokey-looking green-and-grey uniform with a matching hat, greeting her effusively, "Evenin' Ms. Lander!"

Lane introduced me and I shook hands with the doorman, whose name was Arthur. Once inside the tasteful elevator lobby, Lara whispered, "Don't underestimate Arthur. He worked on the docks until he hurt his back. Underneath that blarney, he's a pretty handy guy to have around.

"Last year, I was coming home a little late when some wandering scuzzbucket snatched the purse from a little old woman who was just walking down the street. As he ran past my building, Arthur pulled a blackjack or something from underneath that ridiculous uniform coat and cold-cocked the guy. Then, when the bum's on the ground, Arthur materializes a set of handcuffs and cuffs him to an awning pole until the cops arrive."

I whistled in appreciation. "I've got a new respect for doormen in general and Arthur in particular. I hope you give him a nice tip at Christmas time."

We took the elevator to the 15th floor and got off into a well-appointed, short hall with only six doors visible leading off of it. Her unit was 1504.

Inside was further evidence that Ms. Lander was getting along quite nicely, thank you very much. Her apartment, or condo or co-op – she never said for sure – was elegantly styled, the walls in off-white and muted tints, the furniture some sort of Modern, maybe Danish, comfortable-looking and well-laid out. The room was dominated by two large modernistic paintings, one maybe eight feet long by four feet tall consisting of pastel squares, rectangles and other pointed geometric designs, some interlocking, others free-floating. The smaller of the two, perhaps four by four square featured bold, bright colors in shapes ranging from squiggles to commas to what might have been sperm. I know almost nothing about art. Nonetheless, names like Klee and Mondrian and Oldenburg jumped to mind, although I really had no idea if their respective styles were anything like what was on Lane's walls.

She took my coat and shrugged out of her own before taking me on a mini-tour of her home. In addition to the very spacious living room with picture windows angling toward the park, she had a good-sized dining room separated by a half-wall and ceiling-hung matchstick bamboo screening, a kitchen with restaurant quality equipment and its own breakfast bar, two bedrooms, each with its own bath, hers predominantly in red, the guest room in blue, a service area with apartment-sized washer/dryer combo and a tiny office area that would have looked right at home aboard a submarine, albeit a very chic submarine. Not exactly a bachelorette pad.

Back in the living room, Lane flipped on the stereo and the room filled with quiet classical guitar music. I guessed Andres Segovia. Spotting a bottle of Wild Turkey on her small bar I asked for two or three fingers on the rocks. She made my drink and built a vodka gimlet for herself. After a perfunctory gesture of toast, she excused herself.

"I'd like to stay in my 'Let's have dinner with Bobby McRae' duds but, frankly, I've had this outfit on all day at the office. Plus, the shoes are killing me."

She left me alone with copies of Sports Illustrated and The New Yorker and disappeared into her bedroom to change. If she'd left the room looking like a fashion plate, she returned looking much the same, only more comfortable. Wearing green-and-gold Asian-style silk lounging pajamas and gold slippers, she curled up on the big beige couch across from my easy chair and tucked her feet under her.

"So, do you like my pad?"

"I really like the art, but I don't know whose it is."

"It's mine," she said.

"I know it's yours. I just don't know who the artist or artists are."

"They're me. That's why they're mine."

I was stunned. "Hey, I had no idea you were a talented artist!"

"There are a few things you don't know about me," she said with a smile. "Whether I'd consider myself a <u>talented</u> artist is up for debate. How about the rest of my place?"

"I think it's spectacular."

"Do I hear a 'but' in that answer?"

"Well…"

Lane put her drink down and cracked her knuckles silently, a gesture that she was now going to be serious. "I could live quite well on my current salary at Avante," she began. "But, not this well.

"And, no I didn't get a sou from Jack when we divorced and I haven't become a high-priced call girl, although I understand the hours are great. My father, rest his soul, the successful doctor and even more successful inventor of medical devices, passed away around four years ago.

"Dad left my Mom quite well off and she has very few expenses other than playing Mahjong with the ladies, going on one or two cruises a year and the occasional shopping spree at Nordstrom or Neiman-Marcus. I'm her only heir, may she live to be a hundred. So, I'll eventually get all her estate. In the meantime, Daddy wanted his little girl to be able to enjoy some of the nicer things in life so he left me something separate for my own.

"I was kind of a disappointment to Dad. First, I wasn't a boy. Second, I had no interest in medicine. Hell, I had no aptitude for it. But I graduated from Vassar, which pleased him. I got a good job on my own, which pleased him. And, I always spent the holidays with family. So, I guess on balance I wasn't such a bad kid after all."

We clinked glasses. "To Mom and Dad and the good kid who became a big macher – is that the word? – in show business!"

In a barely perceptible movement, Lane reached out and tapped what looked like a tiny coaster and the lighting in the living room dimmed around thirty percent.

"Impressive," I observed.

"The lighting system came with the unit. Besides, after working under fluorescents all day, I can do with a little soft light at night. So, let's get on to what brings you to New York, then on to L.A. Not considering going back to work, are you?"

I laughed. "Hardly. If I took a new job I'd just be paying all of my salary to Uncle Sam anyway. This trip is personal. Do you remember Jerry Kendall?"

Lane furrowed her brow. "Let's see. I met him a few times but he didn't make much of an impression. Kind of a mid-level grind who was good at facilities and logistics and finance, if I recall. Not a big personality type. He died under some odd circumstances, didn't he? Took off from work one day and showed up dead a few days later in the boonies somewhere in West Virginia, right?"

"Partly. Jerry wasn't a heavy hitter. He was just a guy who did his job, had his fun on the side and basically left most people alone. I had lunch with him every now and again. So, we weren't close. That said, he didn't keel over in West Virginia. It was South Carolina. More specifically, it was on my front porch. And, where I live is pretty much the boonies. I'm in Charleston, but Charleston County, and that covers a lot of territory. It's not easy to find where I live, and actually getting there is a whole other story. Yet, that's where Kendall showed up to die. Interesting, eh?"

Lane shifted around on the couch. "Tell me more. But, first, let me freshen up our drinks."

When she sat back down, she leaned forward and really concentrated on what I had to say.

I edited myself as I went along. She still worked at Avante, so any talk of embezzlement and a cover-up would be a really bad idea and could implicate her down the road. Then, I launched into the saga of the aftermath of Kendall's demise. I suppose I purposely played up the hot blonde who approached me at the beach, and turned out to be an LAPD Homicide detective who's been shadowing me for unknown reasons, and my sexy Japanese-American undercover agent scouring the news on my behalf for any interesting tidbits about the company and its businesses.

When I got to the part about my truck being blown up and my best friend in Charleston nearly being killed in the blast, Lane jumped up, then sat back down quickly in the yoga lotus position. She was clearly intensely focused on what I had to say.

"So, you have no idea why someone tried to kill you. And, you're already well connected enough that the authorities will keep a lid on the situation while you try to figure it out. And, yet, some of your new friends seem to think that you may have been behind everything from Kendall's death to a faked attempt on your own life to who knows what else."

"I don't really think so," I told her. "It's just that a lot of my new friends are in law enforcement or the judiciary. They're trained to be skeptical and suspicious. And, let's face it, I'm still a bit of a mystery man down South. I could turn out to be a homicidal con man for all they know."

Lane whistled in amazement. "That calls for another round."

I wasn't feeling the drinks yet, so I handed over my glass willingly. It came back maybe just a hair more full than the last one.

"If I have the story right," Lane began, "Jerry Kendall was somewhat close to Derrick Pettit, right?"

"Hard to say. Jerry had worked for Derrick for quite a few years and they'd gone on some Vegas trips together and briefly set up a little social club for themselves and a few of their friends. But, Derrick didn't have anything particularly glowing to say about Jerry when I met with him. He actually seemed to be trying a little too hard to distance himself from Jerry and his extracurricular activities."

Lane put an index finger up to her mouth, as if she were about to bite the nail. She quickly though better of that idea and put her hand back under her leg.

"I don't pretend to know Derrick Pettit very well," she said. "I've always thought he was a little bit of an odd duck. Nothing I could put my finger on. He worked his way up through the ranks, is well respected by the other senior execs, and always seems to have kept his operation running smoothly and within budget.

"You're going to laugh at me, but whenever I had to sit with him at a conference or a big luncheon or dinner meeting, the one image I couldn't get out of my mind was the character Sherman Hemsley played on TV, George Jefferson. I almost expected Pettit to break out in singing 'Movin' On Up'!"

I cracked up. "You nailed it. George Jefferson. Derrick does seem like the little guy from the wrong background who found his path to the top and took it. He's not a bad guy, but he's just a bit arrogant and full of himself. Maybe eventually he felt Jerry Kendall didn't live up to the standards he set for himself. Or, maybe he just has a huge ego."

"Funny we should be talking about Derrick Pettit," Lane commented. "I've never really had much business to conduct with him over the years but I got a strange call from him only about ten days ago. He was looking for a press release."

"A press release on what?"

"A press release on him. I hadn't heard about his earning some big promotion or winning any industry award so, naturally, I asked him why a press release on him would be appropriate. His answer was weird. He wanted to get the word out that he would be overseeing the overall facilities and equipment for the Academy at this year's Oscar show."

"Wait a minute, I interrupted. "What's Pettit got to do with the Academy Awards?"

"How soon you forget, my friend. For the past twenty years or so the Academy has been lightening the load on themselves and their venue staffs by recruiting the studios to assign a few key execs to liaison with the contractors and service providers up to and including Oscar night. It's not a big deal. Every year three or four studios rotate into the mix to help out. It's Avante's turn this year, and Derrick's our designated hitter.

"This is not a high prestige job. Granted it takes some time, because the studio guy is supposed to review everything in his assigned area, going over timelines, contracts, deliveries and installations, that sort of thing The idea is to insure that the show itself, which, as you know, is seen by billions of people around the world, goes off without a hitch. Come to think of it, Derrick may be feeling both more stressed and more important now that he can't pass some of the work off to Jerry Kendall."

I was confused. "So, Derrick wanted you to put out a press release naming him as Avante's Oscar night rep and praising him for the great job he's doing for the show?"

"That's pretty much it. Of course, I had no intention of actually sending anything out to the media. There are still a lot of people in the publicity racket who believe that bombarding the press with irrelevant paper is the way to get your clients or your company media attention. Truth is, most reporters would kiss our feet if we never sent them anything, unless it was something truly important and of some real interest to their readers and viewers.

"I listened to Derrick for a few minutes, made believe I was taking notes, and said I'd do what I could. But, with the crush of stories out there these days, I couldn't make any promises. I blew him off and figured that was that. Less than 24 hours later, Derrick's back on my line. He says, 'No pressure sweetheart, but the Oscars are just a few weeks away so if Avante is going to get any credit for our work we'll have to move sooner rather than later'.

"If I could have reached through the phone, I would have strangled the little prick. For one thing, I do NOT like to be called 'sweetheart'. But, the path of least resistance was just to dummy up an official looking one-pager, fax it out to him and let him believe we were moving heaven and earth to get him some ink. Which is what I did."

`Lane took a deep pull on her drink. "Next day, he's back on the phone. Loves the press release. Has one more request. If the release hasn't been shipped out to the media yet, he'd like one itsy-bitsy change. Just to get rid of him I say 'Fine'. Here's what he wants. At the top of the press release, where it lists who to contact for more information on the story, he wants to delete my name or any of my staff and put in 'J.D. Pettit.'. It's an old family joke he says. Just a little fun. I don't care. No one's going to see it anyway. So I agree and send him a new draft with 'J.D. Pettit' as the media contact. End of story."

"Now, that's odd," I replied. "Did you by chance save a copy of that fake press release?"

"Sure, I keep copies of everything. I'm very anal."

When I gave her my patented smart-ass eyebrow raise she snatched up a little couch pillow and tossed it at me. "Cut it out. You know what I mean!"

We had a good laugh. Then I stood up and stretched my legs. "Well, the sands of the hour glass run low. I hope Arthur's still on duty to call me a cab."

Lane was on her feet and standing in front of me, standing a little closer than I would have expected, and pretty much blocking my way. "Unless you have an early morning flight, I'm my own boss now. I can go in a little late if I want. Bobby, all these years and we've never had any real alone time together. Let's stay up. We can talk some more." She paused, for the first time tonight seeming a little unsure of herself. "Bobby, don't leave. Stay with me here tonight. I don't have any illusions. I just want to be with you."

My hands were actually trembling as I held her around the waist and drew her closer to me. Her body was warm and firm as she molded herself to me. She laid her head on my chest, then lifted it up to look me right in the eyes. Her scent was like a distant exotic zephyr. Our lips met and we fell into a deep, passionate kiss. Lane had always been a great friend; now she seemed to want to be more.

After what seemed like an eternity, we broke apart and she stepped back.

"So, will you stay with me tonight, Bobby" she whispered.

At a loss for poetry or even wit, all I could say was "Sounds good to me!"

And, it was.

29

Los Angeles, California

Lane was gone when I awoke around 9:00 a.m. The coffee was brewed and a glass of OJ and a buttered English muffin were on the kitchen table. Her note read, "It took too many years, but it was worth the wait. Be careful. Lots of love, your Lane (Lainie) Lander."

Back at the hotel, I packed fast with an eye to catching an early afternoon flight to California. Before I left, I called a really good local florist and arranged to have some orchids delivered to her apartment. My note read," Some of us are slow learners. But, once we've learned, we don't forget. I'll see you in Dixie." I really hoped she might take me up on my offer to visit Charleston. She'd love my city and I know it would love her back.

As usual, once I boarded the flight to L.A. I got comfortable and went to sleep. I didn't need a drink or any airline meals, but I wanted to rest up for whatever was ahead. Derrick Pettit and his press release gave me the creeps.

At LAX, I took a short cab ride up Sepulveda Boulevard to a crusty old industrial building in a neighborhood that was showing signs of gentrification. The sign out front read "Dutch's Dollies." I'd been there before many times, but seeing the building and its faded pink-and-black sign gave me a lift.

Dutch's Dollies was the business, and the home, of Dutch Van Damm who legend has it has looked and sounded just like his name since he was maybe fifteen years old. That's around the time that he realized his childhood love of anything mechanical, but mostly of cars, could make him a living. He quit school, apprenticed to the most popular customizer in the San Fernando Valley, back then the heart of the West Coast car culture, and learned from the master.

By the time he turned 18, Dutch had opened his own shop, building and tweaking engines, molding custom bodies, flame-painting, installing hydraulics and chroming anything that would stand still for a few seconds. For Friday night cruisers as well as for drag racers, Dutch was indispensable. He didn't work cheap so prospective customers had to have plenty of cash to interest him. But, when he promised a young guy a hot rod like nothing anyone had ever seen before, and faster to boot, he delivered.

Dutch's fame quickly spread up and down the West Coast and he had to take on help. But, he always personally designed and oversaw every customizing job. He even spawned a colloquialism that traveled beyond L.A. Because of his incredible knack of taking an ordinary vehicle and turning it into a work of art and/or a snarling beast at the track, when his creations won at car shows or races, fans would hoot at the losers, "You've been Dutched!" Before long, almost any serious one-up-manship move drew shouts of "You Dutched 'em!"

Dutch's Dollies looked so run down it could have been abandoned. Yet, six days a week it hummed with action. In his thirties, the Dutchman tired of customizing and turned his focus strictly to engines and running components. Over the years, he worked on cars for some of the biggest names in racing, Pensky, Foyt, Allison, Andretti, Petty, Prudhomme, even Paul Newman. All of them. It didn't matter whether the car was setup for Indy, or NASCAR, NHRA or SCCA, the racing fraternity knew that Dutch could help them run faster and better, for a price.

Of course, all that secret building and tuning took place in the back of the huge shop. The front was a tiny office with a side door leading out to a lot filled with about thirty cars that looked as if they'd been salvaged from an auto impound some time during the past half century. Dutch had cars from every decade but his favorites were a few behemoths from the 40s and 50s. Whether they were cheesy sedans or once-regal town cars, his cars all had one thing in common. They were seriously beaten up.

No paint job was unfaded. No convertible top not tattered and repaired with duct tape. Bumpers drooped. Rust ringed the bodies' quarter panels. Grills were bashed in. Door handles were missing. These were Dutch's "dollies," ancient, neglected cars that looked ready for the auto graveyard compactor but, because of Dutch's quiet mechanical skills, were actually many times faster, more drivable and more reliable than anything coming out of Detroit or Japan today.

"Air Force proud of dere 'stelt' airplanes," the old man snorted in his unique Dutch/Valley accent. "I build da stelt cars! You pull up by a Corvette at a red light, he better hold onta his pink slip. My girls fipe 'im out!!!"

He was right. I'd steered the studio to him a few times after I'd heard about him through the grapevine, and I'd rented a few of his cars for some fun weekends in the countryside. Some of them would go 150 mph without breaking a sweat. They'd corner on rails. And, with Dutch's secret scavenging exhaust and muffler system you'd be making about as much noise as a golf cart.

Dutch and I canvassed the lot and he tried to steer me to a '51 Merc whose owner seemed to have lost interest in customizing after ripping off all the chrome and spraying the poor thing with flay, gray primer. I had my eye on a '48 Olds. No one would ever confuse this vehicle with any sort of antique or classic. It was just a tall but dumpy, bulbous, inconvenient two-tone gray two-door coupe with a deep grin in the front bumper and a trunk with the lock punched out and held down by a twisted length of electrical cable. It called out to me.

My credit was good with Dutch, so I drove off the lot on a promise that if I kept the car more than two weeks I'd call. We'd settle up on the rental when I brought it back. First stop was the San Diego Freeway north. Any time of the day, it's hard to reach much less exceed the speed limit. This car wanted to annihilate it. I had to stay in second gear all the way to my exit onto Santa Monica Boulevard to keep it from blow-ing everything else off the road. And, the engine just purred.

I'd booked myself at the Hotel Barclay, a nonde-script hostelry just off Olympic where I'd be unlikely to run into any of my old show biz buddies. I knew the place because I'd once trysted there, unwisely, with a Botox'ed blonde with a New Jersey accent I'd met at a bar. She was hot. She was also married, to a part-time repo man and full-time thug who was currently doing 90 days at County for assault and battery. The victim didn't want to press charges, but her hubby slugged the guy in front of a cop. He had already served 60 of his 90 days. Ours was not a match made in heaven.

Before the hotel, my destination was the law offices of Robert Raskin Partners. A phone call from me might have disappeared in his telephone log. A personal appear-ance, I figured, might get his attention. The parking lot attendant at his office building gave me a funny look as I drove up in my ancient Olds. My money was right up to date though, and that was good enough for him.

I straightened my back and brushed off my clothes outside the main door to Raskin's huge complex of offices, preparing to meet his intimidating receptionist. Then, there she was, big as life and looking twice as mean.

"Good Morning, Ms. Hatchet" I said as pleasantly as I could. You may remember me. Robert McRae? I vis-ited with Mr. Raskin oh, about, six weeks ago."

"It's Mrs. Hatchet."

I resisted the impulse to ask if her maiden name were Sledgehammer.

"Well, I happened to be back in town and I thought it might be possible for me to pick up where we left off. You know, continue our very informative conversation."

She said nothing. I detected a slight sigh. Of what? Exasperation, Frustration, Absolute indifference?

"You may recall that I used to work in Hollywood but I live now in South Carolina. We have a tradition down home of bringing a little gift to someone who's been kind to us. So, I brought you something from Charleston."

I reached into my carryall and took out a small, neatly wrapped package. "Please open it. It's a sweetgrass basket, something that's still a handicraft of the descendants of the Geechee and Gullah people of the Lowcountry. Great for holding jewelry, or trinkets, or… or paperclips. You won't find anything like it made anywhere else. These baskets are even in the Smithsonian."

I realized that I was nervously running off at the mouth. She said nothing. She reached out for the package, opening it as gently as if I had told her it contained a Faberge egg, or nitroglycerine.

She removed the paper and lifted that exquisite little handle basket from its box. She turned it over and around, examining it from every angle.

Unable to control myself, I blurted out, "They're one of a kind. There's a little brochure in the box giving the sweetgrass history. And, a few strands of the actual materials they're made of."

Summoning the courage to stop yammering and look her in the eye, I beheld a transformation. Her eyes sparkled and her grim visage now wore an eye-to-ear grin.

She spoke at last, and her voice even sounded different. "Why, Mr. McRae, aren't you sweet! You didn't have to bring me a present. However, I am delighted that you did. This is just wonderful, and I'll find a place here for it on my desk, where I can use it and admire it every day."

She paused. "You'd have no way of knowing this, but as a little girl, I grew up in rural Georgia. By the time I was ten, my Daddy had taken a job out West so we all moved to Fresno and then down here. I was old enough before we left to know about the slave cultures and how traditions like sweetgrass weaving were handed down from generation to generation. But, I've never before owned a basket myself. How can I thank you?"

I wouldn't have been more surprised if she had come around the desk, given me a big hug, and invited me to come over to her house for some fried chicken and peach cobbler.

Choosing my words carefully, I said "Well, Mr. Raskin and I have a few things in common, people and interests that is. I've come into some new information in those regards that I'd like to share with him. As a few things I'm now aware of are somewhat personal and confidential for the time being, I really have to speak with him one-on-one. Would that be possible?"

She licked her forefinger and flipped through two leather bound calendars. "Well, Mr. Raskin is out of state at a conference until Friday. Then, there's the weekend. He's pretty busy the first two or three days of the week. Are you flexible?

"Yes ma'am. But the issues – situations – I need to make him aware of are somewhat time-sensitive. So, sooner would be much better than later."

She clucked thoughtfully, her eyes poring over the calendars. "When he comes back, his wife and children – he has two exceptional little boys and a darling daughter – go on a ski trip to Park City. Maybe they're being gone might loosen up a bit of his time.

"Tell you what. I'll track him down at the convention and let him know that you need to see him. That you have some important information to convey to him that is for him only. And, that you can work around his schedule. I think we can make this work."

I thanked her profusely. I didn't know whether I was supposed to leave and just check in with her from time to time or to leave and await her call.

Where are you staying?" she asked.

"At the Hotel Barclay. I wanted to stay away from the Hollywood crowd."

The moment I'd given her the name of the hotel, I knew I'd made a mistake. I wasn't registered there as Bobby McRae. I'd done what I'd done many times before when I was with a celebrity we wanted to keep away from the public and the media. I signed in as Donald

Corleone. "The best way to reach me," I fumbled, "is on my cell phone. I'm out and on the move a lot." I gave her the number, and she wrote it down.

"I'm going to do everything I can to get you and Mr. Raskin together," she smiled. "You strike me as the sort of man who wouldn't trouble him with something you didn't consider important. And, I'm sure he admires your graciousness and old school charm as much as I do."

If I'd been wearing a hat, I would have tipped it to her as I headed for the door. And bowed from the waist.

30

Los Angeles, California

The bar at the hotel was a bust-out. The most interesting character there was a theatrically made-up babe who could have stood to lose a few pounds and who hadn't seen 40 in a long time. She kept trying to get guys to step outside with her and have a cigarette, but in this land of obsessive non-smokers, her gimmick didn't work anymore.

As a result, I got a good night's sleep and bounced out of bed early and ready for the day. I had some definite plans and I wanted to get started. After a pretty decent cup of coffee from the little machine provided in my room I got an even better cup plus a bowl of Cheerios with milk and two not-too-stale Danish at the complimentary breakfast bar.

I was wiping the crumbs from my lips and heading across the lobby, past a pair of disconsolate-looking potted palms when someone called out, "Bobby!"

I kept going, assuming that the call-out was for somebody else. The second time, "Bobby!" was louder and more insistent. I kept going, thinking that even if I had been ID'd somehow, I'd be better off pretending that

I was someone else. Then, it was "C'mon, McRae. Over here!"

The jig, as they say, was up. I turned and there was Det. Allison Simmons, seated on an uncomfortable looking puce couch, her long legs crossed and the L.A. Times and a Starbuck's cup on the little table in front of her. She waved me over.

"Hey, man. My feelings are hurt. You come into town and don't even call me. What's with that?"

She was wearing an uncharacteristically dull outfit, tailored, but boring. Light brown skirt and jacket, white blouse with a little ruffle around her neck, and her ever-present bulky handbag, which I assumed contained a "secret" compartment for her service weapon.

"I'm sorry, Allison," I attempted. "I had a few things to deal with here in L.A. and I didn't want to be bothered by running into a lot of people I know or having to retell my little part in the Jerry Kendall mystery. I didn't know if you'd be interested in seeing me or not. I thought that if I were to try to pick up where we left off I'd be better off planning something spectacular to sweep you off your feet." I gave what I thought, and hoped, was a sheepish grin.

"I understand. It's just that I feel kind of funny catching up with you through dumb luck."

"Yeah. How did you find me, anyway?"

Allison uncrossed her legs and patted the couch next to her to tell me to sit down. "I have some interesting news about the Kendall mystery, which I'll share with you in a minute, now that I've found you.

"I got this new information yesterday and my first stop, other than to report to the chain of command, was to Robert Raskin's office. He's an intimidating opponent in court, but a good friend of law enforcement all the rest of the time. And, Kendall was his client.

"I was chatting up that battleax who runs the front desk, and doesn't seem to like anyone. I've cultivated her a bit so now I get at least a somewhat friendly 'Hello'. Well, she knows that I know you through the Kendall case. She promised to give my message to Raskin when she contacted him, and she said that you'd come back and were staying at The Barclay. I thought it was kind of strange that you weren't at one of the name hotels. But, if you're ducking your old buddies, this makes a lot of sense."

I heard her out, then asked, "So, then how'd you locate me. I'm not signed in as Bobby McRae."

"A man registering at a hotel under an assumed name!!! Perish the thought!!!" Allison thought her little joke was hilarious. At least it cracked <u>her</u> up.

"Seriously, how'd you find me?"

Simmons was still chuckling to herself. "Bobby, I'm a detective. Detecting is what I do for a living. I just asked the desk clerk for the register, which he gladly turned over to me once he saw my shield, and let my fingers do the walkin'. Now, for today's quiz, how many guests do you think checked in yesterday, giving their home address as Charleston, South Carolina?"

Simple, but effective, I thought. "So, now that you've nabbed me, what's the news you were looking to share with me?"

She opened her briefcase and glanced quickly at a document she pulled from a folder. "Just this. Most likely, Jerry Kendall had no real connection with the dead Jane Doe, who, by the way is no longer a Jane Doe. He probably met her at a party, or shopping on Rodeo Drive. Who knows? I gather from interviewing some of his associates at Avante that he handed out a lot of his business cards, mostly to hot women. He probably figured if he cast a wide enough net, he might once in a while snag a live fish."

"That's good news," I said. "Looks as if we don't have to try to unravel any sort of deadly conspiracy."

"Not exactly," she replied, shoving the document and the folder back in her briefcase. "It gets more interesting. On a whim, we ran her photo and prints through Interpol. Bingo! Her name was Anna Garcia. She was a Honduran national. And, she was a cop."

I involuntarily whistled through my teeth.

"Yeah. Fascinating, eh? And, it gets better. That's a story for when we have a little more time. Right now, I have to boogie to Orange County to re-interview a couple of material witnesses on a cold case we're trying to close. I'll be back later in the day. What do you say we get together for some drinks and dinner and I'll give you the nickel tour of what I found. That is, if you don't already have a better offer."

Actually, I'd planned to have dinner with Tara Fukimoto, to check out what information, if any, she'd come up with for me. Also, the last time we'd talked, she'd said she was between boyfriends. So, I thought. Who knows? Even so, Det. Simmons was that better offer, bland business outfit or not. I'd call Tara and reschedule. "Uh, sure. That would be great. I can pick you up any time after, say, 6:00 p.m. Just tell me where you'd like to go." I was wondering how she'd react if she wanted to go to Spago and I showed up in my Dutch's's Dolly.

"Tell you what. Let's make it 7:00ish. My place. I'm a pretty good cook and I haven't made a 'covert operator' a home-cooked dinner in a long time. I'm thinking veal, if that works for you."

She could have said "shoe leather" and I would have admitted it was my favorite dish. She wrote down her address, kissed me on the cheek and started to breeze out the door. Pausing, she turned back and asked, "Are you going to the big dedication tomorrow afternoon?"

I must have looked as if I had no idea what she was talking about. "That's right. You don't read the L.A. papers any more. Two p.m. up on Hollywood Boulevard. The LAPD is getting a star on the Hollywood Walk of Fame. For more than a half century of service to the motion picture industry. Nice, eh?"

I told her I'd certainly try to be there, and she left. I sat back on the couch, which had all the comfort of a vinyl-covered bleacher seat and pondered. Why did the police department merit a star on the Walk of Fame. Had they changed the department's motto from "Protect and Serve" to, "Lights. Camera. Action"??? Of course, back before guys like Chief Daryl Gates took over and turned the cops into a more or less paramilitary force, legend has it that the department was under the covers with the big studios from the guy on the beat to the chief and even beyond. So, a star kind of made sense.

I was still smarting from Allison Simmons catching up with me so easily. Maybe I wasn't as good as I thought at this secret identity stuff. Nonetheless, I had things to do and had to be on my way.

I cranked up my Dolly and motored down to Lincoln Boulevard in Santa Monica, home of Quartermaster's, one of the few remaining Army/Navy surplus stores around, and still one of the best. A guy could spend half a day just wandering through the jumbled racks of great stuff. In addition to used, and some new, military gear, the store carried tons of work clothes, mostly used. In no time I picked out a nice, rumpled greenish set of coveralls with "Eddie" stitched on the breast pocket. I added a washed-out Red Man ball cap and a tattered pair of Chuck Taylor sneakers. I was tempted, but resisted for a second time, a pair of night vision goggles. Even used, they ran two hundred bucks.

Next, I drove around the block looking for a locksmith that had been in Santa Monica since forever and that we'd used from time to time to provide special lock hardware for sets or just to break into offices and such we'd locked up and forgotten how to open. Costas, the son of the owner, was behind the counter.

I introduced myself and Costas was cordial but didn't seem to care who I was or what I wanted. If he could turn a buck, that was OK by him. I showed him the key I'd taken from Jerry Kendall's apartment and gave him a song and dance about how my uncle had died and left me all his junk including this safe deposit box key. Unfortunately Uncle Walt had neglected to tell me what bank it belonged to and I…"

Costas had taken the key and peered at it through a jeweler's loupe. "Premier National Bank of California," he muttered, "up on Pico. There's only one."

I was impressed. "You must really know your locks to be able to identify that key as from Premier National Bank of California by just one look at it."

"Yeah. I know my locks. That and if you look real close you can see it's engraved PNBC. That'll be twenty bucks."

A Jackson didn't seem too stiff a tariff to pay for Costas' information, so I forked it over and was back on my way. I detoured around to Wilshire, just for the ride, and pulled into Robinson's department store. I hadn't packed many changes of clothes, so in honor of my command performance at Allison Simmons' place, I bought a pair of tan khaki Dockers and a comfortable blue chambray shirt. Women always said blue highlighted my eyes. I would have gotten an oxford cloth but they're always folded and pinned and mashed and the creases never come out until you wash them a dozen times. I didn't want Allison to think I'd bought a new wardrobe just for her.

On a whim, I dropped by the shoe department and slipped on a pair of Bass Weejuns. I remembered that all the Ivy League types at work loved their Weejuns, so I felt they'd be a nice touch. On the way out, I passed the perfume department where a nice young lady whose makeup looked as if it had been applied by Dracula handed me a men's cologne sample, supposedly with a manly scent. It was probably left over from Valentine's Day. But, it was free, so I took it.

Last stop was the little storefront in West Hollywood of a new and ambitious cellular telephone company, CallCal. They'd started up before I'd left L.A. and were still treading water trying to catch up with the already established carriers. They were hungry.

The showroom was empty when I arrived, except for a young guy in a white shirt and tie with an earnest look on his face. I explained that I was from out of state but planned on moving to Los Angeles very soon. I wanted to explore the options in cell phones before I made a commitment. He was more than happy to oblige and launched into a sales pitch almost all of which flew right over my head. My thoughts were elsewhere.

When my new best friend paused for a breath, I thanked him for his presentation and told him that as of now CallCal was top of my list. Then, I asked for a brochure on their plans and also whether I might get a sip of water as I was a little parched.

"Let me get you some nice bottled water from the back," he agreed genially. "Help yourself to any literature you'd like."

I moved quickly to the little racks on the counter as he stepped into the back room. I grabbed two or three brochures and also a small handful of the half dozen CallCal business cards lined up on a little wall rack. Hallelujah! One of the worker bees in the office was "Eddie

Palmer, Sales and Engineering." I had a match for my coveralls!

I promised Mr. CallCal I'd be in to see him again as soon as I came back to town and got settled. Hey, if I ever got back, maybe I would. Last but not least, I transported all my purchases back to the Barclay in order to shave, shower and get myself ready for Allison Simmons, her promised dinner and her very much promised revelations.

31

At 7:10, fashionably late, I pulled up to Allison Simmons' address. It was a comfortable looking older building on Moorpark, not far from Ernesto's just as she'd said. Like most small apartment building in the Valley, this one had probably a dozen units, encased in that innocuous tan exterior that generations of builders must have thought looked like adobe. At least it didn't have one of those kitchy Valley names like Casa this or Villa that scrawled across its façade in cheesy metal stamping. She'd picked a nice place to live, and the neighborhood was good, too.

I parked my Dolly around the corner and headed for the front door, a bottle of pretty decent Pinot Noir in hand. Flowers hadn't seemed appropriate, but a guest never goes wrong bringing a bottle of wine. There was no buzzer system so I just walked in and checked out the mailboxes to make sure I was headed for the right apartment. Hers was upstairs.

I was about to ring her doorbell when the front door swung open, as if she'd been poised behind it with one hand on the knob. I must have looked startled, because she reached out and grabbed my arm.

"I'm sorry, Bobby. I heard you on the stairs. This is a quiet building. I think everyone but me is 90 years old. Nobody else gets many guests." Then, she kissed me on the cheek. Not a bad start.

"I'm so glad you didn't dress up," she said, "I forgot to tell you that off duty I'm always pretty casual."

Actually, I had thought I had dressed up, at least a bit. As for her, she was fetching if not resplendent in a clingy pale peach dress cinched tight at the waist with an eye-catching expanse of cleavage. Her honey blond hair was piled up on her head in an intricate "do." If this was her casual, I couldn't picture what her formal might be.

Allison was delighted with my somewhat over-priced bottle of wine.

"We'll enjoy this with dinner. First, let's relax and have a cocktail."

I always like it when people refer to "a cocktail," not "a drink." Especially when a woman uses the term. It sounds somehow sophisticated, and elegant. Two people savoring a delicious libation, not just whacking back a few shots to loosen up.

Of course, we didn't actually have cocktails, at least not fancy mixed drinks. Allison fixed herself a gin-and-tonic and poured me a stiff bourbon from a cut glass decanter. My guess was that it was a low-end brand she'd repackaged to make it appear more upscale. Surprisingly, it wasn't half bad.

With her stereo providing a background of smooth jazz, we caught up. She told me about some of the funny, and some of the somewhat dangerous investigations she'd been on. I told her about life in Charleston, the charity balls, the Southern Gentlemen's Club, my attempts at becoming a country squire who fished and hunted and occasionally punished a golf ball. I left out any references to the bomb in my truck or to why, exactly, I'd decided to spend some time back in Los Angeles.

We busied ourselves in the kitchen, me piddling around setting the table while she finished cooking some nice-looking veal piccata with au gratin potatoes and green beans. The wine did go well with the meal.

After a dessert of tiny pastries and peach sorbet, we moved back into the living room and got comfortable, she on a maroon velvet couch, me on a big, dark brown leather easy chair. It wasn't a major decision for us to surrender to another round of cocktails.

I enjoy a good meal, some cocktails and listening to soothing music in the company of a beautiful woman as much as the next guy. Nonetheless, I was anxious to find out what more she had unearthed on the murdered Central American female cop, who evidently was not connected to Jerry Kendall.

I asked, "So, what more did you unearth on the murdered Central American female cop, who evidently was not connected to Jerry Kendall?"

She laughed, like a little girl teasing me to make me guess her secrets.

"Is this what this evening's all about? Were my veal and your wine and all our sparkling conversation just a prelude to a fishing expedition? Shame on you, Mr. McRae!"

I couldn't admit that she was right. On the other hand, I couldn't admit that I really wasn't as interested in the murder mystery as I was in getting over onto the couch next to her to see what might transpire.

"Detective Simmons," I started, "from the moment we first met at Muscle Beach. Or should I say, from the moment you tracked me down at Muscle Beach and led me on by not letting me know that you were an officer of the law until you'd departed, I have considered you a gem, a jewel and a pearl of great price.

"What I mean to say is that you are one fine woman and someone I'd like to get to know a whole lot better. That said, I'm also pretty interested in the unfortunate business of the Honduran cop, which you tantalized me with this morning. When, if I'm not mistaken, you had also tracked me down once again."

Allison actually lowered her eyes and blushed. Or, it could have been the cocktails. "Come over here and sit next to me," she said, easing back onto a comfortable cushion and tucking her feet under her. I didn't have to be asked twice.

"I know our contacts have been few and more than a little bit weird. But, there's always been a method in my madness. From that first time, when I admit I shadowed you, I've been a little fascinated by you. You turned out to be a good-looking guy who had a great job in a glamorous industry. Then, you fell into some big money and just chucked it all to move to the Deep South. Then, you came back to L.A. and started snooping around. I wonder if the detective here is me, or you."

It was my turn to laugh. "I'm no detective, lady. Just a curious sort of guy. I was trying to put a few confusing pieces together. Now, I guess I never will. But I'm glad my two visits back gave me the opportunity to connect with you."

"You're sweet, Bobby. Isn't it a shame that what brought us together had to be various sorts of mayhem?"

"Agreed, but, here's to better times!" we toasted and she refilled our glasses before she went on with her story.

As she'd said, when the Jane Doe murder went cold, she took a stab in the dark and ran what she had on the victim past Interpol. What she got back surprised her. Not only was Anna Garcia a cop, she was a member of an elite squad of national police tasked with locating and eliminating – not prosecuting, eliminating – some extremely nasty and dangerous criminals.

In addition to what Allison had learned from Interpol, she'd called on some good contacts she'd developed with experience dealing with Central Americans, as well as with an astonishingly forthright and helpful commander with the Honduran national police.

"Honduras has been pretty chaotic for decades," she said. "There are at least a half dozen 'rebel' groups in the country, based primarily in the rainforests but with tendrils reaching out into the few big cities. In their own way, they're as rich and as powerful as the central government itself.

"Narco-trafficking has been a major problem at least since the 70s, which is why we've collected a lot of information on these people here in the states. Honduras is a major trans-shipping point for narcotics from throughout the world. More recently, these 'liberation armies,' which is what they tend to call themselves, have branched out into arms sale, and not just handguns and rifles. We're talking heavy ordnance, RPGs, Stinger missiles, who knows what else. What's scary is that they apparently are dealing heavily with some serious bad guys in the Middle East."

According to Simmons' sources, one of the kingpins of the liberation armies is a particularly ruthless and ambitious general known only as "The Cuban." He'd arrived in Tegucigalpa some ten years previously from Havana, which is why he was called "The Cuban," even though there was no clear evidence that he was, in fact, a Cuban national. Some reports claimed that he was North African, and had simply used Castro's island as a stopping off point on his way to creating his own little empire in the jungles of Honduras. The Cuban was number one on the hit list for Ms. Garcia and her elite team, and after chasing him through the backcountry for several years they were no closer to finding him, much less capturing or killing him.

When there was some evidence that the Cuban might have left the country, at least temporarily, Garcia tried to follow his trail. She felt he had most likely headed for the U.S. with Florida as his destination. When that didn't pan out she was ordered to take a closer look at Southern California. That, of course, is where her search, and her life, ended.

"No one here has a clue about who this Cuban is," Simmons continued, "whether he is actually here or whether he killed Anna Garcia or had her killed. But, the odds are pretty good that that's how it went down. So, Jerry Kendall, may he rest in peace, undoubtedly had nothing at all to do with it."

It was a fascinating story, and I let her know it. Almost as fascinating as the lascivious thoughts running through my mind as I tried not to be too obvious about staring at her warm and possibly welcoming body. "That is amazing, Allison. So, there's this evil man of mystery who lords it over the people and the government of an entire nation, who can't be found and can't be stopped and who's believed to be funneling drugs into the U.S. and weapons into dissidents in the Arab countries. Incredible."

"Incredible, indeed," she nodded. "and pretty frustrating to law enforcement here. If he's planning on setting up a branch of his operation in our part of the world, things could get really messy."

"Do we even have any idea of how he operates, how he thinks, what he looks like?"

She sighed, "Like most warlords, or Mafia capos for that matter, he rules through fear and intimidation. He's apparently extremely intelligent and devious. He's said to speak both flawless Spanish and colloquial English and perhaps enough to get around in a few other languages. The Hondurans say he's tall, maybe 6"2" or 6'3. He's probably in his 60s now, but they say he's still a handsome man, strong as a bull, and a charmer when he wants to be. Otherwise, he'd be hard to ID. No known tattoos or any clear identifying marks. There's just one thing. He must have been in some sort of accident because he's missing several fingers and a chunk of his left hand."

The hair on the back of my neck went up. I couldn't believe what I was hearing. I struggled to think what to say next and came up with nothing. Then, saved by the bell. The telephone rang and Allison jumped up. "I'm sorry, I may have to take this."

It seemed impossible, but The Cuban was about the right age, had the same propensity toward violence, and shared the same physical deformity as the long-forgotten fugitive, Shabazz Ali. And, according to reports from the time of his disappearance, all indications were that Ali had taken refuge in one of the hostile countries of North Africa.

Before I could formulate any further thoughts on the subject, Allison stormed back into the room, looking angry and frustrated.

"I'm sorry, Bobby. I wanted this to be a very special night for us. Hollywood Division just found a teen pross in a dumpster in back of a strip joint. Guess she gave a private lap dance to the wrong guy. It's pretty pro forma but someone's got to take down all the details and tonight I drew the short straw. With the paperwork, I won't be through for hours. There must be a full moon tonight. Six Ds on call and all of us are needed."

"I hate to say goodnight like this," she pleaded, "but it's not my decision. Now, I have to do a quick change, rinse my mouth out and slap myself sober. A sector car is coming by in about ten minutes to take me to the scene."

I wasn't saved by the bell. I was screwed by the bell. I told her I completely understood, which I actually didn't. If she had the night off, and this was a routine murder, if a murder can ever be called routine, why was she the detective who had to handle the investigation. Was every other detective out investigating convenience store hold-ups?

She seemed so frazzled that I didn't ask any questions. She went into the bedroom and kept talking to me while she got out of her pale peach clingy dress, which I had devoutly hoped she would do while I was stepping out of my chinos, and into street clothes.

"I'll call you, Bobby. Let me know how long you'll be in town. We'll make this up, I promise."

"It's OK, I understand. The job comes first. I don't know when I'll be going back home. I'll probably be here at least a few more days. We'll work something out."

Then, for no apparent reason, a question flashed through my mind. "Before I go, I meant to ask you. What ever happened to your partner, the one who got suspended."

"He's back on the job," she replied cheerily, "and doing well."

"So, LAPD took him back after all?"

"Nope, he's working Narcotics in Miami."

I couldn't think of anything snappier to say than, "Oh. Well good for him." She came out in her detective clothes and she gave me a much better good-bye kiss than her hello kiss, and I reluctantly hit the road.

I walked around the corner to where I'd parked my hot rod junker and cranked her up. As I pulled up to the intersection I saw Allison quick-stepping down the path from her apartment building, her hair in a swinging pony tail and her "cop bag" flapping by her side. She quickly climbed into a car, but not a black-and-white. An unmarked. At least I think it was an unmarked. It was dark and big and it looked a lot newer and nicer than most unmarked cars I'd seen.

As I drove back over Coldwater Canyon I found myself wondering about Allison's departure and also about how a cop who got suspended pretty recently by the LAPD for some sort of shadowy association with known drug dealers managed to land on his feet with another big city department one of whose biggest problems each and every day is drug dealers.

32

Next morning, there was little time to speculate about Det. Allison Simmons' motives, intentions or mysterious calls to return to work in what appeared to be a late model Cadillac. I had a plan for the day and it hinged on timing.

My assumption was that most working stiffs would be on their jobs by 9:00 a.m. and that folks without jobs would either still be asleep or at least not bright-eyed and eager to scan their neighborhoods looking for potentially suspicious individuals. I slipped into my "Eddie" coveralls and put my little burglar kit and my mini-camera in my pockets along with my tear gas pen, my stun gun cell phone and my very sharp switchblade. For verisimilitude, I added a simple notebook on the cover of which I'd written "Cell Tower Study" in large letters and a pair of thin latex gloves I'd purchased at CVS. I actually had to buy a box of 50 pair of gloves, which mystified me. Why would the average person need so many gloves? To get a job making sandwiches at Subway?

Dolly kicked over smoothly and motored me to Beverly Hills, where I parked on a side street just below

Wilshire Boulevard. I didn't know the exact address of Jerry Kendall's Champagne Castle, but the description Derrick Pettit had given me was enough for me to narrow down the prospects. There weren't many older four story residential/professional buildings with a rooftop "penthouse" left in that pricey area. The second place I stopped at had a little placard by the front door listing a podiatrist, a child psychologist, two residence units on the third floor and on the fourth, "Kendall – CC."

The door to the small foyer wasn't locked and at the end of the short hall was an ancient elevator. I try to avoid elevators, especially old ones, if I'm trying to be cautious. Once you're inside, you can't see out. And, they're noisy, so anyone can hear you coming. If they wait outside the door, when it opens, Ba-da-bing!

I really didn't expect anyone to be lurking by the elevator waiting to pop me, but my alert meter was registering high. I took the stairs up the four short flights. There was only one unit on the top floor, and over the bell, it also said, "Kendall – CC."

I approached quietly and listened at the door. No sound. I rang the bell. Once. Twice. A third time. No answer. Reasonably confident that no one was home, I took a closer look at the knob. It gave a bit and didn't seem very secure. I figured a shim would slip the tongue of the lock and let me in. I told myself I hadn't done this in a while. Actually, I'd never done it, except once or twice in training. Fortunately, it was pretty easy and only took me about three minutes. If anyone had been inside, they certainly would have heard me forcing the shim between the door and the jamb and cursing to myself.

The front door swung open and I eased myself in. Dim light filtered through the dirty windows to illuminate what could conservatively be called a mess. Jerry Kendall's condo had been immaculate, with everything in its place. His "Champagne Castle" looked more like a beer joint at around 3:00 a.m.

I closed the door behind me and looked around. The living room had some kind of papers spread out over every available flat surface. In one corner were three large black trash bags filled with beer cans, wine bottles, pizza boxes and Chinese food take-out cartons. The room smelled like a dumpster.

The master bedroom contained a large unmade bed and two bedrolls on the floor. The second bedroom had a smaller unmade bed and another bedroll. It looked as if quite a few people had been having sleepovers at the place, but probably not the orgies Jerry had fantasized.

I went back into the living room to look for anything that would give me an idea of who had been here, and probably was still here, although not at this moment. Wearing my nitrile gloves, I began lifting the papers, sorting through them while keeping them in place as best I could. A great many seemed to be blueprints or schematics of some sort, although there was no indication of what they represented. A number of the documents on top had hand-written notes in Spanish and circles and arrows at key intersections of what might have been walls or conduits.

I got out my mini-camera and started taking pictures as fast as I could. Very soon I had good close-up images of what I decided were all the important papers. I moved to the kitchen, which had a bunch of dirty dishes in the sink and a lot of pieces of what looked like electrical wire and small metal components on the breakfast bar. I took pictures of them as well.

Then my phone rang. Loud. I'd never bothered to turn the volume down and it sounded like Big Ben echoing through the empty apartment suite. I flipped it open fast and answered in what amounted to a stage whisper, "Hello."

"Is this Bobby McRae," a woman's voice responded. "You sound funny."

"I'm keeping my voice down so I don't disturb the people at the next table," I whispered. "Who's this?"

"It's Gretchen Hatchet, from Robert Raskin's office. Are you sure you're alright?"

"Oh, hi Mrs. Hatchet. I'm fine. How can I help you?"

"Well, I don't think you can help me, but I believe I can help you. Mr. Raskin is back in the city and would very much like to get together with you."

"Excellent. When would he like me to swing by the office?"

"He doesn't want to meet with you in the office. He'd like to have drinks and dinner with you at his home, tonight at 7:00 if that's agreeable to you. His family is away, so it will be just you two. He said to be very casual. He'll just grill up a couple of steaks and you two can talk."

I couldn't imagine why Raskin would want me to come to his home, and feed me to boot. Nonetheless, I agreed and took down both his address and his home telephone number in case anything came up or I got lost. Getting lost wasn't likely. From his address I could tell that he lived by the crest of Mulholland Drive, and there are only a few mini-mansions along that stretch of road. I whispered, "Goodbye" and made a mental note to get Mrs. Hatchet another present.

I put the phone away and listened to see if anyone had heard me talking and might be headed this way. No one was. I went into the master bedroom and poked around a little more, making sure I didn't move anything or leave any trace that I'd been there. If I thought I'd uncovered some interesting clues before, now I started to hit pay dirt. Under a worn T-shirt on the dresser was a Glock 26, fitted with a silencer. Leaning against the nightstand was a 12 gauge shotgun with a sawed off barrel and a pistol grip.

On a nightstand pushed up against one wall were a battery of chargers, one with four walkie-talkie units powering up and the other with four what looked like modified, or maybe just foreign, cell phones, all with glowing green LEDs indicating a full charge,

Against the wall was an unobtrusive object that could easily have been overlooked. It was just a long, thin tube with what looked like a small, rubbery mouthpiece at one end. Next to it were half a dozen sharp and nasty-looking darts and an aspirin bottle sized vial of a yellowish liquid.

I took pictures of everything then made one last sweep through the main room. I'd noticed what looked like a small easel in the corner with a blank piece of construction paper on it. I turned the construction paper over and took a good look at the reverse side. About a third of the sheet included another blueprint or schematic, this one seemingly hand-drawn, but neatly hand-drawn. Next to it was written in big script AVANTE 53. Stapled onto the surface was one page of a calendar, with the date "March 4" circled multiple times in red marker. Today was February 27th.

Only two other phrases were inscribed on the construction paper. The first was in a stylized freehand script, "La Raza – A Revolution in Heating and Air Conditioning Technology." The second was "Ceremonia de los Oscars." My Spanish isn't first-rate, but it seemed to me that this could mean nothing other than "Oscar Ceremony," or, in plain English, the Academy Awards. I shot all this from several angles and headed for the door.

This time, I took the elevator down. No need for stealth at this point. Except, when the door opened I was face to face with a burly Hispanic man about 60 in baggy grey khakis, a wrinkled flannel work shirt and a scraggly beard.

"Can I help you?" he asked.

I was startled but not speechless. "Why, yes you can. Are you the owner of this property?"

"Nope. The manager. More like the custodian. I do maintenance and odd jobs. You lookin' for someone in particular?"

"Not at this time, but perhaps you could let the owners know that I stopped by. I'm from CallCal, the cellular telephone company. I'm sure you have heard of us. We're the fastest growing phone company in L.A."

I handed him one of the business cards I'd pocketed at the company office. He looked perplexed and scratched his head underneath what looked like a fishing hat.

"So, what's that got to do with this building, eh?"

"Well, you see," I vamped along with my mental script, "we're always scouting new locations for our transmission towers. This location looks like a very good one for us to mount an antenna on the roof. It would give us great coverage throughout Beverly Hill and West Hollywood. Of course, we'd pay generously for the right to put our gear up on your roof. I'm sure your owner would be pleased to have some extra income at no cost."

He looked skeptical. "And, of course, as the manager of the building, there'd be a nice monthly compensation to you for keeping an eye on our equipment and reporting any damage or problems.'

His eyes brightened at the prospect of cash. "O.K. then. I'll just let 'em know next time we talk and give 'em your card. How soon you think you'll be puttin' your antenna up?"

"Well, we're still in the preliminary phase. It may take a while. But, based on what I've seen today I'm sure it won't be long. Between you and me this is a prime location, so don't mention this to anyone else. We don't want the competition to beat us to the punch."

He seemed satisfied, so we shook hands and I wandered down the block to where I'd stashed my wheels.

I made a quick stop back at the hotel to change out of my coveralls and into the suit I'd brought, a serious navy blue two button model worn with a blue button down collar shirt, a sincere navy blue necktie with deep red diagonal stripes and black wing tip shoes. I looked and felt like a mortician. Or, a Special Agent of the United States Department of State.

As promised Premier California National Bank was on Pico, a few blocks from Hoover, on the fringe of a very rough and not very English-speaking neighborhood. I arrived at 12:30 p.m., counting on the tellers being busy with customers and the manager most likely at lunch. I was right. The place was packed.

When my turn in line came, I asked to speak with whoever was in charge of safe deposit boxes. A short, round woman in a flowered dress came out from behind the counter and introduced herself as Mildred Lyman. Mildred evidently hadn't gotten the news that her bank had just been voted Most Likely to be Robbed. I apologized for not having recognized her, saying that it had been quite a while since I'd had to access this safe deposit box. Actually, I think I said "my" safe deposit box. But, I hadn't meant to lie to her. At least not about that.

I was ready to show her my credentials and give her a story about having to get into the box as a matter of national security or some such, but I didn't have to. She looked at my key and led me through a buzzer-operated door into the vault area. Taking my key, she said, "Just sign the register and come on back. I'll be at your box."

This was just too easy. I signed my name as "Clifford Irving" and noted an entirely different box number, on the theory that she wasn't going to check anyway.

Mildred used her master key and my key to release the box, which she let me pull out of its slot and take to a discreetly secluded table and chair where I could examine the contents.

"Call me when you're finished," she chirped. And that was that.

The contents of the box were not spectacular. A copy of Kendall's condo mortgage. A copy of the rental agreement for his car. Some correspondence about the Rotary Club. Then, I pulled out a passport. The photo was of Jerry Kendall but the name on the passport was Juan Cardenas. It had customs stamps from the U.S., Mexico, and Honduras. The passport hid a slim volume on idiomatic Spanish, an envelope containing – surprise! – nine thousand dollars. A Kahr Arms compact 9mm pistol. And, a 9mm mate to the cartridge with the strange black bullet that I'd found hidden at Jerry's condo. That was it. That and a pocket calendar with one date marked in red. March 4.

I took a peek to make sure Mildred wasn't lurking around then spread Jerry's belongings out on the table and quickly snapped pictures of everything. Two minutes later, all of the items were back in the box and I called Mildred to put it away.

Before I left, she thanked me for my business and gave me her card in case I had any problems or questions. By now, I had plenty of questions, but I doubted that she'd be in a position to answer them.

33

Los Angeles, California

A quick stop back at the Barclay gave me time to download copies of the photos to my laptop and to dump my little weapons cache. Then, I took a little nap before heading out to Hollywood and the unveiling of the LAPD star on the Walk of Fame.

It's never easy to get a parking spot on Hollywood Boulevard so I turned off a few blocks away from where the ceremony was set to take place, parked in a cash lot and hoofed it down the street. Not surprisingly, the street was closed off with sawhorses and every ten feet there was a police vehicle.

The event had drawn a pretty decent crowd, including just about every television and radio station and photographer in Los Angeles. It took me a few minutes to ease my way toward the front where I could get a good view of the proceedings. Precisely at 4:00 p.m. the dignitaries marched to the small stage that had been thrown up for the occasion. Taking the spotlight were the mayor, the chief of police, several members of the police commission and city council, Captain Terry Bates and a gaggle of popular radio and television personalities. The

Mayor introduced the official members of the dais and each accepted the honor with gratitude and went on for a bit about the great relationship the movie industry and the Los Angeles police had had since time immemorial.

Finally, the big gold star was unveiled, video rolled and still cameras flashed and the star was placed ceremoniously into the pavement not far from the old Pantages Theater. After a few minutes of innocuous Q&A, the big shots dispersed and headed for a little private party at the time-honored restaurant Buon Gusto. I overheard one of the cops telling another that the chief's office had taken over the entire place for a reception for a few hours before the dinner crowd arrived. Otherwise, I wouldn't have known about it. My invitation must have gotten lost in the mail.

It was a nice afternoon for a walk, so I strolled down to Buon Gusto and just kind of lingered in a doorway until the luminaries had all gone inside. Then I put my dark glasses on, braced my shoulders in my serious suit and approached the doorman, who was flanked by two big cops. I whipped out my wallet, flashed my badge and announced myself as Special Agent, State Department, representing the United States government as a guest of the Chief.

No problem. The uniformed doorman stepped aside, parted the velvet rope and commanded, "Right this way, sir!" Inside it was pretty crowded. And noisy. Waiters were circulating through the mob with trays of hors d'oeuvres and glasses of champagne. I have nothing against champagne, but what I really wanted was a real `drink. A few deft maneuvers and I was at the hosted bar and the bartender was more than happy to pour me a double bourbon when I tossed a five in his tip jar.

It was a nice party, particularly since it was free. I saw and talked to quite a few people I'd known from other studios and the media and everyone who knew I'd retired wanted to know what life was like in historic Charleston. I'm hardly a South Carolina historian, but I've learned enough about the city and the Lowcountry to impress folks who had never been there with my knowledge. No one seemed at all interested in what I was doing back in town. They probably thought I was looking for a production deal.

At the front of the room representatives of the Hollywood Chamber of Commerce some studio execs and the police bigwigs held court, telling jokes, slapping each other on the back and, most likely drinking better whisky than I was. Soft jazz played in the background and to one side a large table held a gigantic sheet cake iced with a replica of the Walk of Fame star, the official LAPD shield and the motto, "To Protect and Serve." I wondered if maybe an undercover policewoman would jump out of the cake.

As I was working on my second drink, I bumped into, literally, Captain Bates. "Hi, Bobby," he said, "nice to see you. Glad you could come."

It crossed my mind that even though he knew full well that I lived in South Carolina, he didn't seem at all surprised to see me at a private party for the police in Los Angeles. In fact, he launched into a canned speech about how great it was that the LAPD and the industry had such a wonderful relationship and how honored all of the officers on the force felt to be enshrined on the Walk of Fame. When he took a breath I asked him how things were going for the department these days.

"Terrific, just terrific," he said. "We have a whole bunch of new procedures in place that are making life easier on us and tougher on the bad guys. We've got everything under control. You know, we've learned a lot about big incidents like demonstrations and riots since the Rodney King days."

I had to wonder why, of all the things the LAPD does, he had focused on the department's new found ability to deal with demonstrations and riots. Maybe he'd just attended some sort of major incident training course. We shot the breeze a bit and he moved on. I scanned the crowd looking to see if I knew anyone else. I did. Way across the room, surrounded by about ten guys, was Det. Allison Simmons in skin-tight black leather pants and a lilac blouse, cut very low, naturally. She even had a different bag, in black leather, to match her outfit.

I'm tall enough that I tend to stand out above the multitudes so eventually she spotted me. I got a big wave and a blown kiss, but she made no effort to disengage herself from her admirers and come over to say "Hello." So be it. I'd sort of convinced myself that this relation-ship, if it could be called that, wasn't going anywhere.

Just as I was admitting defeat with the lovely gum-shoe Simmons, I felt a tap on my shoulder. I turned and there was Derrick Pettit.

"Well, Bobby! This is a nice surprise. Glad you could be back here to Los Angeles and on hand to see the industry honor the Los Angeles Police Department. I know that you always had a great relationship with law enforcement, and since you left us I've kind of picked up the slack on behalf of Avante Entertainment. How long are you in town for?"

It occurred to me that Pettit had never been this effusive about me when I was working with him at the studio. Suddenly, I was his long lost buddy and he was thrilled to be breathing the same air as me.

"I'm just in for a few days, Derrick. I had a little business to take care of and I wanted to see some old buddies from the service. I'll be out of everyone's hair and back on the fringe of the marsh before you know it."

Derrick furrowed his brow and looked concerned. Actually, I think he furrowed his brow in order to look concerned.

"I was kind of hoping that you might be planning on sticking around at least through next weekend," he said. "When I saw you from across the room I had a great idea."

I just nodded, so he continued. "Here's what I had in mind. You know the Academy Awards are next Sunday, down at the Hollywood and Highland Center. You know. It used to be the Kodak Theater. Well, naturally, all the major studios have a certain allotment of tickets to the big event, and as this year's liaison between Avante and the Academy, I'm more or less responsible to see that ours are used properly."

I couldn't get the image of Derrick as George Jefferson out of my mind. I nodded again.

"Well, Chuck Lattimore. You remember Chuck Lattimore, the producer, who did so many great films for us…"

Chuck had produced maybe a dozen films, two of which made money. The rest went straight to video.

"…his wife Arlene, you know Arlene, died last year. Cancer. Terrible. So, I had one seat set aside for Chuck at the awards. Long story short, he wanted to go but he's still so broken up over losing Arlene that he's afraid he might lose it watching all those stars going up to accept their awards when Arlene, bless her heart, never even got a nomination."

I nodded twice this time.

"In any event, I now have one free ticket, Chuck Lattimore's ticket, and I have to get someone to take it. You know, the Academy is very strict about the cameras never seeing an empty seat in the audience during the Oscars. That's why they have all those young hopefuls willing to stand for three or four hours just to watch the show and be seat-fillers in case anyone has to throw up or get a drink or take a leak during the show.

"Now, it's not as if there aren't dozens of people who'd kill to get that ticket, even though it's a single and they couldn't bring a spouse or a date. Of course, that puts me on the hot seat because if I give it to one, all the rest will have their noses out of joint and it'll be terrible for office morale.

"So, when I saw you, it was like an answered prayer. If you'll take Chuck Lattimore's seat I'll be giving it to an esteemed former member of our team, an executive emeritus as it were. Everyone who remembers you still loves you so your getting to go to the Awards wouldn't bend anyone out of shape. What do you say?'

Thus far, I hadn't said anything. I guess it was time to open my mouth. "Derrick, I understand your predicament, and I'm flattered that you would think me worthy of helping to represent Avante at the Academy Awards. Unfortunately, I can't guarantee that I'll be in Los Angeles through the weekend. In fact, I'm reasonably sure that I won't be. So, rather than make you a promise I can't keep, I'll reluctantly have to decline your offer."

Derrick was pretty composed, but his face briefly clouded over.

"I'm truly sorry to hear that, Bobby. I want very much to have you on hand with us. I even have a pass for you for the Governor's Ball. You know this is a big deal, don't you? I don't think you've ever gone before. Why not extend your stay just a bit and be a part of history?'"

By now, Pettit was really getting up in my face, which was not easy for him, as his face is a good foot lower than mine under the best of circumstances.

"Bobby, I'm dead serious about this. I want you there. I'm going out on a limb quite a bit by not greasing one of my co-workers with an invitation to the Awards and the big gala. I don't want you to dismiss this out of hand."

"I understand, Derrick, and don't think I don't appreciate your kindness. I just can't guarantee I'll even be in California next weekend and I don't want to accept and leave you in the lurch."

Pettit backed off a bit, looking crestfallen. "OK. I understand. You can't blame me for trying. If you change your plans and change your mind, let me know right away. Better, let me know where I can reach you and I'll touch base in a day or so when you might have a better handle on your plans."

I didn't want Derrick Pettit to have my cell phone number so I just told him I'd be at the Barclay and gave him my room number. Probably a bad idea, but I thought he'd come to his senses in the morning, realize I wasn't kidding and move on.

With some time to kill before my meeting with Robert Raskin, I grabbed a few more hors d'oeuvres and another drink and wandered around the party for a half hour or so. One of the big presentations was a giant, fifteen by ten foot montage of old time, mostly black-and-white photos of the police interacting with the movie folks from around the 1920s to the present.

It was fascinating to see the clothing, the police vehicles and the biggest stars back to the silent era all posed with L.A.'s finest. I've always been a sucker for memorabilia so I got a big kick out of this display. Then, I shook the required hands and made my way down the boulevard to where my car waited to whisk me off to the Raskin fortress.

34

Los Angeles, California

On the drive up the winding portion of Laurel Canyon to the peak at Mulholland, I kept turning the day's activities over in my mind. What was important? What was irrelevant? How much should I tell Robert Raskin? Why did I think it was somehow important to involve him in all this? One thing in particular completely perplexed me. Why was the movie studio's name written on that board in what used to be Jerry Kendall's "Champagne Club" and what did the number 53 after it mean?

Right at 7:00 p.m. I pulled into the circular driveway of the Raskin residence. The house was one of those quintessentially California homes built on the edge of a cliff with most of the structure cantilevered out over an abyss. I wasn't entirely comfortable being in one of these perilously suspended building, but there were plenty of them around and none seemed on the brink of toppling down a hillside.

I parked and crunched across the bluestone driveway to the front door. One push on the doorbell and Raskin himself opened the door. No maid or butler or other servant. I wondered whether he lived more a more Spartan life than I'd imagined or whether he'd just given the help the night off.

"Bobby McRae, welcome" he said, sweeping one arm to usher me in.

Raskin wore tan shorts, a dark red polo shirt with the tail hanging out and designer flip-flops. I was still in my serious suit.

"Guess you didn't get the memo about my being very casual at home," he said with a smile. "Or, you just didn't believe my executive assistant!"

I explained to him that I'd attended the placing of a star on the Walk of Fame for the LAPD plus the after party and thought I should look suitably ceremonial.

He laughed. "O.K. you're forgiven. Just let me hang up your jacket and you roll up those sleeves and ditch the tie. We should both be comfortable."

Obviously pleased with his home, Raskin offered me a quick tour, which I took. The place was impressive. Spacious, with terrific city views through huge plate glass windows. The furniture was all modern and looked showroom new. There was an expansive verandah, also over the cantilevered portion. Best of all, downstairs — these houses always open at street level and have large downstairs areas under the main house — he had two rooms for amusement. One must have made his girls and their friends pretty happy. It held a major league sound system plus a working, old-time jukebox, a tiny dance floor, a pool table and a ping-pong set-up. The other room was an in-home theater with a screen I estimated at around 90 inches, carpeted floor and a dozen luxurious leather theater seats. Being a criminal didn't seem like a very good job, but being a criminal lawyer sure had its benefits.

After the tour, Raskin invited me out onto the overhanging verandah. Between two comfortable chairs obviously meant for us he'd placed a tray of hors d'oeuvres and mini-sandwiches along with an ice bucket, glasses and a bottle of Wild Turkey and a bottle of a single malt Scotch I'd never heard of.

"I thought we could have a snack and a few drinks. If there's anything else you might want, a soft drink, a beer, just let me know."

Bourbon was more than fine for me and he poured himself about three fingers of Scotch, neat. He obviously knew and loved his spirits. The sun was down and the lights of Los Angeles sparkled far below.

"When you said you wanted to see me, one on one, I thought it was important for us to get together. Clearly, you wouldn't have come back to L.A. and sought me out just for the pleasure of my company. Which I hope will be a pleasure in any event. I'm assuming that you have some significant and perhaps confidential information to share with me. I hope to offer the same to you."

He paused, took a long sip of his drink, and sat back reflectively.

I wasn't quite sure where to start and how much I should actually reveal. I had a strong feeling that I needed his help. At the same time, I wasn't sure he'd be willing or able to offer it.

Raskin broke our silence. "You seem a bit hesitant, Bobby. How about this. If you show me yours, I'll show you mine."

That got a laugh from me and we both seemed to relax a little.

I started out. "I've come across some information that leads me to believe that a criminal plan has been hatched by a long-time fugitive from U.S. justice. In brief, I believe this plot may involve mass murder, and soon. Some of the information I have has been obtained in ways that could make it inadmissible in a court of law. So, once I tell you what I now know, I have to be confident that both you and I won't be subject to criminal charges."

Raskin whistled softly. "Even without your details, this sounds like either a dangerous conspiracy or a pipe dream. You aren't subject to flights of imagination are you, Mr. McRae?"

"No, sir, I'm not. And once I tell you what I can, I think you'll agree that I have to take action, and sooner rather than later. Some details I'll have to hold back because I don't want either of us to break the law or be an accessory to breaking the law."

Raskin reached into a folder he'd placed on a small table next to his chair. He took out several sheets of paper and laid them on the table between us.

"Do you have a dollar bill on you?"

"Well, sure."

"O.K. Give it to me."

I did as he asked and he slid one of the papers across the table between us.

"Now, sign this. You don't actually have to read it. It's a very simple agreement naming me as your attorney of record. Your dollar will serve to seal the deal and once you're my client our conversations will be privileged. I'll be bound not to disclose anything you tell me, unless, of course, you tell me you're about to commit a major crime."

I glanced over the document quickly. He was right. It was pretty simple and straightforward. I signed it where he'd thoughtfully placed an "X" with my name typed beneath it.

"I never thought I'd be able to hire such an important and successful lawyer," I quipped.

"Consider it pro bono, if you wish," he replied, taking the document away and sliding another into its place. "Now, sign this."

I glanced over this one as well. It looked like the same document that I'd just signed. Then, at the bottom, where he'd put the "X" for the line I was supposed to sign I read the name below it. It read "MacArthur James Cutter." It was my Army/State Department identity.

I froze with the pen in my hand. "What's this?"

Raskin took another thoughtful sip at his Scotch. "If we're going to have an attorney-client relationship, and if we're going to help each other, we have to be completely honest. I know that in addition to your being Bobby McRae, you are also MacArthur "Mack" Cutter. He has to be my client as well."

I was speechless for a few seconds that seemed like a few minutes. "O.K. I'll sign. But, first tell me how you know about Mack Cutter."

"Do you smoke a cigar?" Raskin asked. I don't particularly like cigars but once in a while I'll try one. I was betting he'd have only the best. And he did. We went through the ritual of cutting the cigar ends, warming and lighting them with wooden stick matches and, finally, sitting back and savoring them thoughtfully.

"Dominican, from Cuban seed," Raskin said, "my favorite. Now, I'll freshen up our drinks and tell you an interesting story."

Interesting it was. It all began with Linus, the somewhat creepy young man from Raskin's office who's shadowed me the one time I'd made my little search of Jerry Kendall's condo. Raskin told me that Linus was an only child, the son of a cousin who was very close to him. He said that Linus was a genius, a savant, who was at the very high end of the autism spectrum. Kind of Asberger's plus.

As a child, Linus had to attend special schools. He graduated from high school at fourteen. UCLA basically designed a program just for him and he lived at home, not on campus, graduating at eighteen. Even with a B.A. he had the social skills of perhaps a twelve year old.

"Linus' family really couldn't cope with him. He was just too smart. He also had an idietic memory, so he remembered pretty much everything that ever happened to him, perfectly. He just couldn't relate to other people. After two years of intensive therapy, he'd improved a lot, although he'd never be mistaken for a wild and crazy guy."

Linus was directionless, but he'd expressed an interest in the law and in government service. Between Raskin himself and his cousin's husband, a one star general in the Air Force, they secured an internship for the kid in Washington, D.C. It paid almost nothing and he lived in a group home with some other "special" kids. But, he was out in the world. Apparently he even had a girlfriend briefly but they broke up over a disagreement over some obscure point in German philosophy.

At work, Linus did so well that he earned a transfer from the Department of Commerce to the State Department, where his almost obsessive-compulsive sense of organization was ideal for a project the bureaucrats had in mind but didn't want to tackle themselves, organizing and cross-referencing thousands of files on past and present employees and others associated with the department. Some of those files pertained to personnel in special services such as the Army's liaison with State.

His internship over, Linus returned to L.A. and Raskin took him on at his law office, while the kid started taking law school courses. One day, Jerry Kendall called to ask Raskin if Linus might like to go to a real Hollywood party, a premiere, and see what the glitterati were like. Raskin was of two minds about the idea, but Jerry was so enthusiastic about helping Linus adjust to the "real" world that he caved in and let him go.

It was an Avante premiere so Jerry had great seats for the show and no problem getting Linus into the tented after-party, an event replete with first and second tier celebrities. Turned out, Linus had a terrific time and even had a few reasonably normal conversations with people, including one hot young blonde he had his eye on. So, it was a success. Jerry also introduced Linus to me, although I have no recollection of meeting him. I shake a lot of hands at these events, plus I likely had one or two adult beverages under my belt.

On their way home from the party, Linus turned to Jerry and said, "You know, Mr. McRae is also MacArthur James Cutter, an Army officer serving in a special services division tasked with projects involving the Department of State.'

Kendall didn't pay much attention to what Linus said, figuring it was just some idle wandering of the kid's strange mind. The next day, he called Raskin to give him a recap of how the gala had gone for Linus. Just in passing, he mentioned what Linus had told him about me. Raskin didn't know exactly what to make of this revelation. But, he knew if Linus said it, it had to be right.

Then, about two years later, Jerry Kendall is dead, under unusual if not outright suspicious circumstances, and I show up at Raskin's office as Bobby McRae asking a lot of questions and clearly not convinced that Kendall's demise was natural and understandable. Small wonder he wasn't surprised when I was back in L.A. requesting a face-to-face meeting with him and now going on about plots and conspiracies and mass murder and the need for secrecy. Small wonder he wanted to have me as a client, so he could keep me close, keep me confidential and maybe keep me from going much further in pursuit of the truth.

I wasn't sure who would benefit more from this attorney-client relationship, but my gut told me it would be the right thing to do. I signed on the dotted line. Then, it was my turn to tell him my story and ask his advice and counsel.

35

Los Angeles, California

I began my story with a question: As Jerry Kendall's attorney and as his executor, would you legally have access to all of his assets, even those not disclosed in his will?

Raskin drew on his cigar and blew a perfect smoke ring. "That's a question that leads us into a gray area. On the one hand, the answer is yes. On the other, it's no. Yes, I have the authority to assess and evaluate all of the deceased's assets, even if it requires some digging to find them. No, I have no right to dispose of them to benefit myself to the detriment of any of his heirs. Is that the answer you wanted to hear?"

"I'm not sure," I replied. Maybe I should be more specific."

"Please do."

"O.K. If you were to learn that Jerry had a safe deposit box in a local bank, as well as an apartment suite separate from his residence that is paid up for the next ten months in advance and which apartment suite was being utilized by persons unknown for purposes unknown, would you be able to get into either or both, legally."

Raskin thought for a moment. "I'd have to say, yes. The safe deposit box would be easy. As soon as I identified myself as Kendall's attorney and executor, I'd be able to open the box and remove its contents as a part of his estate.

"The apartment suite is a little different. Yes, I could demand that I be allowed to enter the apartment and I'd likely be within my rights to remove any items of value as well. But, you say the apartment is being used by persons unknown for purposes unknown. I assume that, absent some written agreement I'm not aware of, they would have to be evicted and barred from returning to the premises.

"My question to you," he continued, "is, what if these individuals are dangerous? I wouldn't want either of us to try to serve an eviction notice without some significant law enforcement back-up."

We both stayed silent for a few moments. I was the first to speak. "O.K. I grasp the general ground rules we'd be operating under. We'll get back to those questions, but, first, I'll take you through the chain of events that led me to you tonight."

Raskin topped off our drinks and I began. He already knew of my skepticism about Jerry Kendall's death on my front porch. He didn't know about how during my previous return visit to L.A. I'd been shadowed by Det. Allison Simmons, who also told me about a mysterious dead Jane Doe with Jerry Kendall's business card on her person and curare in her system. He didn't know why Simmons, at least in my mind, had come on to me and then pulled back abruptly.

I told him how Capt. Bates of the LAPD had seemed very cavalier about Kendall's death, and not at all surprised that I'd be back in Los Angeles asking about it and how my former colleague Derrick Pettit had made it a point to wine and dine me, when we had never been close at work.

His attention perked up when I told him about the attempt on my life that resulted in the blowing up of my truck and nearly killing my neighbor and good friend. He seemed very interested in how through my new found contacts in Charleston the bombing had been kept quiet so as not to alert the bombers of their success or failure.

Raskin seemed to find it amusing that the Judge had rhetorically suggested that in a court of law I might be considered a prime suspect in Kendall's death for a number of coincidental and circumstantial reasons. He also paid attention when I explained that one of the guests at our club, the FBI Special Agent in Charge for South Carolina, had taken me aside and, in so many words, told me that if I had anything to say about the Kendall death, he'd be the right guy to talk to.

I told him how Derrick Pettit had called me out of the blue just to chat and to tell me, oh yes, by the way, Jerry Kendall was a major league embezzler, who made off with as much as a million dollars before his demise but Avante Entertainment declined to prosecute

"You're telling me that a mid-level executive at a – pardon the expression – mid-level motion picture company, was able to embezzle that sort of money and just keep it. No one cared?"

"That's how Derrick put it. The studio didn't want the bad publicity."

When I got to the information I'd gleaned from my handler in the service, I didn't try to hide the source. He already knew that I'd been involved in some covert operations and probably still was, so it made no sense to try to fool him.

Raskin stubbed out his cigar and leaned toward me to listen intently. That's when I told him about Jerry Kendall's secret trips to Honduras via Mexico and what Det. Simmons had told me about the former Jane Doe turning out to be a Honduran special investigator following the trail of a notorious paramilitary leader known as The Cuban. The Cuban headed a paramilitary criminal organization deeply into drug smuggling, arms transfers to hostile states and dissident groups, extortion, kidnapping and murder. According to Simmons' sources, the dead Honduran agent believed she had followed The Cuban to Los Angeles.

It was time for a break, so we retired into the house to enjoy some red wine and an excellent eggplant parmagiana Raskin had prepared himself. He explained that during law school and his early years in practice, he had wanted to eat well but didn't have to money to go out to restaurants very often. So, he'd taught himself how to cook a lineup of dishes that were relatively easy to prepare and that most people seemed to enjoy. When he married, he said his wife was overjoyed that she'd snagged a guy with a decent job and the ability to take over the kitchen duties from time to time.

Over our meal, I continued to fill Raskin in on what I'd discovered, still being careful not to disclose exactly how I came by some of my information. I explained how Det. Simmons had once again tracked me down, even though I was staying at an unlikely hotel under a different name. I also mentioned how she invited me to her apartment for dinner and just when the lights were low, the music soft and the wine flowing she bolted out, ostensibly on a homicide call, but left her home in what could have been an an unmarked car but that looked suspiciously like a late model Cadillac.

Raskin took everything in, making few comments and nodding thoughtfully as if he were dissecting everything I said in order to prepare a court case. Finally, he said, "You've told me a great deal, Bobby. What you haven't told me is what I'd consider really important right now. If that can't be told without your telling how you came by the information, so be it. But, let's not dance around the ring sparring.

"I need to know what specifics, if any, have led you to believe that a mass murder is being planned and that if we don't move fast there'll be no stopping it. Tell me what you know and what you think. I don't care how you got the information and I can promise you that whatever you tell me will be held in confidence."

It seemed that if he were to be willing to help me untangle this riddle, I'd have to level with him about my quasi-legal activities. I took a deep breath and began with my break-in at the Champagne Castle under the guise of a cellular telephone company location scout.

I told him about the blueprints and schematics, the copious notes in Spanish, the firearms and the blowgun with darts and a vial of some yellowish liquid. I told him about the bedrolls and the fast food garbage and the multiple walkie-talkies and odd-looking cell phones on chargers.

I told him about the hand-drawn logo for La Raza Heating and Air Conditioning, about the March 4 date circled in red, about the phrase "Ceremonia de los Oscars" in large hand-lettering and the cryptic, bold inscription "Avante 53."

Moving on to Kendall's safe deposit box, I told Raskin about the false passport, the cash, and the loaded handgun. I specifically did not mention how I got into the safe deposit box. And, Raskin never asked.

Then, I sat back in silence.

Robert Raskin spoke first. "Let's clear the table and go back to the verandah, unless you want some dessert."

I didn't, and we did.

He poured us each a fresh drink and we sat staring at the twinkling city lights. Even knowing how grubby L.A. could be at street level, the enchantment of its lights couldn't be denied.

"Let me encapsulate," he began. "If I read you right, you believe that this Cuban, is planning some sort of action at the time of the Academy Awards, which you'll recall are just a few days away, next Sunday to be exact.

"You've arrived at this conclusion based on a great many pieces of circumstantial evidence. Not bad evidence, mind you. But not enough to put anyone in jail.

"That said, the odds are that even if the people using Kendall's former apartment are The Cuban's henchmen, he won't be anywhere near where they're doing their planning. And, if the place gets raided all the government will have is a couple of illegal immigrants with some weapons that will maybe get them a slap on the wrist before they're deported. All that paperwork you saw could easily be explained in any number of ways. Maybe they were writing a novel."

He paused, and sipped at his Scotch. "You need something more substantial, and if you find it, you have to be careful how you handle it. That apartment is in the jurisdiction of the Beverly Hills P.D. You'll forgive me for saying that they don't boast the best investigative teams around.

"The Oscars will take place smack dab in the heart of LAPD country. But, you seem to have some questions about how the Los Angeles police have acted toward you since you started asking questions they couldn't, or wouldn't answer. Don't get me wrong. I'm usually in an adversarial position with the LAPD in court. But, out of court, we get along just fine. I'd never go out of my way at trial to use some trickery that might make a good cop look bad."

I thought I knew where he was headed, and I was right. In fact, I was a little ahead of him. He said the best bet would be to get the FBI interested in the situation.

It would be a real coup for the office of the Bureau that stopped a terror incident that could have killed hundreds of celebrities live on worldwide TV. But, he counseled, I'd have to go to the FBI with a lot more than my personal gut feeling and they'd be unlikely to overlook my own criminal activities if my leads didn't pan out.

Raskin asked me to really focus on everything I'd told him to see if any one item stood out. Something that might point to a way to get some really hard evidence that would mobilize the FBI and bring down whatever plan the Cuban had in mind.

I told him that the one thing that both leaped out at me and mystified me was the inscription, "Avante 53." Why would my old studio be written down so prominently, and what could "53" mean?

"Does Avante have a Studio 53," Raskin asked. "Is there an office or department 53? Is there any special relationship between the name of the company and the number 53?"

I had no answers. I'd already been with Robert Raskin for several hours. He'd come across as a truly smart man, no surprise, and also as a thoughtful, considerate friend. He'd known my other identity for a long time and had never brought it up to anyone, even me, until it became important to do so. He wanted to see me move ahead with my freelance investigation and come up with enough hard information that the authorities would have to listen and to act. He was one of the good guys.

We shook hands after 10:00 p.m. and I headed back to the hotel hoping for a good night's sleep. When

I hit Sunset and turned west, I saw a white van a few cars back that seemed to have come out of nowhere. For a moment, I thought I was being tailed. Then I wrote that thoughts off as fatigue and paranoia, although that white van did seem to be behind me almost all the way home.

What was really top of mind was that inscription, Avante 53. I felt it had to mean something, something significant. Unfortunately, I didn't have any idea what that might be.

Just as I turned left onto Avenue of the Stars heading toward Olympic, it hit me. The big montage of mostly old black-and-white photos at the LAPD reception. It was just like the one that hung in the main reception area at Avante Studios, except ours wasn't of police and the entertainment industry. It was of photos marking major accomplishments and milestones in the history of the studio.

Right in the middle of the wall-mounted display was one photo that was larger than all the rest. It was a picture of Avante's very first sound stage, a converted barn in the north Valley that was home to the first few low budget potboilers Avante turned out. It was abandoned after a few years because it wasn't anywhere near up to industry standards, and Avante had made enough money that it could have its own lot with state of the art sound stages and themed streets and warehouses filled with props, just like Warner Brothers or Paramount although admittedly fewer and smaller.

But it all had started with that dinky tricked-out barn somewhere around Chatsworth, and Avante had never sold it because it was iconic. Right there in that photo it stood as a monument to great beginnings. And, in big, white letters, it bore the name of the studio and the year it began…'53.

36

Los Angeles, California

When dawn broke, there was no question in my mind where I had to go and what I had to do. I resurrected my "Eddie" coveralls and my cell phone scout identity, loaded my pockets with all my spy and self-defense gear and headed over the hill to the Valley and Avante 53.

I took the Ventura Freeway and turned off at Topanga Canyon Boulevard to head north. I'd been to Avante 53 once before, as a part of the studio's 80th birthday celebration for one of the company's two living founders, Abe Tropp. The PR department had set up a meet-and-greet photo op with the entertainment press out at the old barn. As they say, a good time and some decent media coverage were had by all. I still remembered the funky "pirate map" we'd sent out to the press to help them find the old place.

Between remembering that map and my own general instincts, it wasn't hard to find the rutted two lane blacktop road that meandered into a track that was more dirt than asphalt before winding past Avante 53 and disappearing somewhere into a North Valley no man's land.

When the aged structure came into view up a long, straight stretch of road, I drove on by for about half a mile until the road curved again around a scraggly patch of evergreens.

I got out and worked my way through my meager cover to a point where I could look directly down at Avante 53. I didn't have binoculars, but the zoom focus on my "spy camera" worked really well to give me a reasonably close up view. I panned back and forth, then took a break and just eye-balled the scene below before scanning with the camera again. After about twenty minutes of this, I was convinced that there was nothing moving around the old studio. Plus, I was getting bored. I suppose stake-outs won't ever be my strong suit.

If there were anyone inside, I could be walking into some danger. If I got caught snooping around I was relying on my disguise and my natural ability to appear goofy and confused to convince anyone I might meet that I was just a dippy working stiff.

I drove my Dolly down and parked right in front of the studio. If anyone was going to spot me, it paid not to seem as if I were trying to hide. The front of the studio with its massive sliding doors was really well secured. Heavy industrial strength chains crisscrossed the doors and they were secured by huge padlocks. I noticed that while the chains seemed weathered, the locks looked very new. In any event, there was little chance I'd be able to pick those padlocks and remove the heavy chains without being detected.

I walked around the studio looking for any other possible points of entry. Not surprisingly, there were no other doors. After all, once you're inside a sound stage it's supposed to be virtually sound and light proof. Then, behind a tall bunch of weedy plants that had grown up alongside the building, I noticed a section of the wall that looked to be a slightly different color from the rest of the structure.

I pushed the weeds aside and peered at the exterior wall. It was a different color because it marked a panel about three feet tall and three feet wide. It had to be some sort of access point, maybe where cables once went in from an outside generator or ran out to power some outdoor shots. A closer look revealed that it was held in place only by a few big rusted screws. I trotted back to my car and returned with the old-fashioned lug wrench from the trunk. Sure enough, the flattened end meant for prying off the hubcaps was perfect for removing those screws.

Once I had carefully taken off the panel, which turned out to be made only of painted plywood, I was able to first listen, then, hearing nothing, to climb into the sound stage itself.

There had to be no one inside because the interior was pitch black, as it would have been designed to be. My maglite wasn't powerful enough to illuminate more than a tiny area in front of me, but it turned out to be ideal for leading me to a panel on the near wall with dozens of switches and circuit breakers. I took a chance and flipped two of the more promising switches and, amazingly, some lights went on. The effect was that of a murky gloom, but I could see well enough to move around the building.

Off to one side was parked a truck, a commercial van, actually. I moved over to give it a better look and saw a big logo on its side, "La Raza –A Revolution in Heating and Air Conditioning." Bingo. The same inscription I'd seen at the Champagne Castle. The logo was nicely done, but had some raw edges that indicated it had been done free hand, not with a stencil. Its doors were locked.

I began my search around the cavernous interior past a bunch of old background flats propped against one wall, a few light stands, two big workbenches and what looked like some discarded props. Along the back wall I spotted a big metal cage, about twenty feet wide, ten feet deep and maybe twelve feet tall. It was one of those secure areas where studios put some of the more expensive pieces of equipment that might have sprouted legs if they were left lying around. Apparently petty theft was just as prevalent in the '50s as when I worked in the industry.

The cage door had a hefty closure, but, instead of a padlock, it was secured only by a rusted piece of rebar. I tapped it out and walked inside. Darker still within, I had to use my maglite again and I swept it around the space. It was empty except for two smallish wooden boxes a little bigger than milk crates. I opened the first one and saw it contained a half dozen stacks of bricks, each about the size of, well, bricks.

There were four bricks in each stack, twenty-four bricks total. I slipped on my latex gloves and picked one up. It was heavier than I'd thought and a grayish non-color with no identifying marks. I lifted it up, turned it over and had no idea what it was. Then, I peeled away a corner of its wrapping, which seemed to be something like waxed paper. I gave it a sniff. The odor was slight, but it triggered a memory from my Army training. These bricks were a plastic explosive of some sort, C4 or Semtex most likely. I couldn't be sure.

I rewrapped and replaced the brick very gingerly. There had to be enough explosive here to take down a city block. I was afraid of what I might find behind door number two. When I carefully opened the second box, I saw not more explosives but two heavy steel canisters that looked like industrial fire extinguishers or some sort of super thermos bottles. A separate compartment was filled with wires and electrical equipment.

I stepped back and took a longer look at the two boxes. One was marked – again neatly hand-lettered – "Filter Material," the other "Thermostats." I reopened both and went to work with my mini-camera. The flash illuminated the contents of both nicely. Finally, I lifted the bricks carefully and peeled back a corner of the wrapper on the bottom one. Wishing I'd been carrying my little pocket knife, I snicked open my nasty switchblade and delicately carved out a little slice of explosive, smoothing the hole over as best I could and putting everything back in place. Luckily, I'd been chewing gum and, not being a litterbug, had some paper to wrap the little sample in.

I'd seen enough and figured it was time to hit the road before the Hondurans or whoever decided to make a visit. On the way out I did two things. First, I took some pictures of the van and its logo. Then, I pulled out of my coveralls one of the two GPS bugs I'd bought back in New York, reached under the rear of the van and secured it with its powerful magnet to the bottom of the metal gas tank.

I crawled out of the access door, screwed it back in place, and headed for my car. I was certain that I'd gotten the evidence that would sell my case to the feds. I backed Dolly out onto the narrow road and started home.

No sooner was I headed downhill than I saw a distant speck heading my way from a mile or so below. As I continued on, the speck became larger, appearing and disappearing as the road twisted and turned. Then, it was on the long straight strip I was descending, a white commercial van much like the one inside Avante 53, lurching awkwardly toward me on its small tires and cheap suspension.

As it approached, kicking up a cloud of dust, I continued at the same pace. As they hurtled past me, I gave a friendly wave, as if I'd been out for a ride in the country and was pleased to see another car, although it was a van and its occupants looked more like twenty-something Hispanics than a Valley family looking for a nice picnic spot.

I watched in my rear view mirror and wasn't surprised to see the van stagger through a broken U-turn, trying to stay on the roadway and not tumble off into the weed-filled gullies on either side. Then it was slip-sliding downhill through the potholes, tailing me, although not very secretively as there wasn't a single vehicle between them and my car. Hopeful I hadn't spotted them, I suppose, when they started to catch up they slowed down and stayed around ten car lengths behind me. Pretty tricky!

In a few minutes we reached civilization and the checkerboard of Valley communities and roadways. I'd never paid much attention to the names of Valley streets, other than the important ones like Ventura Boulevard, Reseda, Lankershim and Woodman. Nonetheless, I knew my way around pretty well by sight. So, it was easy to keep the white van guessing as I weaved my way left and right and left again, always heading eastward, with the van doggedly following me, occasionally with another car or two between us.

My guess was that if the occupants of the van had planned on trying to kill me, they would have done so back up on the road to the sound stage. There no one would have heard a gunshot or seen my body being dragged into the van, eventually to be dumped in some remote canyon. They wouldn't try anything like that in the heart of the suburbs.

When I tired of leading this fruitless chase, I looked for a long stretch of curb on a nice, leafy street and just pulled over and stopped. The van slid to a halt around fifty feet behind me. I got out with my little pad and made believe I was making some notations. Two young-ish males started to exit the van. I made a big deal of noticing them and strode back toward where they were halfway in and halfway out.

"Mornin' fellas," I said with a big smile. "You boys from around here?" They apparently spoke little or no English and just looked at me quizzically. I went right ahead. "Reason I'm askin' is that I'm not real good on geography out here in the Valley and I figured maybe you worked out here and could steer me in the right direction."

Again, no response, but the two men were looking both worried and confused. "Oh, I see. You boys speak Spanish! Well, I have to confess I'm not much on your lingo. Maybe I can call your home office and they can help me with some directions. Let me just walk around your truck and see if you've got a number listed."

While they sat in the van, unsure whether to stay in their places or get out, I walked around the back of the van, reached into my coveralls, and slapped my second GPS bug on a piece of the frame just behind the rear bumper. I came around the other side and said, "Nope. I see your number isn't listed. Well, thanks anyway."

I gave them a little salute, climbed back into my Dolly, and went on my merry way. This time, without a white van keeping me company.

Before I headed up Coldwater Canyon, I pulled in behind an upscale strip mall on Ventura Boulevard. I parked in back just in case the Hispanic guys in the van came to their senses and decided to try to pick up my trail. I grabbed a cappucino from a "boutique" coffee shop and got back in the car to make some phone calls.

My first call was to Special Agent Bud Bianco, head of the FBI's Los Angeles office. I identified myself and mentioned that I'd been referred to him by Mike Kelley, Agent in Charge for the state of South Carolina. I was put on hold and after about a minute, Bianco came on the line.

"Mr. McRae. Bud Bianco. Mike Kelley said you might be calling me one day. You're the guy whose truck blew up. How can I help you?"

Trying for a light, personal tone, I answered, "I'm not sure I'd want that carved on my tombstone, but, yeah. Agent Kelley said you were the man to call if I ever had any FBI business in L.A. Right now, the correct question might be not how you can help me but how I can help you."

Kelley's reply sat on the border between interested and annoyed. "Not sure I follow. Fill me in on what you can do to help me."

"It's like this. For the past few months I've been looking into a suspicious death. Make that two suspicious deaths. Plus my truck being tagged with some high explosives. In the course of my investigation, I've uncovered evidence – and I mean hard evidence – of a planned terror attack, very likely masterminded by someone who's been a high value fugitive from U.S. justice for about thirty-five years. The target is a major public and media event and it's in a few days. The Academy Awards. No way I can stop this on my own. I need a meeting ASAP with you to dump this in the FBI's lap."

Bianco was silent for a moment. Then he said, "You're serious, aren't you." It wasn't a question.

"Never been more serious. I didn't go looking for this. I wanted some answers about how a former co-worker ended up dead nearly three thousand miles from home, on my front porch. The rest just fell into place. Now, it's reached critical mass. So, when can I see you?"

Agent Bianco exhaled. "O.K. My schedule's pretty clear tomorrow. How's ten a.m.?"

"Perfect. I'll show you everything I've got. One question. Can I bring my lawyer along?"

"Do you think you'll need a lawyer?"

"I can't be sure. But he's also someone I trust. I think you'll trust him, too."

Bianco agreed and we hung up. Next, I called Robert Raskin to give him a quick rundown on my visit to Avante 53 and tell him I needed him at my meeting with the FBI. He never hesitated. Whatever else he had to shuffle around to do it, he'd be there. Finally, I called Tara Fukimoto to confirm our date that night. I left a message with her service.

37

I'd had a busy morning, yet it was only a little after 1:00 p.m. when I arrived back at the Barclay. I suited up for a good workout at the hotel's small gym, then headed for its even smaller "business center" to use one of their computers and their internet connection.

Their connection was almost as slow as dial-up, but adequate for my purposes. I just wanted to do a search for Shabazz Ali. Typically, the browser brought up thousands of pages of references. After the first few dozen, which told me pretty much what I already knew, I'd had enough.

Just for the hell of it, I tried "Josiah Small." Once again, I found plenty of items, most of which were irrelevant. There was an Alabama preacher, a California performance artist, a butcher shop in Milwaukee and lots more. Idly scanning the items, I spotted one that made me stop. It was a headline from a magazine I'd never heard of: "Detroit Boy Wins State Art Competition."

I opened the item and, sure enough, it was about the Josiah Small who'd morphed into the terror bomber Shabazz Ali. In sixth grade, Small had been a talented and promising artist. His work in oils and charcoal had impressed the judges enough for them to award him the blue ribbon ahead of hundreds of other kids who'd vied for the state title.

The article included four color photos. Two were of Small's paintings, a single eye-catching flower that could have been a Georgia O'Keefe and a landscape with distinct Andrew Wyeth overtones. The kid was good. The third photo was of Small, grinning widely with his head wreathed in a pillowy Afro, standing next to his art teacher, a Mrs. Viola Brown. The final shot was of Small at work on a new canvas. He delicately added a brush-stroke, and he held the brush in his left hand.

If Shabazz Ali had created and hand-lettered the La Raza logo I'd seen at the Champagne Castle and on the two white vans, that would explain their style and also their slightly ragged appearance. He would have either drawn them with difficulty with his badly dam-aged left hand. Or, he would have switched and tried to draw them as a righty.

Either way, it helped confirm to me that Shabazz Ali a.k.a. The Cuban, who planned to blow up the Acad-emy Awards, was the same person as that smiling young boy whose artwork won him a first prize.

With that information under my belt, I went back to my room to grab a nap before getting ready for my date with Tara Fukimoto. I'd just lain down and started to drift off when a phone rang. I grabbed my cell, but it wasn't ringing. It was the room phone. As I reached out to grab it, I assumed it was the front desk wanting to know how long I might be extending my stay.

To my surprise, the voice on the other end chirped cheerily, "Bobby, my boy. Hope I didn't catch you at an inopportune moment."

It was Derrick Pettit, sounding as if he was my new best friend. I answered, "Not at all, Derrick. Just about to take a little nap. What's on your mind?"

"Bobby, I'll be honest with you. I was very disappointed when you told me that you couldn't take my spare seat for the Oscars. I don't think you've ever attended, and it's really something other people would kill to see in person. I thought for sure that with your background in film you'd jump at the chance."

I explained in detail to Derrick how I had little interest in big, Hollywood galas and, even if I loved them, I wasn't likely to be in L.A. on Oscar night.

Derrick wasn't giving up. "Come on, Bobby. Do me a favor. I can't get any senior execs to attend because they wouldn't be able to bring their spouses. And, if I give my ticket to one of the mid-level guys, all the rest of them will be ticked off at me.

"If you haven't got a tux with you, I can get a nice one in your size from wardrobe. You'll see a lot of your old friends and have a bang-up time."

I knew that unless the FBI came through based on my information, a whole lot of people were going to have a "bang-up time."

"I'm sorry, Derrick. I know you're under the gun to fill that seat, but you'll think of someone. Actually something has come up that would make it impossible to accept your offer in any event. So, I have to pass."

Pettit went on some more about how sorry he was that I wouldn't be on hand for Hollywood's big night before I could finally get him off the phone and head out on a new mission.

It had hit me that I had to make a run to West Hollywood and a well-known sex shop to pick something up before my date with Tara.

I'm not a regular at adult stores, although I'd been to this one twice, both times with dates who "just wanted to see what it was like." One time, we were staring into a display case at some sex paraphernalia that we couldn't figure out. A sales clerk sashayed over to help us and when we asked him what the gear was used for he whispered confidentially, "You don't want to know."

In this instance, I slinked into the store as if I'd meant to go shopping for a pair of shoes and had just gotten the wrong doorway. I don't know why I was self-conscious. The clerks at sex shops are more than blasé. They don't care what weird things you're into as long as you pay for what you buy. I made my purchase and left with it tucked into a plain vanilla plastic shopping bag that couldn't have screamed "Sex Stuff Inside!" more clearly if those words had been printed on it in six inch high red letters.

At 8:30 on the dot I parked down the block from Tara's 1930s building just east of Hancock Park. She looked terrific in a saffron pants suit that highlighted her dark complexion. As always, her jet black hair cascaded down her back.

We had a drink, not a "cocktail" this time, before heading for our favorite Thai restaurant up on Hollywood Boulevard. Predictably, she loved riding in the vintage Oldsmobile I'd rented from Dutch. She said it made her feel like the female lead in a film noir. I didn't think it would be appropriate to mention to her that I'd never seen a Japanese female lead in a film noir.

One thing about Tara, much as she loves rubbing shoulders with the big Hollywood names, she is equally enthusiastic about eating, and doesn't care if she dines in a joint that's something of a dive as long as the food is good and keeps coming. Where a woman who weighs maybe a hundred and ten pounds soaking wet could put all that chow was a mystery to me.

The place we were going filled the bill on all counts. It was in a really crappy neighborhood. It was dingy on the outside and beaten up on the inside. Most of its leatherette booths were held together by duct tape. But its menu offered at least a hundred choices, all of them more delicious than the others. We lucked out getting seated in less than ten minutes. By the time we placed our order there was a line out the door.

Tara rambled on about this and that, mostly about her latest networking activities and work possibilities. Much as she'd tried, she hadn't come up with much that was really useful to me about Avante. She did say that she'd spotted several references to the studio's recent quarters in the red.

According to what she'd gleaned from the L.A. Times business section and the trade papers, there seemed to be no apparent reason why Avante should be losing money. The studio had had three money-making films in the past eighteen months, none of which could really be called big budget.

She remembered that one item in The Hollywood Reporter had quoted Avante's CEO as saying that the studio had accrued some extraordinary administrative expenses and expected to be back in the black once those had been amortized. That sounded like corporate double-speak to me, and I was always pretty good at that kind of evasive quote myself.

Over the Pad Thai, Tara suddenly grabbed my hand and squeezed it excitedly. "Oh, Bobby. I nearly forgot to tell you. I'm going to the Academy Awards!"

I was stunned. What had she done to get her to the Oscars? And, why did she have to be going this year? I had to suppress my instinct to tell her to stay away.

"O.K., I'm just going to be a seat-filler," she said. "I know it's a nothing job and it's usually just interns or some executive's daughter or son who does seat-filling. I'm a little too old and a lot too experienced to just jump into any old empty seat when someone leaves the room.

"However, I see this as another opportunity to brush up against a lot of people who can do wonders for my career. And, this year, afterward I get to go to the Governor's Ball. Don't tell me I won't make some great contacts there!"

Tara's enthusiasm, however misguided, was contagious. I actually hoped she might score a hit or two that would catapult her to something that would make her happy. If not stardom, at least a good gig with a nice screen credit. If she survived the Oscars, that is.

We headed back to her place and she pulled out a basket filled with bottles of wine. "I got this from the director on my last shoot," she said.

"Pick out some wine you like and we'll uncork it and have a party as soon as I check my service."

Tara was the only person I knew who didn't have a pretty big time job but had to have a service rather than a plain old answering machine. Also, although she was born and raised in California, she maintained a strong sense of her Japanese identity. She owned two formal outfits with kimono, and obi, and all, and wore them to really fancy parties. Likewise, she didn't own an actual bed. She slept on a not very comfortable thin mattress on her bedroom floor.

I'd picked out two bottles of wine I was interested in trying and was just settling in for a lovely evening and maybe more when she returned from her little office with a distinctly long face.

"Oh, Bobby. I wanted tonight to be so special. I wanted to thank you for always remembering me and to show you how much I care about you."

Then came the "but."

"But, I just picked up my messages and the indie film I've been working on is running over budget so they had to cancel a location next week in Arizona. Now, we're going to compress those scenes and shoot them up in the Antelope Valley. Long story short, I have a 5:00 a.m. call tomorrow morning, which means I have to be up by around 3:30. So, I have to say good night and get to sleep."

Just another "date-us interruptus" for the kid. Oh, well. "That's O.K. sweetie," I said, and meant it. "Work comes first. I may be around for a few more days and if I get a break, I'll call you. If not, we'll get together the next time I'm back on the Coast. And, hey! Work your magic at the Oscars."

After a good-bye kiss that under other circumstances would have promised more, she showed me to the door and that was that.

It was unseasonably warm for March, so I rolled down the window of my Dolly and savored the night air. It was a pleasure to actually roll down a window instead of pushing a button and having it disappear into the door frame. A quick glance at my watch told me that our drinks and leisurely dinner had taken longer than I thought. It was a little after midnight. I hoped Tara was a fast, sound sleeper.

I pulled in to the hotel and, just protectively, made certain that my pepper gas, stun gun and switchblade were at the ready. I didn't expect to be confronted by an attacker, but I had certain suspicions.

That's why I approached my room quietly and listened at the door for any sounds inside. Even when I was just about convinced that the room was empty I slipped the card key in silently and slowly turned the handle.

The instant I opened it a crack I flicked on the light switch, which I had committed to memory as being located just to the right of the door jamb. Light flooded the room and I leaped in, my knife open and brandished. I was alone.

Well, I wasn't entirely alone. There was someone, actually something, in my unmade bed.

I pulled back the blanket and sheet and there was "Ted," the life-size male "party doll" I'd bought at the sex shop in Sherman Oaks. He was in bad shape, only about half the size of his former self. I put on another pair of my latex gloves and carefully deflated him the rest of the way.

I couldn't see it with my naked eye, but I was certain that with a magnifying glass or a microscope, I'd be able to find a tiny pin hole somewhere in his vinyl back. And, the odds were that under his skin, a lab would find a lethal dose of curare. I put him in the plastic bag the hotel thoughtfully provided for dry cleaning and left him in the closet

I had nothing concrete to link Derrick Pettit to someone's mistaken assault on "Ted". Yet, he was the only individual, with the possible exception of Allison Simmons, who knew my room number at the Barclay.

If he were involved in the terror plot, maybe as a result of the Kendall embezzlement – if that's what it really was - I had to assume that he wanted me at the Oscars so anything I knew would be buried in the rubble.

When he hadn't been able to convince me to attend the ceremony after practically begging me to be his guest he could have decided to have me taken out first.

What better way than the same way Jerry Kendall and that inquisitive Honduran cop had been disposed of. If the Cuban or one of his henchmen were enlisted, they wouldn't have had much difficulty getting into the hotel. The front door was only one of several access points around the completely unsecured building. Any decent break-in man could have slipped my room lock easily, and probably even more quietly than I had.

Then, all that remained would have been to see what looked like a sleeping form in my bed, use a silent blowgun to inject it with curare, quickly remove the dart and exit as swiftly as he'd arrived. The only catch was that it was "Ted," not me, under the covers of my bed.

I was sure that Special Agent Bianco and his team would find "Ted" a very interesting victim. I was also very pleased that I'd had the foresight to take my laptop, my camera and my GPS monitor, put them in my gym bag, and hide them under the big old-fashioned spare tire of the Oldsmobile. If whoever handled the blowgun had been of a mind to search the room for any incriminating evidence, he wouldn't have found a thing.

Tomorrow morning, the FBI would be the only ones to see the pictures I had of the hide-out at the Champagne Castle and at Avante 53, and to analyze the sample I'd taken from one of those bricks. Until further notice, Derrick Pettit and The Cuban would assume that I was dead, and no longer a threat. Maybe the FBI could even plant a bogus item in the newspaper about a former studio executive dying unexpectedly of natural causes at the Barclay Hotel. That would seem to seal the deal for sure.

With the 10:00 a.m. meeting looming, I watched a few minutes of the news on CNN and turned in. I slept alone, but I slept the sleep of a man who'd live to fight another day.

38

Los Angeles, California

At the Federal Building in Westwood, Robert Raskin was already waiting for me in the lobby. We took the elevator to the FBI offices and identified ourselves to the receptionist. She told us Special Agent in Charge Bianco was expecting us and buzzed him. Less than a minute later, he came out to the waiting room.

Unlike special Agent in Charge Kelly in South Carolina, an older guy who looked a little world-weary and just a bit unkempt, Bianco looked like a recruiter for an Ivy League college. Brown loafers, grey slacks, a blue blazer, pale blue shirt and a yellow and blue rep striped tie.

"Mr. McRae. Thanks for coming in. Nice to see you again, Bob."

"Likewise, Bud."

"Bob?" "Bud?" It seemed as if Raskin and Bianco already knew each other, and a lot better than I knew either one.

Bianco ushered us into his office, a spacious if not particularly luxurious room looking out toward the campus of UCLA.

"Please forgive me for not exchanging pleasantries; if what you have, Mr. McRae, is as significant as you think it is, we've got to jump on this situation right away. On the other hand, if it's not, we can all part friends and be on our way in time for lunch."

Bianco sounded more than a bit unimpressed so I skipped the dog-and-pony show about how I got involved in my investigation in the first place and cut to the chase.

I took my laptop out of my canvas bag, booted it up and placed it on his desk. Next to it, I put the little gum wrapper in a plastic bag containing the sliver of explosive I'd taken from Avante 53.

`"It would be a lot easier if we could all sit on your couch and put the computer on your coffee table. That way, I could run you through the pictures quickly and explain what you'd be seeing."

Bianco agreed and we all moved to the couch. Before I began my "presentation" I casually dropped the fact that the plastic bag contained what I believed to be a high explosive.

Bianco's eyebrows shot up and his face showed a new determination to focus on what I had to show him.

Before I could click on the first image he asked me to hold off. Pressing the talk button on his intercom he said, "Madeleine, please send in Nick Pappas."

He sat waiting for a moment before Pappas arrived, a thin, cerebral-looking man in shirtsleeves with light olive skin and dark, curly hair.

Bianco introduced Pappas as his office's expert on unconventional weapons, tactics and ordnance. Without preface, he asked the agent to take a look at the substance in the little plastic bag and render his opinion on what it might be.

Pappas opened the bag, unfolded the chewing gum wrapper and examined the little piece of brick I'd pried off with my knife. He turned it over in his fingers, looked very closely, then sniffed the tiny chunk.

"It's pretty obvious that this is a small piece of plastic explosive," he said. "I can't tell you with certainty what it is exactly, but the lab can do a run-up and have a determination in an hour or so."

"Nick," Bianco asked, "this is a very small piece of whatever substance it turns out to be. Based on that alone, could you estimate the destructive potential of, say, a pound or two of the same stuff, maybe more?"

Pappas smiled. "You really don't want to know. For example, if this turns out to be Semtex or C4, a pound or two, if used properly, would be enough to blow up a small apartment building. Any more than that and you're talking about serious, mass destruction."

"Thanks, Nick," Bianco said. "Get me those results as soon as you can. Now, Bobby – may I call you Bobby – why don't you take me through how you came to be in possession of that little piece of bomb-making material."

I started my slide show and walked him through my suspicions about Jerry Kendall's death, the murder of a Jane Doe who died under similar circumstances but was later determined to have been murdered by curare poisoning, and just happened to have Jerry Kendall's business card on her person and later turned out to be a Honduran agent on the trail of a notorious warlord and drug and arms dealer named The Cuban.

I decided that anything I could glean about the final weeks and months of Jerry Kendall's life might help to explain why he died on my front porch in South Carolina, 2500 miles away from where he had last been seen.

I said that I had learned about a two bedroom apartment on an older street in Beverly Hills that Kendall had tricked out as a sort of party palace he dubbed "The Champagne Castle." Even though he was single and had a nice apartment of his own, he must have liked the adventure of having a secret hideaway. He also enlisted at least a few of his friends and co-workers to go in on the expenses of the apartment, on the promise that they'd also be able to use it for their own romantic trysts.

I gained entry to the apartment and discovered that several people had been living there, and not in any party atmosphere. I began showing him photos, one by one.

Bianco was as mystified as I had been, viewing the blueprints, schematics and notes written in Spanish. His interest perked up when he saw my pictures of the weapons, particularly the blowgun and the vial of what was most likely poison for the darts, and the bank of walkie talkies and cell phones neatly plugged into chargers.

Next, I walked him through what I'd found in Jerry Kendall's safe deposit box. The bogus passport. The large amount of cash which fell just below the reporting level. The loaded handgun. And, the pocket calendar with the date of the Academy Awards, as had been the one in Champagne Castle, ringed boldly in red.

Finally, I showed the FBI agent the pictures of the interior of the abandoned sound stage, Avante 53. He was stunned at the amount of what appeared to be high explosive stored in the old building and hazarded a guess that the large, sealed canisters in the safe enclosure might well contain a toxic gas of some sort.

The white van with La Raza painted on its side and purporting to be the property of a heating and air conditioning company seemed to him to tie right in. If there were, in fact, a plan to blow something up, even if it weren't the Oscars, bombers disguised as heating and air conditioning technicians might be able to gain access to the structural underpinnings of a building and place charges where they would do the most damage. They might even have been unwittingly hired to be on the premises working to maintain the building's operating systems.

Special Agent Bianco pondered this prospect for a minute then abruptly detoured the discussion.

"Mr. McRae, Bobby, can you explain how you were able to gain access to the Champagne Castle apartment, the safe deposit box and the Avante 53 soundstage?"

I hadn't thought I'd escape without some questioning. Nonetheless, I hadn't come up with any really good answers. Fortunately, Robert Raskin had.

"My client need not answer those questions at this time. However, I can tell you that as Jerry Kendall's attorney and executor, I had legal access to all of his assets, at least as long as I didn't attempt to turn them to use for my personal benefit. Those assets included the apartment, of which he was the lease holder of record, and the safe deposit box."

Raskin was winging it, and doing it well. Since he wasn't in court or under oath, no harm, no foul.

Bianco nodded thoughtfully, "O.K. For now. So, what about Bobby's little adventure in Avante Studios abandoned sound stage?"

Raskin jumped in again. "When my client retired from his position as a senior executive at Avante, he and the company parted on very good terms. As a result, he was required neither to sign a non-disclosure agreement nor to surrender his various pass keys and access cards to the studio's many facilities."

No question, my attorney was nothing if not quick and glib. Bianco nodded again and sighed as if he really shouldn't have bothered to ask the questions.

"Alright," he said, "I think we have more than enough evidence here to give this situation a more than serious look. Bobby, I'd like to download all of these images onto a disc. You can retain the originals for the moment.

"I expect we'll have the lab results back shortly and that will be one more building block in our case, if we have one. Anything else you might want to add?"

I'd been holding back on this one, and now was the time to spring it. "Well, yes. During the course of my investigation, I ran across information that points to the mysterious and dangerous Cuban as being in actuality a long-time fugitive from justice that the FBI and a number of other law enforcement agencies in the Unites States have been seeking since the 1970s with no success. I am virtually certain that the Cuban is an American citizen who fled the country after a series of killings and bombings, the final one of which took the lives of four of his co-conspirators and cost him two fingers and a portion of his left hand."

Bianco was sitting up virtually at tattention on the edge of the couch.

"I believe that the mastermind behind this current plot – the Cuban - is none other than Shabazz Ali."

Now, I had Special Agent in Charge Bianco's undivided attention. I quickly ran him through what I'd learned from Det. Allison Simmons about what Interpol and the Honduran military had to say about the Cuban. He was believed to have arrived in Cuba from one of the countries in North Africa generally hostile to the West. After a few years on Cuban soil, he had disappeared and emerged in Honduras, where he was apparently well-funded and wasted no time in setting himself up as the head of an anti-government militia.

Over the years, his power had grown and all attempts to capture or kill him had been fruitless. From a base, or bases, deep in the Honduran rain forest, he masterminded drug transshipments throughout North and South America and dealt in arms with other South American insurgent groups as well as militant organizations in the Middle East.

Little was known about his physical appearance except that he was a large man, most probably around 60 years of age, with a badly damaged left hand.

I added that I had noticed that the inscriptions on the sides of the La Raza trucks appeared to be hand-lettered and while competently done, had small imperfections that led me to believe that they had either been done by an artist with a damaged hand or by an artist using his opposite hand. My Internet search had pulled up an old photo of Shabazz Ali, then Josiah Small, winning an art competition and drawing with his left hand.

Since Bianco had been scribbling copious notes on a yellow legal pad while I spoke, I decided to give him a little more information to chew on. I told him about how I had been spotted and tailed – very inexpertly tailed – when I was leaving the Avante 53 site.

I told him how I had been invited to attend the Oscars, then begged and pleaded to attend, by an Avante Studios executive who was serving as this year's liaison to the Academy Awards. I declined his entreaties on two separate occasions. After the second attempt to convince me to attend, I became suspicious.

I rigged up an inflatable dummy in my hotel bed and went out for the evening. When I returned, I found that the dummy had been "killed," presumably by a dart from a blowgun. I reached into my bag and pulled out the plastic wrapped remains of Ted and handed him over to Bianco. 'If your lab can located the pinhole in this dummy and examine the area surrounding it, my bet is that they'll find a significant residue of curare."

Next, I sprung the information that the Avante Studios executive who had been so frantic to get me to attend the Oscars, confided in me, confidentially of course, that Kendall had been embezzling a lot of money from the company but that Avante Entertainment had declined to prosecute him or seek any restitution from his estate.

That information clearly caused another area of Bianco's cortex to light up. The Bureau has a special interest and expertise in cases of fraud and embezzlement and I could almost smell his brain working on other aspects of this whole plot business.

While he mulled over the financial implications of Kendall's alleged embezzlement, and how they might tie in with the bombing plot, the agent mused out loud, "If we only had some way to keep track of their movements over the next few days. Surveillance might work for the apartment, but it would be tricky to stake out the sound stage up in the hills surrounded by open land."

"Oh, I nearly forgot, "I said. I reached into my canvas bag again and pulled out the tracking monitor.

"I don't know how well this gadget works. I paid a bundle for it in a New York City spy shop. I managed to put tracking bugs on both of the La Raza vans I'm aware of. Maybe your people can see what it's effective range might be and use the bugs to keep an eye on the Hondurans."

Special Agent in Charge Bianco gave me a look that said, "What in the world can I expect from this guy next?"

Instead, he actually said, "That's great. I'll have the tech guys give this a close look. If it's any good at all we'll start tracking the vans right away. Thanks for thinking ahead and giving us a little advantage."

Before we ended our meeting, Bianco explained that if our leads panned out, and he suspected that they would, the Bureau would be putting on a full court press, including bringing in additional agents, including counter-terrorism and explosive experts to support the efforts of the L.A. office.

"Naturally," he continued, "we'll have to have at least a conversation with the Beverly Hills police. The apartment's in their jurisdiction. We'll have to call in LAPD as well. The sound stage should be in Northwest Division and the theater is in Hollywood Division. We'll still take the lead but we can't cut them out and, frankly, we could probably use their help."

I understood his concern but had to explain my personal position a little. "I know LAPD will have to be involved, but I have a few concerns about opening up to them too much or too soon."

Bianco was puzzled about why I would be wary of the Los Angeles police. I explained to him my unexpected surveillance and encounter with Homicide Detective Allison Simmons on my first trip to the city after Kendall's death. I wondered why she had shadowed me in the first place, why she had revealed herself to me and why she had also more or less come on to me only to back off.

Then, there was Captain Bates' seeming indifference to Jerry Kendall's death and my mission, if I could call it that, to find out more about how and why he had died. I'd known Bates for years and yet he just shrugged off my interest in the case. Granted, it wasn't his problem, but he could have offered me at least some guidance.

Finally, there was Det. Simmons' finding me on my second trip, even though I wasn't registered at the hotel in my own name. Also, her inviting me to dinner then, just as things were warming up, taking a phone call and telling me she had to go in to work because of a fresh homicide. And, as I accidentally saw her leaving her apartment, she got into not her own car or a black and white but what appeared to be a late model unmarked Cadillac.

Bianco agreed that my encounters with the L.A. cops had been a little sketchy and promised to be discreet in what he told the department, and how. He said to stay close and keep my cell phone handy. He expected to be contacting me in the next twenty-four hours to let me know next steps. Then, he strongly suggested I move out of my hotel and not leave a forwarding address.

He offered a few nights at a safe house the Bureau maintained in the city but I declined. It was a generous offer, particularly since he wasn't yet convinced that we were on to a serious crime about to happen. But, I had little interest in the Spartan accommodations of a safe house or the round-the-clock surveillance I'd have.

We all shook hands and Robert Raskin and I left the building. On the way out, he said, "This could be big, Bobby. I'm rearranging my schedule for the rest of the week so I can be available if I'm needed or can be helpful in any way. I recommend you take Bud Bianco's advice and get out of your hotel. When you're settled somewhere else, give me a call and let me know where I can find you."

Before nightfall, I'd packed what little clothing and gear I had and left the Barclay. Just for the hell of it, I drove down to Long Beach and got a room aboard the Queen Mary. The old ship is docked there permanently and isn't going anywhere. I just thought it would be fun to hide out on a famous luxury liner.

39

Long Beach, California

My decision to switch hotels to The Queen Mary was a good one. The old ship was beautiful and my "stateroom" was luxurious. Plus, the hotel was filled with tourists, making it one of the last places anyone would come looking for me, assuming that anyone was still looking for me. After all, whoever knocked off good old "Ted" might still be under the impression that I was actually dead. Of course, if the bad guys thought I had been working with the law, they might have guessed that my murder had been kept quiet and not leaked to the news media on purpose.

Because I still felt very much alive, I ate a hearty breakfast in the main dining room and strolled around the ship, admiring the polished brass and the gleaming mahogany railings. After around 45 minutes of admiring, I'd pretty much covered everything I wanted to see and was getting antsy.

I got my car and motored over to the 405 Freeway, heading south. The weather was still nice for March, temperature in the low 70s and skies as clear as they ever get in the Los Angeles Basin. Laguna Beach seemed like a good destination. I hadn't been there in years and it was a great place to prowl art galleries and arts and crafts shops and feel like a hippie free spirit reborn. I even ran across a street musician playing his violin with the case open for tips, and a street artist drawing caricatures for $25 a pop.

I didn't really need a caricature, so I dropped two singles in the violinist's case and went into a cozy, local looking coffee house. Aside from offering a selection of caffeinated beverages, the place was about as far from a Starbucks as a coffee shop could get. Instead of Formica topped tables and uncomfortable chairs, it offered couches and easy chairs and weathered, beat-up coffee tables. There was also a very eclectic collection of magazines to thumb through while whiling away the day, from the New Republic to Reason to Newsweek and Funny Times.

I ordered a huge café mocha, added four sugars, and sat back in a comfortable chair that looked as if it had been taken from somebody's grandfather's house. The coffee was good, but after a few minutes of flipping through magazines, I realized that all I could focus on was what was happening back in L.A.

It was already Thursday. The Academy Awards were coming up on Sunday. The FBI seemed interested in the evidence I'd uncovered, but the Bureau didn't seem to be breaking into a sprint to do anything about it.

Maybe I was wrong. Maybe all these bits and pieces I'd found out about were unrelated, circumstantial and irrelevant. Maybe there was no plot of any kind at all and I was just a conspiracy theorist who got lucky and found a few nuggets to support his paranoia.

I didn't need another coffee, but I ordered it anyway, adding five sugars this time. I sat back and let my mind wander. I almost wished that I was a smoker, because this would have been an ideal scenario for me to be blowing smoke rings while I pondered what all of my little adventures really meant. Of course, in Southern California about the only place I could smoke a cigarette these days would be on top of a wind-swept mountain peak with an exhaust fan at my side and a ring of air fresheners around me. Even as a non-smoker I could recognize a nanny state when I saw one.

I sifted through the pieces of the puzzle. Jerry Kendall is found dead on my front porch. Jerry Kendall has made a number of trips to Mexico and, apparently, to Honduras. Jerry Kendall, at least according to Derrick it, was a big-time embezzler who was discovered, but not prosecuted, by the company he embezzled from, my old company.

If Jerry Kendall were cooking the books with a number of fake accounts – and they would have had to be numerous for him to have embezzled as much money as Pettit claimed he did – wouldn't Derrick have noticed it? Wouldn't he have called Kendall on the carpet and put a stop to him before he ran wildly out of control?

According to Robert Raskin, Jerry Kendall knew through the eccentric genius Linus Parkin that I had a second identity and was a member of a special Army unit assigned to missions on behalf of the State Department. What if Jerry Kendall realized that he was into something way over his head and didn't know where to turn? What if he'd found out where I live, flown cross country, and come to see me in the hope that I might be able to help him get out of a jam? What if it had become obvious to some people that Jerry Kendall had developed cold feet and he'd been followed and silently disposed of before he could get to me with his story? Could that explain why my truck was bombed? To dispose of me in the event that Kendall had somehow spilled the beans to me before his ill-fated trip to Charleston?

Why had Detective Allison Simmons tailed me and approached me at Muscle Beach on my first trip back to L.A.? Why had she told me about the Jane Doe who had died in a similar fashion to Jerry Kendall but whose death had later turned out to be by curare poisoning? Why had she come on to me and then abruptly backed off?

Why had she gone to the trouble to find me at my hotel, even when I wasn't registered there as Bobby McRae? Why had she told me the story of how the Jane Doe had been a Honduran agent following an internationally wanted criminal? Why had she made a point of asking if I would be attending the LAPD's ceremony at the Hollywood Walk of Fame, when there was no good reason for me to have known about it or to be invited to it? Why had she come on to me again and once again abruptly backed off, leaving her own apartment ostensibly to work a homicide and being picked up by someone in a nice luxury car?

Where did Derrick Pettit fit into this picture? Jerry Kendall reported to him, and Jerry Kendall was in charge of a wide range of facilities, procurements and contractors for a good-sized Hollywood studio. Could Kendall have listed La Raza as one of his "paper" vendors, funneling funds through that account to…whomever? Being accredited for some period of time as a contractor in good standing for Avante Entertainment would have given the bogus company a good deal of credibility, credibility that could have lead others, including the Academy, not to question its credentials.

Those credentials would put La Raza and its men in a position to access some remote areas where few people ever go except those workmen who keep big buildings running. Those labyrinthine basement areas would contain not only potentially corruptible systems such as heating and air conditioning but would also be where the support structure that held up the entire building was open and obvious and vulnerable.

Why was I tailed from Avante 53? Why was there an attempt on my life using the same methodology as the killings of Kendall and the Honduran cop? Why was Derrick Pettit so desperate to have me attend the Oscars?

Was The Cuban who I thought him to be and, if so, why after decades of successfully eluding the United States' authorities, would he take the chance of returning to America and hatching a plot to attack the Academy Awards? It just made no sense.

Suddenly, I was aware of someone standing over me. I looked up, and up, and up. It was a very vertical woman, close to six feet tall. She was wearing a pale blue eyelet short sleeve blouse over an ankle length gray skirt with threads of maroon and dark blue running through it. On each arm were about a half dozen bangle bracelets. She was plain, with long brown hair that hung below her shoulders. And she had a big, terrific smile.

"Is your coffee alright?" she asked.

"Uh, sure. It's fine. Why do you ask?"

"Well, I noticed that you've been sitting there for about twenty minutes and you haven't taken a sip."

"Oh, well, it's my second cup" I said.

"I know. I made it for you. Why don't you let me warm it up "

That sounded like a good idea so I handed it to her and she went behind the counter. About two minutes later she came back with my now steaming cup.

"Pretty fast. Throw it in the microwave?"

She laughed, a very pretty laugh.

"Not in this store. We don't nuke anything. I warmed it on the stove. Are you new in town?"

I told her I was just visiting for the day, that I hadn't been in Laguna Beach in a few years and wanted to see if it had changed.

"It's pretty much the same," she said, "only better. If you thought this community was artsy before, you'll be surprised how that aspect has grown.

"We're filled with talented artist and writers and musicians. Are you any of the above?"

For reasons that escape me, I replied, "No, ma'am. I'm a secret agent and I'm hiding out from some folks who seem to want to kill me."

The look she gave me sent the message that she figured I was just a wise guy, giving her a stupid answer to an honest question.

I was about to protest that I was telling the truth when my cell phone rang.

"Excuse me," I said, then, "Hello Special Agent Bianco. Thanks for calling. I got out of town just as you recommended. What's new?"

I turned to the tall woman and said, "Excuse me. I have to take this."

She was already backing away, keeping an eye on me, as if I might go completely bonkers and start raving about black helicopters coming in for a landing.

Bianco told me his people had analyzed the little specimen I'd given them and determined that it was Semtex and in the quantity I'd described would be sufficient to take down an entire city block. His people had also enlarged my photos of the blueprints, schematics and notes, translated the Spanish, and concluded that the plan was, indeed, to launch a terror attack against the Academy Awards ceremony.

"We're going full bore on this, Bobby," Bianco said. "We'll be taking the lead, but it's imperative that we meet with LAPD to coordinate everything. I've talked to my opposite number at the PD and found out that they've already put a plan in effect.

"He didn't want to be too specific, claiming it was a local response to a local situation. My guess from what little he could tell me is that they're expecting some sort of large scale demonstration against the Oscars as symbolizing the so-called false values of Hollywood.

"I wasn't about to tell him what we're chasing down, at least not in a telephone conversation. We've set a meeting for tomorrow morning at 10:00 a.m. at Parker Center. Some of the brass and all of the key commanders will be on hand and I'll be bringing a few of my top agents. We'll listen to what they have to say, then drop our bomb, literally and figuratively."

Special Agent in Charge Bianco told me it was important that I attend, but that he'd feel more comfortable if I'd stay out of sight until then. Another night on the Queen Mary wasn't exactly tough duty, so I agreed. We were to meet at the Federal Building at 9:00 a.m. and go downtown together. Then, Bianco tossed me a little curve ball.

"Bobby, while my team was at work on the evidence you presented us with I did some checking of my own on you. I was stonewalled at first, but, contrary to what you may have heard, sometimes we do share information with other agencies and they tell us things that can help us do our job better. And, to be completely frank, I had a head start based on some sleuthing by friend Mike Kelly in Columbia did on you after he met you at that club meeting."

I was waiting for him to tell me what he'd discovered, but he remained evasive.

"Let's just say that I now have a little better insight into how and why you were able to gather as much evidence as you did. I'm not sure I want to know your methods. That said, I'm convinced that you can be trusted and that anything you did was for the right reasons."

I quickly changed the subject by asking him what the dress code would be for our meeting with the LAPD. He answered, "Fatigues, helmet liner, web belt and canteen."

It took me a second to realize that he was just making a joke, a not so veiled reference to my Army career. Then he told me not to worry. The FBI would be the "suits." I could dress any way I wanted.

He advised me not to volunteer any information unless asked a direct question and to let him do the talking. He also made it clear that in no way would I be cut out of the operation, but, because I wasn't a sworn officer, I couldn't carry a weapon and he couldn't intentionally put me in harm's way.

I understood. To all intents and purposes, I was still a civilian. Neither the Bureau nor the LAPD would want me in the line of fire if close quarters trouble broke out. I was pleased that Bianco included me in his planning and didn't try to shuffle me off to the sidelines after all the work I'd done.

I agreed to his terms and told him I'd stay out of town again that night but he reachable on my cell.

I closed my phone and took a long pull on my coffee, which had started to get cool again. I glanced up at the tall barista and saw that she was back behind the counter and on the telephone.

She was probably talking to her boyfriend. On the other hand, she could have been calling the local constabulary to report a weirdo who let his mocha coffee get cold and claimed he was a secret agent on the lam from some bad guys.

Just in case, I swigged the rest of my brew, slapped down a five dollar tip and hit the road. I had a few cocktails and a nice dinner to look forward to aboard the Queen, and I wanted to get a good night's sleep so I'd be fresh for the morning meeting.

40

Los Angeles, California

Special Agent in Charge Bianco and I drove downtown to Parker Center in his official car. Several other special agents were driving separately and meeting us there.

We were met by a veteran sergeant with plenty of decorations on his crisp uniform. He took us upstairs to a large, unadorned conference room with one long table surrounded by not very comfortable-looking chairs. And one end was a breakfast set-up: a coffee urn, two large pitchers with water, orange juice and glasses and, incredibly, a tray heaped high with donuts.

All I could think of was that these cops must have studied Cliché 101. That said, the donuts were delicious, especially the apple fritters.

The Deputy Chief was on hand and at first I thought there was no one in the room ranked lower than Commander. Then, I spotted Captain Terry Bates. We all milled around a bit then the Deputy Chief asked us to be seated.

The Deputy Chief thanked the FBI for arranging this meeting and expressed the department's long time respect for and cooperation with the Bureau. After those pleasantries, he shifted gears.

"I'm sure you are concerned, as we are, about the possibility of a disruption of the annual Academy Awards ceremony. To be frank, I can't see why any such disturbance would fall under the FBI's jurisdiction. Be that as it may, we welcome your input and assistance if needed, but we believe we have a plan in place to contain and neutralize any problems in the area of the Hollywood and Highland Center."

The Deputy Chief told us that the Department planned a media briefing at 3:00 p.m. which would lay out in general terms how the LAPD was prepared for any eventuality on Sunday night. Then, as chief media spokesman for the department, he turned the proceedings over to Terry Bates.

Bates introduced himself again, put on a pair of bifocals, and read from a press release he'd prepared for that afternoon.

In essence, it stated that the LAPD had become aware through a confidential informant and several other sources that a potentially large scale demonstration against the Oscars was in the works. He said that the Department's best information was that the demonstrators would be drawn from a number of otherwise unrelated activist groups including PETA, Friends of the Earth, the Congress of Racial Equality, some anarchist organizations and even several motorcycle clubs and politically-savvy Los Angeles street gangs.

The idea was not that any one group take the lead or that all the participating groups mass at one place. The plan was for each group, most likely at a specific time or at a specific signal, to march on the Auditorium from different points of the compass so that the ceremonies would be surrounded on all side by demonstrators.

Bates said that while the LAPD did not necessarily anticipate any violence, precautionary measures had been taken to anticipate and defuse any incidents before they could escalate and cause harm to persons or property or disrupt in any way the internationally televised Oscar proceedings.

The press release noted that the entire force had been placed on alert and that specialized units including elite crowd control officers, SWAT, the Mounted Platoon and the Bomb Squad would be assigned to create and maintain a perimeter at a sufficient distance to insulate the ceremonies from the protestors while allowing them their Constitutional right to free speech. In passing, Bates mentioned that the Los Angeles Fire Department would have at least two trucks on hand, presumably to hose down any particularly rowdy demonstrators. Also, the Air Support Division would have a helicopter with thermal imaging and forward looking radar capability stationed above the area.

With a hint of a wink, Bates concluded by revealing that the LAPD had some other tactics available but didn't want to alarm anyone by mentioning them in a general press release.

Bates sat down, looking pleased with himself, and the LAPD brass and relaxed and smiled.

Then, it was Special Agent in Charge Bianco's turn. He opened by thanking the LAPD in return for attending this important meeting. Then, without skipping a beat, he said, "You plan is impressive, if a street demonstration were the biggest concern we had to face. Unfortunately, it's not.

"While it will surely help to have an extraordinary police presence outside the Academy Awards, it won't help to deter what we now believe will be a far more serious attack from within."

The LAPD brass all began shifting in their seats and looking worried and uncomfortable. But, before giving them any further details, Bianco left them hanging while he introduced his colleagues.

"More than twenty FBI agents from offices as distant as Denver, Kansas City and New York City are already on site or en route. All are specialists in various aspects of this operation. Plus, the entire Los Angeles office will participate, headed by my professional colleagues here with me today, special Agents Jenter, Reedy, McCarthy and Speizman.

I'd never officially met any of them so I gave them the once over as they were introduced. Thin, balding, with a scholarly appearance, Jenter was likely a tactician. Burly, with close-cropped hair, Reedy looked like a street fighter. Taller than me, in fact one of the tallest men I'd ever met, McCarthy had a strange look in his eye. He could have been either a computer geek or a trained assassin. Take your pick. Special Agent Speizman was, very obviously, a female. She looked as if she'd been poured into her trim, navy blue suit. A red-head with a slightly crooked smile, she gave off the vibe that if she had to use her weapon, she'd probably shoot low just to teach the guy a lesson.

Lastly, the Special Agent in Charge acknowledged me. "Also assisting the Bureau, or, perhaps I should say the Bureau is assisting him, is the man whose solo investigation uncovered the incredible plot we are now working to dismantle and defuse. Some of you may know him as Bobby McRae, a former motion picture studio executive. For the purposes of this operation, you will know him U.S. Army First Lieutenant MacArthur Cutter, who is also a Special Agent in an elite team assigned to service with the U.S Department of State.

All I could think of was that yet another nail had been hammered into the coffin of my "classified" secret identity.

The LAPD honchos didn't seem particularly interested in the introductions. But when I was put in the spotlight I saw the Deputy Chief scowling and whispering in Terry Bates' ear.

Bianco continued. "I'll get right to the point gentlemen. There is a criminal conspiracy to detonate high explosives in, under and possibly around the theater during the Academy Awards ceremonies this Sunday night,

"Largely as a result of Special Agent Cutter's single-handed efforts, we know who the players are, we know how they plan to execute this disaster, and we know how to thwart them and bring them to justice.

"Most important, we now know who is the mastermind behind this plot. He's someone you may recall personally from the 1970s or may have read about in the annals of terrorism in America. Currently known as 'The Cuban' he is almost assuredly the most successful fugitive from justice in the history of the United States, the elusive criminal whose signature was bombings that killed several officers of the law and dozens of civilians, including several of his own co-conspirators, Shabazz Ali."

"Excuse me, Special Agent," the Deputy Chief blustered. "This scenario you've presented to us seems patently preposterous. Do you mean to tell us that while we have, on good information, been preparing for serious street demonstrations a plot has been hatched under our noses to kill hundreds of people, mainly international celebrities, during a live worldwide telecast?"

"I'm afraid that's exactly what I'm telling you," Bianco countered calmly. "The Bureau isn't acting on admittedly vague information from a confidential informant or any other sources.

"Thanks to Special Agent Cutter, we have hard evidence of this terrorist group's very specific plans. We know how they expect to execute those plans. We even know what specific explosive they plan to employ to destroy as much as they can of the auditorium while the Oscars are on the air around the world.

"The one piece of the puzzle we don't yet have is what Shabazz Ali is doing in this country after all those years when there's still a price on his head everywhere in the USA. We don't know how he got into the country either. And, we don't know what his motivation might be in hatching a conspiracy against the Oscars.

"Also, while we can identify his co-conspirators, while we know where they have stashed their weapons of mass destruction, and while we have them under surveillance and are remotely tracking them at this moment, we do not know where exactly Shabazz Ali is hiding out. Our hope and expectation is that when we close in on his underlings, they will lead us directly to him. Then, he will be under arrest, on his way to conviction and to federal prison after more than a quarter century on the run."

The Deputy Chief seemed visibly shaken. "I'd like to suggest that we take a brief recess in order to discuss among ourselves the information you've brought to us, Special Agent Bianco.

"If that's acceptable to you, we will adjourn to another area and you can remain here. We'll reconvene in, say, thirty minutes?"

Bianco agreed with that suggestion and the LAPD team filed out of the conference room silently. I was glad they'd chosen to meet elsewhere and left us where we were. They'd left the snacks behind and I wanted a second cup of coffee and a chance to sample a cake donut and maybe a bear claw.

While the cops were meeting, and most likely beating each other up. Bianco filled me in on the plan he and his A-Team had put together during the past

24 hours. I had the impression that none of them had gotten much sleep.

They'd reached a consensus that the Hondurans would be on the front lines, doing all the dirty work. It was very unlikely that Ali would show himself either beforehand or even at the time of the planned explosions. Most likely, he'd be somewhere in Los Angeles watching everything unfold on TV and ready to beat a hasty retreat out of the country and to the safety of the Honduran rain forest as soon as he'd seen the deed done. Only then would he take credit for the carnage.

That's why we had to let the plot unfold and not make any moves on the bombers until it became apparent that their plot had failed and they high tailed it to wherever Ali was hiding out and everyone attempted the flee the U.S.

All agreed that it was not likely that the explosives would be planted until the last possible moment. To do so even as early as a day before the ceremonies would leave too much opportunity for them to be discovered.

Special Agent Jenter had met with the key officials at the Academy and given them a story about a possible inside attempt to do something embarrassing on Oscar night. No one bothered to ask why the FBI would be concerned about a black eye for the Oscars. They just wanted to cooperate.

As a result, the Bureau already had two agents assigned to the auditorium as janitorial help. They were wearing janitor's uniforms and actually helping get the old building ready for the big show. They were also keeping their eyes open for any suspicious activity and scouting locations where explosives might to the most damage.

Additionally, Jenter had learned of an eight hour lockdown, from 10:00 p.m. Saturday night until 6:00 a.m. Sunday morning, when no one but essential personnel, principally security staff and any technical workers who had to resolve last minute problems, would be allowed in the building.

It seemed obvious that this window of opportunity would be the most advantageous for the bombing team to arrive on a pretext of fine-tuning the heating and air conditioning systems, conveniently located in the bowels of the building, in order to swiftly place their charges and detonating devices, conceal them, and leave.

Best guesses were that the La Raza team would hit the Auditorium around midnight. Not too soon after the lockdown, and not so late that they'd have to rush their work.

They'd be scrutinized by remotely monitored mini-cameras the FBI would emplace quickly right after the lockdown. Also, two of the uniformed security guards at the theater would actually be Special Agents Reedy and McCarthy.

Once the charges had been placed and the La Raza team had left the building, the FBI would roll up in a truck loaned to them by a food provisioning company and park at the loading dock in case the Hondurans had left anyone behind as a look-out on the place.

They'd quickly unload a team of bomb specialists and two explosive sniffing dogs. All of the explosives would be removed and replaced with similar-looking blocks of inert modeling clay, again on the off chance that anyone came back to check on the bombs before showtime.

Before dawn, the Bureau's agents would be out of the building and all of the explosives would have been neutralized. When the conspirators attempted to detonate their charges, nothing would happen. As best the Bureau's technical experts could assume, the detonation attempt would most likely be by radio frequency, possibly by means of a cell phone or similar electronic device.

Just out of curiosity, I noted to Bianco that Special Agents Jenter, Reedy and McCarthy already had specific assignments, but nothing had been said about Special Agent Speizman.

Bianco responded, "She'll be handling details in the office. Then, on the night of the Oscars, she'll be stationed backstage to look for anything unusual that might be happening in the midst of all the action between that area and the media room where the winners are taken after they've received their statuettes.

"We've gotten permission for her to dress appropriately and mingle with the models who escort the winners offstage to meet the press. I think she'll fit right in, don't you?"

He actually grinned a bit. So did I. Special Agent Speizman looked more concerned about where she'd conceal her gun.

41

Los Angeles, California

When the cops filed back in, they'd added two new members. The first man through the door was Chief Barton Barnes, known universally although not to his face as "Dirty Barry." Widely regarded as a hard core law and order guy, his MO had always been to lock 'em up first, and worry about the niceties of the arrests later. His people had had their share of cases thrown out, but in the two big cities where he'd served as chief before being hired by L.A. when arrest rates went up, crime rates went down.

The other newcomer was an officer I was already familiar with, Detective Allison Simmons.

Chief Barnes sat in the middle of the long table, flanked by his senior staff. Det. Simmons took a chair toward one end and behind rather than at the table.

Barnes gave Bianco and the FBI team perfunctory greetings and thanks before launching a thinly-veiled attack.

"Tell me if I'm correct. According to the FBI, the Los Angeles Police Department's exhaustive preparations for potentially violent demonstrations at the Hollywood and Highland Center during the Academy Awards have been in vain. This is because at the eleventh hour the Federal Bureau of Investigation has uncovered a plot by a foreign national presumed to be a fugitive from U.S. justice and some unnamed co-conspirators to blow up the building during the live television show."

Bianco was unfazed. "That's not entirely correct, Chief. The Bureau has no information regarding the street demonstrations LAPD has prepared for. That doesn't mean they can't or won't take place. So, the department's gearing up for that potential eventuality seems entirely appropriate.

"On the other hand, we now have knowledge and hard evidence of a serious threat directed against the awards ceremony itself from within. I apologize for sharing this information with the LAPD at this late date, but the pieces just fell in place over the past forty-eight hours."

The Chief's demeanor seemed to soften just a bit. "So, are you saying that we should call off our counter-demonstration plans and simply stand aside while the Bureau moves in to break up this bomb plot?"

"Not at all," Bianco countered. "The Bureau would like the LAPD to keep its plans in place and for Captain Bates to hold today's media briefing as planned.

"The announcement in the press that the LAPD is aware of a possible demonstration and prepared for it might actually dissuade some or all of the groups planning to take part. Additionally, an increased police presence in the area around the auditorium might throw the plotters off balance, make their task more difficult and perhaps assist in their eventual capture."

The Chief nodded his head, but wasn't finished with his questioning. "Special Agent Bianco, I follow your logic. However, I'm at a loss to grasp how you came by your so-called hard evidence of a bomb plot and whether your source is reliable.

"My understanding is that whatever evidence exists was brought to the Bureau's attention by someone outside law enforcement, some sort of vigilante, a lone wolf who for reasons best known to himself decided to look for trouble when no one in authority was aware of any brewing."

Bianco began to look just a bit irritated. "You are correct that an individual acting on his own initiative uncovered the evidence we are relying on. But that individual, Special Agent MacArthur Cutter is neither entirely outside law enforcement nor is he a so-called lone wolf. He is a team player.

"Cutter is both an officer in the United States Army and a decorated member of a special unit tasked with missions on behalf of the State Department. He relied on those confidential and classified sources at his disposal to sort through a number of clues that led him to piece together the case that he presented to us as soon as he was certain of his facts.

"As I mentioned, Lt. Cutter is first and foremost a team player. He has asked for no special recognition for his service to his country or to his hard, lonely and dangerous work in unearthing this current conspiracy. For the record, there have been two attempts on his life during his investigation, one a bombing at his home in South Carolina and the other a curare blow gun murder attempt at his hotel here in Los Angeles just three days ago. His credentials are impeccable."

Chief Barnes made one more attempt to undermine the Bureau's position. "Special Agent Bianco, the first LAPD officer to encounter Lt. Cutter was Detective Allison Simmons, who has just joined this meeting. Det. Simmons, could you please fill everyone in on your contacts with the Lieutenant?"

Simmons stepped up to the table and cleared her throat. "When I became aware that Lt. Cutter, who I knew then as Bobby McRae, had come to Los Angeles to look into the death of his former co-worker Jerry Kendall, I made it my business to seek him out. I met him for the first time at Venice Beach."

"Why is this relevant?" Bianco interrupted.

It may or may not be relevant," Barnes snapped. "Outside of yourself, perhaps, Detective Simmons knows Cutter, or McRae, better than anyone in this room. I'm simply attempting to establish his bona fides. Proceed."

"At first, I didn't identify myself. I subsequently provided him with my name and a means to contact me at headquarters should he need my assistance.

"Because of the death of a Jane Doe in our jurisdiction who was carrying one of Jerry Kendall's business cards on her person and because of the nature of her death, which bore similarities to Jerry Kendall's death in South Carolina, I provided Mr. McRae with this information.

"I also had a dinner meeting with him in the Valley during which time we discussed aspects of the two deaths, one ruled of natural causes, the other clearly a homicide."

"And, when Cutter/McRae returned to Los Angeles," the Chief prompted.

"When I learned from Interpol that our Jane Doe was actually a Honduran agent tracking a major criminal wanted in that country, I visited Jerry Kendall's attorney, Robert Raskin, to let him know that there was apparently no direct link between the murder victim and his client.

"Mr. Raskin was not in the office but his administrative assistant volunteered the information that Bobby McRae had also attempted to see him and she gave me the name of the hotel where he was staying.

"I went to his hotel and discovered that he was not registered there. On a hunch, I asked if there were any guests from South Carolina. There was one. I assumed that for whatever reason he was traveling under an alias and waited at the hotel until I encountered him.

"Because neither of us had the time to discuss new developments in the former Jane Doe case, we agreed to have another dinner meeting, this time at my home."

"And, during that dinner meeting," the Chief interjected, "would you say that Cutter/McRae was still very interested in seeking some link between these two deaths?"

Simmons looked down at her feet and replied almost breathlessly, "Yes sir. But, I believe that he was principally interested in me."

I'd have sworn that she actually blushed. I didn't know how good a detective she was, but she sure was a pretty good actor.

Special Agent Bianco nudged my leg under the table, turned his head slightly and whispered behind his hand, "Good taste!" Who knew he had a sense of humor?

All business again, Bianco asserted, "This is all very interesting but I don't think we really need a minute-by-minute recital of Cutter's Travels.

"The bottom line is that, acting on information provided to him by Detective Simmons as well as by his own confidential federal sources, Special Agent Cutter took it upon himself to obtain and furnish to the Bureau everything we need to stop a catastrophe and put one major league bad guy and several of his flunkies behind bars for a very long time.

"Now, unless the LAPD has any more questions to ask or guidance to give, I'd like my colleagues and me to be able to get back to the business of law enforcement.

The top brass all glanced around the table at their counterparts, hoping that someone might have something to add. No one did.

"Good," said Bianco. "I'll take that as your agreement that the Bureau will handle this operation and that the LAPD will focus on street demonstrations. Naturally, we'll seek out your assistance and rely on your special expertise as needed. It's always been my pleasure to work side by side with the outstanding professionals of the LAPD."

On the way back to FBI headquarters, the Special Agent in Charge and I exchanged small talk.

"You know, I'd be just as comfortable with you calling me Bud. The Bureau loves this Special Agent and Special Agent in Charge stuff but for normal conversation it's just a pain in the ass. What would you like me to call you?"

I thought for a moment. "Well, now that I've become a true son of the South, how about Bobby Mack?"

"Jeez. Now I've got a comedian on my hands. So, tell me 'Bobby Mack,' did Allison Simmons really shut you down?"

"That's cruel," I said. "Every time I saw her she was coming on to me. Then, nothing. I usually do O.K. with the ladies. I mean, I'm no George Clooney but…"

"More like George of the Jungle."

"Hey, now who's the comedian?"

I was starting to think that in addition to being a buttoned-up FBI agent, Bud Bianco might turn out to be a pretty good guy. Then, he switched gears, so to speak.

"So, what's with that heap you're driving? My grandfather used to drive a car like that, right after World War II."

"Be careful what you call a heap, Agent Bianco," I countered. "My Dolly would eat a Mercedes 560 alive and be a lot more fun to drive, to boot."

"Now I get it. You know Dutch, and that Oldsmobile is one of his custom jobs. Smart move renting from the old Dutchman. He must know you pretty well. He doesn't hand over his really good cars to just anybody."

I was impressed that Bianco knew about Dutch. Of course, he was the FBI after all. Aren't they supposed to know just about everything?

"While I think about it, where are you staying for the next two nights? I know you laid low pretty successfully the last two, but I'm still a little concerned. Twice, these guys have tried to knock you off and twice they haven't been sure whether you were dead or not. They might figure three times is the charm."

I told him I'd checked out of the Queen Mary hotel and hadn't made any new plans. I kind of thought I'd go back to someplace familiar and convenient, like one of the show biz hotels in Hollywood or Beverly Hills.

Bianco put on his worried look. "Those hotels," he said, "are really too big and make it too easy for strangers to mingle with guests and access the rooms, particularly with all the out of towners and media here for the Oscars.

"I'd sooner see you in a smaller, out of the way place. Easier for you to monitor and for us, too, if need be. If you don't want to stay in a safe house, I could probably put you up with one of our agents."

"Great idea," I responded enthusiastically. "How about Special Agent Speizman?"

Bianco nearly ran his car off the road. "After what happened to you with the lovely Ms. Detective Simmons, you'd want to try to room with Speizman??? You must be a glutton for punishment!"

I admitted I'd only been kidding. Well, half-kidding. I told him I knew a quiet little B&B not far from the beach in Santa Monica. I'd call when we got back to the office and see if I could get a room for the weekend. He was good with that.

Back at headquarters, we hooked up with the other four agents on his first team. They were seated in a small conference room around a table piled high with deli sandwiches, sides, chips and soft drinks. They must not have had as many LAPD donuts as I'd had.

Just to be polite, I forced myself to grab a ham and cheese on rye, half a turkey club, a bag of barbecue chips and a Dr. Pepper. I used to be a Pepsi guy but I'd learned that Dr. Pepper is the unofficial soft drink of the South, especially for breakfast.

After we'd chowed down, Bud called a business meeting. First order of business, what to do with me.

"Bobby Mack," he began, while the other agents looked at him quizzically, "when we break today I'd like you to secure those accommodations we discussed. When you're settled in, let me know.

"Tomorrow's going to be both intense and boring. Mostly surveillance, both on site and remote. By the way, those trackers of your work fine. Not the most sophisticated pieces of equipment but they'll let us tail the vans from around a half mile back so they'll never spot us. Thanks for that.

"Since there's no real job for you tomorrow, why don't you take in a movie or play a round of golf. Anything that will keep you busy and be unexpected. I'll call you if anything unusual happens."

I could tell he knew I was disappointed at being cut out of the action.

"Oscar night's a different story," he went on. "Sunday morning I want you here no later than 10:00 a.m. We'll go over everything at that time. In brief, you'll have to be at the auditorium by noon to get fitted for your tuxedo.

"The Academy is being very cooperative with all our efforts, including using you. They're making up an Oscar name tag for you as Mack Cutter. Officially, you'll be a supervising usher, so you have to look like one. You won't actually have to do any ushering, though."

"I can't arm you," he continued, "but you'll have a radio with an earpiece so we can stay in contact. You'll be our eyes and ears in the rear of the auditorium. Agent Speizman will perform the same function backstage."

He paused and a sly smile crossed his lips. "I considered putting you backstage with Agent Speizman, but I wasn't sure she'd be able to keep her hands off you."

The other agents cracked up and Agent Speizman gave Bianco a coy smirk as if to say, "Maybe I would, maybe I wouldn't." Lucky for me we were all getting along.

Everyone adjourned to another room where several out-of-state agent specialists were already gathered.

I decided a personal appearance at the B&B might work better than a cold call and headed for my car. As I cranked it over and pulled out of the FBI parking lot, I found myself musing, "I wonder what Special Agent Speizman is doing <u>after</u> the show???"

42

Saturday was a wash. I appreciated Bud Bianco's suggestions, but a round of golf didn't appeal to me. Plus, I didn't belong to a private club and getting a tee time at a municipal course would have meant sitting around waiting all morning. I scanned the Times for a movie or two that might be worthwhile and came up with nothing that interested me.

For most of the past week, I'd been running for daylight, trying to get past obstacles to arrive at some answers. Now, I was supposed to just sit back and let the FBI handle all the action.

I couldn't just hang around the bed and breakfast all day so I got into the Oldsmobile and headed up Pacific Coast Highway with nowhere special in mind. Unless it's blocked off my tons of rocks and dirt as it is every year or two by California's well-known landslides, PCH is a nice relaxing ride.

Before long, I'd passed Santa Barbara and was about to turn around when I decided to make it all the way up to Pismo Beach. It's a long ride from L.A. but I had a whole day to kill.

When I got there, the sun was shining and the skies were blue. At the shore, it was a little chillier than I'd anticipated, so I pulled on a sweatshirt to go for a long walk on the sand.

When I found myself back at the pier, I realized I'd gotten pretty cold. I found a little café that didn't look like a tourist joint and went in for a warming drink. I wasn't really hungry, but I couldn't pass up a bowl of steamed Pismo clams. They're the signature food of the town and rightly so, absolutely delicious and some as big as your fist.

Maybe it was the clams, or, possibly, the second or third bourbon, but I started developing telephonitis.

My first call was to Special Agent in Charge Bud Bianco's cell phone. He answered on the third ring.

"Bud, it's Bobby Mack," I said, trying to sound cheery. I knew already that he liked the Dixie nickname I'd come up with and would probably call me that forever.

"Hey, Bobby Mack! Where are you and how's everything going?"

"I'm up at Pismo Beach eating giant clams and drinking giant bourbon," I said.

"No, seriously, where are you?"

"I just told you. I couldn't decide on anything to keep me busy in L.A. so I took a drive. If you've had Pismo clams, you know it was worth the ride. So, what's new with you?"

Bianco paused a moment. "Listen, Bobby Mack, I know you'd rather be here despite how good those clams are. But, trust me, keeping a low profile is your best bet for now. You'll be right in the heart of everything tomorrow."

"I know," I said. "It's just frustrating to be on the outside looking in. Can you tell me anything about how the operation is going?"

"I can't discuss details on the phone. That said, you should know that all of our specialists are in town and have their assignments. We're counting down on the timetable we discussed and we don't anticipate any hitches.

"By the way, your trackers are giving us decent eyes on the subjects and we've got spotters on that old place in the hills. Everything's cool."

He wasn't able to tell me much, but what he did say put my mind at ease. Everything was moving along smoothly. The real action was still set for some time between 10:00 p.m. tonight and 6:00 a.m. tomorrow morning.

Next, I tried the Judge, back in Charleston. I knew I'd have to be careful what I told him. I just wanted to let him know where I was and that I was close to coming up with some answers to Jerry Kendall's murder, since it now was clearly a murder, and maybe more.

His home office phone rang half a dozen times and I was just about to hang up when his rich, molasses baritone voice reached my ears.

"Pinckney, here. To whom am I speaking?"

"Judge! It's Bobby McRae," I almost shouted. I must have sounded way too excited, because his next words were, "Now, Bobby, Calm yourself down, hear."

I told him I was excited because a lot of strange and interesting things had been going on out here, but I couldn't get into specifics. The Judge gave me a moment to quiet down. Then, he said, "Bobby, I've been on the phone with Michael Kelly off and on for two days. He's had to be discreet but he's given me a little briefing on what the Bureau's Special Agent in Charge out there has told him.

"You do realize that when you suddenly popped up with your theories and what you claimed to be evidence Bud Bianco had to contact his good friend at the FBI office in Columbia to find out whether or not you were a crackpot."

I couldn't think of much else to say other than, "So, what do you think so far, Judge?"

Again, Judge Pinckney weighed his words. "I think that your resourcefulness, determination and daring have exceeded my already rather high expectations.

"If what fractional information I have been provided proves out, it appears that in less than forty-eight hours a great many questions will be answered and a great many people may be in your debt.

"For now, all I can do is wish you good luck and God speed and encourage you to go after your quarry tenaciously and take no unnecessary chances."

The Judge had a way of making even simple statements sound eloquent. I thanked him for his good wishes and his concern and we both hung up.

I was running out of people to call, so I tried Tara. Amazingly, she was at home on a Saturday afternoon. I wished her well for her "Academy Award debut" Sunday night and hinted that I might even see her there at the theater.

She was thrilled. Well, she was thrilled about being at the Oscars and maybe mildly excited about possibly seeing me there. To her credit, she said that maybe after the ball we could go back to my hotel, or to her place, and recap the night's activities. Nudge, Nudge, wink, wink. For once, it was me who had to say, "Gee, I'd love to, but I think I'm going to have a very early, very busy Monday."

I'd done enough damage for one night, and dark had started to fall. On balance, between the clams and the drinks, I had a warm and comfortable feeling, despite my anxiety about the day ahead.

I paid up, slipped the bartender a ten for his generous pours and strolled out the door into the parking lot. Where I stopped cold.

An LAPD black-and-white cruiser was creeping through the lot and it came to a stop right behind my Dolly. My first reaction was to reach in my pocket for a mint, which I didn't have. Then, I realized that they couldn't bust me for DUI because I wasn't driving yet and because they were L.A. cops in Pismo Beach. Somehow, that thought didn't make me feel any more comfortable.

I flashed through the other options that came to mind, none of them good. There was no place to escape. The Pacific Ocean was to my back and even if the water hadn't been around 40 degrees the nearest place I could have swum to for asylum would have been maybe Portugal.

The cop car's driver side window rolled down and the officer called out. "Excuse me. Could you please step over here for a minute."

He was being awfully polite. As I started toward the cruiser, he stepped out and his partner came around from the other side. The driver had in one hand what looked like some official documents. The other cop was holding what appeared to be a map. At least they didn't have their guns drawn

When I reached them, I tried one of the oldest and stupidest moves around. I talked out of the side of my mouth in the hope that I wouldn't bowl them over with Maker's Mark fumes. They didn't seem to notice. Or care.

"Evening officers. How can I help you?"

The driver spoke first. "We have an arrest warrant." Those were five words I hadn't hoped to hear.

He held out the official-looking documents. "I'd like you to take a look at this."

I gingerly took the papers from his hand, trying to focus through the bourbon and the dim light. After what probably seemed like a long time to the cops, I said, "I'm sorry. I don't understand."

It was the second cop's turn to speak. "We came all the way up here to serve this warrant and take this guy in, but we couldn't find his street on the map.

"We were either going to go into the bar and ask around or see if anyone outside could help us. This car has the only California tags in the lot, so we pulled in by it figuring maybe the owner would come out. I guess that's you."

It suddenly registered why the name on the arrest warrant wasn't mine. "Geez, I'm sorry guys. I'm not from around here. I just drove up for the day from Santa Monica. Guess I can't be any help."

Unable to stop babbling, I asked, "Aren't you fellas way out of your jurisdiction?"

The driver just snorted. "You got that one right. Only reason we're up here at all on a dipshit aggravated assault warrant is because the vic was the Chief of D's nephew. He didn't trust the locals to bring in this desperado."

We all had a little laugh about that, especially me. My laugh was so relieved it was almost hysterical.

"O.K. sir," the other cop said. "Thanks anyway. If you're heading back to Santa Monica tonight, buckle your seat belt, drive carefully and…maybe pick up some Tic Tacs."

Both cops thought that was pretty funny and I had to go along with the joke. But, first chance I got I was going to pull over and buy some mints.

I headed back home, parked at the B&B and walked down Santa Monica Boulevard to a spot I'd always liked, but hadn't hung out at often enough, The Crown & Scepter. If you didn't know that you were in California, you'd swear you were somewhere in London. Every Brit in town, and there are plenty of them, drops by The Crown & Scepter, especially when one of their football matches is on telly.

I ordered steak and kidney pie and the first of what would become several pints of Smithwick's lager.

By the time I finished my meal, I had three or four new best buddies and the topic, as it will, turned to darts. The competition was on!

People who hang a board in their rec room and toss darts have no idea how complicated true British pub darts can be. Because I'm a Yank, we settled on the quickest, and perhaps the easiest, version. Every player starts out with 301 points, and the object is to score points to reduce that number to zero. Which you have to reach exactly.

Long story short, I was doing better than I deserved. Maybe the lager was loosening me up. I won a few, lost a few, got some applause from my mates, gave some in return, and bought a few rounds for just about everyone in sight. What the hell; it's only money.

I'd lost track of the time and was about to start joining in on some old music hall tunes when I realized I should be wandering home soon. I had time for at least one more game. As I lined up my first toss, I felt a sudden tingle coursing down my left leg. My dart flew over the target and harpooned a Guinness poster at least eight feet up on the wall.

For a split second, I thought I was having a stroke. I grabbed for my left leg and found a bulge in my pocket that could only be…my cell phone. I'd turned the ringer off and put it on vibrate and it had gone off unexpectedly.

The Brits had a good laugh at my insanely wayward dart and everyone wanted to buy me a pint. I graciously offered to drain one but excused myself for a moment to answer the call. I had to step out onto the street to escape the din.

It was Bud Bianco, and he was speaking very quietly. I thought, 'Why is he speaking so quietly. He's in his office."

Maybe his speaking voice was a little theatrical, but his message was straightforward. A La Raza van had been tracked to a location about three blocks away from the auditorium. It was parked on a side street at the moment, but the FBI expected the bombers to head into the building soon.

I wondered why they'd be going in so early. I squinted at my watch and saw that my free day had slipped past me. It was almost midnight. If the FBI team were right, the bombers should be making their move some time in the next few hours.

The pub would be hopping until 2:00 a.m. but it was time for me to call it a night. Well, maybe after one more pint.

Before he rang off, Bianco said that I shouldn't expect to be hearing from him again until morning. If everything went according to plan, there'd be nothing to report. If it didn't, he'd be too busy scrambling looking for a Plan B.

I wished him good luck and ambled back into the pub to say my goodnights.

43

Los Angeles, California

Last night's fun and games were long forgotten when I jumped out of bed at 7:00 a.m. and headed downstairs for as much coffee as I could swallow. I wasn't due at FBI headquarters until 10:00 a.m. but I was way too anxious to wait. I pulled into the lot at 8:30 a.m. and had to restrain myself from banging on Bud Bianco's door before 9:00 a.m.

The office was already humming. My guess was that no one had gone home since yesterday. When I was ushered into Bianco's office, my assumption was confirmed. The Special Agent in Charge, dressed in rumpled chino pants and a polo shirt with its tail hanging out, was bleary-eyed and in need of a shave. He waved me over to a chair while he finished a phone call.

"You that bird after the worm?" he asked, half smiling.

I admitted that I woke up early and couldn't wait to come in, find out how the operation had gone, and see what I could do next to help.

Bianco jiggled the intercom on his desk and asked that we be brought two large, "very large" coffees. The receptionist brought them in almost immediately and Bianco took a swig of his and leaned back in his chair.

"Actually, I'm glad you came in early. I'm going to have to go home soon to clean up and try to get a few hours' sleep. Before I do, I just about have time to update you."

Bianco said that the La Raza van pulled into the parking structure just after 2:00 a.m. Four men in work uniforms got out and wheeled a commercial dolly and a large industrial cart up to the security guard at the elevator leading to the underground areas of the building. He gave their credentials a look, found them in order, and let them proceed.

All four exited the elevator at the sub-basement level, where they were picked up by two of the FBI surveillance cameras. The rolled their gear down a long hallway past a table where two janitors, actually agents Reedy and McCarthy, were having lunch and playing cards. The La Raza men paused by the "janitors." At least one of them must have been an English speaker, unlike the two I'd encountered after my break-in at Avante 53. He said a few words to the disguised agents. They smiled and waved him on. And they went back to their lunch and cards.

A few minutes later, the "janitors" tossed their sandwiches and soft drinks, pocketed their playing cards and grabbed their mops, buckets and cleaning chemicals. Having established themselves as a couple of harmless, goofing off maintenance employees, they planned on doing their mopping and polishing within sight of the La Raza team, wherever they went.

That's how it worked out. Between the surveillance cameras, the two FBI agent/janitors and another pair of agents disguised as prop masters banging together some last minute sets for the telecast, the La Raza men were never completely out of sight.

According to Bianco, the perpetrators were both quick and efficient. It was often impossible to see exactly what they were doing and how they were placing their charges but where they were placing them was clear. A team of ordnance specialists and the K-9 handler were watching on a remote feed.

"These guys obviously took serious notes on visits over recent months, "Bianco said. "When our guys went in they actually had some difficulty identifying the charges because they were housed in worn metal boxes and other sheathing that blended in with the existing circuit boxes and terminals located throughout the sub-basement."

The Special Agent in Charge said that his team had recovered twenty-seven separate charges, most of them placed on structural elements where they could do the most damage. Each had both a timer and a radio-frequency detonator. The bomb experts determined that the radio frequency signal was to activate the timers, not the actual charges. That way, someone close by could remotely set the timers in motion and still be able to escape the building or the area before the explosions.

The really nasty business, Bianco said, was the industrial fire extinguisher sized canisters I'd photographed at Avante 53. Although the lab hadn't had time to analyze their contents safely, the bomb team was certain that they contained an aerosol, weaponized nerve gas, possibly sarin or ricin.

The canisters were placed in a dry sump pit close to the main air conditioning complex and connected to it by a flexible hose concealed under an old tarp. The canisters had sealed valves with their own timers attached. They were set on a shorter "fuse" than the six minutes of the timers on the charges, so they would begin releasing toxic gas even before the actual explosions.

The FBI had used my homing trackers and visual surveillance to follow the van back to the Avante 53 building, where the big sliding doors were opened and it disappeared inside.

"Now, we wait," Bianco said. "We all agree that the devices they placed have to be activated by a strong signal. That means that the sender has to be either inside the building or close by outside."

"There are a couple of things that can happen. One, we nab the perps with the RF signal device. Two, when the building doesn't blow, someone gets sent inside to the sub-basement to find out why, and we snag him. Three, when the building doesn't blow, everybody realizes their scheme has been uncovered and runs for the hills.

"Then, we track anyone and everyone we can in the expectation that we can arrest them, but not before one of them leads us to Ali."

Bianco got up to leave and sent me down the hall to a conference room. Jenter, Reedy, McCarthy and a couple of guys I didn't know were sitting around eating Danish. Reedy and McCarthy and the other guys looked exhausted. I turned to them and quipped, "Those lap dancers wore you guys out, eh."

McCarthy gave a hearty laugh that sounded somewhat like a horse's whinny. "Asthma," he explained. Reedy just glared at me as if he couldn't decide whether to chuckle or rip out my windpipe. Maybe that was just his normal expression. Jenter looked as fresh as a guy about to lead a Boy Scout troop on a hike in the mountains. Obviously, he hadn't been up all night.

Jenter presided over a table loaded down with tactical gear. "You know, you aren't allowed to carry a weapon," he said.

I'd already taken care of that, leaving my megaswitchblade back at the B&B. I figured the tear gas pen and the concealed stun gun didn't count.

Jenter handed me a small radio with a belt clip and a long twisty cord attached to an earpiece and a tiny wrist microphone. He made a big deal out of showing me how to run the twisty wire under my clothes so it wouldn't be obvious that I was with law enforcement. I wondered how many people in the 21st century would see a guy with an earpiece attached to a twisty cord and <u>not</u> think he was in law enforcement.

"This radio has two channels," he explained. "Channel One is the general channel. Everyone can hear everything. Channel Two is for one-to-one communications. Unless you're told to switch to Channel Two, you'll only have to worry about Channel One."

I thought, "Fascinating…"

"Now, Special Agent in Charge Bianco's call sign is 'Popeye.' Don't ask. He gets to choose the names. You are 'Team Player,' which he also selected. You don't have to remember anyone else's call signs. If you need to speak to everyone, just say 'All ears!'."

Next, Jenter handed me a plastic placard that said "FBI - -OFFICIAL BUSINESS" in six inch yellow letters on a blue background. It had hooks on the back to attach to a car's driver's side visor.

"Parking's a bitch at these things. Best bet because you'll be arriving way early is to park up one of the side streets. Then you'll have a fighting chance of getting out before the crowd or at least by next Tuesday.

"Oh, and here's something else that will make your car look more official." He reached into a big cardboard box and pulled out a rotating red flasher, a mini-version of what we used to call on cop cars a 'gumball machine.'

"You'll probably never have to use this, but it has the look of authority. To operate it, slap it on your roof, it's got a strong magnet in the base, plug it in to your DC transfer outlet and hit the switch on the right."

"The DC transfer outlet?" I asked. "What's that on a 1948 Oldsmobile coupe?"

He thought for a moment. "That would be your cigarette lighter."

That seemed to cover just about everything. I had some time to kill before I was expected at the Hollywood and Highland Center Theater so I stuck around to shoot the breeze with the three agents I knew and the others who'd been part of the tactical team locating and neutralizing the explosives.

They were an interesting group although at first reluctant to open up to me about their work. Once I told them the information Special Agent in Charge Bianco had already given me, they loosened up.

Because of all the first rate surveillance and the bomb-sniffing dog, it had taken them just a little over an hour to remove all the charges. It took almost another hour to replace them with bogus charges in the event that anyone tried to check on them. The actual explosives were taken in a bomb disposal van to a remote site in nearby Griffith Park until they could be moved to a military facility.

The agents didn't seem inclined to talk about how they wound up in the FBI or how they'd learned their particular special skills. They seemed even less inclined to ask me who I was and why I was sitting in the FBI office asking them a lot of questions.

I did have one more question before I headed out. "I don't see Special Agent Speizman here. Where is she today?"

Special Agent Reedy actually bared his teeth in a smile, although it seemed reminiscent of the smile on the face of a shark just before it bites your leg off.

"She's getting her hair done."

44

Hollywood, California

When I pulled up to the police barricade at twelve noon, the street in front of the theater was already filled with cameras, lights and broadcast technicians. I had the impression they'd been on site since dawn.

Between the visor placard and my special agent credentials, I badged myself past the sawhorses easily. Ignoring Jenter's advice, I went straight to the valet parking station at the complex.

I showed the young guy in the red vest my badge and told him I needed to be in the best possible spot for quick access in case I needed it. And, I had to keep the keys to the car. His look said "Fat chance" until I slipped him the picture of Ben Franklin in my hand and told him if he took care of me there'd be another one for him on my way out. He found me a spot marked "Absolutely No Parking" and said, "Have a nice day."

The theater itself was already humming with activity. I asked where I could find wardrobe and was directed backstage to a staircase leading down to a lower level where the dressing rooms were located. On my way to wardrobe, I passed a door marked "Makeup" and stuck my head in.

Already there were half a dozen makeup artists on hand, pulling the tools of their trade out of big, rolling suitcases and setting everything up at their stations. I recognized one of them, a middle-aged woman with magenta hair I'd met on one of our sets.

We did the Hollywood air kiss acknowledging each other and I asked her for a favor. I told her I'd gotten out of the movie business and gone into journalism. I was writing a behind-the-scenes feature on the Oscars for Rolling Stone and didn't want to be recognized. Could she help me change my look just a little bit?

With nothing else to do until some of the celebrities showed up, she was happy to oblige. Fifteen minutes later I walked out with some sort of powder in my hair to temporarily darken it, my eyebrows and sideburns filled in, some pale lip gloss and a touch of tan make-up base on my face, neck and hands. I turned down the offer of a pencil-thin mustache. She was good. I looked in the mirror and although I still looked like me, anyone just glancing at me in a crowd wouldn't be sure. I added my fake eyeglasses for effect and voila! I was transformed.

Not surprisingly, the wardrobe department was just about perfect. They'd laid out for me a crisply pressed tuxedo, complete with ruffled shirt, cummerbund, bow tie, links and studs and even a pair of patent leather shoes. Everything fit.

My "dresser" sent me along to an administrative office back on the main level. There, I picked up my

90th Academy Awards official tag, a plastic breast pocket badge identifying me as "Mack Cutter, Usher Coordinator." I was in business.

I spent the next hour or so roaming around the huge theater, getting my bearings and checking out any doors, windows or other obvious access points. Once people started arriving and the red carpet part of the telecast was underway, I'd position myself just inside the main door, where I would have sightlines across the span of the seats and, with a half turn, out to the street.

After I'd convinced myself that there was nothing I'd overlooked in the theater itself, I took a walk backstage just to orient myself to that area. Compared to the theater, backstage was stark and functional and a bit confusing. Trying to get back to the main entrance, I turned a corner and discovered something even more interesting, at least for the moment.

Evidently, the Academy didn't want its worker bees to starve. They'd set out a groaning board of a buffet with sandwiches, salads, cookies, candy bars, soft drinks and more. Just leaving the table with a plate piled high was Special Agent Speizman.

Reedy had been right. She'd had her hair done. No longer pulled back, her scarlet tresses cascaded in waves over her shoulders. She wore what I'd have to call a deep blue sheath with a mandarin collar, one bared shoulder, a long slit up the opposite leg and a necklace with a single, large opal.

The long hair and the collar hid her twisty wire and earpiece. The long sleeves of the sheath concealed her mike. The only items that might have pegged her as a cop were her slightly overlarge purse, holding her weapon, and her shoes. On a night when just about every woman in Hollywood would be wearing spike heels, Speizman wore a pair of flats built for comfort <u>and</u> speed.

Not sure if we were supposed to acknowledge each other, I asked her "What would you recommend?"

Speizman thought the question over for a moment. "The roast beef sandwich is good. But forget about getting a decent rye bread in L.A."

Sensing an opening, I countered, "Ah, not an Angeleno, then. So, where are you from?"

She finished a healthy bite of her sandwich before answering. "Chicago. North Side. Now, that's where you get good bread. Of course, you get the Cubs, too."

Her lips caressed the rim of a diet soda can. Or, at least that's how I saw it. "I'm surprised you let Bud Bianco talk you into standing post at the back of the room. According to the notes I read you were invited twice to be a guest, by your boss, Mr. Petite."

I was quick to correct her. "He's not my boss. Just a colleague. Admittedly, he's not very big, but his name isn't 'Petite.' It's Pettit. P-e-t-t-i-t."

She licked her soft, alluring lips. "Well, maybe they changed it. Dropped the 'e' and added a 't.' Maybe they were all little and didn't like being named 'small.'"

I grudgingly admitted that maybe she had a point. Then I threw in, "You have an unusual name yourself. Ever think about changing it?"

"Nope. It's an asset. When people meet me, they never forget my name."

I gave her another good look. I thought to myself, "When guys meet you, I'll bet your name isn't the only thing they'll never forget about you!"

Agent Speizman shimmied away to find a spot to enjoy her lunch. I had to wonder how she'd be able to sit down in that dress.

I was left to contemplate enjoying a roast beef sandwich without decent rye bread.

45

Hollywood, California

I didn't have much time to chow down and relax. Outside, the red carpet was ready to go and on the dot of 6:00 p.m. the celebrities began arriving. As always, the broadcast network, this time ABC, held down the best positions. Everyone else had to push, shove and struggle to get their cameras, microphones and still cameras in position to document the annual star fest.

I positioned myself at the top of the broad staircase and watched the scene unfold and the VIPs worked the media line before wending their way into the theater. It was not as if I'd never seen actors and actresses before, but I have to admit I enjoyed seeing people like Denzel Washington, Gary Oldman, Meryl Streep, Frances McDormand – looking a little less like a bag lady than usual for some reason - Woody Harrelson and Daniel Day-Lewis hoping to humbly rub the noses of their fellow thespians in their own Oscar wins.

Of course, I already knew most of them either from working with them on a film or just hitting the cocktail circuit. All the same, I enjoyed watching them strut their stuff for the cameras as if who they were and what designer they "wore" was a huge deal.

By the time WillemDafoe, Emma Stone, Nicole Kidman, Jennifer Garner, Octavia Spencer, Christopher Plummer and Stephen Spielberg had sashayed past me, I'd started to lose interest in celebrity spotting. I couldn't afford to let my mind wander. I had to be alert to anything out of the ordinary.

Of course, it wasn't likely that Jordan Peele or Mary J. Blige would be smuggling in a radio frequency detonator. Now, Nick Nolte…him I wouldn't have minded giving a pat down just to be on the safe side. But he wasn't nominated and I never saw him wander in.

The pre-show started right on time, 6:30 p.m. precisely, a little later than usual because the awards show itself had been bumped back to an 8:00 p.m. start for arcane reasons best known by the Academy. And today in Hollywood the sun was actually shining bright.

Jimmy Kimmel was on stage for the actual show as the emcee – second time. He'd done a good job the year before, but this would be the test – the big enchilada for the popular late night host who'd become something of a lightning rod for his frequent political commentary. This time, he'd likely tone down the rhetoric and do a great job. As long as he wasn't blown to pieces along with all the other stars.

Truthfully, I'd never been a big fan of flashy awards shows. Sure, an Oscar, even a nomination, can give a shot in the arm to a film's box office. When I worked at Avante I was thrilled for us to have a winner. It was terrific for the company's bottom line. Yet, the idea of a bunch of egotistical millionaires getting together to slap each other on the back while stabbing each other in the front, always left me a little cold.

Another reason I've tried my best never to get roped into attending any of these shows is that they're like the Super Bowl. You think it would be absolutely fantastic to be on hand, live and in person. Then, once you are, you realize that you would have enjoyed it more sitting at home and watching it on TV in your underwear.

Between film clip montages, songs from film scores and strained introductions the whole program just kind of groaned along. Even though the presenters were all famous actors and actresses, some stumbled trying to read the Teleprompter and most delivered their lines like second graders reciting the Pledge of Allegiance. I expected a lot of squishy political statements and "Me Too" campaign approvals from these geniuses and wasn't disappointed.

The one element that could have caused a mini-crisis was the gimmick of taking a handful of "stars" across the street to ambush a captive audience in another theater. Working with the producers, the feds had this under control. Special Agent Bianco had called in a few favors and the new "audience" was peppered with undercovers from agencies such as ATF while LAPD earned their keep by securing everyone's march across the street.

After that tepid "tribute" to the folks who cough up their dollars to actually go to movie theaters, the Oscars reverted to being just another TV awards show, where no one knows what camera shots the director will call for so no one is supposed to leave their seats. If they did, the camera might inadvertently show an empty place or two, which would reflect poorly on the Academy Awards' image of being so important that everyone privileged to attend would be glued to his or her chair. Just the argument Derrick Pettit had made to try to convince me to attend as a guest.

Naturally, when you've been in the spotlight for three or four hours, including the red carpet arrivals, and the show is just droning on about various awards that don't actually involve you, the human tendency is to want to hit the rest room, sneak out for a smoke, or look for some place to get a drink. That's probably why the Golden Globes are more popular among the attendees. You can leave your seat. And you can certainly get a few drinks.

This night, after around the half-way point of the show, each time there was a commercial break, a dozen or so people jumped up and headed for the back of the theater. Their quick exits were the cues for the seat fillers, like Tara Fukimoto, to zoom down the aisles and jump into those empty chairs, so if the break ended before the celebrity returned the viewing audience would be none the wiser.

So, that's where I focused my attention. Guests leaving their seats and seat fillers taking them were the only signs of any activity in the theater, other than what was taking place on stage.

The radio had been strangely quiet. Bud Bianco had called several agents requesting them to switch to

Channel Two to update him on the situations at their positions. Finally, it was my turn.

"Popeye to Team Player, over."

I quickly replied, "Copy, Popeye, over." He didn't ask me to switch channels so he either thought it didn't matter whether all the other agents heard what I had to say, or he specifically wanted them to hear what I had to say.

"Update the status at your position, over."

"Quiet here. A few people leaving their seats temporarily but not leaving the building. So far, all of them have returned and been accounted for. Over."

"Roger that, Team Player. In total, how many logo vans did you count at the two locations you investigated. Over."

That question seemed to come out of left field. "Two total. One at the primary location and one headed back to that location from somewhere unknown. The second van tailed me into a neighborhood in Canoga Park and left when I confronted the driver and passenger. That's when I tagged their van with my bug. Over."

"Two total. Thanks Team Player. Popeye out."

There had to be some specific reason why the Special Agent in Charge suddenly had to know how many vans La Raza had in Los Angeles. He also didn't want to say why he needed to know, and he also wanted every other agent on this assignment to be aware of my answer.

The awards presentations had been going on for a little over two hours and I was getting tired of just stand-

ing around watching the proceedings and counting people going to the rest room and then back to their seats.
I'd never make it as one of those event security guys who
stay in one place through long, boring sports events just
hoping that some drunk fan will give them a reason to
toss him out of the stadium.

My mind was definitely wandering. For no apparent reason I found myself wondering why one of my
favorite actors hadn't done anything in the past few years
to deserve a nomination. F. Murray Abraham.

At that moment, something weird happened. I'd
like to say that a bell went off or a light bulb appeared
over my head. It was more like a pop-up graphic. In one
corner of my brain I saw the cover of an Avante Entertainment annual report.

Each year, when it was published, I always looked
through my copy carefully. I wasn't all that conscientious.
I just wanted to check the corporate executives listing to
see that my name was spelled right. That's the page that
my mental copy of the annual report flipped open to.

I was right there. Bobby McRae. Next was Charles
A. Nelson. Irving Nussman. Michelle Oliver. Dr. Paul
Parrish, Phd. And, Derrick Pettit. "J." Derrick Pettit.

Special Agent Speizman's off the cuff remark about
a family changing its name because they didn't want to be
known as "small" suddenly started to make sense. As did
Lane Lander's story about Derrick Pettit's strange press
release – the one listing the contact as "J." Derrick Pettit

Unexpectedly, my radio crackled again. "All ears.
This is Popeye. No need to respond. Just listen.

"Chase vehicle has a pair of buzzards in sight, now eastbound on the Ventura Freeway. If they're headed here, ETA is around thirty minutes. I'll keep you posted. Over."

So, the La Raza perps were on the move. I could almost feel the FBI team stiffening up in preparation for some action. I wondered if The Cuban would be in one of the vans. I decided it was unlikely. His flunkies might screw up, even be caught. He'd be close enough for them to reach him pretty quickly if they had to abort their mission and try to escape but far enough away to "get out of Dodge" without them if he had to move fast.

Bud Bianco's next transmission wasn't as calm and collected as before. There was frustration in his voice as he told us all "One buzzard has peeled off onto 405 South. We're going to lose signal. Working on a link to CHP to keep a lookout but not engage. The other bird is flying right our way. Out."

Popeye was back on the air. "All ears, perimeters listen up. Chase has its bird landed at a gas station on Franklin. No word on how many it was carrying or whether they're still in the nest. Chase team will observe on foot and report."

Our situation was changing rapidly. Bianco's next communication was "No one in the nest. We lost them. They've got to be headed this way. LAPD reports small knots of demonstrators at various locations around the theater. Not the monster showing they expected. But, even small groups could give the subjects enough cover to move in close and even try to enter. If you spot 'em, don't lose 'em. But do not engage them unless absolutely necessary. Clear? Over."

His message was met with a chorus of affirmatives. About ten minutes passed without an update since the van had been spotted parked on Franklin. The show was slowly winding down. I figured that if they made a move, it would have to be very soon.

On stage, the Oscars forged ahead. I hadn't seen many of the films, mainly because when I left Hollywood, I took my name off the comp list for nominated features. I'd actually gone to a theater to see "Three Billboards Outside Ebbing Missouri," which was pretty impressive. So I felt good when Sam Rockwell and Frances McDormand picked up statuettes.

The award for Best Picture would be coming up next, then the show would wrap. It was already running late and would go for way more than three hours. The smart money was on "The Shape of Water," which I'd skipped because the "thing" in the trailer reminded me of the "Creature from the Black Lagoon." But with Warren Beatty and Faye Dunaway due to make the presentation after their previous year's blunder, no one was going to want to miss this finale.

The lights went up for the last commercial break before the big announcement. The moment they did, I spotted one tuxedoed figure stand and step into the aisle. He started toward the back of the theater and the main exit, holding a big white handkerchief up to his face and coughing loudly.

I was afraid that the FBI team might have missed a gas canister and some sort of nerve agent was rapidly filtering into the audience, with this lone guy the first casualty. I worked my way past a couple of hired security guards standing around doing nothing much and moved across the back of the theater to try to intercept him.

For someone in distress, he was moving pretty fast and I'd barely made it to the top of his aisle when he was there too. Through his coughing I could hear him cry out, "I need EMS!" As he raced past the pillar where I'd posted myself I recognized him even behind his handkerchief. It was Derrick Pettit!

A few quick steps and I was at his side. I grabbed him by the arm. "Derrick! What's the matter?"

"Gotta get EMS!" he yelled through his handkerchief. He must have suddenly realized that I'd called him by name. His head swiveled and he stared me in the face. "Bobby?"

So much for my great disguise. I needed to find out what was going on, whether he'd been affected by some toxic gas. Then, I heard a shouted command from behind us. "Let him go!"

I spun around and came face to face with Det. Allison Simmons. She shouted again, "Let him go. He's ours!"

I squeezed Pettit's spindly arm harder while I tried to figure out what she meant. Wasn't the FBI in charge of this operation? If he was going to be arrested, why did LAPD think he would be their collar?

Simmons back pedaled a few paces. She was dressed for the occasion, complete with an official Academy Awards credential attached to her sleek, maroon dress. Two things gave her away: her detective shield at her waist, visible when she swept back her short jacket, and her right hand buried deep in a little bit too large Vuitton shoulder bag.

She glared at me and shouted, "I'm not kidding. Turn him loose. I don't want to have to use force."

I thought, damn! She has her hand on her gun!

Simmons squared her shoulders into a Weaver shooting stance. "Don't do anything stupid, Bobby." Strike two for my disguise. "Turn around and put your hands on your head."

I dropped Derrick's arm and turned around, reluctantly putting my hands on my head. Next, she said, "Back up toward my voi…"

She never finished the word "voice." Her command ended with what sounded like "Uhhhhhn" which was accompanied by what had to be a body hitting the hard floor.

I whirled around and found her crumpled in a heap with her service weapon on the ground next to her. Standing over her was Tara Fukimoto

"Hi, Bobby," she said cheerfully. "Why'd that bitch pull a gun on you?"

I stammered, "What are you doing here? What did you do to her? How did you do it? Do you know she's a cop???"

Tara just smiled. "You needed help. During the war, my whole family was in the camps. When they got out, they made sure we all studied karate, even the girls. I've got a black belt. But that was just a rabbit punch. So, she's a cop. She'll be OK in a minute."

I said, "Tara, get the hell out of here, now!"

She smiled. "O.K. my job's over. Nobody leaves their seats when Best Picture's coming up."

I ran over to one of the security guys, who must have been so engrossed in the show that he didn't even notice the drama a few feet away.

"Hey! There's a lady cop down in the lobby. She needs help, now!"

While he figured out what to do, I ran past Allison's prostrate body and did something I knew right away I'd probably regret. I scooped up her gun and stuck it in my belt.

46

I ran to the top of the stairs, swiveling my head to try to spot Pettit. He had a head start and was quick-stepping it down Hollywood Boulevard. For a guy who was desperate for medical attention, he'd dropped the handkerchief from over his mouth and was doing a good imitation of the Olympic race walk, just casual enough not to attract the attention of any of the cops stationed all over the street.

I saw him cross Orange and thought, "Well, he's in luck. There's an EMS ambulance parked right there."

He reached the ambulance and the rear door swung open. A hand reached out, grabbed his and hauled him in. This was a rescue technique I'd never seen before. Before the rear door could swing closed, the ambulance had pulled away from the curb.

I raced down the stairs and around the corner toward the parking garage. Wardrobe's fancy tuxedo shoes weren't helping my hundred meter time. My car was still in its great spot.

Fumbling with the keys, I climbed in, cranked the big motor over and blew past the frantically waving valets. By the time I made it onto Hollywood Boulevard, I could still see the flashing lights of the ambulance in the distance. Getting through the police barricades must have cost them a minute or two.

Fifty yards ahead, two cops were beginning to muscle the sawhorses into place to hold back the meager crowd of sign-waving demonstrators. I had no choice.

I flipped on my red emergency flasher, leaned on the horn and flashed my headlights. The cops stopped hauling the sawhorses and whipped around to stare. They must have thought they were seeing the ghost of a late '40s cop car bearing down on them at full tilt.

They jumped out of the way, the protestors tried to scatter, and I made it through just nicking one sawhorse enough with my bumper to send it skidding into the crowd.

Now, I had the ambulance in sight, but I had to stay back so they wouldn't make me as a tail. I killed the flasher, knocked off the headlights and slowed down. I was pretty sure I could keep them in sight. After all, my Dolly looked like some old junker that would most likely have been driven by their grandfathers.

At Fairfax, they took a left, heading south. They were using their light bar but only occasionally hitting the siren. They wanted to move fast, but not draw too much attention to themselves. I stayed well back but was still able to keep up.

For the first time, I had a chance to try to raise Bud Bianco. I hit my send button and yelled, "Popeye. Team Player. Come in. Come in. Over!"

Instantly, I heard the FBI agent's voice, much calmer than mine. "What is it, Team Player?"

"I'm in my car. I've got buzzards in sight and I'm tracking them at a distance. We're headed south on Fairfax."

Bianco replied, "What's going on? Why did you leave your post? The show's ending and nothing's happening here!"

"I spotted Derrick Pettit running out of the theater and climbing into an ambulance. It looked like a set-up. He could have been the trigger man."

Bianco radioed, "I hope you're right. If you are, that's all we've got."

His transmission was filled with crackling. I answered, "I think I'm heading out of range. I'll keep pursuing and fill you in later."

"Roger that. I'm standing by. How can we help?"

At first, nothing came to mind, other than alerting the 101st Airborne. Then, it hit me. "Can you get through to the LAPD and see if their chopper can look for us. They're in an LA County EMS ambulance. The buzzards from the van must have overpowered the crew and carjacked it. Tell the cops my guess is we're headed for the Santa Monica Freeway."

Now, he was barely audible. I picked up "chopper… ambulance..freeway"Then, my radio went dead. So, I was on my own, with no way to reach the FBI. I'd just have to keep following them and hope for the best.

We passed Canter's Deli and turned right onto Beverly Boulevard. Twice, I had to hit my red gum ball briefly to get around some slower cars. I used it sparingly in the hope that whoever was in the ambulance would be looking forward, not back, and wouldn't get spooked.

We took Beverly to La Cienega and turned left, heading south. I was still about four car lengths behind them and trying hard to keep at least one vehicle between them and me.

For some reason, Allison Simmons' words kept running through my head. Ordering me to release Derrick Pettit, she had said, "He's ours." It started to make sense. She didn't mean "He's ours" as in "We want the collar." She said, "He's ours" meaning Pettit was working with the LAPD!

Now it added up. He had to be their confidential informant, the guy who'd gotten the LAPD all hot and bothered about big demonstrations at the Academy Awards. The guy who'd conned the cops into putting their resources and their attention outside the theater, where he'd managed to round up a few hundred so-called demonstrators, not inside, where his colleagues had placed their explosives and nerve gas.

In his own way, little Derrick Pettit might turn out to be one of the masterminds behind a failed plot that could have wiped out most of Hollywood's biggest stars.

This realization was just setting in when we reached the 10 Freeway and headed west. Unless they were going to the beach, or to Los Angeles International Airport, which they clearly weren't, there were not many other good options. They'd run out of freeway in a few minutes.

On the Santa Monica Freeway, the ambulance speeded up and I could hear its siren come on. They must have figured that the CHP would be less likely to stop and question an L.A. County EMS ambulance than the LAPD. Hell, the highway patrol would probably offer them an escort.

We were still traveling not much over the speed limit. The ambulance was hitting around 80 mph and I was keeping pace in a different lane with at least one car shielding me from them. Eighty was a trot for the engine Dutch had put in the Oldsmobile. I could have caught the ambulance, pulled in front of it and done jumping jacks all day long. I almost wished they'd try to get their van over 100 so I could pull alongside and flash them the bird from my nondescript vintage coupe.

Driving at freeway speed helped clear my head. Now, I now had a solid guess as to where they were going. If The Cuban, his buddies and Derrick Pettit realized their weapons of mass destruction had turned out to be duds, they'd be looking for the fastest way to get out of California to somewhere safe.

They wouldn't be standing in line at LAX to buy tickets on AeroHonduras. They'd have no chance of driving to Mexico or Canada. They could have a boat moored somewhere but they'd have to outrun the Harbor Police, the Coast Guard and half the U.S. Navy off the coast.

No, if these guys had planned ahead to get away, whether or not their plot worked, they'd have some sort of plane at the ready and the direction they were headed it would have to be warming up at Santa Monica Airport.

Santa Monica is a well-equipped, modern general aviation field with lots of private planes hangered there and any number of charter planes and pilots. Since it's not a commercial aviation field, there would be no hassles with Homeland Security or any delays getting off the ground. It had to be Santa Monica.

We were running out of road and the exit that would lead into the airport was coming up fast. I remembered that I had my cell phone with me and that special Agent Bianco's cell number was captured from his call yesterday. It was worth a try.

I dug the phone out and scrolled through its options while keeping one eye on the ambulance. I called his number up and pressed "dial." It took five rings for him to answer. It must have been noisy on his end. "Bud, it's Bobby Mack" I shouted, completely forgetting our radio protocol.

"Talk to me, Bobby Mack."

"So, where the hell's the LAPD helicopter," I shouted. "I'm all alone here hanging out to dry."

"I got LAPD dispatch on the horn right away. They understood the situation and diverted their chopper. Last I heard, they couldn't find you on the Hollywood Freeway."

"No, no," I said, frustrated. "I said my guess was that they'd head for the Santa Monica Freeway, not the Hollywood!"

Bianco paused, "Oh, shit. That's when you went out of radio range. Give me your 20 and I'll get ahold of them pronto."

"On the 10 Freeway, Barrington's coming up. We're headed for Santa Monica Airport. At least that's my best guess. Got to hang up."

I thought I'd lost them while I was on the phone. They'd just pulled around an eighteen wheeler hauling concrete drainage conduit.

Sure enough, the EMS ambulance left the freeway at Bundy Drive and headed straight for the airport. They were far enough ahead that I lost them again briefly. The Olds' brakes barely squealed as I cornered fast onto Ocean Boulevard, took a right onto Donald Douglas Loop and slammed the brakes on just outside an open gate to a runway.

Dead ahead was the ambulance, pulled up next to a sleek business jet. It could have been a Beechcraft or a Citation or a Lear. I'm no good at ID'ing airplanes. But it wasn't tiny and its two big engines, their turbines already whining, looked like they could get it fast deep into Mexico or even northern Guatemala.

The plane's little boarding steps were down and one of the men from the ambulance was climbing them. I gunned the Olds and raced onto the tarmac, parallel to where they were loading. I swung around and started to cross behind the ambulance when an arm stuck out from the open door. It was holding a shotgun.

One loud blast and my rear window disappeared.I had time to think, "I'm glad they didn't have an automatic weapon." That's when I lost control and crashed through a hedge and into a chain link fence,

The impact stalled Dolly, but when I recovered, pumped the accelerator and turned the ignition key, she turned right over. My front bumper was caught in the fence. I couldn't just climb out and try to pry it off. I couldn't see the ambulance and any one of those guys might be coming after me with his gun.

Trying the only thing I could think of, I slapped the car into reverse, popped the clutch and gunned it. At first, the tires slipped and smoked then caught and the car rocketed backward, taking a big chunk of the fence along with it.

They certainly weren't making chain link fences like they used to. Or bumpers.

I steered back onto the airstrip, pushing the tangled mess of fence and branches in front of me, sparks flying everywhere. Up ahead, the boarding steps were up and the plane's door was closed. Over the roar of my own engine I could hear a change in the sound of the pitch of the engines. They were ready to taxi and take off.

I headed for the plane at full speed, chunks of chain link fence breaking off and peppering the windshield. The plane's door opened slightly and an arm stuck out, again holding a weapon. I hit the brakes, spun the wheel hard right and heard the Brrrt! Brrrt! of something fully auto. Slugs ripped across the left side of the car but the old bus was made solid and nothing penetrated through to me.

It was obvious that these guys were playing for keeps, and that I wasn't going to be getting any help. So much for Det. Simmons' sidearm. I wasn't going up against a machine gun with nothing but a 9mm pistol. Now, the plane was rolling a little faster as it moved into position on the runway.

In another minute or so, it would be squared away for its take-off and I'd be out of luck. My last ditch hope was to do something they'd never expect. Until it was airborne, my ride had a lot more speed than their plane. These private planes would be hitting maybe a hundred twenty miles an hour when they went wheels up. I could go 140 mph easy.

Suddenly, the airstrip lit up like midday. The LAPD "eye in the sky" had arrived. I thought, "Sure. Now you show up!"

I didn't have time to wait for the cops to do any-thing. I raced past the plane, did a K-turn and stopped dead in their path. We were 50 yards apart and neither of us was going anywhere.

The pilot was slicker than I'd bargained for. He didn't need the whole runway to take off. He swung left and speeded up, planning on juking around me and using what was left of the runway for a full power lift.

As he turned, so did I. Checkmate. Then he got smart. He turned right and I had to move with him, which gave one of his passengers a chance to open the door and get off another quick burst at me.

Either I'm a great driver or he was a lousy shot because none of his rounds hit Dolly. But, I still had to get cover in case the shooter's aim improved. I roared past the plane, did another hard turn, and came up on its left flank about twenty yards away.

Just for a moment, the thought flashed through my mind that the crew up in the helicopter must have been amazed to see what was going on down below.

With Dolly stopped way off to his side, the pilot must have thought he'd shaken me. He straightened out in the center of the runway and started to roll faster toward take-off.

That's when I yanked on the seat belt Dutch had thoughtfully installed in the car, even though they hadn't been invented when it was built. I was as secure as I was ever going to be.

As the plane started to pull even with me, I punched the accelerator. In two seconds I was in second gear doing 30 mph. I stuck my left hand out of the car window and emptied Allison Simmons' sidearm at the cockpit.

In four seconds, I hit 40 mph. In five seconds, two tons of Detroit steel going 50 mph slammed into the plane's fuselage right where the front wheel sticks down from its pointy nose.

I remember hearing a tremendous bang. That's when the lights went out.

47

University Medical Center, Los Angeles, California

The next time I opened my eyes, it was Tuesday. A nurse with gentle brown eyes was standing next to me, taking my pulse. Her hand felt cool and comforting.

"Good afternoon, Mr. McRae. How are you feeling?"

"Pretty good," I croaked. My throat felt as if I'd swallowed a pound of sand.

Nurse told me that my vital signs were almost normal, and that was a good thing. I just nodded my head in agreement.

"You have a visitor outside. Do you feel up to seeing him?"

I said, "Sure" and she went to bring him in. It was Special Agent in Charge Bud Bianco.

He'd brought me a can of Diet Coke and a beef and bean burrito.

"Sorry the burrito could be a little cold," he said smiling. "I bought it this morning thinking you might be awake."

No matter, it tasted great and the Coke went down like a fine wine. My throat began to feel a little better.

Bianco explained that I'd been brought to the hospital by ambulance, "and, not the EMS truck at the airport. That's evidence."

I'd been registered under my own name and listed as a civilian employee working for the Bureau on a sensitive project. Hence, the secrecy about my "automobile accident" and the 24 hour guard posted outside my door.

He told me the doctors said I was a very lucky guy. The windshield of the Olds had been popped out, apparently by my head, and they thought I might have had brain damage. But, preliminary tests showed that I didn't. I knew I'd been called hard-headed. Now I had proof.

"It's like the newspaper headline after Yogi Berra got beaned," I quipped. "Doctors examined his head and found nothing."

That actually got a laugh from Bianco. I offered him a bite of my burrito, but he declined. "These days, I'm not particularly fond of anything from south of the border."

That even got a smile from me. Bianco told me that in addition to my head injury, I was pretty banged up. When I tried to move in bed, I had to agree. I had bruises on my bruises and pain in places I'd never imagined I could have pain. The good news was that I only had a broken collarbone, a few broken ribs and no internal injuries.

That said, he told me that I'd be in the hospital for a few more days. The doctors wanted to run more tests and the Bureau needed to debrief me on the final hours of Oscar night. He said he'd fill me in on all the details from his end in a day or two. For now, all I needed to know was that no one got away.

Then he pulled out a folded copy of the Los Angeles Times. The huge front page headline read, "FBI Thwarts Terror Plot At The Oscars" with the subhead "Most Wanted Fugitive Captured After 37 Years."

I couldn't focus well enough yet to read more, but Bianco told me that my name had never been mentioned.

"It's not that we didn't want to give you all the credit you deserve," he said. "The situation was just too complex. And, we were leaned on a bit by the Army and the State Department to keep you out of it."

I told him not to worry. It wouldn't be the first time the Army had wanted to sweep me under the rug. His raised eyebrows told me that he hadn't learned everything when he had me checked out. To make me feel better about the whole incident, he told me that I'd be getting an official commendation from the Director himself.

"It won't mention specifically why you're being commended and it won't even get you a free cup of coffee. But, it'll look great to hang on your wall."

Agent Bianco let that sink in. Then, he added, "While I'm passing out kudos and all, I have a few more things to fill you in on.

"First, preliminary indications are that the Honduran government is so thrilled to finally have the Cuban taken out of action that they're likely to be giving you one of their highest medals. Another goodie you can't do anything with but that will look good in your obituary, you should pardon the expression."

Bianco was on a roll and really enjoying having me at his mercy. He reached under my bed and pulled out a large, brown-wrapped package. "Oh, and this is for you from your new friend, Special Agent Speizman. If I'm not mistaken, it's a Chicago rye bread. Why that, I have no idea."

Well, that's a nice overture, I thought to myself. Maybe I did make a pretty good impression. I asked Bianco, "How the heck did she get a rye bread here so fast?"

He took way too much pleasure in informing me that, "She had it shipped here on one of our inter-office flights. She knows someone in our Chicago office. Her fiancé."

Having had his fun with me, Bianco paused and actually looked around furtively. You would have thought he was a lawbreaker and not the law. He cleared his throat. "Uh, one thing, just between you and me, Bobby Mack.

"Well, just before you smashed into the jet, when you unloaded that 9mm into the cockpit, you winged both the pilot and Shabazz Ali, who was riding co-pilot."

"Damn!" I exulted. "And I haven't practiced in months!"

Now, Bud Bianco looked flustered. "No question it was good shooting, particularly under the circumstances. Of course, now we're having a little problem explaining how a supposedly unarmed civilian plugged a major terror suspect, with an LAPD-issued pistol."

"I'd like to help you out, Bud," I said, "but somehow the recollection of how that weapon came into my possession has been wiped from my memory. Must have been that hit to the windshield."

Bianco sighed, shook his head and left. A few minutes – or hours - later a candy striper came around offering me some magazines and candy bars. The drugs the doctors had me on helped me lose track of time. I took everything I could, figuring this could be a long, boring stay.

By Wednesday, I was ready to get up and out and head home. Unfortunately, my opinion and my wishes weren't shared by the medical staff or the FBI. The docs had some more poking and probing to do and the Bureau had lots of questions.

Over the next few days, I was interrogated, "interviewed" is the politically correct term, I suppose, by Bud Bianco, the Special Agents in Charge from the Sacramento and San Francisco offices, a Deputy Director who'd flown out from D.C., an ATF agent and a guy from Homeland Security who wouldn't tell me exactly what his job was.

Everyone asked pretty much the same questions, and they all had stenographers who took down everything I said. I was starting to think that I was the perpetrator, not the Cuban.

In between grillings, I had a chance to make a few calls. First, I tracked down Tara Fukimoto, thanked her for her help when I really needed it, and told her just to keep her mouth shut. If the LAPD had no idea who'd cold-cocked their detective, I wasn't about to tell them. I'd plead amnesia.

Next, I reached Lane Lander at her office in New York. She was beside herself. Since Monday morning she'd been through a monsoon of media, all looking for answers. Her version of the official company line was that Derrick Pettit had been under investigation for several months for possible improper financial practices among other concerns.

The company's findings would be made available in their entirety to the FBI, the SEC and any other relevant investigatory bodies. Avante Entertainment knew nothing of his involvement with any foreign nationals or any plots of any sort. Of course, at that time at least, she could have had no inkling that the company's disgraced senior financial officer was also the brother of the notorious Shabazz Ali.

She knew I was in Los Angeles and she knew I'd had misgivings about Pettit and his possible connection to Jerry Kendall's death. Naturally, she wanted to know if I was somehow involved in his arrest. I told her I'd had a few meetings with the FBI and that they had nabbed him after they thwarted the Oscar night bombing plot.

I told her how much I missed her and how sorry I was that she got caught in the meat grinder over this story. She sighed and admitted, "Well, that's my job."

Before I hung up I promised that as soon as I knew more I'd tell her everything I could, ideally over cocktails and shrimp and grit somewhere below the Mason-Dixon Line. It wasn't exactly the offer she'd been looking for, but she said she'd think about it.

One unfinished piece of business was my vehicle, Dutch's Dolly. Because Bud already knew the Dutchman, he broke the news and offered to have a wrecker deliver the car as soon as the evidence techs were finished with it. He vamped around how the car I had rented ended up helping to capture an international terrorist by smashing into a private jet.

Dutch wasn't hearing anything of this. He said he'd be right up to L.A. to meet with Bud and survey the damage. Within hours that's what he had done, and Bianco said he left with a big smile on his face. The old Dutchman said he'd replace the windshield and most of the body damage but leave the bullet holes in place.

He told Bianco that he'd triple the rental on his very own "Bonnie and Clyde car" that captured America's Most Wanted Fugitive.

By Friday, I'd been picked over and probed by the best of the best, both lawmen and physicians. I was ready to get back home.

Around 5:00 p.m. Bud Bianco came by. I'd just gotten back to my room from my physical therapy session. Turns out there's not a lot more you can do for a broken collarbone and some broken ribs.

He told me I was free to leave, but warned that I'd likely be called back to Los Angeles to testify some time down the road when the principal perpetrators went on trial. He'd try to keep me out of the courtroom, but he couldn't promise.

I already knew that Shabazz Ali would be tried for attempted mass murder as well as for the crimes he was wanted for when he fled the country. Ironically, there wasn't much chance he'd ever see a courtroom himself, much less a federal prison. Turned out he has stage 4 cancer of the pancreas.

Castro's best doctors over in Cuba had examined him and told him there was no cure. He had only a few more months to live. So, he probably planned the Oscar bombing as his last hurrah.

Derrick Pettit, a/k/a/ Jebediah Derrick Small, wouldn't be getting off easy. He had his health but he also had charges against him not only for the attempted mass murders but for fraud, criminal conspiracy and embezzlement.

The four Hondurans would be deported and turned over to the Honduran authorities. They'd probably wish that they'd been convicted and imprisoned in the States.

The LAPD escaped with nothing more than an embarrassment for having been duped into planning for huge demonstrations outside the Academy Awards when the real danger was inside the theater itself. Captain Bates actually found a way to cover up the fiasco and get the department some credit for creating a diversion so the FBI could do its job, then swooping in to assist with the airport capture with its helicopter eye-in-the-sky.

It was a great piece of spin. Unfortunately for him, it was Terry Bates' last official spin. Because he was the principal supporter of the demonstration debacle, he was allowed to quietly retire with his full pension. Rumor has it that he's already lined up a new job. As chief investigator. For Robert Raskin.

As for Det. Allison Simmons, she resigned from the force and moved to Miami to be with her former partner, who, as it turned out, was also her very serious boyfriend. Captain Bates hadn't approved of her dating the guy, much less thinking of marrying him, which is why he cooked up the phony suspension that got him out of town in the first place.

Why did he care? Bates wasn't being protective of one of his officers, and he didn't have eyes for Simmons himself. It was a well-kept secret, but it turns out she's his daughter. While he was at the Academy, Terry had a fling with a hopeful actress and she wound up pregnant. A good Catholic, she wanted to keep the baby so she moved back home. Bates faithfully supported the child and visited every year or so until she was an adult and wanted to come to L.A.

Although she kept her mother's name, he was proud when she told him she wanted to be in the LAPD just like Dad. She proved to be a really good cop. Of course, having a captain for a father didn't hamper her career at all.

Conspicuously absent from the official summary of the events was Simmons' role in the demonstrations debacle. Almost a year before, she'd met Derrick Pettit while she was working on a grand theft investigation at the studio. He'd pegged her as an ambitious cop eager to make her mark and move ahead. He also sensed that she might still be a little naïve. When the time was right, he planted the mass demonstrations story with her and kept up the heat once the department started buying into the scam.

All that explained why she always seemed so interested in me, but never came through with the goods. At least, I think that was it.

As a parting gesture, Bud Bianco said that if I didn't mind leaving Saturday afternoon, he could get me a ride back to Charleston on a Bureau Gulfstream. I thanked him profusely for his magnanimous gesture and told him I'd be honored to fly the friendly skies of the FBI. However, as departure was almost 24 hours away, I wanted to check out of the hospital and into a really nice hotel in time for happy hour. And, I did.

After a few huge drinks with umbrellas in them and a pleasant chat with a lovely, friendly cocktail waitress at Trader Vic's, I looked up my buddy Jerome Ravenel's number and gave him a buzz. He was happy to hear from me and to report that my rustic abode remained safe from harm.

He told me that a bunch of the guys would be gathering at the clubhouse Sunday afternoon for a few drinks and some chow to swap their assessments for the prospects for a good fishing season along the Intracoastal and up the Wando. I told him to save me a rocker on the porch.

That's when I noticed some writing on the damp cocktail napkin under my drink. It read "I'm off at midnight" and concluded with a dainty smiley face. I looked across the crowded room, caught the cocktail waitress' eye, and gave her one big thumbs up.

Then, I thought. "Sounds good to me!"

48

Manigault, South Carolina

The flight back East was a delight. I never realized that when they weren't collaring bad guys, FBI agents really knew how to live. It was late when I made it home at last. I looked forward to hitting the sack and getting a good night's sleep in preparation for Sunday afternoon's gathering. First, I wanted to check my phone messages.

I'm not a great phone communicator so I had only a few messages, two from ladies I'd dated, one from a charity asking if I'd be attending their upcoming fundraiser, and another from my mentor, Col. Matthews.

Matthews said, "Sorry to be calling on your home phone, Bobby. There's no message machine on your secure phone. By the way, when are you going to return that thing? They're not cheap, you know.

"Anyway, without going into specifics, I want to commend you on your great work out in Los Angeles. You made us all proud and you made us all look good. Oh, and you'll be getting a package in a few days from this office with a few things you'll need. Best wishes and congratulations…*Captain* Cutter."

I was stunned. I'd expected maybe a reprimand and instead I'd gotten a promotion. All I could say to myself was, "sounds good to me!"

When I got to the clubhouse around 4:00 p.m. the next day almost everyone in the group had already assembled. I guess Jerome never mentioned that the festivities would begin at 3:00 p.m.

I poured myself a drink, took my appointed rocker on the porch and shot the breeze with my new friends. Before long, Sam Archibald broached the question.

"So, you've been out on your old stomping ground for a few weeks, rubbing shoulders with the Hollywood rich and famous. Tell us all about your trip."

"Well," I began, "I visited the artists' colony at Laguna Beach. I ate some great clams up at Pismo Beach. I saw a few old friends. And, I had a couple of interesting dates."

I looked over at Judge Pickney, whose prodigious eyebrows were raised at the blandness of my travelogue.

I gave the venerable jurist a wink adding, "Oh, and I even got to put on a tuxedo and actually go to the Academy Awards!"

www.ingramcontent.com/pod-product-compliance
Lightning Source LLC
Chambersburg PA
CBHW050611170726
48283CB00001B/199